WAITING ON THE RAIN

CLAUDIA CONNOR

Waiting On The Rain is a work of fiction. Names, places, and incidents either are products of the author's imagination or are used fictitiously. Any resemblance to actual events, locales, or persons, living or dead, is entirely coincidental.

NOTE TO READERS

Dear Readers,

I am so grateful to you for going on this journey with me. Beginning with the McKinney family, and moving into the Walker brothers.

Ava's character has been living in my mind for years, almost as far back as Matt and Abby. When I got to know Luke Walker, I knew they were meant to be together.

Luke felt broken, tainted somehow, and didn't want anyone to see him. Ava doesn't look at him, can't *see* him. But in the end she sees him more clearly than anyone else.

Ava was a joy to write. It did require a lot of research and I was lucky to find several people more than willing to help.

Also, when I was in college at Auburn University, I spent a year planning to get my master's in Deaf Education. That later morphed into Early Childhood

Education, but during that time, I took a class on general disabilities.

The professor offered extra credit to anyone who wanted to spend 24 hours blindfolded. Always up for an adventure, I was eager. He gave me a blindfold and a cane, wished me luck and told me he'd see me on Friday and off I went. I began later that evening and I didn't cheat once. I truly wanted to experience it.

It. Was. Hard.

Two things stood out. One, I had to rely on others for help. This was 1992 in a small college town. The campus offered transit from one side of the campus to the other, but there was no handy app to find the transit I needed or when it was coming. I couldn't easily call for help because we didn't even have cell phones then!

Luckily, I had a boyfriend with a car, so he dropped me off near my classes. Navigating through an enormous building, up an elevator and to my classrooms, some of which were auditoriums, was a challenge to say the least.

The second thing that stood out was the loneliness. At night, when dinner was over and my boyfriend left, it was just me in the dark and the quiet. I couldn't watch TV. I couldn't read myself to sleep. There were no podcasts then, I had no audio books. And even in the classroom, surrounded by people. I was in my own dark world.

I know that my 24 hour experiment in no way

compares to living with a sight impairment, but it made an impression on me and I've never forgotten it.

I love Ava and Luke and I hope you enjoy their story as much as I enjoyed writing it!

Sincerely,
Claudia
Xoxo

SPECIAL THANKS

A very special thanks to Dr. Chad Cullison, O.D. of Cullison Eye Care, Germantown, TN. His expertise and interest in making the facts regarding Ava's sight accurate are greatly appreciated. Any and all mistakes are my own.

For my girl, Jamie.
Keeping me sane, keeping me moving, keeping the faith.
Xoxo

1

Luke Walker stood in the bathroom of Marco's Supper Club men's room, staring at himself in the mirror as the cold water ran over his hands.

He'd crawled through South American jungles when he was barely old enough to qualify as a man, tumbled out of airplanes, and blown doors with blocks of C-4. He'd eaten sand in Afghanistan, Iraq, and Turkey and a few more places the US government wouldn't want him to admit he'd ever been.

At times it was fun, the training, the adrenaline rush, the bullshitting with the guys. Other times it was haunting.

But there was always another day. Morning came and there was another mission. That's why guys hated going on leave. Not because they didn't want to see their families but because if you didn't keep it tight, keep moving, planning, reloading, the darkness could creep in. As brave as they were, they feared being smothered by that darkness. And that's where he was now, where he'd been the past few months.

Retirement, permanent leave. Trying not to get smothered and doing his damnedest not to let it show.

At the moment he was trying not to let it show as he washed baby barf out of his dress shirt. There'd been too many toddlers and babies belonging to his little brother's wedding party to not have one tossed at him. So, with the women in the wedding party posing for pictures, he'd gotten the barfing one.

Hard to believe a human who weighed less than twenty pounds could contain so much...stuff. He was an Army Ranger for God's sake and had smelled some acrid stink, but this was getting to him.

The bathroom door opened, letting in the sounds of a wedding reception in full swing.

"Hey, man."

Luke gave a head nod to the man as he passed on his way to the urinals. He squeezed out his dress shirt then held it under the hand dryer. His undershirt could probably use a good wash as well but the scars of war brought looks, if not questions, neither of which he was in the mood for.

Ten minutes later he was back at the makeshift bar, watching his younger brother bump hips with his new bride. The happy go lucky jokester who never met a lady he didn't like now settled down with a kid. Nora's, and now officially Zach's. A cute little guy who was somewhere between one and two and who'd stolen the show toddling down the aisle as ring bearer.

They seemed in love, Zach and his new wife. *Wife.* Good, Lord. He shook his head at the thought. His older brother Nick had a wife now too. His baby sister, Hannah, *was* one. And this was life, he thought, taking a sip from the cold amber bottle. This was *normal.* People meeting, people linking up with one another. And today's normal had been a small wedding in a Catholic Church followed by a reception at a supper club that served a lasagna dinner then offered a makeshift bar and parquet dance floor.

"This next one is a ladies only dance," the band leader announced. "If you've got man plumbing get yourself off the dance floor."

The band moved into a new tune. The females at the bar whooped and laughed, pushing their drinks into the nearest man's hand so they could throw themselves into the shifting shaking mass of women singing about respect, spelling out the word.

Women filled the dance floor as quickly as the men vacated. A mass of white dress shirts, in various degrees of tucked, the ties around their necks loosened, if not lost altogether. He'd left his own penguin suit choker on his assigned table. And nearly every one of them made a bee–line to the bar.

Some he recognized as Zach's fire station buddies, others were part of the McKinney clan his sister had married into. The noise around him ratcheted up as the men called for their drinks. The quick moving bartenders set small plastic cups and bottles on the bar, serving everyone as fast as they called out their order. Nothing said party like an open bar at a wedding. As much as he wished, it just didn't say it to him.

He'd been easing into civilian life for months now. Or trying. Maybe not trying hard enough since the civilian skin didn't fit quite like his Ranger skin had. But then he hadn't been non-active military for more than twenty years. He'd been a kid when he'd signed up. A wild, immature, overly emotional kid with a chip on his shoulder so deep he was shocked he'd been able to hold a rifle. But he had.

He'd held a rifle and held it steady. He'd learned to navigate— day or night— run obstacle courses, and rucked miles until a lot of the anger had been sweat out of him or buried under exhaustion. Maybe that's why civilian life was hard.

He checked his watch. Almost nine. He figured at least two more hours before the bride and groom departed. The day had begun with a wedding party brunch at eleven this morning and his duties as groomsman hadn't slowed since then. He'd surpassed his social limit hours ago.

He perused the other side of the room dotted with large round tables where he'd survived the seated dinner portion of the evening. White table cloths, spindly green and pink floral somethings sticking up out of skinny glass tubes in the center of each one. Kinda cool, he thought, though it hadn't blocked him from even one of the nine people seated with him. Might have been better altogether if he'd built a walled garden around himself, like the folders he'd set up as a child when the class took a test.

But he'd nodded, even forced a smile when appropriate and tried his best to look like everyone else when on the inside he still felt gritty with sweat after operating in a middle eastern sandbox.

He'd been firm on not bringing a date and gave points to his sister the wedding planner. She hadn't pushed. Instead she'd paired him up with one of the bride's coworkers who was old enough to be his grandmother. Another point for Hannah.

There'd been a time when his hormones had raged and the thought of bridesmaids would have made him think *good time*. Now there was nothing raging. His blood didn't run hot or cold. Sometimes Luke wondered if it was running at all.

Not for the first time, he looked around him and thought what the hell was he doing here? Not in the building, or in the state of Virginia, but in the country.

Was it too late? Could he call his commander, tell him April fools? Just joking? Why had he thought he could be anything other than a soldier? But he had thought that. Or had thought he wanted, that he *needed*, to try.

His gaze skimmed over the room. Most of the women were on the dance floor while a scattering of people sat at one of the large round white cloth covered tables. Older couples, one he recognized as Zach's fire chief and the chief's wife. A blonde sitting alone, nursing a drink, not facing the dance floor— which was odd with all the commotion going on. This place was a people watching gold mine, if you were into that kind of thing. Maybe she wasn't. Maybe like him she was feeling the sensory overload. He couldn't see much of her. Just her back with her long, pale hair flowing down, past the top of the chair.

Out of the corner of his eye, Luke saw Nick make his way over to the bar. He ordered himself a beer and gave Luke a chin jerk in greeting. They stood like that, side by side, facing opposite directions. To say they'd butted heads way back when, would be putting it mildly. At seventeen, Luke had had no interest in listening to Nick, his nineteen-year-old newly appointed guardian.

Nick got his beer and turned to look out over the room, taking a long swallow from his drink. Luke noticed his brother scanning the room, locating each of his three babies before he spoke. "Holding up the bar or drinking it dry?"

Nick's tone was easy, not accusing so Luke tamped down his automatic bristling at his brother's question. Told himself not to read too deeply into it. Before he came up with a response, Zach was there.

"My man!" Zach shouted as he hooked an arm round Luke's neck. "I'm going to need you to kick it up a notch. Turn that frown upside down."

Zach pivoted, turning them both back to the dance floor. When his gaze zeroed in on his bride, a goofy grin spread across his face as he watched Nora move. "That's my wife," Zach said. "I love saying that —my *wife*."

It was a wonder his grin didn't split his face. Luke couldn't really imagine being that happy. It was kind of creepy.

One of Zach's fire station buddies who'd also been in the wedding party joined them and rolled his eyes. "How many times can you say 'my wife?'"

"More than you," Zach said to his single friend. "And hey, without Dallas, that makes you the only single brother. Hey, Nick." Zach leaned across him. "Luke's the only single bro on the premises."

Nick raised an eyebrow at Luke then cut his eyes to Zach.

Luke raised a finger to the nearby bartender. "Can we get some water over here?" It wasn't the first time he'd thought of Dallas being absent today and hoped Zach wasn't hiding too much disappointment at his twin not being here for his big day. Dallas, the quiet thinker, the introverted scholar, who'd shocked them all by going to police academy, then taken a job offer up north. And was now deep undercover and pretty much out of contact.

The bartender filled two clear plastic cups, set them on the bar.

"Drink some water, Romeo," Nick said. "Don't want you disappointing your bride tonight."

"What?" Zach picked up one of the waters. "Lot of

women here. Can't you get even one to dance with you."

"Not trying," Luke said.

"I don't think you could get a girl to dance with you if you were. Not with that scowl on your face." He downed one of the waters and started on the second.

"Maybe not." He didn't feel like he was scowling. It was just his face, but he mustered up a smile for his brother.

"I love you, man." Before Luke could dodge, Zach grabbed him in a head lock and planted a kiss on his face.

"Okay. Maybe some more water."

"Nope. Don't need it. I'm high on love."

Luke could only shake his head. The band ended the ladies only dance and called the men back out onto the floor. The men obliged, maybe because the women were all dressed up, slightly tipsy, and dancing in heels.

"I'm going to dance with my wife." Zach finished his second water and joined his bride, but not before he reached into his wallet and slapped a crisp bill on the bar in front of Luke. "A hundred says you can't get one woman to dance with you."

Luke just stared at it.

"He's going to regret that," Nick said with a shake of his head.

"Yep. If he remembers." Luke slid the bill into pocket with every intention of keeping it for his brother. Or maybe he'd slide it into the cash box on the gift table.

Nick's wife Mia curled a finger at Nick in a come hither gesture, as she made her way to the bar. She took the beer from his hand, downed a swallow and handed it back. "Who's got the babies?"

"One of Nora's coworkers there," Nick said, pointing with the bottle. "The others are with Mrs. McKinney and... whoever that is sitting beside her."

"It's not every day we have a hundred hands ready and willing to hold babies." Mia took the beer again and finished it, then set the empty bottle on the bar. She took her husband's hand. "Let's make it count."

Luke watched them go back to the dance floor. He'd always liked Mia, all the way back to when she and Nick had first started dating in college. She'd come into the picture soon after their parents had been killed in a car accident and had brought a bit of soft, but fiery, female to the house. She'd also seemed to get Luke in a way no one else had.

He was glad to see them back together and it was fun to watch such a tiny little thing keep his brother in line. One by one the bar flies thinned out, leaving Luke alone. He nursed his beer, thinking he'd like to switch to straight whiskey which led him to think he'd like to be drinking that straight whiskey alone. But he wouldn't. He was afraid to start a slide down that slippery slope. He'd known more than one good man who'd left the military only to find new demons.

Don't think about it. Not now. Not at his little brother's wedding. If he thought too hard, let the feelings or the knowledge of just how numb he felt, he might go for that whiskey.

He'd held it together all day. Family, food, smiling for the camera in constricting clothes. Kids running, wiggling, adults of all sizes talking over the music, laughing. Things that shouldn't seem foreign to him but they did. Which made him feel even more like a fish out of water.

He nearly smiled, picturing a fish flopping on land, gulping and gasping for air. Described him pretty well. And made him wonder again, *what the hell am I doing here?*

Luke watched Matt McKinney dancing with one of his little girls. Impossible to keep them straight—the man had something crazy, like seven kids. This one looked to be around six or so and had a wild head of brown curls. She'd served as a flower girl in the wedding. Luke couldn't help but smile when he saw she'd lost not just her crown of flowers but her shoes too. Matt held the little girl's hand, guiding her in a spin around his finger.

The man looked exactly right doing it. Enjoying himself, completely at ease. But Matt had also been in the military, so was he a sign that normal was within reach for men like them, or was he a glaring example that Luke wasn't made like that?

He'd been around the McKinney's a handful of times. The man brought his girl out to ride at Hannah's barn pretty regularly and his sister had mentioned Matt no less than ten times since Luke had been back.

You know, Stephen's brother Matt was in the military.

You know, Matt McKinney left the Navy after almost as many years as you.

And the kicker—

Stephen's brother Matt seems really happy. Followed by the silent, pleading questions he imagined. *Are you happy? Can I help you be happy? What can I do?*

More than anything, he hated knowing Hannah worried about him.

Matt didn't stare at him as his family tended to do, but still, there was friendly concern. Luke didn't want concern. Didn't want people trying to get inside his head. Wondering if what he'd seen in war made him stand apart. Even now, Hannah watched him from the dance floor, motioned for him to come join them.

He raised his beer as an excuse and forced a smile. It was what he'd seen, and done. But that wasn't the only reason. His sister rolled her eyes and to his great relief turned her attention back to her husband. The two of them danced in a group with Nick and Mia, then shuffled their way over to include Zach and Nora. As a whole, their moves were pathetic, but they did it together, moving and laughing.

All these years he'd had his team, but while he'd been gone his family had been making their own connections. Making their own unit.

It looked like everyone in this room belonged to someone. He was the odd man out. He drank, looking around, proving his theory. His gaze landed on the blonde again. Raucous laughter erupted from her table, the two couples sitting opposite her looked to be having a great time but she seemed apart somehow. Like him, on the outside. And why the hell was she sitting alone? Her date ditch her?

Her hair was so pale it was almost white and hung midway down her back, straight as a waterfall. Her body was angled enough that he could see one arm resting on the table, perfectly still. The other women were in constant motion, raising drinks, spooning in desserts, talking animatedly with their hands. He didn't think he'd ever seen a woman sit with other women and be so still. Still waters run deep, he thought, and searched his mind for the rest of the poem.

He tried to watch the dance floor, but his eyes kept coming back to the woman at the table in... he didn't know what you'd call the color. Pink champagne was the closest thing he could think of. The type he'd seen the bridesmaids toasting in delicate glasses. Whatever it was, it was quiet like her. Soothing in all this noise and movement. He also noticed the back of said dress draped and dipped nearly to her waist leaving a good bit of her back bare.

"Luke!" His brother Zach called his name from the dance floor, enthusiastically waving him over. "Come on man!"

Luke read his lips more than heard him over the music and the crowds' Sweet Caroline chorus. Luke gave him a chin jerk to show he'd heard him, and again raised his bottle in a kind of salute and an excuse.

He was good where he was, or good enough, holding up the bar, watching the revelry, and would have preferred to stay there all night. Until he saw Hannah and Zach with their heads together, then Hannah's worried expression aimed his way. The same one he'd been getting since his return.

Worried glances, hushed voices, and the watching. Always watching him like he was a ticking bomb and they were afraid he would blow at any second. It made his skin crawl. He didn't need their worry, didn't need to be coddled and tip-toed around. No one looked at him in the Rangers. No one worried about Captain Walker, First Class. Here, it seemed everyone had time to sit and look and ask.

The tables were mostly empty now, leaving only men who flat out refused to dance, people holding babies, and a few small clumps huddled in deep conversation. As his gaze roamed the room, he caught sight of the blonde again—just in time to see her stumble at the far end of the cookie table. Too much champagne would do that and she wasn't the only one who'd overindulged tonight. Not that he was judging.

He continued watching her, noting again how still she stood now that she'd regained her balance. He hoped to God she wasn't about to pass out face first into a platter of ladyfingers.

Feeling a sense of purpose, he set his near empty bottle on the bar and headed off to avert potential disaster.

As Luke got closer, he saw she had a small plate in

her hand. An empty plate. He'd admit there were an overwhelming amount of choices, but he'd never seen a person deliberate quite so...deliberately.

"Can't decide?" he asked as he came up beside her.

She lifted her chin slightly, and he was hit with blue eyes. Seriously blue. But those blue eyes didn't come close to meeting his.

Oh, yeah. She's toast.

Luke watched her intently, noted that even in her heels he was a head taller than her. He also noted it wasn't just her eyes. The lady had a face and she still hadn't answered him. Finally, she lifted the empty plate she held in one hand and held up the end of a white cane in the other.

"Hard to make a choice when I can't see them," she said with a soft smile and a shrug.

Can't see them? She didn't seem that drunk, now that he was up close. But there was something... Her eyes looking in the direction of his face but not quite meeting his eyes.

"I'm blind," she added casually. Like she was just throwing it out there to see where and how it landed.

"Oh," he said, remaining absolutely still. For a beat, he stared at sky blue eyes that looked perfectly normal before snapping out of it. "So, if I put some cookies on there for myself you won't notice?"

"Nope."

She smiled and it was so devastating it nearly knocked him back a step.

"Someone walked me over, then there was a kid emergency and..." She shrugged again. "I'm not quite sure what to do now."

"I can help with that. Are you familiar with the cookie table phenomenon?"

"No. Well, I've heard talk tonight, but I can't really picture it. I'm beginning to think I should just skip it. If you could help me get back to my table—"

"No." No way was he walking her back to leave her sitting alone. "I mean, you really shouldn't skip it. And going on my personal experience from my sister's wedding last year, the best way to attack this is to survey the choices first, get a game plan. You don't want to fill up your plate then find something better at the end."

"Good point."

"Do you want to... Or should I..."

"It works best if I take your arm." She slipped the loop at the top of her cane over her wrist and held out her hand. "If that's okay."

"Yeah. Sure." She raised her right hand, touched the sleeve of his shirt at his elbow then found his bicep. Her small hand held him not tightly, but firmly enough that she wouldn't lose him.

"This good?"

"Yes. Thank you."

"So, evidently," he said, starting down the row.

"This cookie thing is big in Ohio and Pennsylvania. And for some reason, it's big in the McKinney clan. Since my sister married a McKinney, we're reaping the benefits once again."

"Oh. Your sister's Hannah?"

"Yep."

"Which makes you brother of the groom?"

"Right again. And even though neither my brother Zach, nor his new wife Nora, is a McKinney, when the McKinney's hear wedding, they make cookies. And women, being competitive as they are, when one bakes, they all bake."

"You seem to know a lot about it," she said, smiling.

He smiled back then remembered she couldn't see it. "My sister talks a lot. Okay. There's about five, maybe six tables lined up end to end."

"What do they look like?"

"Um... Let's see... Well..."

Her body brushed a platter laying too close to the edge and she jerked back. "Crap!"

"No problem." Luke reached across her to catch it just before it tipped. "As you can see, or tell, the tables are full to overflowing. That's one thing. There are plates and platters covering the tables, and even more set up on things to make them high."

"A very manly description," she said, teasing him.

"Okay, some are on stands about yay high." He took her hands, raising one to give her an idea of the size. "And there are random little candles in between some of them."

"Yikes. Glad I didn't risk my life for a cookie."

"No, shit. Would have sucked if you'd gone for a cookie and grabbed fire. You, know," he said, pausing to look at her. "When I first came over here, I thought you were two sheets to the wind."

"You *what*? You thought I was *drunk*?" She laughed. "So you came to save me from myself or save the cookies?"

"Both."

"Hmm." She slid her eyes in his direction. "I guess that's fair."

"Okay. We're to the end. Now that we've gotten an idea of our choices, we go back to the beginning and load up."

"All right, but I don't really have an idea of my choices."

"Good point. I'll do a better job on the second pass. You hold the plate and I'll fill it."

"Sounds like a plan."

"Okay. First up are some long, skinny log rolls. Hard. Maybe filled with some kind of nutty mixture."

"Sounds good."

"Okay. We'll do two of those. We can always come back. Next are some white balls. Looks like they've been rolled in powdered sugar."

"Yum."

"I agree. Four of those."

"I like how you describe things."

"Really? How's that?"

"Well, not like a food critic, but like..."

"Like a man who eats?" he suggested and got another smile out of her.

"Exactly."

"Here we have some white things. Round, crispy, maybe some jelly in the center? I think we need more information." He took a bite. "Yep, jelly. Strawberry. Want to try it?"

She pressed her lips together to hold back a laugh. "I'll wait."

"Good thinking. Let's take three."

They continued like that, with him describing, sometimes tasting, while she held onto him with one hand and held the plate he filled with her other. She said no to a few, and yes to most.

"No shit," he muttered.

"What?"

"Nothing." Ava was staring blankly at the table and he immediately regretted his *nothing*. Everything, *anything*, he saw was something. Something she couldn't.

He grabbed a bag. "Here," he said, and put her hand around it. She took it, turning it, feeling the thin, onion like paper. She ran a finger along the sides and bottom then the delicate scalloped edge at the top.

"They're white," Luke explained. "And right in the center there's a fancy Z and N in gold. Zach and Nora."

She smiled and held it out to him. "Cute."

"Yeah. Cute," he said, but he wasn't looking at the bags. "Okay, I bet you'll go for these. Chocolate, and

going by the shape of them I'm guessing maybe chocolate covered Oreos."

"You're right. I do say yes."

He was reaching for the chocolate covered circles
when she tripped, let out a gasp and gripped his arm
almost upending the plate.

"Whoa." He gently righted her, catching their plate
and barely squeezing it onto the edge of the table
between platters. He looked down to see what had
tripped her up just in time to see two little feet in white
shoes and short white ruffle socks make a swift retreat
under the floor length table cloth.

"Ahh. Looks like we have a cookie bandit." He let
go of her arm and knelt then raised the table cloth a
few inches. Three pint sized bodies sat, their laps full
of cookies, powdered sugar and chocolate rimming
their mouths. He chuckled, thinking that's exactly the
kind of thing he and his brothers would have done.
Luke couldn't remember their names, but he did
recognize two of them as the McKinney twins, along
with another blond headed boy who looked to be
around five.

Ava knelt beside him, reached her hand out to
touch a small white buckle shoe. "What is it? Are there
mice under the table? With shoes on?" The kids
giggled. "Smells like mice and..." She sniffed. "Did the
mice get into the powdered sugar?"

"Don't tell," a little boy said.

"Hmm. Maybe you need to practice your escape
and evade tactics," Luke told him.

"I know how. We play with our dad and I told Caroline not to stick her feet out. Who's that?"

The boy pointed at the woman kneeling beside him and Luke turned his head. God, she was beautiful. Even if he had known her name, he wasn't sure he could have answered.

"Ava. I'm Ava."

"Luke. Walker."

"Hi."

"Hi."

"We did our job anyway," the kid said, interrupting their slightly awkward and belated introduction. "Mom said after we could have cookies."

"Did she say to have them under the table?"

"She didn't say not to."

The girl drew her feet farther under the table and shoved a small cookie into her already full mouth. Maybe sensing their cookie raid was soon coming to an end.

"Well, number one in evading is don't get seen which means you have to keep your feet all the way under the table. And when you leave, crawl to the ends so you don't trip anyone and make them drop their plate. No sense wasting cookies, right? You do that and I won't tell. Deal?"

"Deal. But why would they be wasted?"

Luke laughed. Good question and one he'd leave to the parents, he thought, and straightened, bringing Ava with him.

"Sweet kids," Ava said. "Or maybe I should say,

smart kids. Did you ever hide under tables eating cookies?"

"I might have. You?"

"Not tables, no. But I did keep a lock on my closet to hide the Cocoa Pebbles from my pig of a brother."

"Smart kid."

With Ava beside him, they continued their gathering then took the bounty back to her table.

"I'm guessing you were in the wedding party?"

"Yep. Got the tux, the choking tie, the whole deal."

"You don't like weddings?" she asked, as they got back to her table.

"Nothing against it," he said pulling her chair out. "But I could do without a thousand pictures."

"You don't have to stay with me," she said, taking her seat. "I can manage the eating."

He respected that, and she genuinely didn't seem to mind being left alone. Even so, he was in no hurry to leave. "I'm sure you can," he said and took the seat beside her. "But you've got my cookies. Or maybe you came with someone," he added, again wondering why she would be here alone.

One side of her mouth curved up. "If I did, would you fight him for the cookies?"

God, her eyes were blue. A clear, pure, summer sky blue. Add to that, she had the kind of face that made a man want to straighten his tie if he still had one on. He might surrender the cookies but it would be damn hard to surrender her.

3

L uke's voice was deeply male and Ava felt the warmth of him, felt the slight shift in the table and heard the faint slide of fabric against fabric as if he was leaning his arm on it. Even sitting, his voice came from slightly above her head. "Never mind," she said, kicking herself and reaching for her glass of water. She'd left at exactly twelve o'clock when she was facing the table. "You don't have to fight anyone."

"Are you kidding? After all the time we spent making the perfect plate?"

She smiled, pretty sure by the sound of his voice that he was looking right at her. She'd thrown out the blind bomb and he'd handled it. As far as she could tell, he hadn't even fumbled. Unless he was just very good at covering. Some people were. "Well, you're in luck. I didn't come with anyone. Hannah invited me. I think she feels sorry for me."

"That's—"

"No, not because I'm blind," she said quickly. "Just because she feared for my sanity. I'm only in town helping out after my dad's knee replacement."

"That's tough. How's it going?"

"It's going. But, like you said, it's tough."

"Mmm. How do you know Hannah?"

"I've been riding at Freedom Farm for a couple of weeks now. A gift from my sister-in-law."

"Huh. How do you like it?"

"I like it a lot." Ava picked up her fork and ran it over the plate of cookies, feeling them through the utensil. "Where should I start?" She tapped the tips of her fork over the plate. "What's this one?"

"That's the powdered sugar ball. A butter ball, I think they're called."

"Mmm. What do you think? Should I go for it? I don't usually just pop unknown foods into my mouth. My brother says I eat like a squirrel. Or a rat."

"That's brothers for you. Here. A fork's not going to work." He took the utensil from her.

"Just so you know," she said, "If I was alone, I'd be fondling the hell out of these cookies."

THE WORD FONDLING had certain images coming to Luke's mind as he guided her soft, cool hand to the cookie she wanted. "There." He watched her lift the ball to her mouth, felt his pulse jump as her lips parted then closed around it.

"Mmm. I love these," she mumbled around the mouthful. Then laughed, spraying out a puff of powdered sugar before she slapped a hand over her mouth. "I'm tho thorry!"

"Not a problem." He bit back a chuckle and popped the same cookie into his own mouth, unable to stop looking at her.

"Okay. That was amazing," she said. "Maybe worth getting burned for." She reached for another one and stopped. "Sorry. I don't want to touch your cookies."

"Our cookies. And go ahead. I've been in the army. We eat with our hands all the time. And trust me, you'll be the cleanest person that's ever ah... touched my cookies."

She laughed clear and bright and held her hand out. "Hit me with another one."

Had he ever been so entertained eating cookies with a woman? Not just entertained, but captivated. "Can you see it at all? Shit," he said the second the words were out. He just wanted to know about her, but... "Sorry. That was definitely not PC, and I..." He shook his head at himself.

"It's fine. And fair, since I'm touching your...cookies. And the answer is, no. I'm one of the few blind people that have no sight at all."

He stared at her, drinking his fill. "You'd never know it."

"I know. It's a nerve thing, a disconnect is the easiest way to explain it, between the optical nerve and my brain. My eyes— the muscles, the corneas and all are actually normal."

She angled her face down to her plate. Strands of silky, blond hair fell around her face, blocking his view. He was still kicking himself for even asking, but her eyes were so far from normal. Beautiful didn't cut it either. They were extraordinary. The purest, brightest blue. Uniform in color. No speckles of another color, no variation.

She looked at the plate of cookies, or seemed to, and they sat a few minutes without talking. Chewing on cookies, listening to the band, sudden movements of people around him catching his eye, but not really paying attention.

He'd rather look at her. What could it be like? To see nothing? Just darkness? Even crawling through the darkest of nights he had night vision goggles. And maybe it wasn't darkness that she saw. "Where'd you come from?"

"New York."

"Ooh."

"What? You don't like the city?"

"By city you mean millions of people? Streets that smell like sewers? Horns blasting?"

"Wow. I'm going to take that as a no. Are you the brother that just got out of the military? Hannah might have mentioned her brother situation," she added with a smile, when he didn't immediately answer. "FBI. Army Ranger. Firefighter. Cop. Poor girl." She smiled again. "I imagine the military's loud."

"It is. Different though because I'm the one making the noise." He held his breath, hoping she didn't ask for details the way some people did.

"Well, city life's not for everyone. Hannah mentioned you're building the cabins for her camp. That's nice."

She smiled, her eyes not meeting his exactly, but close enough and whatever tension he'd felt eased.

"How about one of those mini cannoli things," she said, aiming her fork at the edge of her plate.

He gave her one, took one for himself. He was about to ask her how city life worked not being able to see anything when his sister caught his attention from the edge of the dance floor. With both of her hands locked tightly in Stephen's, Hannah pointedly dipped her head at Luke, then jerked it toward Ava. Luke pretended he didn't understand this weird sign language she was giving him. Luckily, Stephen spun her around before she got a crick in her neck.

The music slowed and the opening chords of a well-known song played. "The band's good," she said, reaching out carefully for her glass of ice water.

"Yeah. They are."

She took a sip, then carefully, put it back in its place.

He looked past Ava's shoulder and Hannah was back again, this time pointing animatedly at him, then at Ava, then the dance floor. Yeah, yeah. He got the message. And okay fine, he could manage one dance. He'd never hear the end of it if he didn't. "Let's dance."

"Nah. I'm good."

"Aww, come on. If you step on my feet, I won't even notice."

"Well, thanks for that, but—"

"But what? I'm the black sheep of the family," he said. "If anyone's looking, they'll be looking at me." He slid his chair back from the table and stood.

"Why are you the black sheep?"

"A story for another day. Come on." He touched her arm lightly to guide her up beside him. "If we sit here debating it'll be over and then you'll be crying on your cookies."

"*Excuse* me? I will not be crying if I don't get to dance with you, but fine." She scooted back and stood. "You'll have to help me navigate," she said, adjusting her hand.

"No problem. Truth is, I'm not much of a dancer so I'll get us through the maze and you can take it from there?"

"Deal."

4

L uke moved slowly, doing his best to be mindful of Ava as they made their way to the dance floor. "I can see why you'd need a guide. This is a minefield." He pushed a chair in that blocked his path so he could lead her around the one in hers. Her shoe caught on something and her grip tightened on his arm.

"Hold up." He bent, saw her heel——the type designed to make a man beg—was caught on a chain attached to a small purse. The hem of her dress hit just above her knees, and he patted her calf, felt the firm, smooth skin there and— *Get a grip, Walker.* "Lift up. Okay, got it." With the danger averted, they continued. "Diaper bag straight ahead," he said, steering her clear.

Finally, they stepped off the carpet and onto the wood of the temporary dance floor. "Made it," he said, turning to face her.

She angled her head up toward the sound of his

voice. "We did. Thank you."

"Now it's your turn." He waited for her to make the move, noticing every detail while he did. The way the silky fabric hung from the narrowest of straps and draped over her breasts, leaving the pale skin of her chest bare. Not nearly as revealing as some and twice as sexy. He watched her chest rise and fall just above the edge of her dress, bare except for a small silver heart on a delicate chain. Small diamond studs sparkled at her ears.

She reached out slowly until her hand touched him just below the center of his chest. There was power in her delicate hand, he thought, as she slid it slowly up his chest and it was suddenly hard to breathe.

"You've lost your choking tie," she said, her unseeing eyes following the path of her hand until she found his shoulder.

"Yeah." He took her right hand in his, slid his other around her waist over cool slippery fabric. Then farther until he felt the warm, smooth skin. With the slightest pressure on her lower back, she moved into him. Her face was turned so that just a little more, a little closer, and she'd be resting her cheek against his chest.

Hard when I can't see them. The words replayed in his mind.

She couldn't *see*.

He knew guys who'd lost eyes to roadside bombs. Had seen bloody faces, charred skin. His concept of blind was so completely at odds with the woman in his arms. She wasn't injured, wasn't broken. And right now he didn't want to think about anything other than how it felt to dance with her. And it felt pretty damn good.

Her body was soft against his, her scent fresh and sweet and utterly female.

She turned her face toward his chest, squelched up her nose just a little and sniffed. "Do you have a baby?"

He groaned. "I know. I stink."

"Not stink. Exactly."

"My nephew barfed on me and of course my brother thought it was hilarious." Looking up at him, she smiled again and even without seeing, there was laughter in her eyes. Was it wrong to stare when she didn't know he was staring? He hoped not because he couldn't stop himself. Without a pause, the band moved right into another slow song for which he was grateful, because he wasn't quite ready to let her go.

Ava felt his hand, firm and warm on her lower back. She felt the buzz along her skin at the feel of his big, hard hand gripping hers and the rise of muscles in his shoulder under her other. Each sway of the music brought them closer together.

Luke's fingers curled around hers and he brought their joined hands to his chest. There was strength and competence in the way he'd led her to the dance floor and in the way he held her now. Close, but not too tight. He made her smile. Surprising given the way she'd felt about men the past year. And even more surprising was the hot, little thrill that skated up her spine at the feel of his hands on her skin.

He certainly didn't seem to have two left feet as he'd alluded to. Of course the kind of dancing they were doing was probably more a reflection of how the man moved off the dance floor. *Not* where her mind needed to go.

The tempo picked up but he made no move to leave. Instead he took both of her hands and stepped back, until her arms were straight out.

"Interesting song choice," he said, and she heard the laughter in his voice.

He pulled her back in and they both sang the chorus about a couple with suspicious minds. He had a low, smooth singing voice.

"You lied," she said. "You do know how to dance."

"Well, I haven't smashed your toes, so that's something. But then you can't see me." He turned them in a circle. "I could be horrible."

She laughed. "True."

A new song started up and from the murmurs around her the crowd approved.

"And.... that's my cue to vacate the dance floor," Luke said.

"What? Why?"

"Oh, um. People are lining up like they've all practiced this one and I definitely have *not*. Want a drink? Or we can go back to the cookies?"

"A drink's good."

. . .

With Ava's hand tight in his, Luke started to lead her between the first and second line of dancers toward the bar. He hadn't gone more than a couple of steps when he felt her resistance and looked back. Her brow was furrowed and the hand he wasn't holding was out to her side as if she was feeling her way in the dark. Because, damn it, that's exactly what she was doing.

"Sorry." In the span of one dance, he'd already forgotten. He backed up, slipped his arm around her waist, pulling her into his side effectively steering her through the crowd toward the bar. He pulled a stool out at one of three high tops situated between the dance floor and the bar. "What'll you have?"

"Um... A beer? Something light?"

"Got it."

He was back in less than a minute with two cold bottles. "They were out of cups. Sorry."

"No problem."

Luke watched her reach out, feeling for the bottle. She found it before he could apologize for just clunking it down on the table for her to search for.

"This guy bothering you?"

Luke didn't bother turning to look at the voice behind him, just hooked a thumb over his shoulder. "My brother, the groom, and his idiot firefighter friends."

"I take offense to that," one of them said. "Why don't you introduce us to your friend?"

Before he could, his sister was there.

"Ava! I'm so sorry!"

Hannah slipped an arm around Ava's waist and they gave each other the quick and easy hug of girl-friends. If his sister was shocked he'd actually asked Ava to dance, she covered it well.

"I told you I'd be right back and then Will needed a change and I couldn't find his bag. I didn't want to ask Nora or Zach and—"

"It's fine. Really."

"I guess you found someone else."

"Yeah. Or he found me."

"Rescued you," Luke said.

Ava rolled her eyes, and lifted the beer to her lips.

"I think you should know," Zach said, leaning in. "My brother here is ugly as a troll. Uglier."

"Really? Well, that changes everything."

She turned her head in his direction and when she smiled he felt a clutch in his gut. He was still staring when Mia walked up.

"Nice to meet you, Ava," Mia said. "Hannah's mentioned how much you're helping her with camp preparations."

"Oh, not much," Ava said, turning the bottle in her hands. "Just answering a few questions."

"Are you kidding? You've been a lifesaver, but we're not talking about that tonight. I'm on a break from all things stressful."

"Where's Will now?" Mia asked.

"Nora's friend from work took him. She's changing

his clothes, bless her. Hey, you guys should hit the cookie table."

"We did," he and Ava said in unison.

Hannah gave him a curious look. "Well, make sure you fill a to-go bag, or two. The McKinney women are obviously used to baking for an army. Please don't make me haul all those cookies to my house."

"Why doesn't Zach haul his own cookies?" Nick asked.

"Because he and Nora are leaving on their honey moon tonight. But," Hannah held up a finger. "I could stash all the leftovers in their freezer instead of mine. Then Nora can gain twenty pounds instead of me."

Nick shook his head. "Why are women always worried about gaining weight? You can put cookies in my freezer any damn time."

"Mine, too," Zach said.

"Thank you both for your sacrifice. But still," she said, turning to Ava. "Please, make a few bags to go. You could take one to your dad."

"Thanks, he'd love that."

The group chatted a few more minutes, before he and Ava were left alone to finish their beers. The band leader announced it was time for the tossing of the bouquet and called all single women. There were laughs and squeals as some women rushed to the dance floor and some were pulled along. The band leader called again, cajoling all the women to get up and get out there.

"You're not going for that?" Luke asked.

"Ha. My hand eye coordination isn't the best."

"Sorry."

She waved it off. "You wouldn't catch me out there even if I could see."

"Why is that?"

"Because getting married is the last thing I would ever do. And if I want flowers, I'll buy my own."

He'd bet there was a story in there somewhere. He heard it in the tone and in the words she didn't say. He was tempted to press on that, dig for answers. Not smart for a man who didn't want anyone digging into his.

A dark-haired woman walked swiftly up to their table. "Hey, Luke, Ava. Sorry to interrupt but have you seen any kids by chance? About this high, she held her hand at hip level. Blond hair? Probably into mischief?"

"You might check under the cookie table."

She sighed. "Not again."

"Hey. You didn't hear that from me."

"Thanks," she said and went off in that direction.

"Was that Abby?"

"Uh...I'm not sure of her name. Married to my sister's brother-in-law, Matt. You know her?"

"I've met her. She brings her daughter out to ride."

And she remembered by the sound of her voice. Luke wondered how many people he could pick out by their voice alone.

"I should make those to-go bags before I forget." She reached around her, then froze. "Shoot. My cane is at the table."

Luke took Ava's hand, wrapping her fingers around his bicep so that she walked beside him much like an escort. Her steps were tentative and hesitant and he slowed his pace to meet hers.

"Would it be better for you to walk behind me? Tuck your hand into my belt?"

He instantly imagined her small fingers slipping into the band of his pants and... "Never mind. I'm not asking you to put your hand in my pants."

Her lips twitched. "Sounds like you were," she said, her voice light and teasing.

They filled two bags for her parents then Luke led her back to her table where they'd left their cookies. And funny thing, he felt lighter, freer, with her on his arm than he had all day.

"Luke! Hey."

One of his brother's groomsmen approached him and Ava back at her table. Big guy, with a head of thick, wavy black hair. Bull, he thought his name was Bull.

"We need you outside, man. Nick said you had more stuff in your trunk."

"Right." And in the past thirty minutes he'd completely forgotten about his responsibility on the finishing touches of the bride and groom's car. "Well..." He scooted his chair from the table, hesitated.

"Go," Ava said with a wave of her hand. "Please. I'm sure your brother will appreciate the 'stuff' you have for him." She grinned knowingly, then gestured to her cookies. "More for me."

"Don't eat them all."

"I make no promises."

As soon as **Ava** was sure he was far enough away, she dropped her forehead into her hand and took a deep breath. Wow. The man was... potent. And he was her friend's brother. She shook it off and felt for her bag on the table. Finding it, she pulled out her phone.

It had to be getting late. She'd gotten a ride with Hannah from the wedding to the reception, and had tentatively accepted a ride home though she wouldn't put her friend out. She probably had a million things to take care of and she'd been sure she'd be ready to leave well before that. Though after meeting Luke she wasn't as ready as she had been.

She was just about to check her phone for the time when Hannah was beside her.

"Ava! Hey. Come on." She leaned down, a hand on her shoulder, obviously primed to drag her out. "We're doing the whole send off thing."

"Oh, that's okay. I'll just hold down this table. And hey, I was actually about to call for a ride. You don't need one more thing to do tonight."

"What? No, don't do that." Hannah sat in the seat Luke had just left. "Nora's and Zach's co-workers have volunteered to hang til the end and make sure all the gifts are loaded. My sole responsibility is to get their son home and tucked in without noticing they're gone. No small task, but we'll be heading out soon. And come on, you can't miss this! It'll be fun!"

It might be, she thought. But it would also be a mass of people moving through doors and over curbs, all anxious not to miss something that she couldn't see anyway. "I'm good where I am. Honest."

"I could guide you through it."

"Thanks, but no. I was just about to check on my dad." She smiled at Hannah's sincere offer, knowing she meant it. "Go! You can't miss seeing them off."

"Okay. If you're sure."

"I am." When she was alone again, she asked her phone for the time, then the weather for tomorrow. She started to google a place nearby where she could do some indoor swimming for exercise. She loved the horseback riding and would be forever grateful to her sister-in-law for setting that up, but she needed to get in some real cardio.

She could do a local search with voice commands, no problem, but it was still a little loud in here to be getting directions so she dictated a quick text to her best friend, Maddie, instead.

EATING COOKIES. Wish you were here.

LUKE STEPPED BACK and took an approving look at the finished product. The crowd was gathering, ratcheting up the noise around him with festive chatter and laughing.

"He's going to kill you when he gets back," Hannah

said, coming beside him.

"Worth it."

"Okay." Hannah looked around. "I'm going to give the girls a few more minutes to pass out their petals and then give the signal for Zach and Nora to come out."

Stephen joined them with his arms full of toddler. "Damn, sorry I missed the finishing touches." He had Nora and Zach's son Will on one arm and his own son Mitchell sleeping on his shoulder.

"Where's Ava?" Luke looked around, realizing she wasn't there and that he'd expected her to be with his sister.

"She didn't want to come out. I tried," she added firmly.

"I'll get her."

"I don't think she wanted to fight the crowd," Hannah added with a hand on his arm.

"I'll fight it for her," he said, already heading back inside.

"Well," was all Hannah said, sharing an equally curious look with her husband.

There were only a handful of guests still inside. Two women holding babies, a younger man standing over a kid in full out melt–down mode. And Ava. He wasted no time making his way over.

"Show's outside."

Ava jumped at the sound of his voice and he cursed himself. He'd often been told he moved like smoke. "Sorry." He dropped into the seat beside her. "Hey."

"Hey."

"Come on. I don't want you to miss this."

"It's okay, really—"

Nope, it wasn't okay. And he couldn't really say why it bothered him so much to see her sitting alone but it did. "Come on." He stood, pushing his chair all the way in, making sure it was out of her way. "They'll be coming out any second and I don't want to miss the look on my brother's face when he sees his truck."

"Then you should go. I can't just run out there. You'll miss it."

"Neither of us will miss it. Trust me." He wrapped his hand around her upper arm, gently, just to give her a nudge.

She stood, feeling around for her cane. He picked it up, held it to her left hand and put her right hand around his arm, again like an escort. He led her faster than she might have liked but time was of the essence. "I've got you. I promise. There's a clear path to the door. I'll tell you when we get there."

He pushed out the swinging doors and the cool night air rushed at them. The volume had risen with the anticipation and the crowd had split to make a path down the center for the bride and groom.

"Nice job," someone called out to him with a nod to Zach's truck.

The onlookers had split into two sides, leaving a path for the bride and groom. He led Ava right down the center of it and to the left, taking a spot at the end between the decorated truck, and Nick and Mia.

"They're going to kill you," someone else said.

"I take it your work was a success," Ava said.

"I'd say so. I'm particularly proud of the giant, blow–up penis on the roof. And I might have filled his suitcase with condoms, after I zipped–tied them closed."

"Nice."

"Yeah. Oh, and we've got these." He reached into his pocket for the paper cone he'd snagged for her, a bit smashed now. He gave the opening at the top a quick reshaping then touched the flower filled cone to Ava's hand. "It's rose petals. To throw at the happy couple, I'm told."

She took it, sniffed and smiled. "I'm not sure I'll hit the mark, but thank you."

He looked around at the boisterous crowd, most had come out with drinks still in their hands. "You'll do as well as anyone here. I'll tell you when."

She turned her head, and hit him with a smile so sweet he missed his brother's initial exit. But the crowd whooped and cheered and Zach and Nora jogged hand in hand under a shower of pink and red petals.

"Okay, now!"

Laughing, Ava flung out petals, missing the happy couple by several feet.

"How'd I do?" she asked him.

"Perfect."

Zach paused at his truck, threw out some good-natured curses when he saw what had been done, then scooped his bride up into his arms and stuffed her into the front seat. With a wave and a couple of laughing threats aimed at his groomsmen, he rounded the hood, joined his bride and they were off.

"Whew!" Hannah said. "Good times, but I'm exhausted. We need to get these little party animals to bed." Mitchell was now awake and crying a pitiful, weary cry.

"Okay," Ava said. "I'm ready. I just need to get my purse."

"I can get it," Hannah said. "I've got to grab the boys' bags."

"I'll get the car." Stephen strode off.

Hannah touched Ava's arm. "You want to come with or wait here."

"Um..." Ava shifted, brushing her arm against Luke's. "I'll wait here."

Hannah's eyes met Luke's, silently confirming he'd wait here with Ava and he nodded. Weird, he thought, to be silently communicating with his sister.

"Okay. I'll be back in five and Stephen will be here with the car. Need anything else?"

"I don't think— Oh! The to-go bag of cookies. They're on the table."

"Got it."

Luke watched his sister, a mother, a wife, walk swiftly back inside and felt a wave of pride. Then he turned back to Ava and felt something else. She shivered beside him and he angled his body to block hers from the wind. "I should have gotten your coat."

"I didn't bring one. Didn't expect it to be this cold. Guess I should have."

It'd been a warm day for early March but it had to be in the fifties now. If he'd still had his jacket on he'd have given it to her. "You sure you don't want to wait inside?"

"No. It's fine. By the time we get in there it'll be time to come back out."

They were so close. Almost as close as they'd been dancing, but they weren't touching.

"Thanks for the dancing and the cookies," she said. "It was fun." Her lips curved a little, but her eyes still focused just beyond him.

"Yeah. It was," he said, surprising himself that he meant it. He wasn't even touching her, and his pulse was pounding. Her lips were so rosy, looked so soft. He wanted to find out if they were as soft as they looked. He wanted to taste her.

"And thanks for hanging with me," she said. "And saving me from looking so pitiful your sister felt she had to babysit me."

"Me, too. All of it. The hanging, the looking pitiful."

She breathed out a little laugh and smiled. "I doubt you ever look pitiful."

"You'd be surprised." His heartbeat ticked off the seconds. The urge to touch her was so strong, he stuck his hands in his pockets. This was the most he'd felt in way too long. *Well, make a plan, Walker. If you want to see her again, make a plan and make it fast.*

"Ava!" Hannah yelled.

Luke nearly groaned, nearly suggested they should go for coffee, or... He didn't know. Couldn't think of anything that felt quite right. Then Hannah was doing a light jog up to them in her heels.

"Ava. I'm so sorry but I forgot about the extra car seat and we took out the back row so we could help with the gifts." Hannah handed Ava her purse, phone, and two bags of cookies.

"Oh, that's okay," Ava said, completely unruffled. "I'll call an Uber. I do it all the time." She already had her phone out.

"I feel awful," Hannah said. "I really do. Why don't you let Luke take you home?"

"Oh, no. Really. My parents live ten minutes from here. It's not a big deal."

"I'll take you," Luke said.

They went through the dance of *you don't have to* and *I don't mind,* with Hannah there thanking Luke and encouraging Ava to accept.

"I totally vouch for him," Hannah added.

Ava wasn't worried about that. Not really. She'd been with him for a while now and he seemed perfectly nice. Definitely wasn't drunk. And it's not like she didn't get into cars with strangers all the time. But she didn't *need* him to.

"Please," Hannah said.

"Okay." She might not need it but Hannah obviously did. "Well," she said turning to Luke. "Guess you're taking me home."

"I guess I am."

5

L uke walked Ava to his truck and opened the door for her. He was trying to figure out if she needed guidance getting in, if he should describe it or touch her or... And then she was already in.

He reached up, grabbed the seatbelt and was just about to stretch it across her body when she reached to do it herself. Her hand caught him in the arm at the same time her cheek turned into his hand. They both froze.

"I can buckle myself," she said, with just the hint of a smile but her eyes were definitely laughing.

"Right. Got it." Cursing himself, he rounded the hood and got in. The second he cranked on the engine, Luke Bryan blasted through the speakers.

He immediately turned it down. "Sorry," he said again.

"Like it loud, huh?"

"Well, I was uh… driving to the wedding earlier. Or the pre-wedding photos… I had the windows down and… Yeah."

"I listen to loud music when I'm nervous."

"I wasn't nervous."

"Oh. Okay. I just thought wedding so…I would have been nervous."

"You ever listen to Luke Bryan?"

"No. I don't know this song. I don't listen to country music really."

"Mmm. You're missing out." He glanced over at her face, noticed her nose scrunched up in an apologetic smirk. Adorable.

He let the music play, let the song finish out between them as he drove out of the lot and turned onto the main rode. "Okay, fine. I was nervous."

She grinned but didn't do a *told you so*. "Country, huh?"

"Sometimes," he said, lying because it was pretty much all he listened to. "We can listen to whatever you want. The controls are all right here." Should he take her hand? Guide her to them so she could choose what she wanted for herself? "The music and if you want heat or air."

"Got it," she said, and looked like she was trying not to laugh.

He didn't blame her. He was acting like he'd never had a female in his truck before.

"Well. That was fun," she said, having pity on him.

"Yeah. A busy day all around, but not too bad."

"I appreciate the ride."

"Sure. No problem." Why the hell was he so edgy? He'd held her in his arms earlier now he couldn't handle being two feet away. He could still smell her, even over the lingering baby vomit faintly clinging to his shirt.

Her parents' house was just as close as she'd said and they were there in under ten minutes. He searched the mailboxes lining the quiet residential street for the number she'd given him. He found it, turned into the driveway. The home sat on a medium sized lot, a neat one story, red brick and white siding. He cut the engine, came around and opened her door offering his arm when she got out. Getting the hang of this, he thought to himself.

"Well. Thanks again," she said as they scaled the three brick steps to the front door.

"You're welcome."

Ava turned to open the door and he waited behind her. She wasn't the sort of girl a guy met and walked to the door a few hours later to cop a kiss. He thought about holding his hand out for a shake but that was ridiculous.

Or did she want him to kiss her? God knows he was dying to.

Ava stepped inside and hesitated, looking back at him. There was something he wanted to say, but he didn't know what it was and it didn't come to him fast enough.

"Goodnight, Luke."

"Good night, Ava." And with that, she closed the door.

6

"Damn it," Ava said, tripping over a pile of laundry then banging her knee on the corner of the coffee table. Breakfast dishes clanged in the sink followed by her mom's profuse apology as she hurried in from the kitchen.

"Are you okay, sweetie?"

"I'm fine," Ava said, forcing a smile through gritted teeth.

"Are you sure? I'm just out of practice since you're never here. I keep forgetting."

"Yes. Positive." Ava rubbed at her knee, ignoring her mom's subtle mention of her lack of visiting. "It's okay, Mom." It'd been three weeks now, and if her mom had picked up the clutter, it had reappeared. Or maybe it multiplied. Even though she'd grown up in this house, it was her parents' space, and it made her even more anxious to get back to her own.

"Where's your cane?"

"It's in my room," she said stepping cautiously around the table. She wasn't used to having to rely on her cane in her apartment. She knew where everything was and wasn't. Could move confidently through the clear paths she left for herself. "Hey, I'm going to grab a shower."

She counted out twenty–two steps down the hallway to her old bedroom and grabbed what she needed before crossing the hall to the bathroom.

She closed the door behind her, turned the lock. She hadn't lived at home since she was eighteen. At thirty–one, she didn't need her mom poking her head in while she was naked.

When she'd been young, her mom had been meticulous about the house and keeping Ava's paths cleared. A constant problem for her older brother who had a habit of dropping backpacks and shoes where he stood.

She was just coming into her bedroom, her wet hair wrapped in a towel, when she heard her best friend's ring tone on her cell. Sliding her hand across her dresser, she tapped her phone twice to answer the call. "Maddie. Hey."

"When are you coming back?"

Ava dropped the towel and grabbed some underwear. "What?"

"I said, when are you coming back? I've had the worst two days of my life, beginning with walking out of my apartment without my purse and thus locking myself *out* of my apartment—"

"Oh, no."

"Oh, yes, and then having to beg Funky Frank, the landlord from hell, to let me in. Then getting waylaid after work by Nosy Nina to go to Russo's for a beer, because obviously we're best friends now after she bummed a tampon from me at work."

Ava chuckled as she pulled on jeans.

"Yeah, laugh it up."

"I'm sorry. But you could have said no. To Russo's, not the tampon."

"Yeah, right. And have her whine to everyone that I don't like her because Ben started talking her up after he ghosted me?"

"I am sorry." Maddie had been her best friend since the first day of third grade when she'd shoved a boy for calling Ava clumsy as she tried to navigate a new classroom. Maddie'd had to sit out recess as a punishment. Ava had sat with her and in fifteen minutes their friendship had been cemented.

Over the years they'd grown as close as sisters, maybe closer. She didn't think she would have survived middle school without Maddie. It was hard enough to navigate the subtle nuances of pre-teens for a sighted person, but when you couldn't see, couldn't read the body language, it could be deadly.

"How's Mister B?"

They'd been friends long enough that Maddie had dropped her last name down to one letter. "Good. Better. I'm going to the rehab place this morning. If he does well, I think he'll come home tomorrow or the next."

"That's good news. Then *you* can come home."

"Yeah. And not that simple." Ava grabbed a plain long-sleeved T-shirt— she didn't have a sense of the color except that she knew Maddie had labeled it white which she knew went with any other *color*.

Maddie had helped her organize her closet with braille labels that Ava made and attached to the hangers, as well as small tags inside the clothing. She couldn't show up at the United Nations wearing the bottoms of one pantsuit and the jacket from another.

"I miss you," Maddie said, the pout clear in her voice. "Ryan couldn't help them?"

"He has been helping them. And Connie, too. But I can't leave him to do everything." Her sister-in-law and brother, both attorneys, did a lot. Enough to make her feel like she needed to come home and take some of the weight.

"Well, it was his choice not to move away."

And her choice *to* move away, Ava thought guiltily.

She pulled out a pair of short leather boots. She moved her fingers quickly over the braille label stuck to the bottom near the heel where it never touched the ground, confirming they were the ones she wanted.

She knew that certain items and combinations were ones she'd worn to certain events so she had memories of wearing them, even if she couldn't see them. That gave her a sense of knowing what she was wearing. Like the dress she'd worn to the wedding. The one she'd worn when she'd danced with Luke.

"Why are you complaining anyway? You're still in the city," she said, running her hand to the right, lightly touching the few hanging items she'd brought from New York.

"It's not as much fun without you."

"Well, I miss you, too." Ava's fingers paused when they came to the cool, satiny fabric. If she brought it to her face would she smell him? She leaned in, sniffed. Yep.

"Are you dying of boredom?"

Ava smiled, thinking of Luke. "They're keeping me pretty busy. Nothing fun. Calling the insurance company, vetting the bills, getting special bathroom equipment delivered. Oh, and taking care of Rocky," she said, of her parents' Shitzu.

"Aww. How is Rocky?"

"Hanging in there, my little angel. He's sixteen, takes meds three times a day and wears a diaper."

"Yikes. Still riding horses? I bet you smell like a barn."

"Yep and I do." She sat to pull on socks. "I've even scooped manure."

"Any sane person would ask why."

"One, to get out of the house, two to get out of the house, and three—"

"To get out of the house."

"No. Number three is I actually like it."

"Well that's scary and you've obviously been there too long. When are you coming back?"

"I don't know. He's already behind schedule because of the infection. I'd hoped he'd be home and settled by now. I feel like I need to stay long enough to get him back on his feet. Or at least until he doesn't need someone here twenty–four seven."

"Meanwhile I don't have anyone to drink Friday cocktails with."

"That's no reason to sit at home," Ava said, tugging up the side zippers on her boots. Not exactly riding boots, but they worked. "What about Sabina? Or Katy?"

"I didn't say I was sitting at home," Maddie said with a laugh. "And I have met the random guy here and there. None worth a second drink. But I need you here. I need my wing woman. I need you to listen for their lies."

A knot curled in Ava's stomach. "I'm no lie detector." Her faith in her ability to read people had been thoroughly shaken in the past year. Everything had been shaken. Having your husband wake up one day and say he didn't want to be married to you anymore would do that.

Maddie blew out a breath. "Sorry." Like a true friend, Maddie held savage disdain for Ava's ex.

"Hey, maybe you could come down here for a visit. You could ride a horse."

"I don't think so. Ooh! How was the wedding? You did go, didn't you?"

"I did, and it was good. Thanks again for mailing the dress."

"No prob. Was it cowboy themed?"

"I don't know why you think this is the country. You lived here half your life. Norfolk is twenty minutes away."

"Anything not the city is the country. Besides, my passport says NYC."

"Well, it was nice. There were fresh flowers, a great band at the reception. Oh, and this cookie table. You wouldn't believe it. Rows and rows of cookies. Luke gave me the tour—it was that many cookies— and we piled our plate until they were falling off. You should've heard him trying to describe each one. There was this one—"

"Whoa, back up. Who's Luke?"

"Hannah's brother. She's the one that has the barn and—"

"Yeah, yeah. I got that. I want to hear more about Luke."

"He was nice. Sweet. We danced."

"Oooh. And?"

"And... I don't know if I'll see him again."

"But he's Hannah's brother, right? This horse thing is making more sense now. Save a horse, ride a cowboy."

"Ha." She hated that talking about the wedding made her think of Blake. She shouldn't be hurt after all this time. She wouldn't be. She shouldn't even be angry, but she absolutely would not be hurt. "Blake emailed me."

"Asshole."

Ava smiled in agreement.

"What the hell did he want?"

"Oh, you know. Just checking in. Asking about Dad. He asked me to call him."

"God, I'd really like to hurt him. Can I please? Just a little?"

"You know you wouldn't last an hour in a cell. There's no Starbucks in prison."

"True."

"At least for the time I'm here I don't have to run into him." Because he also worked at the UN, but in the IT department. It was a big place, but since the divorce she ran into him at least once a month. Or maybe more than that. After all, how would she know?

His parting words to her as they'd left the attorney's office had been, *I hope we can be friends.*

She'd been so shocked by his *hope,* she'd stumbled getting into the elevator. Had violently rejected his quick offer of help with a jerk of her arm. She'd never felt her blindness so keenly, never felt so small, so... lacking. All she'd wanted was to get away. Away from him. Away from the feelings she was afraid to admit were still there. She'd loved him for five years. Why couldn't she turn it off like he had?

"Here's an idea," Maddie said. "Take the cowboy for a ride. Exorcise the demon that is your ex."

The idea had merit, Ava thought, but digging out from under a failed marriage took time. And so, *so* much emotional energy. She was better off being alone. Her phone dinged with a time reminder. "Oh, shoot. Hey, I need to go. Mom is dropping me at the rehab place while she goes to an eye appointment."

"Okay. Hug Mr. and Mrs. B for me."

"I will. I miss you."

"Miss you more."

She ended the call, felt for her small silver studs on her dresser and put them in her ears.

Take the cowboy for a ride.

She wouldn't deny she'd felt a tug in her belly when she'd danced with Luke. Couldn't deny she'd been disappointed when he'd dropped her off without so much as a kiss on the cheek, which was insane. She needed to keep her life simple. She'd had way too much complicated in the past year. And she wasn't at all sure kissing Luke Walker would be simple.

"Thanks for doing this Ava," her mom said as they drove to the rehab facility. "I've had this appointment for ages and I don't want to cancel."

"Of course. That's what I came for."

"I don't know." Her mother sighed the heavy sigh of the martyr. "I should be there. I can cancel this eye thing or change it."

"Mom, you said you'd been waiting for months to get in to see this doctor. It'll take you months to get another appointment."

"I know. I just can't believe it worked out like this, today of all days."

"I'll make a note of every single thing his doctor says, I promise. I'll even record it on my phone if you want. I think I can record and take notes at the same time."

"You know your father won't ask any questions."

Ava smiled thinking of her affable father. He'd be coming home tomorrow, assuming his doctor gave him the pass to continue his physical therapy at home after today. "I'll ask them." And she would ask again about getting some in home help. Her parents didn't have the extra money to hire someone to come in, and so far the insurance wasn't paying.

"Okay. Your brother said he'd get here if he could, but it was doubtful," Ava's mom said, as she pulled to a stop under the awning of the rehab facility. "Do you need me to walk you in?"

"No. I'm good," she said, evenly and with a smile, but jeez. How did her mother think she survived on her own? Only by the grace of God, would probably be her mother's answer. Ava gathered her purse and her guide stick.

"The door is straight ahead. Maybe twelve steps."

"Okay. Thanks." She'd been here four times. It was actually slightly to the left and sixteen steps.

"I can just walk you in. I've got time." She put the car in park.

"Mom. Please. I've got it. Go."

"I'll be back to get you in two, maybe three hours depending."

Ava stopped outside the car, her hand on the open door. "I'm going to the barn for a riding lesson after this."

"Ava! That's thirty minutes away. I don't know if I—"

"Mom, I'll be fine. Promise." She'd waited until the last minute to tell her mother this.

Ava closed the car door before her mother could argue, drew in a deep breath and made her way in. The automatic doors opened with a whoosh and she was blasted with that sickly smell of hospitals and rehab facilities. Overly sweet cleaning supplies that couldn't quite cover up the stale smell of sickness and old people. Her dad wasn't that old and he wasn't that sick. She'd be glad to get him out of here.

Blake's hospital room hadn't been like that. As the renowned transplant facility in the country it had smelled clean, fresh, new. That had been a happy time, even with the nervous anticipation.

"You're getting eyes!" she'd said for the fourth time, squeezing Blake's hand.

"You're repeating yourself," Blake had said, but gave her hand a return squeeze.

"I know. I just can't help it." She couldn't have been more excited if it was herself just hours away from a corneal transplant. Her husband, her blind husband and best friend, could possibly be able to see in a few months.

"It might not work," Blake said.

"I know. And I know you have to be realistic, but you also have to be positive."

"I am."

"Positively realistic?"

This time when he squeezed her hand he kept on squeezing. "I love you."

"I know. I love you, too. For better or worse."

"For better or worse," he repeated.

"Yep. But I think this is about to be for better. I really do. The best." She clasped her other hand around their joined hands as if by touching him she could lend him her strength.

Blake took a deep breath and let it out. She knew he was nervous. He'd put in for a double corneal transplant four years ago and they both knew the odds and the risks. His body could reject the transplants, among other things. She knew regardless of how many times he reminded her, and himself, that it might not work, how devastated he would be if it didn't.

"I'm sorry you're not a candidate," he said softly, interrupting her thoughts.

"What? Blake, don't. You know I'm happy for you."

"I know. But I feel guilty."

"That's stupid. And you're not generally stupid."

He laughed softly. "Thanks. You know what I'm looking forward to seeing most?"

"Yes. Me. You told me."

"True. But specifically, your eyes. I want to see your eyes." He touched a gentle finger to her brow, ran one *smooth fingertip down to her lips. "Then your smile. Then..." His finger continued down her neck, her chest.*

"I get it." She smiled and covered his hand with her own, stopping him from going any lower. "I hope you like what you see."

"No question." He rubbed his thumb over the wedding band he'd placed on her finger almost a year before. "I couldn't do this without you, Ava."

"Ava!" her dad called when she reached his room. "Hey, baby girl."

"Hi, Daddy." She leaned over to kiss his cheek. This was real love. Unconditional and lasting.

7

L uke drove a second replacement post into the ground and secured a cross board to either end. He'd taken some time off from working on the first of the campers' cabins this morning to replace a few rotted sections of fence. There were four turn–out paddocks, each one about half the size of a football field and each one had at least a couple posts that needed attention.

He'd been up before the sun had burned away the dewy mist of dawn when the world was blanketed in a soft gray. The trees in the distance blurred around the edges. Now the landscape was a pallet of greens instead of grays. The heavy stillness of fog replaced by a gentle breeze that had every new blade of grass swaying with life.

He tried not to think it was the perfect place for the enemy to hide. Tried not to slide his hand over his hip and be reminded that he didn't have a gun if death rose up out of the field and started shooting at him.

He didn't close his eyes. Couldn't force himself to do that, but he did concentrate on breathing normally, slowing his heart rate. *Not a war zone. Not a war zone. Not a war zone.*

He scanned the expanse of raw land. Horses made soft noises or stood stock still, heads down. No sign they sensed danger. He inhaled the scent of damp grass and fresh manure. Sometimes, even here, he swore he smelled diesel exhaust, burnt rubber, and smoke.

The sky overhead was clear, clear and blue and he couldn't look at it without thinking of Ava's eyes. The sun was warm now and he'd traded his sweatshirt of earlier for short sleeves. After two more screws at the bottom, he gave the post a good shove, assuring himself it was solid.

He stretched his neck and looked down the fence line. He'd walked almost the entire way from the cabin to the barn. Might as well see if his sister needed help with anything else while he was here. Keeping busy was the best coping strategy. Assuming he needed a strategy to cope.

He entered the barn through the open back doors, passing stalls on his way to the office. He'd passed three empty stalls before he heard his sister telling someone what a handsome boy they were.

He stood just outside the stall, watching her stroke the big gelding.

"And such a good boy, too. Yes, you are."

"You talking to me?"

Hannah turned at the sound, then grinned over her shoulder. "Well, you're moderately handsome, though you don't hold a candle to Newman."

"Mmm. Careful he doesn't step on you."

Hannah rolled her eyes before turning back to the horse. "What are you doing here?"

"Nothing. I was just working on some fence posts I noticed were loose. Thought I'd see if you needed anything else."

"If you're going for best brother award, you're in the lead." Hannah grabbed the pitchfork leaning outside the stall and scooped up a fork full of manure laden straw.

"Here. Give me that." Luke stepped up to take the pitch fork from her. She didn't let it go.

"I can do it."

"I know you can."

"Then let go."

"Fine," he said, raising his hands in surrender. He still saw her as two with hair sticking up all over her head in golden tufts. His brothers had been tight once, even if the years and miles he'd put between them had killed that. But his baby sister, he'd missed her entire life. Funny how regret could grow once it started.

At fifteen, he'd been in awe of this tiny little thing his mom had brought home. A lone girl in a house of teenage boys. He remembered how his mom had fussed over every detail for months. How he'd moved into Nick's room so his mom could make the pink and white nursery of her dreams.

A surly teen to his core, it'd been hard to keep up his angry shell when Hannah gave him her toothy slobbery grin or patted his cheeks with sticky fingers. She wouldn't remember any of that. Given what had happened the night he'd left, he should be grateful she was too young to remember.

Unless Nick had told her.

"You know you always had your fingers in your mouth."

Hannah gave him a curious look, wrinkled up her nose. "Well good thing I broke that habit."

"So you say."

Hannah rolled her eyes again and Newman dipped his head over the half door. Luke ran his hand over the silky neck of Hannah's newest Gelding. "How's he settling in?"

"Good, I think. He's a good boy, aren't you." The old horse, dipped his head. "He'll be good for the kids to ride. He's strong. We'll just need to get to know him, let him get to know the area. I've neglected Winnie lately. I think she's getting jealous. You know, if you have time, maybe we could go ride together."

"Okay."

"I'm also looking into getting a donkey."

"You're going to put a kid on a donkey?"

"No, dork. Not for riding. Someone who runs an animal rescue called and asked if I had any room here. So I'm thinking maybe. I'll just make sure he's as sweet as they say he is. Anyway, I'm thinking of moving Newman into that front turn–out. I think Pete would make a good friend for him."

"Horses need friends?"

Hannah shot him a too kind look over her shoulder. "Everyone needs friends, Luke."

She looked at him just a beat too long, probably wanted to ask if he'd been sleeping again to which he would lie and say yes. But thankfully, she didn't ask and turned back to the horse. He rarely came over to the barn during the day, preferring to work alone on the cabin. But he did try to check in when he knew Hannah was going through morning chores before her first riders of the day arrived.

"Before I do that, I need to make sure that back right corner is secure. I've let it go because Banjo's not going anywhere, but I don't fully trust Newman."

"Already done."

She stopped, stared at him. "Seriously? Luke, you're already doing too much."

"I don't mind," he said, looking away.

She closed and latched the bottom half of the stall door, then leaned the pitchfork against the wall and rose up to kiss his cheek. "Then you're a good boy, too."

"Yeah, yeah." Luke took the wheelbarrow from her and rolled it out, dumped the pile.

He wasn't used to it, his sister's affection. Often wondered how she was able to give it so freely to a brother she barely knew. Maybe there was some kind of subconscious memory from her two-year-old self.

However self-absorbed he'd been, he'd loved her ridiculously, even if he hadn't known how to show it.

When he came back into the barn she was pouring grain into Newman's feed bucket.

"I started on the bunk beds last night. I went by your measurements, but you might want to take a look, make sure it's what you had in mind."

"That's awesome. And it makes it seem *really* real." She moved on to the next stall. "I still wish you'd stay with us. There's no need for you to rough it."

"And risk seeing Stephen's bare ass? No, thanks. I'm good, really. I like it, it's quiet. And it's hardly roughing it."

Hannah had offered the couch in the small house she shared with Stephen and their one–and–a–half–year–old a hundred times. No way did they need someone sleeping on their couch. He'd spent a week on Zach's before his brother's lease ran out and he moved in with Nora and Will.

Luke considered it a stroke of luck that his sister needed help building cabins for her camp. So he'd thrown his sleeping bag down on the foundation and spent his days, and nights, building walls.

Hannah was still looking at him. Trying to read him? Wondering if there was a reason he'd rather be alone in the quiet? He forced a smile and that seemed to satisfy her. "Insulation's in. Most of the interior walls are finished."

Along with his brothers, Stephen, and a couple more McKinneys, they'd gotten the thirty by forty–five foot space framed and dried-in in a weekend. With Matt's direction—and some help from YouTube, Luke had managed the plumbing. Matt McKinney had sent over one of his guys for the electrical.

"You don't even have a kitchen table."

Hannah said it like it was the worst thing in the world. He wouldn't point out all the places he'd eaten. "I will soon. I'm working on one with some of the scrap pieces."

"I don't know where you're finding the time to do all this, but I'd like to see it. And I still need to pay you for the lumber and nails and... whatever else."

"Don't worry about it."

"Luke. You're not doing the work and paying for the materials too."

Despite a few nonprofit grants, he knew she and Stephen were putting most everything they had into this place. "I may have lost the receipts."

"Luke! I need those receipts for taxes."

She turned to him again and he caught mild annoyance in her eyes, not pity. Progress.

"Sorry. I'll remember next time." Like hell he would. He had money from twenty years of service. Except for a truck and a cheap apartment, he hadn't had any reason to spend it. Other than helping out Hannah and Freedom Farm, he didn't have a reason now. "Where's Stephen?"

"He's dropping Mitchell and Will off at his mom's for a few hours."

"The honeymooners are back tomorrow?"

"Yes." She paused on her way to the office and gave Winnie a scratch between the ears. "I think Mitchell is going to miss having Will around. It's making us think about trying for a second."

"Trying what for a second what? Oh. Um." He straightened. Was she actually looking at him like she wanted his opinion? "Well, I don't know about that."

"You mean you don't *want* to know about it."

"Yes. I do. *Not* want to know, I mean."

She laughed as his face went hot. He took a step back. "Do you want help with turn-out, or not?"

"Yes, but first I could use some help with my To-Do list. Honestly, it's starting to make me crazy."

He followed her to the barn office, stopping in the doorway. She sat down at her desk piled with miscellaneous papers and pulled out the notebook he knew was her camp to-do list bible.

"I'm waiting on call backs from two suppliers, hoping for donations," she said, making a note in her book. "Stephen's brother Matt has offered to help and I've got you, but... am I crazy? To think I could do *this*? I mean what am I thinking? I need strobe lights in the cabins for the hearing impaired and braille everything for the blind. I want to get as far along as I can before Ava leaves so she can go over everything and tell me what I've missed. She's going to help me get the nameplates ordered for outside the stalls.

"Every path needs lighting and braille markers. I'm scratching the dining hall for now—each cabin will eat breakfast and dinner separately. We'll do picnic style for lunches."

Luke shrugged, pretending not to notice the mention of Ava. "It's camp. Kids are supposed to rough it." He snagged a cracker from the open package on his sister's desk. He rarely saw his sister eat a real meal.

"I know, but a lot of these kids require extra consideration. They have medicines that have to be refrigerated and dietary restrictions and—" She pulled at her hair. "I am crazy. I truly am. To think I could have all of this done by June. Certifiable."

"I don't think you're crazy. You can add cabins as you go." He shrugged. "Consider this first summer a trial run." She'd already had a summer day camp, now she was looking to expand to overnight. It made sense and it would open it up to a lot more kids who didn't live close enough to be driven back and forth every day.

"Well, I was definitely crazy to think I could have had this up and running by last fall."

"I agree, that was a long shot."

She sighed. "Yeah. But that's good about the bunks. Thanks, really. It's a huge help and I can't wait to see them."

"No, problem. It's working out on my end, too." Because he wasn't ready to make the leap of signing a lease or buying a house. Plus, the thought of having nothing to do during the long nights made him edgy.

"I'm lucky you're here," Hannah said. "And I'm glad

you're here. Even if you weren't helping I'd be glad. So glad."

He almost said, *me, too*, but he didn't want to lie. He wanted to be glad. He wanted to feel like this was right, that it was where he was supposed to be, but the truth was, he just didn't know. He couldn't tell his baby sister that nothing felt right and at least twenty times a day he was sure he'd made a mistake leaving the military.

"Yeah, well. I don't have anything else to do, so..." He shrugged, shifted, angling for the door and escape. The long look Hannah gave him made his insides squirm. Guess saying you didn't have anything to do struck another worry chord in his sister's heart. And wouldn't it? Most grown ass men had direction. Purpose. Most forty-year-old men didn't walk away from the only career they'd ever known with absolutely no plan. *Shit*.

But his sister was staring at him, waiting on some kind of answer or reassurance. "Just kidding," he said, and raised his hand, thinking to ruffle her hair but ended up giving her an awkward pat on the shoulder. She was twenty–seven, not two. "I'll get going on the bunks." He purposefully left off that he had an appointment later. If he told her she'd ask what it was and he didn't want to say.

"Okay. Hey."

He stopped at the door, half afraid she somehow knew.

"Ava's coming out to ride later."

His pulse might have jumped a little at that news but he was confident he didn't let it show. "Okay."

"Just thought you might want to come say hi. You two seemed to hit it off at the wedding. She doesn't know many people here," Hannah added when he just stood there. "I think she's getting a little stir crazy with her parents."

He blinked. "Okay."

"Jeez," Hannah said. "Go. Get out before you talk my ear off. You can take Big Al out with you."

He made his escape, clipping a halter and lead rope to Big Al, a small Shetland pony. He walked Al out to his paddock to join Hazel for some spring grass and sunshine. He hadn't thought much about horses before coming here, but he liked them well enough. They watched, considered, taking in their surroundings, their jaws moving in slow circles as they chowed contentedly on grass.

"Okay, big guy, go do what horses do." Al stood still in front of him, his head lowered for a scratch between the ears. "Okay, fine. But you do know you're not a dog, right?"

Al bobbed his head as if answering which was kind of creepy. He kept rubbing the course strands of the pony's forelock, and squinted up at the sky. What would he do if he saw Ava again? Since he was on his way to a psych appointment, or transition counselor, as the military liked to call it, it was probably best for both of them if he did nothing.

"Okay, Al. That's all you get. Some of us have work

to do." Again, as if Al understood him, the pony turned and ambled off, lowering his head to the grass.

Luke left the paddock, secured the latch behind him, thinking of Ava. Ava with the blue eyes, soft skin and a smile that killed him.

8

It was a thirty minute drive to the nearest office of Veterans Affairs In order to finalize his retirement, or any type of discharge, and receive benefits, all soldiers had to make six meetings with a transition counselor spread over the course of three months.

They wanted vets to check in, touch base, and hopefully get men and women to see the benefit of reaching out for help before it was too late. They also helped with civilian job placement and dealing with the differences encountered in civilian life. Sometimes it was just to talk. His least favorite thing to do.

He didn't resent the new program. Much. He didn't need it, but he knew guys who did. The suicide rate among returning veterans was staggering, so he had to appreciate the effort. Even so, he'd asked if he could just do all six of his hours in one day. Not the way it worked, so this would make his third appointment.

He'd waited a month to get started. Okay, closer to two, but he was in it now.

Financially, he wasn't pressed to get a job. The only thing he'd ever bought was a cheap house he didn't sleep in enough for it to matter, and a truck. But he wouldn't deny he needed a plan. Couldn't deny he felt at loose ends.

It often felt like all his ends were loose and flying when he preferred things be tied down tight.

"What's up doc?" Luke said, entering the small office at the end of a dank, cinderblock hallway.

"As I've told you before, I'm not a doctor," Gary said with a shake of his head and an easy smile. "Have a seat."

"Right." Luke took the shit brown and puke green upholstered chair across from Gary. Gary Drummond. Military–Civilian Transition Coach was his official title. He had nothing against Gary, a former marine. He actually liked the guy. But however they dressed it up, Gary was a therapist, and even if neither of them said the word, they both knew it.

Luke looked around the office. The beat-up pine desk. Low metal filing cabinet with a first-generation Keurig on top and a tall ceramic mug that said *My Wife Thinks I'm Hot*. A tall bookshelf on the wall to the left held more crap than books. But there in the center was a medal in a box. He wondered if that was to remind people like him that Gary had indeed served. Help build rapport? A tangible way to say, *I know where you're coming from*?

Fifty-ish, Gary was on the shorter side, stocky, with a thick beard and saggy brown eyes that had him always looking like he was recovering from an all-nighter. The wire rimmed glasses, loose fitting khakis, and white and brown checked dress shirt made Luke think nutty professor. "You put in for a bigger office yet?"

Gary sat back, smiled again. "You don't like my office?"

"Mmm." Luke cracked his neck side to side. He hadn't seen him in the winter yet, but fully expected to see the same shirt layered with a navy sweater vest. Weird he noticed so much about Gary's clothes. "At least you have a view."

Gary looked over his shoulder at the window behind him. An air conditioning system blocked any view if there was one. He turned back, steepled his fingers. "You survived the wedding."

One good thing about Gary was he didn't shuffle through papers like he was trying to remember who you were.

"Appears I did."

"See." Gary spread his hands. "Told you there was nothing to worry about."

"Who said I was worried?"

Gary sat back with a friendly expression. That was one thing he *didn't* like about Gary. He saw too much. "They both said I do and now they're married."

"You happy about that?"

"He's my brother. Why wouldn't I be?"

Gary shrugged. "Just making conversation."

Luke rested his elbows on the armrests, steepled his fingers, mirroring Gary. He waited for Gary to pose a question. Gary waited too. A standoff, Army versus Marines. As a Special Forces fighter, Luke figured he had the upper hand.

"Anything eventful?" Gary finally asked.

"You mean did I get drunk and stumble into the cake singing *Sweet Caroline*?"

Gary laughed. "Weddings are rife with wayward relatives."

"Well, I wasn't the wayward one. Didn't stab anyone with my salad fork." *Not even the fifth person who'd asked him about life in the Rangers, or the sixth one who'd clapped him on the shoulder and said it must be nice to be back.*

"Anyone stumble into the cake? Take the band's mic to make a drunken statement of love?"

Luke huffed out a laugh. "You've been to wild weddings, Doc. But, no. Nothing eventful, unusual, out of the ordinary, or unexpected." Except Ava. Ava had been unexpected.

Gary leaned back in his chair into what Luke now thought of as his non-threatening pose. "You mentioned last time you didn't know why you were here. In this town specifically."

Luke raised a brow. "Jumping right in today, huh, Doc?"

Gary lifted his hands in a small, hey, I'm innocent gesture. It was a harmless enough question. Not even a question really, though every comment Gary made was meant to elicit a response.

"Reconnecting with family can be hard. Especially when you've been gone so long."

Luke said nothing. It didn't feel like reconnecting exactly. He hadn't ever been connected to his brothers as an adult. This was more like repeatedly seeing people you were supposed to have a deep connection with but didn't. He hadn't shared a Christmas or birthday with his siblings in over twenty years.

Somewhere, deep down, maybe he'd thought that if he came back, he could go back to that time. Do what he should have done, been who he should've been. Too bad life didn't work like that.

"Sometimes going to weddings makes people start thinking about their own future."

He looked back to Gary. "Is going to a wedding what made you want to get married?"

"No. I met Laura, fell in love, and then I wanted to get married."

"Please. Tell me more."

Gary chuckled. "Here. I've got something for you. Even if you are a pain in my ass."

While Gary shuffled through a pile of papers on his desk, Luke thought about what he wasn't saying about the wedding. That he'd felt more in those moments with Ava in his arms than he'd felt in weeks. Maybe years.

But there'd been something there with Ava before the song hit the second chorus. Before he'd even asked her to dance. Beyond beautiful, she was funny, smart, easy to talk to, and relaxed. And in turn she relaxed him. And maybe she'd needed him, just a little.

Timing is everything, isn't that what people said? But *time* was also everything and you never knew how much of it you were going to get. He'd seen that time and time again. "What were you thinking about just now?"

Luke's mind jerked back, but on the outside he showed no sign Gary had interrupted his thoughts. "Nothing."

Gary sighed. "So, civilian jobs I thought might interest you." He slid over a sheet of paper.

Civilian job. Why did that sound like such a dirty word? Maybe because he felt guilty for being on the outside and out of danger. Now *that* was something Gary would love to talk about.

Luke gave the list a quick look.

"Operations research analyst," Gary said, tapping his finger at the top of the page. "This could be strategizing business plans and best practices for an organization. It's a job that comes naturally to a lot of Rangers who've been trained in logistics and military strategy. These are research-intensive jobs that involve investigating a company. It'd be primarily behind a desk—"

"No. No desk."

Gary looked up from his paper. "Okay. No desk. That narrows things down a bit." He looked back to his paper. "Training and Development Managers. Corporations have finally figured out that Rangers make especially good trainers, teaching others to think strategically in a fast-paced environment. It involves assessing employees—"

"Nope. Don't want to assess anyone and I don't want employees."

"They wouldn't be your employees, but got it." He made an X next to that one. "What about security?"

"Paul Blart?"

Gary laughed. "I wasn't thinking mall cop, but if that interests you..." He shrugged.

"Would I get a Segway?"

"Maybe." Gary sat back. "Are you staying in this area? Have you decided that?"

Luke made a noncommittal sound, shrugged.

"It's good to have family. A support system."

Luke nodded even as he thought Gary was making a great argument as to why he *shouldn't* stay. He didn't want his siblings to support him. Emotionally or otherwise.

"Okay. Moving on. What about law enforcement?"

"No, thanks."

"You know," Gary said, taking a sip of his coffee. "It's a good thing you're so easy to work with. Otherwise I might feel like I'm not good at my job. What about teaching?"

"You mean *kids*? Among other reasons, I'm not qualified."

"Maybe not, but with minimal hours through Troops to Teachers, all offered online, you could be. High school math. History. Maybe geography. Share your knowledge, and shiny personality, with the next generation." Greg smiled and slid the typed sheet of paper across the desk.

Luke took it, folded the sheet precisely in half, then slid his finger along the fold. He'd come back bodily whole when a lot of men hadn't. And what was he going to do with that? One more thing to feel guilty about.

"Thanks," he said and folded it precisely again. "I appreciate the effort here."

Gary sighed, tapped his fingers together. "How are things with the family?"

"Great. Other than the looks they share when they don't think I'm looking. Like they're afraid I'm about to blow and they don't know whether to sacrifice themselves and jump on top of me or run."

"Are you worried you're going to blow?"

Was he? He didn't think so. And maybe that meant something was wrong with him. "No. And that wasn't right. None of them would run. Not my older brother who no doubt thinks I'm here because I got kicked out for some reason, not even my baby sister who wants to pet me and feed me and worries if I'm sleeping enough."

Seconds passed in silence and Luke sighed. "Go ahead. Ask. I know you have to."

"I don't have to," the man across from him said with a hint of defensiveness.

Luke waited.

"Okay, fine," Gary said and huffed. He leaned forward to open his notebook. "How are you sleeping?"

"Like a baby."

"Dreams?"

"Dreams?" Luke raised an eyebrow. "I'm not sure we know each well enough for that."

"Smart ass."

"Okay. Rarely, but when I do, they're wet dreams."

Gary cracked a smile at that, and shook his head. "My wife is going to love this when she types up my notes."

"What?"

"Kidding. What about sex? Have you been... intimate with anyone since you've been back?"

"Definitely not going there." Luke leaned back, stretched his long legs out in front of him. "But if there's something *you* want to talk to *me* about, I'm here for you."

"God, you are such a pain in my ass."

Luke smiled. "What can I say?"

Gary pushed on. "Nightmares?"

"You know, Gary, you asking me this every time I see you is starting to give me a complex. *Should* I be having nightmares?"

"What do you think?"

"I think I saw some messed up shit. Wouldn't a normal person dream about it? Think about it?"

"There's no normal. There's just you."

"Sorry, Gary, but that's a load of horse shit. If it was all normal you wouldn't ask."

"Not true. I ask because if you were, even though it's normal, it might help to talk about it."

"And if I'm not?"

"Then you say, 'I'm fantastic, Gary. Thanks for asking.' Unless it bothers you that you're not."

Luke muttered a curse under his breath. This is why people in general baulked at seeing a shrink. If you weren't screwed up about something when you went in, you were when you came out. "What about you? Do you have nightmares?"

"I used to. Not so much anymore."

Luke hadn't expected Gary to answer. He should have.

"When something happens that we'd rather not think about, it's natural to internalize it when we relax our mind."

"Uh, huh. And look at that." Luke raised his left wrist and the thick black wrist watch. "My time's up."

Gary tapped on his own watch. "Almost. Any questions for me?"

Will I always feel marked because of what I've seen and done? Will I ever stop feeling like people can see it just by looking at me? "Nah, I'm good."

"Okay, just a few tips then. I may have mentioned them before. Yoga, meditating, and hey, riding, since you have horses at your disposal. Even a simple walk can help you assimilate back into civilian life. Help you appreciate and rediscover what you might have missed."

"I was seventeen when I enlisted."

"I saw that. Underage." Gary frowned.

"Yeah, well. I wasn't much of a rule follower." His parents were dead and all he'd needed was a guardian's signature, which was his nineteen-year-old brother, Nick. No one in the recruiting office had looked too hard at his forgery. "And I wasn't doing a lot of meditating."

"Look at my shocked face. But that's a good point. You were young, so take some time to figure out what you're interested in now. Above all, give yourself time." When Luke didn't respond, Gary sighed. "You don't have to do it alone. If you don't feel like you can talk to me, then someone else. Trust me, it's better than holding onto it."

"Okay." Luke stood with the list in his hand. "Thanks again for this," he said sliding it into his back pocket. "And don't look now Gary, but someone's messed with your toys again."

At Luke's gesture, Gary looked over and saw his original Stretch Armstrong was in fact doing obscene things to the Bionic Woman.

THE STIFF WIND blowing west to east helped with Ava's sense of direction as she made her turns. It whipped the strands of hair that had escaped her braid across her left cheek. Hannah's voice, calling out directions, was directly in front of her.

She'd already made four passes around the riding

ring at a walk, then two at a trot. Even walking was a thrill, feeling Banjo's big body beneath her. Hearing his breath, breathing in his scent. She hadn't ridden in so many years, and then only at camp once a summer.

"Keep your seat," Hannah called. "Use your legs to keep him moving."

Ava did her best to follow Hannah's instructions. As much as she was focusing, her mind still jumped to Luke every now and then. When it did, she jerked it right back. They were two adults who'd shared a couple of sexually sparked hours together. Well, there'd been sparks on her end.

She wasn't going to do anything as stupid as ask Hannah for his number. And she didn't really expect him to ask for hers. After all, she'd told him she was only in town until her father was back on his feet.

"Okay, Ava. You're approaching four ground poles. Keep going just as you are. Good. That's great."

Ava felt the slight change in the horse as he came to something he had to pay more attention to but he kept his even one two gait.

"Okay," Hannah said, her voice following Ava down the ring. "You're nearing the end of the center aisle. Make a left turn and come down the outside. You'll come to the low cross bars midway down."

Ava felt a little tickle in her belly. She'd walked the entire course before she ever got on the horse today so she had a sense of where everything was set up, how high the cross rails were. Not so high that Banjo would have to jump over them, but he would have to pick up his feet to high step which would change the rhythm. Not an Olympic worthy jump by any means, but it was something she'd never done before, and a challenge.

"Good. Heels down, close your legs. Strong back, chin up."

At Hannah's direction she made a conscious effort to drive her heels farther down in the stirrups and squeeze her calves to the horse's sides.

"Cross bar coming up in three, two, one."

The horse's gait changed but she was ready for it.

"Beautiful!" Hannah called out. "Keep posting straight ahead toward me. Okay. Start a gentle turn left, ninety degrees in three, two, one."

The horse was so familiar with going around this ring, he could probably do it without her, but Ava guided him, posting up and down in time with his trot. She made the turn with a light tug on the left rein and a slight shift in her leg position. Hannah also moved so that her voice was still in front of her as she made the turn.

"Bring him to a walk. Great job."

By the sound of Hannah's voice, Ava judged her to be about six feet ahead. A few more steps and she drew the horse to a full stop.

"You're a natural," Hannah said, patting Banjo's neck. "How did it feel?"

"Great. I think I confused him a little when I made the turn just then."

"I couldn't tell. But if you felt it, try to focus on

sliding your outside leg forward a hair while squeezing more with your inside calf."

"Okay."

"Let's pick up a trot and go through the same thing again."

By THE TIME Luke had picked up the supplies he needed and made it back to the barn, it was after three. He could still get in maybe four hours before it got too dark. Then he'd switch to inside work. And hope he could get to sleep before the sun rose.

A lot of guys got in the habit of staying up late to avoid sleep and dreams and then sleeping all day. Made it hard to hold a job that way. That wasn't him or he'd been determined it wouldn't be.

He parked outside the barn and got out, almost leaving his truck running while he grabbed the specs he needed from the office, but turned off the ignition at the last second in case Hannah had a chore for him. He lived for chores. The more the better.

The warm air blew his hair off his forehead and he took in the blue sky and again thought of Ava with eyes that didn't see him. And wasn't there something appealing about that? That she couldn't see him. Even in the short time they'd spent together, it had felt like a reprieve. That if he was indeed marked by war, she wouldn't see it.

Before he made it inside the barn, he heard Hannah calling out instructions in the riding ring and changed direction to watch. It wasn't a child in the saddle, it was an adult and not just any adult, he realized as he reached the fence. An unmistakable pale braid hung mid-way down her back from under the riding helmet.

Hannah stood several yards away from horse and rider. There was no lead rope, no lunge line as he'd seen her use with the McKinney kids who came out for lessons. This was Ava, riding around the ring on the giant chestnut. He propped his foot on the bottom rung, watching intently.

"Your balance is great," his sister was saying. "Focus on driving your heels down just a little more, engage your core and you'll be ready for the jump when it comes."

Jump? What the hell? He dropped his foot back to the ground, poised to jump over the rail.

"Keep coming around and I'll count you off as you go over the ground poles. Okay get in your two point."

Ava raised her bottom out of the saddle, body tilted forward, back rod straight, her heels indeed down as Hannah had said. She held her position as the horse trotted over three poles on the ground then went over the cross bars. It wasn't more than two feet but he held his breath.

Damn. She looked like she'd been riding her entire life. Maybe she had, but how the hell did she do it?

"That was great," Hannah said. "Let's end there. Good job Ava, great form. And good job Banjo."

Hannah and Ava both patted the horse's neck.

When Hannah began leading them in his direction, Luke stood stock still. He should retreat to the office, get what he came for and get gone. But he didn't. He couldn't.

This was a different Ava than he'd met at the reception. And he was just as interested in this jeans and T-shirt version. The wide smile on her face and the slow rhythmic rocking, rocking of her body atop the brown gelding held him. He had a flash of her straddling him, her long hair hanging down, her body rocking, rocking.

Shit. Ava might not be able to see him, but his sister could and she was looking right at him, her eyebrows raised, and a curious grin. Luke made a hasty retreat to the office.

"Hey," Hannah said, joining him in the office.

"Hey. I forgot to get the specs for the appliances."

"Right. Sorry." She shuffled through a stack of papers on her desk then snapped her fingers and walked to the dented file cabinet. "I'm actually very organized."

"Yeah. I can see that." As she pulled open the drawer and rifled through folders, Luke heard the clip clop of horse shoes on the cement barn floor.

"Forget it. I can come back. Finish up with Ava."

"I am finished. Ava's got it from here, and.... Got it." She handed Luke an envelope. "Stephen said he'll help you this weekend, but I told him you wanted to see them now. Oh, hey, before I forget. Have you seen Tom the cat recently? I haven't seen him in days."

"No, sorry. I'll keep my eyes open."

The office phone rang and Luke gave her a wave goodbye. The open barn doors on his left, led to his truck—he was just feet away. But halfway down the aisle to the right was Ava. He could say, hi. He could go. He glanced down at the finger tapping a fast beat on his thigh.

Who the hell was he kidding?

He turned right.

9

A va was off the horse now and Luke had a clear view of her in blue jeans that followed the contour of her long legs all the way down to short black boots. The long-sleeved white T covered by a thin, blue down vest shouldn't have been sexy. But even covered head to toe, he knew what her bare skin looked like, felt like.

What to do... Did he announce himself? *Hey. It's Luke.* Or just, *hey* and she'd know? He watched as she removed her riding helmet, then ran her fingers over the barn wall until she found a hook to hang it on.

"Don't stare," she said, taking him by surprise.

"What?"

"I said don't stare. It's rude."

"How do you know I was?"

She turned toward him, tilted her head and God, it looked like she could see him. The only giveaway was the aim of her eyes, just a little off his face.

"Were you?"

"No. I was thinking."

"Liar," she said with a smirk, then did some quick flick with the leather stirrup strap and slid the iron up to meet the saddle. That done, she started behind the horse. Banjo shifted on his feet.

"Hey! Careful walking behind him!" Luke took two long strides forward, going for the horse's halter to hold him steady.

Ava calmly laid her hand on the horse's rump, then stared in Luke's direction. "Oh, is this the *back* of him?" She cocked her head, patted the rump. "I thought it was his head. Good thing you told me."

"Right. Sorry." Of course she knew where she was. And now that he took a minute to take in the situation, she was walking behind the animal exactly as he would have, with a hand on his hind quarters.

"And you know, you're lucky your quick move and grab didn't get me kicked. You should really be more careful around horses."

She was wide eyed, her tone playful and teasing, and he felt like an idiot. "You're right. Sorry."

Before he could say more, Hannah came out of the office, breezing past him.

"Hey, Ava. I need to run up to the house, Mitchell fell and bumped his lip. Hopefully I'll be back before you leave. If not, great job today." Hannah touched Ava's shoulder gently as she passed and the women shared a smile. "Just put Banjo in his stall when you're done."

"Okay, thanks, Hannah."

"Bye, Luke."

He watched his sister leaving, wondering how the hell she could just leave Ava here alone. Alone with a horse? She knew what she was doing, but still. The horse could shy unexpectedly and she wouldn't see it coming. He could kick her and she'd be alone here.

"I can hang out for a while." He was looking at Ava so he caught the flash of annoyance on her face before she turned back to the horse.

"Sure, whatever," Hannah said, her mind clearly on her baby. "Bye." She waved over her shoulder.

When Hannah was gone Ava stopped and turned to face him. "I really don't need you to stay."

"Of course you don't." He got it, people acting like you needed a sitter, but no way was he leaving her in a barn alone with a thousand pound animal. "It just so happens I've got stuff to do."

"Stuff." She sent him a skeptical look over her shoulder. "Like?"

"Like... check the feed levels."

"Check the feed levels?" She turned her face toward his, amusement and challenge in her expression.

"Yeah." To prove it, he went into the feed room opposite the office. There were bags of grain and buckets. A board listing what each horse got and how much. Regular grain, oats and honey. He forced himself to stand there at least a minute for show before he came out.

"What'd you find out?" Her lips were pressed together like she was holding back a laugh which just made her dimples stand out even more. Pale strands that had fallen from her braid hung like a wispy frame around her face. She looked disheveled, a touch sweaty around her hairline and so beautiful he couldn't stop looking at her.

"You're staring again."

"No, I'm not." He cleared his throat. "Sorry. The feed situation's good by the way."

"Well, that's a relief."

He watched as she tugged and unbuckled the leather running beneath the horse's belly. Flipping it up and over the seat of the saddle, she reached up with both hands and lifted the saddle from the horse's back.

"I'll get that," he said, and stepped up to take it from her just as she swung around with her load. The force of the impact knocked her back half a step.

"Shit. What are you doing?"

"I'm helping you," he said, steadying her with his hands on her upper arms.

"No. You're getting in my way."

"Okay." He stepped back motioning for her to pass, then realizing she couldn't see that. "After you."

She walked with the saddle, holding the twenty pounds up at chest height like it was nothing. And then he noticed exactly how she was walking with her hands too full to use her cane, or even hold one out to feel her way. Instead, she slid her left elbow along the barn wall and he heard the murmuring under her breath.

"Nine, ten, eleven, twelve."

So soft it was almost a whisper. She stopped on fourteen and made a left turn right into the tack room.

Intrigued, he followed her in, heard the counting again.

"Four, five, six…"

"What are you counting?"

Her brows grew together in annoyance, and the whispering stopped but her lips were still moving.

He stood there trying to figure it out, how she knew where and what. Everything he did relied on his sight. When he'd met her he'd been surprised, and intrigued. And maybe it just hadn't hit him that this was her always. Her everywhere, every single day. Everything she did was in the dark. Or was it in the dark? Being blind didn't necessarily mean dark and he wanted to understand.

Ava stopped, strained to raise the saddle up high enough to rest it on the empty rack. Then she turned and started back so fast he didn't get out of the way and she ran right into him. *Again*.

"*Seriously*? You weren't nearly such a hoverer at the wedding reception. I think I liked you better then," she said, then eased her words with that sexy smirk she had.

"Sorry. Really. My bad."

"Look, I can't carry things with two hands and use

my cane at the same time so if you want to help, then stay out of the way."

"Got it. I'm just... interested."

"Really? In what?"

He followed her back out, making sure not to stand in her way. "How you do it? How you know what to do and where to go without seeing?"

"Can you tie your shoes with your eyes closed?"

"Yeah."

"Same thing." She moved back to Banjo and took the halter hanging next to his head.

He doubted it was the same thing. I mean how many times did a person tie their shoes in a lifetime? Too many to count. She couldn't possibly repeat every motion that many times.

He could take apart his gun and put it back together in the dark. Maybe. But could he get from point A to point B? Hell, no. And how much courage did it take to step off into the unknown?

With the blue, nylon halter hanging on her left arm, she expertly unbuckled the bridle behind the horse's ears, slid it over and down, then gently let the bit fall out of his mouth.

When it was off Luke reached to take it from her, but she already had the leather hanging on her right shoulder as she slipped the halter from her left arm to the horse's head. She buckled it into place, gave Banjo a stroke down his white striped face and turned toward the tack room with the bridle.

He got out of her way this time, but followed her,

stopping just outside the tack room. He watched her run her fingers over the hooks on the wall, touching each one until she found the one she wanted and hung the bridle.

She came out with a brush and ran it and her hands over the horse's head, neck, sides and down each leg. When she was satisfied, she tugged on the end of the leather lead rope to unknot it from the hook and turned to lead Banjo to his stall.

She secured him inside, murmured something softly to him, then came back down the aisle with the white cane she'd had at the wedding. She held it like a pencil, using her fingers and wrist to move it in a wide arc along the ground about two feet in front of her. She continued, walking with confidence to the tack room.

At the risk of being yelled at, he stayed out of her way and followed her. The room was jumbled and crowded with riding gear. Helmets and saddles, bridles and halters, hanging on hooks and a pile of saddle pads piled on a trunk against the back wall.

Special modified saddles hung on another wall and a shelf lined with stacks of foam blocks of various size and shape. He'd seen Hannah use these to help children remain upright in the saddle.

The scents were familiar to him now. The oil and leather, stronger in here than horse and hay. Even with the pile of saddle pads and rarely used blankets in the — "Well, I'll be damned."

"What?"

"The cat." He made his way across the room to

Tom, the fat cat. His body was mostly white mixed with large puddles of black and four white paws. Even his face was half black, half white. "It's Tom, the cat Hannah was looking for."

"Oh?"

He felt Ava come to stand beside.

"Hey, buddy. We thought you were lost." He stroked the cat from head to tail. Ava reached out and after a tentative touch, she did the same. "You were just off tom cattin', weren't you? Doing what Tom cats do."

Ava rubbed her hand over the cat's belly.

"You might want to lay off the mice, though."

She paused, then rubbed the belly again. "Are you sure this is a tom cat?"

"Well, his name is Tom. I don't guess I know exactly what a tom cat is. Why?"

"Because I'm thinking Tom might be a Tina and that Tina is very pregnant."

"No, shit." He rubbed the cat's belly as Ava had. "Huh."

Tom stretched, liking the belly rubs. "You sure he's not just fat?"

Ava lightly ran her finger's over the cat's nipples. "I'm pretty sure." She gave Tom one more scratch under the chin then turned back to the shelving. "You might want to tell Hannah she's going to have more than one cat soon."

"I'll do that." Luke left Tom and watched Ava. A rack of wooden shelves lined the wall closest to the door and held rags, saddle soap and hoof oil. Three wooden caddies lined one shelf and held brushes and hoof picks. Ava felt her way along the third shelf from the floor until she found what she was looking for.

"Look, no offense, Luke, but I don't need a babysitter."

"I can see that. Would it be wrong for me to offer to help or are you going to snap my head off? I happen to know everything in here's not labeled in braille."

And I don't want to leave yet.

"There are other ways to find things, but no. It's not wrong." She took a rag and an old metal can from the shelf. "You can hand me the bridle I used today."

He did and she sat with it on an old black trunk in the center of the room. She carefully unscrewed the rusty lid, covered the hole with her rag and tipped the can. Then she didn't just set the can beside her on the trunk as he might. She screwed the lid back on, and when she put the can down, she did so deliberately, sliding it from the edge and back.

Again, he never would have known she was blind, not unless he was really looking. She didn't look right at what her hands were doing, just in the general direction.

"You know, it could be a half hour or more before my ride gets here. Are you going to stand there staring at me the whole time?"

"No. Maybe." He smiled. Her eyes were even bluer, bigger, than he remembered. Her mouth...he shouldn't be thinking about her mouth.

She sighed, and continued working the bridle for several minutes. "Are you a cowboy?"

That made him laugh. "What? No."

"Oh. I just thought..." She gestured at the floor. "Your boots."

"Ah..." He took a seat on the trunk beside her and looked at his feet. "Still no. Just handy that I already had these."

"Do you have a hat?"

"Like a cowboy hat? No." Did she look disappointed? Maybe he should get one. "Why do women always want to date a cowboy?"

"Do they?" She angled her head toward him. "I hadn't heard that. Did you take a survey or something?"

"No. Just a guess. There was this guy in my squad, he'd never seen a cow in his life but he wore the boots, the hat, laid on the southern drawl like he was from Texas or some shit even though I'm pretty sure he'd never been to Texas. Anyway, seemed to work for him."

"Worked for him, huh?" Her lips twitched, trying not to smile and it turned him on. "And what works for you?"

"Hmm...Cookies usually does the trick."

"Funny," she said, refolding the rag. "I thought Army Rangers were kind of like Navy SEALs. I wouldn't have thought you guys needed an angle. Don't women pretty much drop their panties right in your beer?"

"Um…" He opened his mouth. Closed it. "Where did you hear that?"

She laughed out loud at his obvious embarrassment. "Forget it. I was just messing with you."

She reached for the can, brushing her hand along his thigh as she did and jerked her hand back. "Sorry. If you're going to sit right beside me you run the risk of being touched."

Being touched? If she only knew how many times the thought of touching her again had crossed his mind.

"No problem. Here. I'll—" He fumbled to hand her the can which she didn't need him to do and only succeeded in making it more awkward as their hands bumped.

He watched her work. Her fingers deftly moving over the leather, not at all like her heart was beating out of her chest because their hands had brushed. She had pretty hands, slender but strong with short unpainted, nails with clean rounded edges. No rings. "You know if you needed a ride home, I could take you."

"My brother insists. As annoying as it is sometimes it's easier just to let him. I'm sure he's almost here. He's not entirely happy his wife gave me a bundle of riding lessons."

"Really? Why? You're obviously good at it."

She angled her head at him again.

"I saw you riding when I pulled in."

"Oh. Well… thanks. He just worries I guess," Ava said. "It is weird though. Growing up my brother was always the one I could count on to let me do stuff. He's gotten super protective since..."

"Since what?"

"Oh... um nothing. Do you ride?"

"I can." He'd like to get back to why her brother had gotten so protective but he let it go for now. "So your brother lives here, your parents live here. I'm going to guess you're from around here."

"Yep. Born and raised."

"How did you end up a city girl?"

"I went to college in upstate New York."

"Why there?"

She slid him a sideways glance. "You're a lot nosier than you were the last time I talked to you."

"Just curious." And he liked talking to her, listening to her. The woman was good company. "But hey, if it's a secret..."

"I went to Cornell on a swimming scholarship."

"No shit?"

She laughed. "No shit." She shrugged. "I'd always liked swimming. It was a safe way for me to play I guess, to be not careful and not constantly hear, *be careful*. Then it grew into more, the speed, the competition. It was the only time I could be fast, that I could really push myself and go all out. So I got a scholarship to swim."

"Nice. Were you good?"

"Yeah, I was good." She slid him a grin. "State champion in Butterfly. Twice." She held up two fingers.

"Impressive."

"Thanks."

"So, what do you do in the big bad city?" He was being nosy, he realized but he couldn't seem to help himself.

"I'm an interpreter at the UN."

"Really? Interesting. You work with a particular country?"

"I interpret for all types of meetings between US officials and... anyone they want to talk to."

"How many languages do you speak?"

"A few." She smiled like she was pleased with herself.

"How many is a few."

"Seven at the moment."

"Wait." He held up a hand. "*Seven*? What are they?"

"Four of the six official languages at the UN... French, Spanish, Italian, and English. I'm not fluent in Arabic or Chinese."

"Slacker."

"I know, right?" She smiled. "But I do speak Portuguese, Russian, and German. I can even send you a message in morse code if you want."

"Oh, yeah? I might be able to send you one back." He had a vision of the two of them, in the dark, naked, knocking out code. He smiled at the thought. "Sounds like a cool job."

"It is. I learn a lot in preparation, reading documents on a wide array of subject matter. Economy, law, geographical situations in regions and countries. And then interpreting for closed sessions there's always the unexpected that I didn't prepare for like a sudden interest in Japanese opera or the discovered common love of raising guinea hens. Never a dull moment."

He nodded as she spoke. "Wow. I had no idea." He'd accomplished a lot. Was proud of all he'd done, but he hadn't gone to college. When it came to that type of knowledge, he wasn't in her league. Not even close. "Do you speak pig Latin?"

She gave him a funny look. "Uh, I could probably understand it, but I'm not fluent."

He smiled. "My brothers and I made up this secret language. Well, we thought so." Funny he'd forgotten that and how many hours they'd spent up in their old tree house.

"I've actually applied for a new job. Not because I don't like the UN, but just for something different. It would be more direct work, more detailed. I love what I do, but this would have the potential to make a real difference. Diplomatically speaking."

Her smile faltered, her expression going from excitement to worry as a little pinch formed between her brows. "Problem?"

"Not really, no. It's just that, one, I may not get it, and two, I haven't told my parents and they already hate the idea of me in New York."

"Why would a new job matter if you're already there?"

"Because the new job's not in New York. It's in Italy. Rome, to be exact. Though I'd be traveling to China, South Korea, Spain. France." She stopped her wiping and laid the rag in her lap. "I want it," she said, her face full of determination. "I've loved New York, still do, but...Sometimes you just need a change, you know?"

"Yeah." He knew. "So from one overgrown city to another."

"What can I say? I'm a city girl. It's like I can *see* in the city, if that makes sense. I can't see in a small town with no noise, no scents."

He gave an exaggerated sniff. "Plenty of scents around here." She smiled and it nearly knocked him off the edge of the trunk.

"I'm not saying small towns aren't nice, it's just not for me. Where's home for you? I know from Hannah your family didn't start out here."

"Mmm. For a long time, nowhere. Anywhere."

A long moment of silence followed.

"Well, anyway, it's not a sure thing, but fingers crossed. My parents still haven't forgiven me for never coming back after college. I've been in New York ten years and I swear every day they're waiting for me to get murdered. If I don't get this other job then it'll be back to NYC and that'll have to be enough."

He wondered why the look on her face told him that wasn't enough.

He was still thinking when Ava stood and moved to return the now cleaned bridle to its hook and tripped over his outstretched boot. It happened fast. He made a grab for her but not before she rapped her forehead on the edge of a shelf hard enough to make her wince.

uch. Ava threw up her hand, touched the spot. She heard Luke curse then felt his hands on her arms.

"Let me see."

"It's fine. Really." She stepped back. "Not your fault. I should have steered around." The spot above her brow throbbed, but what had her heart running wild was Luke.

"Going to leave a mark," Luke said. "Maybe a bruise. Damn. I'm sorry."

"I'm used to it," she said, waving it off. "I don't bruise easily."

"Run into a lot of things, do you? I ran into a clothing rack sticking out like that once. Metal with a sharp end. Cracked my head on it good."

Ava felt him move in closer, close enough that she felt the heat coming off his body. He stroked his thumb gently over the spot and the pain was all but forgotten.

He smelled of the barn and sun and male. She felt his warm breath on her forehead. She'd wanted him to kiss her when they'd stood outside waiting for Hannah. She wanted him to kiss her now.

The familiar scents of the tack room surrounded her, usually calmed her. But right now the over-whelming scent was Luke. Different than he'd smelled at the wedding reception. No more baby spit up. No cologne. But he smelled male. A pinewood scent. And God, her heart had been thumping since the minute she'd heard his voice standing in the barn aisle.

His hand moved down to cup her cheek and when she felt his finger touch her bottom lip, her eyes fluttered closed. One hand came up to touch his chest. She leaned in...

And too late realized it wasn't a kiss he was after.

"Sorry," Luke said. "You ahh... You had a bit of something on your lip there. I—"

Mortified, Ava jerked away, mumbled a thanks. She was an idiot. An awkward idiot thinking this man was coming in to steal a kiss when that was probably the furthest thing from his mind. No way to know when she couldn't see his face, couldn't read his expression.

She felt around for her cane, desperate to get away.

"Ava, come on. That was my fault. I didn't mean to scare you."

"You didn't scare me, Luke."

"I startled you. I—"

"Just stop. Please."

They both knew that's not what happened. She'd

misread the situation. Not the first time. And she was afraid if she didn't get away from him now she was going to cry in front of him.

She pushed past him, found her cane, then holding one hand out for extra protection, she walked out of the tack room. And right into Hannah.

"Ava."

"Hi. Hey."

"Your sister-in-law is here. I was just coming to tell you."

"Great. Thanks. I'm ready."

As she was leaving, Ava could just barely hear Hannah ask Luke, "Something going on you want to tell me about?"

She didn't catch Luke's reply.

"Ryan got held up," Connie said, explaining why she was there instead of Ava's brother. "And I'd say that's a lucky break for you."

"Really? Why?"

"Because," Connie said, when they were both in her car. "I walk in a barn to get you and you come tearing out like your ass is on fire." She tapped her finger on the steering wheel. "Interesting."

"I was in a hurry," she said, fastening her seat belt. "And why is that interesting?"

"That's not. The man who came out behind you looking like he'd just stolen the last cookie from the cookie jar... *That* was interesting."

It was embarrassing and it jerked her back to a time with so much uncertainty she sometimes wondered if she would ever completely shake it. The humiliation, the feelings of betrayal. Luke hadn't betrayed her, but he'd... What? Rejected her?

No, not really. But wanting Luke to kiss her made the wound of Blake's rejection fresh and raw. And it infuriated her.

Connie drove slowly up the gravel drive. "I'm looking at you and I don't see any hay in your hair."

"Why would I have hay in my hair? I was cleaning tack."

"Uh huh. Looked like more was going on than wiping saddles."

Ava could hear the grin in her sister-in-law's voice.

"Want to share?" Connie asked, pausing before turning onto the main road.

"No," Ava said, knowing she was pouting.

"Well, can I just say, wow?"

Ava turned her hot face to the window. "You can."

"Hey." Connie reached over. "Did something happen? Do we need Ryan to kick someone's ass?"

"No. Nothing happened. I thought... Never mind."

"What? Just tell me already!"

"I thought something was about to happen, but I was wrong. He was just getting something off my face. My mistake."

"Mmm. Well, men are stupid. Want me to tell you what he looks like? Just for kicks?"

She really did. And some of the embarrassment was replaced by curiosity. "If you must."

"I must. Okay... Tall, for starts."

"I know that much."

"Oh, really?"

"Yeah. I danced with him at that wedding thing."

"Ooooh. Danced with him."

"Jeez. Stop making me sound like I'm in middle school."

"Hey, I'm just describing the man. You're doing the rest."

"Right." And Connie had known her a long time. She'd been with her brother the past ten years, married for the past eight.

"Okay, where was I? Tall, hair a little on the long side. Not enough for a man bun. More like he's missed a few haircuts. Doesn't look like he has a typical office job."

"He's military. Or he was."

"Mmm. Well, big, built. And hot. I can say that as a happily married woman. Your brother is civilized handsome. This guy is wild, rugged cowboy, ex-military hot."

"A cowboy," Ava muttered under her breath.

"Huh?"

"Nothing." She didn't know looks, but she knew in terms of comparison. The same as so and so, or different than. She knew tall or short. Big or skinny. Messy or grungy or neat.

They'd had dolls, she remembered, in preschool or therapy. Some with beards to feel. Other with curly hair and straight hair. There were different shaped eyes she could run her fingers over. Color never mattered except in comparison—same as hers, different than mine. "Thanks for picking me up."

"No problem. I don't mind. Gives us a chance to catch up."

"I know, but I could have called a cab or Uber. I hate that Ryan's the stubborn one and you got stuck with chauffeur duty."

"I know you do. Get over it. Ryan wants to have a baby."

"*What*? Talk about change of subject."

"I told you I wanted us to catch up."

"Well... wow. What do *you* want?"

"I don't know."

"I thought you two had decided not to have children. I know you don't want to give up your practice." Connie was a prosecuting attorney and loved it.

Connie's cell phone rang through the car. "Shit. I need to take this. I'm sorry."

"No problem." She didn't mind being left to her thoughts. *Her brother with a baby.* Ava smiled. She'd be an aunt. There'd been a time, a very short time, when she'd thought she might get the chance to be a mom herself.

11

"Sorry for staring," Blake said to the waitress.

Ava could hear the smile and fun in his voice.

"I just had an eye transplant, so I'm seeing everything for the first time."

He told almost everyone they met. She got it. Of course it was exciting. Of course he was staring at everything new. *Oh, my God, Ava, you should see the skyline tonight. You should see the river. I wish you could see...*

Didn't matter what. It was everything.

It had made her smile at first. Eight months later it was getting... tiresome. And more and more Blake sounded agitated when she didn't respond with the same level of awe.

You just can't understand how beautiful it is, he'd say, giving up his description. *It's not at all like I'd pictured. The people, the buildings.*

And on and on it went. He wanted to go to movies and

art galleries and she was more than happy to go. But he almost seemed disappointed in her somehow.

"Oh, wow," the waitress exclaimed. She had a young sultry kind of voice that Ava imagined went with an attractive face. "That's amazing. Then you've got someone else's eyes?"

"Well, they're mine now," he said, and Ava suddenly hated the waitress because she knew Blake and she knew he struggled with that aspect of the surgery. The fact that the only reason he could see was because someone else had died.

"You have really interesting hair," Blake went on, not sounding bothered by the waitress's comment at all. From there her husband and the amazed waitress with the interesting hair talked on and Blake's tone gradually changed from innocent to something else.

Twisting in the sheets, Ava came awake in her childhood bed. A dream. But a very real one. She checked the time on her phone. Too early to get up so she turned over, wiling herself to go back to sleep. It wasn't happening.

She replayed that scene with Blake again. And the part before the waitress had come over. When Blake had quietly admonished her for touching her steak. *"Babe. Don't."* It was something they always did, a double check to make sure they didn't fork up something they'd want to spit in their napkin.

That's why it was so easy to be with Blake. But not anymore. Now she was an embarrassment.

She tried to go to sleep, but the scene with Luke in the barn came to mind. She wouldn't have minded kissing Luke. Lord he'd smelled good and she hadn't forgotten those shoulders from their dance at the reception. It was funny really, a funny miscommunication. Unfortunate she couldn't work up a laugh.

FIRST ON LUKE'S list for the day, after coffee, was to walk the wooded route that Hannah was thinking to use as the campers' path to and from the barn and the cabins. He wanted to get a feel for the distance and the terrain. He'd come back with an odometer later. After he bought one.

He made his way through the wooded area, bypassing the back pastures. It didn't add much distance if any and it was shaded which would be important in the summer. To the left and up the hill was Hannah's house and to the right and down a little way was the front of the barn. If she decided on this route, it'd save some work since they'd be using a portion of Hannah's gravel drive. But then maybe having kids anywhere near a road used by cars wasn't a good idea.

Maybe he'd just go tell Hannah what he thought now. And if he happened to score some breakfast, that'd be a bonus. He made the left turn that would take him up the shaded gravel drive. Tall pines interspersed with dogwood and maple lined either side keeping it in perpetual shade.

He climbed the porch steps, rapped his hand on the door once then walked in. And was nearly blinded.

"Shit!" His hand flew up to cover his face but not fast enough to save him from seeing his sister straddling the kitchen chair her husband was currently sitting in.

"Jeez," Hannah said. "Knock much?"

"I *did* knock! And I'm leaving now." With his hand still firmly over his eyes, he turned to find his way back out the way he'd come, had a flash of Ava trying to find her way, and heard his sister laughing behind him.

"Oh, good grief. It's not like we're naked."

"Well, we almost were," Stephen grumbled.

Luke heard a chair scrape on the floor and lowered his hand to take a peek. His brother-in-law was leaning back against the counter, scowling, a mug of coffee in his hand.

"Sorry," Hannah said, walking to the sink. "We've both told you you're welcome anytime. And you are."

"*Any* time is a stretch."

Hannah shot her husband a look. "Want coffee?" Hannah offered, walking over and giving her husband a hip bump out of the way.

"It's the least you could do."

"What brings you by unannounced and uninvited?" Stephen asked.

"Behave yourself," Hannah said, and handed Luke a mug.

"I don't even remember. I'm wiping out the last ten minutes. My eyes are burned."

Hannah rolled her eyes and laid pieces of bacon in a pan. "You do know how you got your nephew right?"

For the first time he noticed his nephew sitting in a high chair poking in Cheerios. "You sure you should be doing that in front of the kid?"

Hannah smiled and took a swig of coffee. "You take the moments when you can. You'll understand one day."

"Bite your tongue," Luke told her.

"You two watch the bacon while I get myself dressed." She pressed a kiss to her husband's lips and left the men to tend to breakfast.

They stood a few seconds not speaking. Stephen at the counter flipping the sizzling bacon. Him sipping his coffee. Mitchell eating Cheerios like it was the last food on earth. It reminded him he'd wanted breakfast. "Put in a few extra pieces, will ya?"

Stephen grumbled about him being a mooch but did it.

"Hey, I'm the one doing all the building that I was supposed to be *helping* you with."

"True. And I appreciate it. Things have gotten busy at work. I'm closing on houses as fast as Matt can flip them."

"Toast?" Luke asked, as he dropped in a piece for himself.

"Sure. Hannah mentioned she interrupted something the other day." He turned, with what was his standard grin. "Between you and one of her riders?"

He'd been half trying to forget it and half trying to

figure out what to do about it. "What did she think she was interrupting?"

"She didn't know but she also said Ava—that's her name right? — Well that she didn't look happy and you looked like you'd just been kicked in the teeth. Not her exact words."

"*Excuse* me!" Hannah came in, narrowed her eyes at her husband. "I told you that in confidence."

Stephen lifted a shoulder. "Just making conversation, babe. Being friendly."

"Right."

Now it was Luke's turn to grin. He picked up an egg from a black wire basket on the counter and held it out. "Blue eggs? What kind of chickens lay blue eggs?"

"Different kinds than lay brown or white eggs, I suppose," Hannah said and strode to the counter, topped off her coffee. "I got them from a lady who sells them at a little farmer's market stand. Her property actually backs up to ours."

"Huh." Luke turned it in his hand and put it back.

"I told her about the camp and all. She didn't seem too happy about it."

Luke opened a drawer for a butter knife, found spatulas and whisks and moved on to another. "Maybe she's old, doesn't like kids."

"No, not old. But I did get that feeling on the kids. Whatever. I'm still hoping to work out something with her for fresh fruit and vegetables for camp." Hannah opened a drawer, handed her brother a knife. "Have you remembered what you came here for?"

"It's coming back to me. I walked the route from the cabins to the barn, taking a cut through the woods."

"Okay. What'd you think?"

"I think it had possibilities. And I won't know for sure until I get an exact measurement, but I don't think it'll be that much more expensive. It'd give nice side cover in the summer, add some natural walk interest."

"I love that."

Luke grabbed his toast and went to the fridge for butter. "I need to walk it with an odometer."

"I can get my hands on that," Stephen said. "I'll drop it by later today."

"That works. As soon as I know I can work up some materials prices for you."

"You know," Hannah said. "Speaking of prices, I got a generous check in the mail from the man who donated Newman."

Luke took a swallow of coffee. "Nice."

"It was. And interestingly enough, that check came wrapped in a sheet of paper with a note." Hannah eyed him over the rim of her mug and he didn't miss the gleam in her eye.

After taking a long slow drink of her coffee, she turned, opened a drawer and pulled out a sheet of pale pink paper. She held it up to read.

"*For Luke—* in swirly handwriting. And there's a phone number." She sniffed the paper, clearly enjoying herself then held it out to him. "You know if her father and I hadn't been there, I think she might have jumped you right in the barn. She was cute."

"Cute my ass. More like a tiger and she looked at me like I was a piece of meat." He looked at the paper and thought of the horse donor's daughter. She looked to be in her twenties, sharply dressed in a white blouse tucked into tight, dark jeans and little brown boots with mile high heels. She was a looker for sure and no doubt she knew it.

"Not interested?" Hannah asked. "Wouldn't hurt you to go out on a date."

"No, thanks. Not my type."

"Oh? What is your type? Could it be blonde? Blue eyed, maybe?"

"I'm leaving now. I don't know why I even help you."

He strode to the door, taking his toast and bacon with him. And possibly a grin on his face.

12

"That's enough," Ava's dad said, and grunted as he dropped back into the chair.

"Nope. Three more," she told him, touching his calf gently. "Come on, you can do it. Raise your foot. Come on, Dad, really raise it."

He groaned. "Fine. It's up."

"Okay. Hold," she counted to five the way she'd heard the therapist do it. "Are you holding it or trying to pull one over on me?"

Her mom rushed in—she always seemed to be in a rush. She gathered the dishes beside her dad's recliner, took them to the kitchen and came back to pick up and stack magazines on the end table. "I'd never get him to do these exercises. He'd be sniping at me the whole time."

"Dad never snipes," Ava said, smiling at her dad.

"Hah." She wrapped an arm around Ava's shoulder.

"We love having you here. I hope you know we appreciate it."

"I do, and you're welcome."

"Do you really have to go back? I know it's a great job, but—"

"No, Mom. I'm sorry, but this is only temporary, and..."

"And what?"

"Nothing."

"What's this nothing? You can't just say nothing."

"Oh, God." She nearly smacked her palm to her forehead. Why had she said anything?

"Ava?" Her mom was waiting.

"I may be getting a new job. I've applied for one anyway."

"Oh?"

"It's not here, or close," she said quickly before her mom could get her hopes any higher. "It's actually in —" She braced herself "— Italy."

"What? Ava Lane! Italy? What in the world could you possibly have to do in Italy?"

She was an adult. She would remain calm. "I would have a job there, if I get it. I don't even know if I will which is why I shouldn't have said anything." This didn't need to mirror the battle of wills of her childhood. She made herself smile. "It'd be great really. You and dad could visit."

"Ava." Her mother's tone wasn't just shocked now, but disappointed. A hundred times worse. "Isn't New York far enough away from us?"

"I'm not getting away from *you*, Mom. That's not why I live in New York."

"She's an adult, Nance. Leave her alone."

"I am leaving her alone. I'm just asking questions for heaven's sake. I'm sure there are places around here that need translators. Just the other day my friend Carol said how she'd seen a translator at the airport."

Her mother sighed again and Ava heard her sink onto the couch. She didn't bother explaining the difference in translator and interpreter, but went to her, touched her shoulder. "Please don't worry. I probably won't even get it."

Same thing she'd said about the swim scholarship. Same thing she'd said about the job in New York. Her parents had always supported her, encouraged her to try but then, at least for her mom's part, had seemed surprised when she actually succeeded. Like it was safe to tell her to try because she didn't think she'd actually make it.

She bent to kiss her mother's cheek. "And hey, you and Daddy have always wanted to travel. If I do get it, I could be your home base as you two gallivant over Europe."

"Your dad can't make such a long flight."

"Ah, Nance, come on, now. I'll be fit as a fiddle in no time."

Leave it to her dad to insert the positivity. "I probably won't even get it, so you don't need to get upset about it. I'll get your water, Daddy." With her cane and her hand out, she went to the kitchen as fast as she could, wishing more than ever that she was home, in her own apartment, where she could walk swiftly and freely without having to feel for every cautious step.

"I have a riding lesson at three, if that's okay."

"Sure." Her mother was pouting. She could hear it in her voice.

And if Luke was there, she'd just avoid him. Or not avoid him. She didn't need to avoid him. She'd be perfectly pleasant.

IT WAS ALMOST four when Luke stopped by the barn on his way home from the lumber yard. The clouds off to the West were dark and there was a flash of lightning. A spring storm he thought, pulling to a stop in front of the barn. He'd just make sure Hannah didn't need help with the horses before heading to the cabin. The thought of a cold beer on the porch as the rain blew by held more than a little appeal.

A gust of wind whipped his T-shirt and hair as he stepped out of his truck. He made his way through the open doors just as there was another flash followed by a deep rumble of thunder. Closer now.

As soon as he stepped inside the barn he saw her. Ava stood just outside the barn doors at the opposite end so that the dark square of barn wood framed her silhouette in the outside light. Her hair was held by a band at the base of her neck but the wind blew wisps of it around her face. He tried to ignore the quick stir of excitement he felt at the prospect of seeing her again.

Moving toward her, he passed two horses standing in the aisle, saddled and ready, their lead ropes tied to rings on the wall. Odd, he thought, then heard his sister's voice in the office. From the one-sided conversation he could make out, she was talking to a prospective client.

He watched Ava a moment, her face lifted to the sky. A second later, a crack of lightning struck followed by a boom of thunder close enough to shake his bones. When Ava didn't move to come in he strode toward her.

"Hey. You looking to get struck by lightning?"

She only smiled, not turning toward him. "Feels good."

He stood beside her, felt the distinct downdraft of cooler air preceding a storm.

"I like the rain," he said.

The thunder rolled again, no closer than the last one.

"Do you think it's going to rain?"

"I don't know."

"That's what I'm waiting on. It's been a really long time since it rained."

Come to think of it, she was right. But that didn't explain what she was doing. "Are you doing some sort of experiment? Collecting rain samples?"

"No. I just told you. I like the rain. I like to feel it on my face."

He leaned back against the doorway, crossed his arms over his chest and just looked at her. God, she was beautiful. Wild now, with her hair flying around her face, not tame or innocent as he'd thought the first time he'd seen her.

And damn it. He had no business starting anything up with Ava. Didn't even know what he was thinking of starting. It'd been so long since he'd had even the most casual relationship. Really, it had been a long time since he'd had anything at all with a woman.

"I try to imagine what it might look like but it's hard. I try to imagine what it looks like falling. What it's shaped like."

What could he tell her? He didn't know that he'd ever thought about it enough to describe it. But he could describe her. Oval shaped face, wide forehead completely exposed now with the hair blown back. He'd like to catch all that flying hair, hold it in his fist. It looked so silky, so free.

"So, do you think it will rain?"

The question pulled him out of his thoughts. He looked at the sky. "I don't know. Might be toying with us, circling around." He knocked his cap against his thigh. He wanted to say something else, he just didn't know what it was.

He looked down his hat and smiled. "I have a hat now."

"Oh, yeah?"

"Yeah. Not a cowboy hat, just a... you know. A regular hat."

"That's good. Keeps the sun off."

"It does." He zeroed in on a piece of hair that had fallen from her elastic band and hung over her cheek. He wanted to touch her, just to brush his hand over her cheek.

"I think it's moving away," she said, her disappointment clear. "I can feel a breeze, the warmth of the sun. Falling snow, which I love. But my favorite is feeling the rain. Oh, well."

He looked to his right, saw the dark clouds dissipating. He would have brought it back if he could. "Sorry."

"That's okay."

"Is this something you do often? Stand outside, waiting for rain?"

"Depends what you consider often. Seems like it rains more in New York. And maybe I don't need to stand in the rain so much there."

"And you need to stand in it here?"

She blew out a breath. "I need to breathe. It's harder to breathe here. Back under my parents worrying eyes. And no, I can't see the worry, but I hear it. I can feel it. I have limitations, I know that. They're just glaringly apparent here. Makes me feel less capable, more blind, if that makes sense. Or maybe just makes me feel like a child."

"Funny."

"Really?" She slid her unseeing eyes in his direction then back to the horizon. "Happy to amuse you."

"No, not funny like that. Just funny because... I guess I'd say the same. Hannah, my brothers, they look at me like I'm one step from the edge. Kinda makes me want to go over, just to piss them off."

Of course Gary thinks it's in my head. Maybe it is. He wondered what Ava would say to that. "You don't do that," he said.

"I don't do what?"

"You don't look at me like that."

She smiled over. "I don't look at you at all because I can't see you."

"Maybe that's it. Maybe it's not. You don't *see* me, but you look."

There was some kind of electricity in the air that had nothing to do with the storm. He felt it every time he was within three feet of this woman. But there was also a tension and he wanted to be rid of it. "You still mad at me?"

"What?" She swung her face to his. "When was I mad at you?"

He gave her a look, quickly realized that wouldn't help her memory and sighed. Damn he talked a lot around her. "Couple days ago. Tack room."

"Right." Ava let out a suffering breath and groaned. "Can we please not talk about it?"

"Sure. After you answer my question."

"Fine. No. I'm not mad. I was embarrassed. Okay? I didn't see… I couldn't see to know…" She sighed, shook her head. "I misread. Not the first time and I was more mad at myself than at you."

"Because you thought I was going to kiss you."

Her head whipped around to his again, her eyes wide. "Oh, my *gosh*! Please!"

He took a step closer. "If that's what you thought, you didn't misread." He touched her hair, just a dance of his fingers down the strands blowing over her cheek. "I'd say you read it just right."

Her mouth opened, closed. It might have been funny, the way they both stood there not knowing what to say next. Might have been, if his heart wasn't beating so damn hard.

"Hey, Ava!"

Ava and Luke both turned at the sound of Hannah's voice.

"Hey, Luke. Didn't know you were here."

"Yeah. Just stopped by to see if you needed any help." He pointed to the sky. "Thought it might rain."

"Thanks, that was sweet. We thought it might rain too."

"Looks like the storm's passing," Ava said.

"Yeah, that's just what I was coming to say. I think so too, but I checked in with the sitter to see if she could stay longer. She can't."

"Oh." A shadow of disappointment fell over Ava's face. "Well, that's okay. Another time."

"I'm really sorry," Hannah said, touching her shoulder.

"Don't worry about it."

Luke looked back at the saddled horses and put two and two together. He could volunteer to watch his nephew. Or...

"I can take her."

Both women swung their faces to him. His sister's eyes were wide, her brows raised.

"What? You guys had a ride planned, right? I can ride. I'll take her."

"That's okay," Ava said. "Really. We can just do it another time." Her face was still a picture of regret as if he hadn't just offered to fill in.

"Will your brother be able to pick you up earlier?" Hannah asked Ava.

"I'm sure he will. I'll call him."

Annoyed, Luke lifted his hands. "Am I invisible here?"

Hannah stared at him. "You're serious."

"Of course I'm serious."

"Okay. Well...Ava, are you good with that?"

"I guess." She looked at him, seemed be looking right at him this time. "If you're sure you don't have—"

"I don't. Let's go." He was done with the back and forth. He moved to untie Newman and started leading him down the aisle. Hannah and Ava did the same with Hannah's horse, Winnie.

When they got to the end of the aisle and outside, Hannah paused with the reins and waited for Ava to mount up. "Winnie's a good girl. Sure-footed and dependable. She'll do whatever you ask," she said, giving her filly a pat on the neck as Ava took the reins. "And Newman, he's a good boy but he may get antsy if there's more thunder."

Luke put one foot in the stirrup then swung his leg

over. He'd done a little riding as a boy at camp and at his uncle's. He'd done a lot more since coming here. He wasn't worried. At least not about himself. But as Hannah handed him the lead rope attached to Ava's horse he felt the weight of responsibility.

No turning back now.

13

They rode several minutes in silence. Nothing but the plodding steps of the horses and the creaking every time he adjusted himself in the saddle. He didn't know what had possessed him to do this. Except he hadn't been ready to go get that beer and sit on his porch. *Alone.*

Because it wasn't going to rain, he told himself. That's why his great idea had shifted to going for a ride.

"I told my parents about the job."

"Ah. Italy." Luke peered at the ground in front of Winnie, scanning for any potential obstacles. "How'd they take it?"

"Not good."

"What is it about family that can make you feel so damn guilty?"

"They definitely have a knack for it," Ava said. "Maybe I push back more because I've always been too aware of their concern and maybe they hold on tighter because I push.

"Being here, around people constantly trying to help me... It's just hard to pretend I have a normal life when I'm here. Hard to pretend that I *am* normal. And jeez." She shook her head. "Sorry for unloading on you."

"No problem." He guided Newman to the left around what looked like a mole tunnel. He guided Winnie over with him by the lead rope he held.

"It's your own fault," she said. "You're too easy to talk to."

"Back 'atcha."

She let out a long sigh and turned her face up to the sky. "But I can do it. For another month, I can do it."

"What happens in a month?"

"I get back to my life."

"Right." And if that wasn't a reminder he didn't know what was.

"Can we go faster?"

"You want to go faster?" He grinned over at her. "Sure."

With his hand holding tight to the guide rope attached to Winnie's bridle, he picked up a trot, then a gallop. They flew across the open field, horse hooves pounding. He was exhilarated. Flying across a field on horseback could do that for a person. But not him, not lately.

It was the woman beside him. The wild laughter

and wilder hair flying out behind her. Wanting to know what it was like for her, he closed his eyes, just for a second. Less than a second. That was all he could stand it. The not knowing what was coming, the lack of control. Moving through the wind and not seeing. Like dropping through a dark sky with nothing but a packed wad of canvas on your back.

How the hell did she do it? But the smile on her face told him she was more than doing it, she was loving it.

They rode across the back field, over virgin grass, toward the rising woods. The horse's hooves pounded out a perfect rhythm, the cool air brushed over his skin. Even though it was cooler, he was sweating a little. He'd felt responsible for the men under him, but this was different. This was Ava.

He knew she'd hate it, but he couldn't help thinking she was helpless in this moment. If he dropped the rope she'd be a ship without anchor. No idea where she was or where she was going. No way to find her way back. But he wouldn't drop the rope. Hell. Even with the death grip on the guide rope, he wanted her closer, like on Newman's back with him would be good. In front of him, his arms tight around her.

When they neared the grove of trees, he eased Newman back into a trot, then a walk. Winnie followed agreeably. Ava was breathing hard, harder than the horse.

"That was amazing. Thank you."

"You're welcome." Her smile was the brightest he'd

ever seen. Her entire face seemed to be smiling. Her cheeks flushed from the wind and excitement.

"I don't often get to go fast, not like that. I mean that's why I swim, because I can go all out, push my body in a way I can't running. But it's not like this, with the wind in my hair. It's freeing, it's... never mind."

"Tell me."

"I don't know how to explain it. It doesn't even make sense. I can ride a roller coaster, I love riding roller coasters, and it's not so different I think than a lot of people who ride with their eyes shut tight. But I wouldn't have been able to do this, to race across an open field on my own. To feel in control? Knowing I could slow Winnie if I'd wanted."

They reached the trees and the horses walked gingerly in and out of trees, picking their way over the ground.

"Mmm. It doesn't smell like spring here like it does in other places, does it?"

"I guess not." Gary's suggestion of going for a ride, taking a walk had sounded like a crock to him then. But Ava noticed everything. And he wanted to give her more. There's enough pine needles and leaf cover from last fall to keep the grass from poking through.

Their saddles creaked as they walked slowly down a path Hannah used often. They moved in silence except for the horses' steady four beat rhythm.

"There's a stream ahead. So small it nearly dries up in the heat of summer."

"But it's not dry now?"

"No."

"Can we stop and get off for a minute? Or if you don't have time, we don't have to."

"I've got nothing but time." He pulled Newman to a stop and swung off and to the ground. Then giving the horse's face a light rub, went to Ava's side. She was already swinging her leg over.

He stood there, ready to help her down, hold the horse. Had the urge to catch her around the waist and lower her down. But she didn't need that. Or want it. He stepped back to give her room.

She swung gracefully off the horse, her jeans hugging her cute little butt, her hips, and all the way down her legs. He wanted to kiss her. Tried to remember why they'd just decided it was best not to when she landed softly on the ground beside him.

"Ava."

"Yeah? Luke?" She said when he didn't answer.

"Nothing." He secured the reins of both horses to the saddle, leaving them to graze a bit. "Let's walk. There's something down here I think you'll like."

He took her hand and the connection between them zinged, swift and true as a sniper's round.

Her fingers squeezed his before she let go and moved to take his upper arm.

"Right. Forgot." He'd partly forgotten, partly wanted to hold her hand. He slowed his steps to match hers. "Too fast? Too slow?"

"Perfect."

He led her through the trees, over uneven ground,

and the farther they got the more uneven and roots and rocks. Holes from animals.

"Watch out through here." He switched his hold so that his left arm was around her waist and offered his left for her to hold onto. She tripped a few times as they picked their way over exposed roots and uneven ground.

"Maybe this wasn't such a good idea."

"I like it. Definitely don't do much walking in the woods in New York."

"Okay, watch your step here," he said when they reached the stream.

"Okay. I'm watching."

He cringed at using the word *watch* but she was smiling, concentrating as she picked her way, with his help, down to the water. He took both her hands and walked backward slowly, leading her.

"Step down. Again. And one more."

"I hear water. Is it a creek?"

"Yeah, just barely."

"Nice. I like the sound."

"You like the sound, you like to stand in the rain. I'm beginning to think you're obsessed with water."

"Not obsessed," she said, still smiling. "I just like it. Can we sit?"

"Sure."

They sat on the bank, just feet from the shallow creek. It was no babbling brook, but she looked so happy to be there he strained his ears, trying to hear what was making her so happy.

They sat that way a long time. Side by side, shoulder to shoulder just listening to the sounds of nature.

"This is nice." She ran her hand over the mossy ground like she was in her own world and he wasn't the most important thing. He wanted to be in it too. Wanted to be wherever she was.

She dug her fingers into the earth beneath the moss. "I'd like to have a garden but there's not really room inside my apartment. Even if there was, it's not the same as digging in dirt, smelling it, feeling sun."

"Or the rain."

"Exactly. I've been in the city so long I forgot what this sounded like. I mean there are parks, but there's always the noise in the background. And it smells different."

"I hated it at first, all the quiet."

"I'm sure it's very different from where you were. Or not. I don't know where you were."

"Middle East mostly. And it's about as different as two places can be." She wasn't asking, wasn't digging for details. Just talking, and he felt like talking back.

"Isn't it hard for you? Living in the city? And I hope that doesn't offend you, or sound like your family," he added quickly. "I don't doubt you *can* do it, I'm just trying to imagine how."

"No, it's not hard. It's easier in the city."

"Okay," he said and stared at her profile. "*That* you're going to have to explain because I've been once, and it was like trying to maneuver through a drunk circus."

She smiled. Her hair skimmed over his shoulder, his cheek. He was sorry when she brushed it back.

"You get used to it. But for me, public transportation is number one."

"You ride the subway?"

"A lot of times. But most places I can walk."

He shook his head in awe of her. He seemed to do that a lot.

"The subway's not hard after you learn the system. I know the stops. I know every corner on the streets I walk. I can tell where I am by the scents, the sounds."

"What about taxis? I damn near got killed and I could see them coming."

"Well, you can't just step out into the street," she said with a laugh. "There are talking crosswalks in the city, something you don't find in small towns. They countdown, tell you when it's safe to cross, but usually I just feel the tide of the crowd moving and I move."

"Keep in the center. Let the ones on the outside take the hit from a crazy cabbie. Good strategy."

"There are no parking lots to walk across. The entire city has sidewalks. I know I come out of my apartment building, turn right and take thirty–eight steps to the grocery store. I go left fifty-nine steps to the bank. There are delis, and coffee shops, everything I need right on street level. Seventy–three steps past the grocery store is my favorite coffee shop."

"And a grocery store? How does that work? Because

again, I can see and it still takes me an hour to find everything I came in for."

"Believe it or not, there's an app for that. It actually reads objects in view of my phone, tells me how far away they are. It can even read prices."

"Amazing."

"It really is. I'm actually dying for a chocolate croissant. Major withdrawal going on here. The major thing is I can do everything myself. Get anywhere I want to go by myself. The city is like freedom. I miss that almost as much as I miss my friends. My job. I can't just go out and get a cannoli when the mood strikes."

"Does it strike often?"

She smiled. "Too often. Oh! And bagels and lox. You just can't get a real bagel here."

She'd closed her eyes as she'd spoken, rubbed her lips together in a way that made him jealous of a bagel.

"Sounds like you only live in New York for the food."

"That's definitely a benefit. But it was liberating, moving to New York. Sure, it was scary at first, but growing up I always had to rely on someone to take me where I wanted to go. First my parents, then my brother. Then finally my best friend, which was way better than my brother, but still. I couldn't just decide to go out for a snack. Couldn't run out for shampoo or tampons."

"Okay... not touching that last one."

"Such a guy," she said and smiled. "They want me to stay, my parents," she said after a long moment. "I know they do. But more than not being able to go out and get my coffee and croissant, I don't want to become dependent on them again."

"Are you afraid you would?"

"They'd want me to be, and... I don't know. Maybe I would."

"I don't think you would."

"Thanks." She sat up, picked another blade of grass, ran it through her fingers. "I do like it here, the peacefulness of it, but I'd never make it out here. Too isolated. No sidewalks."

"Mmm." Made sense. But for some reason it bothered him to hear her say it.

"So the cowboy life suits you?"

"I'm not quite a cowboy. But yeah, I think this suits me. Still..."

"What?"

"I don't know," he said after a moment. He sighed, and just let it out. His truth. "I'm still not sure I made the right decision, leaving the Rangers."

"I don't know much about the Rangers. It seems all the movies and books have Navy SEALs."

He'd seen some of the movies. Some of them were a joke. Some of them were actually pretty accurate. "It's similar. Except for the water." He wondered again if it was easier to talk to her because she couldn't see him. Or because she was a woman. Or maybe it was because she was leaving soon and that took the pressure off.

"I loved it and it was good for me. It's what I needed at the time. The rules and the rituals. The danger, the action, jumping out of planes, running obstacle courses. There was the challenge in strategizing, the adrenaline rush. And the toys," he added with a small smile. "The constancy of nothing being constant. Being with men I considered my brothers." And he felt guilty about that, because for years he'd been closer to them than his own brothers.

"If you loved it so much why are you here?"

"Well, that's a question isn't it," he said staring at the creek. "The best answer I have is, it was time." He shrugged. "It just seemed like it was time. Time to reconnect with the family I've mostly avoided. And there's one reason for the black sheep."

"Baaa," she said, making him smile when he would have thought it impossible a second earlier. "Avoiding the family will definitely put you on the naughty list. I should know."

And just that easily, she took the heaviness away. Luke glanced at her, saw her eyes were focused on a spot just across the creek, but not seeing. No one had asked the question quite like that, so directly. Or maybe they had and it was just her asking that didn't bother him. Maybe because it seemed like everyone else who asked was on the inside. Except Ava.

"Did you stop loving it?"

"No. But... Something about it changed or I changed. Or both. It seemed more and more I was looking at the guys just coming in and thinking, *You're too young to be here. Go home.* And God, that makes me sound old." He breathed out a short laugh.

Ava was quiet for a long minute. "I guess even if it was time, it can still be uncomfortable."

He nodded, then remembered she couldn't see. "True. I was a kid when I left. I felt like a man. I wasn't, obviously, but at seventeen I was trying to be. According to Nick I was doing a piss poor job of it. I wanted to be a man like my dad. I just... I was so damn mad. It felt like I should have been able to *do* something. Should have been able to stop it."

"Your parents' car accident," Ava said softly. "Hannah told me. I'm sorry."

He felt the rage inside him build and squeezed his hands into fists until they ached. "I wanted to kill someone. I think that's part of why I joined up. Not just to get away from home, but maybe to outrun the rage. And the pain, though I wouldn't have admitted it then.

"I wasn't there when the sheriff came to say our parents had been hit head on by a drunk driver. I was out. Breaking rules, breaking curfews, not caring that it made my parents worry. Then it was too late. Maybe that's another reason I came back now. I didn't want to be too late. Again."

Quietly, in Ava's way, she reached over, laid her cool hand over his clenched fist. Her hand was so small next to his, her skin so much lighter than his sun baked and work roughened ones. Cool and soft. At first he didn't move, just breathed. Then slowly, little by little, the tension eased until his hand relaxed. He turned his hand over and linked his fingers with hers.

"Where would you go if you didn't stay here?"

"I don't know. When I decided it was time to leave, I didn't think about going anywhere else. Hell, maybe that's why I left. I was thinking about family, or thinking I was glad I had no ties. And then it hit me that was bullshit. I *had* the family. But the ties, those were something I'd have to make myself."

"And here you are," Ava said. "The way Hannah talks about you, I'd say you're well on your way with those ties."

"Yeah," he said, thinking it was exactly the right thing to say. He couldn't stop the smile creeping across his face.

"Is it okay for you? Being back?"

"It's okay. Different. Strange. It's getting easier lately. The work on the cabin helps. Keeping busy. And that's enough about me." Luke was ready to hop off that topic. "Tell me, how does someone go about becoming fluent in seven languages?"

"Hmm...How did I learn so many languages... Mostly it was just a lot of time on my hands. Something I started doing as a kid. It seemed to come easily." She shrugged. "It was kind of a game, how many and how good I could be. Maddie, my friend, her grandmother lived with them for a while and she spoke German. She tried to teach Maddie and me. Maddie would get bored and go watch TV or play Xbox. I stayed.

"As many hours as the other kids could play video games, I could listen to her, learn from her. Then at night, or riding in the car with my mom, I'd listen to language podcasts. It was a hobby, when you boil it down. I was good at listening."

"And you turned listening into a career."

"Yeah. I guess I did."

It was already cooler with the cloud cover, but getting cooler still as the day slipped into evening. The wind rustled the new leaves above them. There was something about sitting here with Ava in the quiet that he didn't usually feel in the absence of sound. A peace, he realized and a quiet mind.

"What does it look like here?"

"Hmm... Well, there's trees, a lot of them."

"Tall?"

"Yeah. Some pine, those are the tallest. And some others. We're sitting under a River Birch right now. There's more of those here along the water. One of my favorites."

"Why?"

"Why is it my favorite? Well, their leaves come out early so it's like a sign of spring. I guess that's one reason. And they make a really cool sound in the wind." He looked up at the tree then at Ava. She listened to every word he said, cocked her head in a way that made him think she was cataloging every detail.

"It's more like hundreds or thousands of little leaves shaking... No. Fluttering. The branches get really skinny as you move to the ends of each one so they sway in the slightest breeze. Then later, as it gets closer to autumn, the leaves turn yellow just before they fall. They also have this weird peeling bark." He reached out to his left, stripped off a piece, and handed it to her.

She rubbed it between her fingers. "It feels like paper. You're good at this. At describing."

"You think?" He'd been talking not even realizing what he was saying. He just wanted her to see. To know. To smile. "There's a Dogwood here and there. Not blooming yet. I guess they don't get enough light in here."

"So it's dark?"

"No, not dark. Not like night. Just shaded. There's sunlight, but it's blocked. Of course now it's cloudy so it's kind of... gray I guess." He looked over at her, taking in their surroundings solely by what she felt and what he said. "Is it always dark for you?"

"I'm not sure my perception of dark is the same as yours, but whenever I had tests and the doctor would say she was shining a light in my eyes. Nothing changed so, I guess that means I don't see light. Which means I see darkness?" She shrugged. "I don't know."

"I'm sorry."

"Don't feel sorry for me."

"I don't. But can I just be sorry?"

"You can. But it's all I've ever known so.... So if you feel sorry for me—"

"I said I didn't. You don't need me to. I knew guys—know guys—who lost their sight, an eye or a leg, an arm, and I know that pity is the worst. They don't want it, they don't need it. You don't need it. I got that within about five minutes of meeting you."

She smiled. "Thank you."

"I guess that means you were never scared of the dark," he said, going for lightening the mood.

"I wasn't scared at night, I guess like some children are, because that's when it's dark, but…"

"But what?"

"It's not the dark that's scary exactly. It's more the unknown."

He reached out, took her hand, linking their fingers. "Does everything feel unknown?"

"No. And I'm not feeling scared right now." She grinned over at him and damn it, there was that clutch in his belly again, a hitch in his heart beat.

"That's good. And that's not why I'm holding your hand."

14

Ava felt something whisper between she and Luke, then more than whisper. It sparked and she felt her heart quiver. She'd felt this spark with him before, when she'd danced with him. When she'd thought he was going to kiss her. There was a fluttering in her stomach thinking about what he'd said. *You weren't wrong.*

She hadn't wanted a man to touch her, hadn't even thought about it in so long. It was that far out of her scope of possibilities. She'd slammed that door and slammed it hard. Locked it. It bothered her that she'd consider opening it even a crack. But maybe raising the window. Maybe? Just a little? A bit of fresh air? That didn't sound so dangerous.

"Tell me something else," he said.

"Like what?"

"Anything. How did you know I was staring at you the other day?"

"I didn't. I never know, not for sure. You could have been staring at the horse or your phone, then wouldn't I have felt dumb?" She laughed softly. "When I'm on the train I don't know if people are looking at me, making eye contact and wondering why I'm looking right through them. I don't know if they're watching me, looking at their phone, reading a book. Did an old man smile and I didn't respond and made him sad? My cane's not always visible in a crowd. I can't wear a sign. Or I guess could," she added with a short laugh.

"Sounds lonely."

"It can be. There's no shared eye roll between strangers when someone's rude in line. There's no, *Damn, it's cold*, when I pass someone on the street. Or if there is, I'm not sure they're talking to me. If they're not touching me, if they don't speak my name and address me, it's like they're not there."

Luke pulled her hand over farther to hold it in both of his. "I'm touching you now."

"I noticed." A light breeze kissed her skin and the leaves high above her swayed with it. Her fingers itched to touch Luke's face, to feel his cheeks against her palms. Did he shave every day or was there some scruff?

"But I'm still thinking about it," he said. "About wanting to kiss you."

He was looking at her now. She knew it, felt his breath on her face.

Then Luke took her face in his hands, pulled her in until his lips hovered just over hers. "Scratch that. I *need* to kiss you." He cupped her cheek, whispered her name like a question.

"Okay." She'd barely whispered the word before his lips touched hers. Her heart did that fluttery thing again and her mouth opened under his. The air was cool, Luke's lips were warm, smooth, and firm. There was nothing hesitant about it. It was hot and hard. She gripped his shoulders and held on, not thinking of past hurts. Letting herself take this pleasure that was kissing Luke Walker.

As the kiss went from a blasting take off to leisurely cruising, she slid her fingers around his neck, up and into soft, thick hair that just reached his collar.

She felt a lovely liquid feeling flowing through her, a flying and flipping in her stomach. She heard the low groan of pleasure in his throat. Her fingers curled into the shirt over his chest as she desperately needed something to hold onto.

She must be crazy, *crazy,* to be here doing this, but she didn't want to stop. She wanted more. Her heart scrambled with the sudden intensity and she couldn't think with his hand gripping her hair in his fist. With their mouths fused, his other hand made a slow slide up her side, until his thumb brushed just under her breast.

The longer he kissed her, the longer she wanted him to. Her fingers tensed on his thigh and she let him lead her. He laid her back on the ground, followed her over to her side. He took her mouth again as his hand skimmed slowly up her thigh, slipping under the edge of her shirt.

Then his phone was ringing. They both ignored it. It continued, a ring tone that was hard and loud, breaking the magic of the moment. Reluctantly, she loosened her hold and he pulled back to answer it.

"Luke, where are you?" Hannah asked. "Is Ava with you?"

"Of course she is. Okay," Luke said and hung up.

Ava cursed under her breath as he ended the call.

"Your brother's there. I guess they were looking for you. Us."

"I heard," she said, already standing and wanting very much to crawl into a hole.

Without a word, she took his arm and he led her to Winnie. She mounted and sat waiting for Luke to do the same then gather Winnie's lead rope.

They rode back, but she didn't laugh this time. It felt like the magic between them had been broken. Because she wasn't *normal*. She was thirty–one and her big brother was here to pick her up.

AVA HAD BEEN MOSTLY quiet on the ride back. Lost in her own thoughts, maybe? He'd definitely been lost in his. He was in trouble. Deep trouble. The longer he'd kissed her, the dimmer all the reasons became for not getting involved. On any level. But hell, he thought, approaching the barn, he didn't even know what level they were on.

The second they were inside the barn, Hannah was there, taking the reins of Ava's horse. Luke swung off of Newman and led him to the metal ring hanging on the wall outside his stall.

"Sorry," he heard Ava say as she dismounted. "We lost track of time."

A tall, lanky man stood in the aisle of the barn. His sandy blond hair was neatly trimmed, matching his dark dress pants and long sleeve dress shirt with tie. His brows were pinched together over pale blue eyes as he eyed his sister then Luke.

"Not her fault," Luke said, coming up beside her. "I went the long way. Didn't realize it was so long."

A beat passed with the man sizing him up. Luke held out a hand. "Luke Walker."

The man stepped up and took Luke's offered hand. "I'm Ryan Bennet. Ava's brother."

"Well. Nice to meet you."

"I didn't expect you to be out riding," he said to Ava. "I had thought..." He laughed to cover himself. "I guess I thought you were riding around a ring or something."

"I usually am, but—"

"Ava knows what she's doing," Luke said, noting Ryan's gaze shift to the dried leaves in Ava's hair. The man's expression went from slightly annoyed to highly suspicious. Luke smiled at him, then reached out nonchalantly and pulled a twig from Ava's hair.

"Good grief." Ava huffed. "If you two are having some kind of stare down, pissing contest, you can knock it off."

"Just a small one," Hannah said pleasantly. "How was the ride?"

"It was great," Ava said with a genuine smile. "Winnie is a sweetheart. I'm sorry you got pulled away from home. We should have come back sooner."

"She is and not a problem. It's easy to lose track of time out there." Hannah slid her eyes to Luke and he read the question there. *Just what were you doing that you lost track of time?*

"Thanks for stepping in," Ava said, but she wasn't looking at him.

"No problem."

Luke watched her take her brother's arm and walk out of the barn. One part of his brain said it was a good thing her brother had interrupted. The other part of his brain said, bullshit. Then again, he lost all sense around that woman.

Ava got in her brother's BMW, slammed the door, and buckled her seat belt. She didn't speak until he had the car turned around and was climbing the hill. "I'm sorry you had to wait but please don't treat me like a child. It's bad enough I have to have my brother come and pick me up like I'm one of the kids Hannah works with."

"I'm not treating you like a child," Ryan said, pausing before he made the turn onto the main road. "I'm looking out for you. Like I should have looked out for you in New York."

"You mean with Blake? Thanks for that. Just remind me again that a sighted person would have seen it coming."

"I didn't say that."

"Didn't you?" She sighed. "Forget it."

"Why were you riding with Luke and not Hannah? I thought she was the instructor or whatever."

"Because we'd planned a trail then we waited out what looked like a storm coming. By the time it passed she needed to go relieve her sitter. Luke was there. He offered."

"Mmm. And you were late because you went the long way?"

Ava drew in a long-suffering breath at her brother's skeptical tone. "Well since I can't see, I'm not sure which way we went, but we did stop off and talk for a bit. I'm allowed to do that, right?"

"Shit," her brother murmured like an apology.

"It's fine. And I am sorry, okay? I'm sorry you had to wait and I do appreciate the ride. I just wish I didn't have to *get* a ride. It makes me feel like a child."

They were both silent for a moment and she felt slightly guilty for her brother's discomfort.

"I'm not getting involved with him, so no need to fight for my honor or anything. I won't be here long enough to get involved with him or anyone else. Dad's doing well," she said, to get the conversation moving away from herself and whatever she might be thinking about having or not having with Luke. "We did his therapy this morning and he did great."

"I heard. Mom said she didn't think he was doing it right, or for long enough."

"Of course she did. But you know how she is." Ava shrugged. "She worries, especially when she's not in control. "

"I'm worried about Mom doing it all."

"She's not doing it all," Ava said.

"For how long? Do you know yet when you'll be going back?"

"I originally asked for eight weeks. It's already been three. I could maybe get another four, but I can't ask for more than that. That'd be three months and I need the paid leave to pay my rent." Her boss knew about the consulate job she'd applied for. He'd actually given her a raving recommendation. She didn't want to put him in a bad position by asking for too much.

"You know you could find something around here."

"Right. A lot of diplomatic translators needed around here? Please don't start."

"It wouldn't have to be diplomatic. Hospitals need translators. The District Attorney's office, and... other places."

"You sound like Mom. Please don't give her any more ideas."

"Fine. Is it so bad I miss my little sis?"

"Yeah, right. If I lived here you wouldn't have time for me and you know it."

"Not true, but okay. I don't want to fight with you. It's too sad when I always win."

"In your dreams."

They were silent a while. She thought he might bring up the baby Connie had mentioned, and debated if she should.

"I've been worried about you," he finally said.

"Why?"

"*Why*? Because he hurt you. That's why."

"It was a long time ago," she said.

"It was a year ago. He hurt you, Ava, and I'm just saying… be careful."

"I am careful." *So careful I don't plan on letting anyone close enough to hurt me like that again.*

Which is why the way she felt when Luke kissed her terrified her.

"I also heard about Italy," her brother commented.

"Great."

"Mom's in a royal tizzy."

"Mom's in a royal tizzy when the market doesn't have her preferred brand of yogurt."

"True."

She spent the rest of the drive thinking about Italy. She hated to think of it as a fresh start, because that would imply that she needed one. She didn't. But a change was good, especially one as exciting as Italy.

Exciting changes.

Luke.

She sighed. What would have happened if her brother hadn't interrupted? As nonchalantly as she could, she ran her right hand into her hair, searching for leaves. She could still feel his mouth on hers, the weight of his body.

Instead of obsessing over a kiss in the woods, and with a man who felt and smelled and kissed like Luke Walker, she spent the rest of the drive feeling frustrated over the need to be carted around everywhere. She'd much prefer contacting Uber or another riding service than relying on someone else and their schedule.

It was exactly like she'd told Luke, it made her feel small, less than. There'd been a time not so long ago her husband, her best friend, had made her feel like that more than anyone.

It was that day, the day Blake hadn't picked her up that she'd known it was over. Or she should've known.

She'd told Blake she could take the bus, or a cab, but he'd insisted.

"No way," Blake had said. "No bus. I'll pick you up."

He'd been all about driving since the surgery, even in the city where it was a nightmare. Or so he said.

She waited on the sidewalk, Blake was already late and she felt a little turn in her stomach as her bus pulled away. The nearest metro was eight blocks away which is why she'd offered to take a cab. Or the bus that had just pulled away. But Blake had texted twice that he was on his way.

By the time he finally got there she was an ice cube. A pissed off ice cube.

She got in, slamming the door of his new car.

"Sorry," he said. "So much traffic you wouldn't believe it." She could tell by his tone he was smiling. Never having the option to drive before, driving in traffic was fun for him.

"I could have been home by now. If you say you're going to pick me up, do it. I could have gotten a cab thirty minutes ago."

"Are you saying you'd rather be in a cab?"

She huffed frustrated and let her head fall back. It'd been a long day. "I'd rather be home."

"I knew this was gonna happen," he said clearly annoyed. "I knew eventually you were going to get upset about it or, I don't want to say jealous, but—"

"Are you kidding me? I'm not jealous that you can see, Blake. I'm happy for you. I've been nothing but happy for you this whole time." Why was he trying to pick a fight when he should be apologizing? But it seemed all they did now was fight and make up.

"Everything's different now," he said softly.

"Really? Why is it different? Because you can see and I can't?"

"Yes, Ava! Yes, it's different! I'm sorry but it is. I can't be responsible for you."

"*What*? I have never once asked you to be responsible for me. Ever. You *offered* to pick me up. I waited for you. If you can't come or you don't want to come, then don't offer. I'll take the train or a cab or the bus like I always have."

"Okay," he'd said with a heavy sigh. "Okay, you're right. I'm sorry."

But deep down she knew that wasn't the problem. That wasn't the reason. The truth was, he could see now and he could see that he didn't want to be with her anymore. It took him two more excruciating months to admit it.

15

"Yo," Luke said, answering his cell.

"Hey," Zach said on the other end. "Why can't you return a text?"

"I'm driving," he said, reaching to turn down the radio. "Safety first."

"Right. You've been driving since yesterday."

Luke ignored that. "What's up?"

"Darts at Dudley's Thursday night."

"With your guys? Sure. I could do that."

"No, not my guys. Hannah has decreed we're going to do something as a family. She said she doesn't feel part of the group, that we do stuff together, yada, yada."

"The only stuff we do is working around the farm."

"I told her that. And she said she feels left out because we do guy stuff."

"Well, isn't drinking beer and throwing darts kind of a guy thing?"

"Right," Zach said. "Let me know when you tell her that because I want to watch."

"Mmm," was all Luke said, thinking better of the *guy thing* comment.

"It's important to her," Zach added when Luke didn't reply.

Luke sighed.

"Come on. It's a couple of beers. A game. You can do that."

"I've got a lot to do on the cabin."

"You can spare a couple of hours. Come on. She's been trying to fix it so all our schedules match up for weeks."

Luke tapped his finger on the steering wheel.

"If you say you can't go because you have to work on her cabin, she'll probably cry or something."

"That's low."

Zach laughed. "You'll manage. I'll even give you a few hours Saturday to help you make up the time."

Luke appreciated his brother's confidence in him and there were a couple of things he could use a hand with. "Okay. Deal."

He hung up, turned the radio back up, but continued to tap his finger on the steering wheel. *Family night.*

They'd had those, he remembered, when he was young. Lots of them before Hannah had been born. His parents with four boys. Then maybe a couple with Hannah, a toddler, then... They were gone. Just like that. No more family nights. No more hair rumples from his mom. No more how was your day from his dad. Just... gone.

The music in his truck was replaced by the music in his head. Church music. Funeral music. Too loud and too optimistic.

The church had smelled of candle wax and the incense usually reserved for Good Friday and Easter. He'd mostly thought it was cool, but not on that day. On that day it had made him sick. The smooth wooden pew was hard but he didn't shift like he usually did during Mass. The starch in his collar scratched his neck but he didn't pull at it.

Coughs echoed hollowly. People sniffed and blew noses. Dim, cloudy–day light came through the stained-glass windows on either side, leading to the front of the church. His dad's coffin was covered in white and a lot of green. His mom's in white and green but with pink mixed in. To tell them apart since the coffins were the same?

Some of his friends were there, most with their parents; a few he knew weren't even Catholic. A good excuse to skip school, he thought. He'd skipped school a few times, made his dad look at him with disappointment in his eyes.

There'd been a lady right behind him belting out the words of returning home and being with God. He hadn't sung, not a word, and it had taken all his strength not to turn around and tell her to shut the hell up.

His younger twin brothers, Zach and Dallas, had

cried and accepted the hugs of the people who'd come to say they were sorry. His older brother Nick had held a crying Hannah.

He'd held nothing. Nothing but anger and regret.

Ava was just getting into bed with an audio book when her phone buzzed with an incoming call. Not expecting any calls tonight, she'd turned the audio off that would have announced the caller.

She sighed, considering leaving it until tomorrow. But it could be work. Could be Luke, she thought, though he didn't have her number and they hadn't spoken since they'd gone riding three days ago. Not that she didn't still think about that kiss.

With a sigh, she put aside her iPad and grabbed her phone to answer.

"Hello?"

"Hey. Ava."

Blake. Her heart didn't thump like it did when she was with Luke. It stopped, as if just hearing his name froze her in a place she hated being.

"Hi," she said coolly. She really needed to tell him to stop. Stop calling, stop emailing. But wouldn't that seem like she wasn't over him? She didn't want him to know just how badly he'd hurt her.

"Just checking in. You didn't return my email."

"Sorry. I've been busy."

"I get it," he said cheerfully. "How are things going? How's your dad?"

"He's good." *As if you care.* Her parents had been almost as heartbroken as she had. She hated knowing that part of their hurt was because they thought Blake had been their daughter's only chance at love. At a normal life. And they couldn't have been happier when he'd regained his sight.

Now our daughter who insists on living in a faraway city will have someone to take care of her!

"Yeah? That's good. How long do you think you'll be down there?"

"I'm not sure yet."

"Oh, well. I wanted to tell you that um... Well..."

Good grief. He always stalled when he was nervous. Like when he'd dropped her coffee on the way home or broken the butter dish. Again. She used to try to help him out. Fill in the blank with something funny. She had no desire to help him now so she let the silence hang.

She couldn't imagine what was so hard for him to say. After all, he'd managed pretty well telling her he didn't love her any more, that he wanted a divorce. That he'd found someone else. Oh, he'd hemmed and hawed but he'd gotten it out.

"I've asked Emily to marry me. She's um... well..." He let out a nervous laugh. "We're having a baby."

Everything in her slowed. Her breathing. Her blood flow. She should say congratulations. She tried.

She opened her mouth, but the word just wouldn't come out.

He hadn't said *Emily's* pregnant. Not *Emily's* having a baby, but *we're* having a baby.

And hadn't she known he'd be like that? An all-in, hands on kind of dad. If he could see, that is. Because they'd decided together *not* to have kids. That it wouldn't be fair for a child to have two totally blind parents and even more than fairness, they'd both been concerned about safety.

"Ava. Say something."

"What do you want me to say? Congratulations, I guess, would be the right thing."

"I know you think that's part of the reason things didn't work out between us, but—"

"Things didn't work out between us because you met someone else, Blake. *While* we were still married." She didn't know if he'd cheated physically, didn't trust him when he said he hadn't and wasn't sure if it mattered. He'd moved on to someone else right under her nose and she hadn't even known.

He didn't want to be married anymore. He'd found someone else. When the day had come, she couldn't even say she'd been shocked. She didn't fight it. He'd move out, she'd keep the apartment—it had been hers to begin with anyway. And a week later the papers were signed.

And *shit*. Now she'd made it sound like she wasn't over him. But damn if she'd let him turn things around now to make himself feel better, like it had been some kind of mutual decision.

"Okay," Blake said softly. "You're right. But I hope you know I didn't plan it."

I didn't plan on this. I didn't mean for it to happen. I wish I didn't feel this way. I wish I still felt the same.

Meaning, I wish I still loved you. God, that had hurt. She pressed a hand to her chest at the memory of that pain.

Plan what? Finding a woman whose eyes worked? Someone to have a family with?

Because that's what he'd done. He'd always said having a baby wasn't a good idea for *two* blind parents. After he'd gotten his sight back, he'd decided even one blind parent was too much.

No. She gave herself a shake. She wasn't going to let herself fall into this pit again.

"You know what? Forget it," she said putting a brightness into her voice. "I'm happy for you."

"Ava—"

"No. Really. And congratulations," she added, without choking on the word.

"I don't know how many people you keep up with from work so I just... I wanted you to hear it from me so you weren't blindsided."

"Not hard to blindside the blind," she said, forcing a laugh.

"Ava."

"I'm joking." Or trying to. And it might be the United Nations with serious work, but there was still office gossip. She wanted to get away from that, too. Far away. Italy away. "Thanks for telling me. And ... good luck. With everything."

She ended the call before he could fall into his usual spiel that he still cared about her, that he hadn't meant to hurt her.

She still hadn't decided if it mattered. Would it have hurt more if he'd stopped loving her on purpose?

She'd nearly convinced herself Blake was just another asshole and she was like so many other women who'd have fallen for one. A player. A liar. But then she'd had to face the truth. He wasn't a terrible person. She hadn't been deceived that way. He'd just stopped loving her. He'd wanted a different kind of life, one where he and his spouse could go jogging in the park, stroll through an art museum and argue the merits of Picasso over Rembrandt. But bottom line, he'd gotten his sight back and then he'd stopped loving her.

Putting her phone aside, she reached for her iPad, determined to get lost in someone else's story.

16

"Can you hang this one for me?" Ava turned in the tack room and handed the bridle she'd just wiped down to Kylie, another little rider.

"Sure. I'm glad we rode together today," Kylie said.

"Me, too. It was fun."

"I wish we could have our lessons like that every time."

Ava smiled. "Well maybe we can do it again. I bet if you asked Hannah she'd say yes." When Ava felt the little girl brush against her, she opened her arms and pulled her into a hug. The top of Kylie's head just reached her waist. Her body felt small in the thin sweater.

"I'm glad you're here," she whispered into Ava's side.

Ava felt her heart melt. "Me, too."

"I'm glad you can't see me."

Ava's stomach clenched at that gut-wrenching wish. She knew Kylie had come for riding therapy after a devastating house fire. Ava knelt down. "You know what? I wish I *could* see you. I wish I could see your smile."

"I can't really smile. The skin is too tight."

"Hmm. You know moving your mouth isn't the only way to smile."

"It's not?"

"No. Your eyes can smile, and your voice. I can't see if a person is smiling, but I can tell when someone is happy by their voice and by what they say."

"I can see you," Kylie said. "I like it when you smile. It's so pretty."

Ava laughed. "I bet you're smiling now, aren't you? "

"Yes."

"I knew it." Ava reached out, touched the side of Kylie's head. Just skin. No hair. She pulled her in for another hug. "How about I finish cleaning the tack and you go ask Hannah about our next ride?"

"Okay!"

Ava listened to her go and reminded herself she never wanted people to feel sorry for her. But still, she couldn't help thinking, poor little baby. She remembered what Luke had said. *Can I just be sorry?* She figured that was okay. She could be very, very sorry for all of Kylie's pain.

LEANING against the barn wall just outside the tack room, Luke watched Kylie leave. She hadn't even seen him when she'd come out and turned left to his sister's office. He was pretty sure Ava didn't know he was there either. The two of them had been in animated conversation about Disney princesses when he'd walked up.

Not wanting to interrupt had been only one reason he hadn't walked in. He'd seen Kylie around before and no matter how much he tried to act like he didn't see her burns, he was terrified he did a piss poor job of it. That she could feel him looking.

One side of her face was nearly indiscernible it was so badly burned. Like melted wax over bone. There was no ear on that side. The shape of her nose and mouth were altered and she had only a tiny opening for one eye. Her left arm and hand were just as bad.

He knew the riding therapy was good for her to stretch the scarred skin, good also to be with animals but it was hard to watch her struggle, the way her mouth pulled in pain when she tried to follow his sister's directions. He'd barely spoken to her because he didn't know if he could without crying.

So he'd been standing out here, gathering his courage to face a child that had way more of it than he did. And listening to Ava talk and laugh with her like she was any other kid.

Luke moved into the tack room. He saw Ava pause as he got closer, figured she heard the clomp and scuff of his boots. He stopped a few feet away, but didn't say anything for a moment, just taking her in. She was in jeans again, dark ones today and a sage green long sleeved shirt.

"I can hear you," she said.

"I didn't say anything."

She smiled over her shoulder. "Silence can be loud."

He moved closer, noticed her breathing change, knew she felt him. Had she thought of that kiss as many times as he had? Had she thought of doing it again, as he had?

He could smell her amid the barn smells of horse and hay and leather. A fresh, spring scent, that he now knew came mostly from her hair. What would she do if he leaned in now, drew her in? "You were great back there," he finally said. "With that little girl."

"Kylie?" With her hands full, she attempted to blow a strand of hair off her forehead. Luke did it for her. His fingers brushing over her skin.

"Yeah, I guess. Kylie. I've seen her here before and I didn't speak to her. I didn't know what to say," he said softly. "I wish I couldn't see her burns."

She angled her face up to his, tilted her head. "Bad, huh?"

He drew in a long slow breath and let it out. "Yeah."

"I knew someone at camp once that was burned. She let me feel her skin and it was smooth. She said it was red and ugly but I don't know the color red and smooth skin is usually a good thing so it's hard for me to imagine it."

"It's...shocking."

"Why?" Her brow furrowed, as if she was trying hard to understand.

"Because it looks so different than how it should, I guess. It looks painful, maybe mostly because I know the intense pain that comes from a burn."

She nodded. "I guess there are some things I'm glad I can't see."

She moved away from him, but there was something there before she turned away. Something in her eyes. He watched her fiddle around with cans and brushes, not really doing anything of purpose which wasn't like her. "Something wrong?"

"No. Why?"

"Just a feeling."

She stopped and Luke watched the play of emotions in her face. There was pain there, as she bit her lip. *Come on, he thought. You can tell me.*

He was about to press her when Kylie came skipping back in.

"Ava! Hannah said we could ride together next week. We just have to pick a day."

Ava smiled brightly. "Great."

"Hey, Kylie."

The girl paused and looked up at him like she'd just noticed he was there. Or maybe she was surprised he'd spoken. He really didn't think the times he'd seen her that she'd noticed him. "Hey, Kylie, you want to see something?"

"What is it?"

"Come over here." He turned to the back corner of

the tack room then looked over his shoulder to see if she as following. She wasn't. "It's over here. Come on, Ava. I'll show you too."

"Okay," Ava said, drawing out the word. "Come on, Kylie. Let's go see what the mystery man has over there."

Ava held out her hand and Kylie took it.

"Okay. It's right back here, behind these saddle pads." He knelt down, guiding Ava with a hand on her back who in turn tugged Kylie down.

"Kittens!" Kylie saw them immediately. "Can we hold them?"

"I don't know about that. They're pretty young."

"So Tom turned out to be a Tina?"

Luke watched Ava's face. "Yeah. Proud mama of six babies."

"They're so cute. I want to hold one."

"Maybe just a little touch. How about that?" He stroked his hand over Tom's head and down her back. "You okay with that, Tom?"

Luke reached down demonstrated, giving one of the tiny bodies the lightest touch with one finger. Kylie did the same.

"Aww. They're so little. Ava you should pet one."

"Yeah, Ava. You should pet one." When she lifted her hand, he took it. "You'll have to get closer."

She scooted closer to him, up on her knees, and he guided her hand to the kitten. He couldn't help but think that the last time they'd been this close, she'd been kissing his brains out. She stroked once, twice, then laid her fingers on the kitten, feeling the life.

"Kylie, your mom's here! Ahh," Hannah said. "You found Tom."

"Can I show my mom?"

Luke straightened. "Sure."

Ava stood and together they went into the barn aisle to make room for Kylie, Hannah, and Kylie's mom.

Ava's hand was still in Luke's and she didn't pull it away. She smiled up at him. "Looks like you found something to say."

"Tom helped me."

"You did good," she said, of his interaction with Kylie, then squeezed his hand before letting go.

Ava went back to Banjo waiting in the aisle and Luke followed. He started to offer help, but she didn't need it. When she finished untying the blue nylon lead rope, she led Banjo to his stall and in. She unbuckled the matching blue halter slipped it off of the horse's head and after a bit of love for Banjo, came back out into the aisle.

"My sister's planned this thing," Luke said. "An outing, family thing."

"That sounds fun." Using her cane, she went to hang up the halter and lead rope.

"Yeah, well. I was thinking maybe you'd want to go."

She stopped what she was doing. "Oh. Well." When she'd been kissing him, all common sense had flown out the window. Now it was back, and now the insecurities crept in. She figured he was looking at her, but how? Like he wanted to kiss her again? There was no way to tell. He was being friendly, and friendly was good. But it didn't answer the questions.

"It's causal. Sports bar kind of deal. You'd be doing me a favor," he added. "You know. Moral support and all."

He leaned an arm against the wall beside her and Ava smelled him. She cursed her heart for the way it tripped and galloped whenever he was close.

The door to Hannah's office opened and Luke straightened.

"Luke, stop harassing my students."

"Not harassing. Just saying hi. And bye. Bye, Ava."

"Bye, Luke. Wait. Wait a second." Was she really going to say no? When she wanted to go?

She hated that Blake's call would make her second guess spending time with a man she liked. And why the hell not? Why the hell shouldn't she go? She liked him. God knows she could use a reason to spend an evening outside the house. Hannah and Luke's brothers' wives would be there. "I'd like to go."

"Okay. I'll pick you up at six."

"Tonight?"

"Tonight."

17

It wasn't like Ava to fuss about clothes. For the most part she stuck with black on the bottom. Black pants, white top. Black skirt, black jacket, colored top.

But she wasn't dressing for work or the barn. She would have paid big money to have Maddie here now to give her advice. Casual, he'd said, so she'd start with jeans. It would be a fun night out with a man she liked. A man she was attracted to. A man she had no future illusions about and who had none about her.

She ran her hand over her shirt options. Most of these she could tell by feel. A few of them had the neck tag cut in a certain way that distinguished one from the other. She knew from Maddie that black with jeans was always good. Or white.

She chose the black then switched to the white with short brown boots. It wasn't as if she had other plans. If she didn't go, she'd be sitting in the living room listening to reality shows with her parents.

Something about Luke challenged her. Maybe it was just the challenge of getting back out there, proving to herself that she might have been down for a while, but she wasn't out.

Maddie had trained her in make-up application, or more often done it for her, when they were twelve. She smiled at the thought of what she must have looked like. Though according to her friend, it hadn't been much worse than anyone else.

These days she stuck to a light mascara, very carefully applied. After which she made sure to clean her fingers since she had to feel her way there. A couple of light swipes of blush and a little gloss on the lips and she was done. She decided a quick FaceTime with Maddie was in order.

"I have a date," she said as soon as the connection was made. "I need a make-up check."

"Okay, bring the phone a little closer. There. Turn to the side... Other side. Good job. Now tell me about the date. The cowboy?"

"Yes. And it's not really a date, it's a family thing. A group thing."

"Gotta start somewhere."

"Yeah." And by the way he kissed her, Ava didn't know if that was a reason to go for it or a reason to run.

"Just do it. Get it over with."

"Wow. How romantic," Ava said. "Assuming we're talking sex."

"We are and this could be the perfect way to get back in the saddle so speak. Break the man fast."

"Maybe." Ava laid the phone on the bed and went for her shoes, short brown boots with a four-inch heel. "Are you on the subway?"

"I had to go into the Brooklyn office this morning."

"Mmm." Ava came back to the phone, and zipped up each boot. "You know, I really don't know why I'm making it so complicated. We're both single, we're attracted to each other."

"Then stop making it complicated. You're not going to fall in love with the guy. Just have sex with him, leave him pining."

No, she definitely wasn't going to fall in love, but— the doorbell rang and she ended the Face Time. She grabbed her cane and her leather wristlet that held her phone.

She'd planned on being at the ready to avoid exactly this. This, *date comes to meet the parents of a grown adult,* scenario. But before she made it down the hallway she heard her mother opening the door and saying hello, in a tone she might have used for a door to door salesman. As if she'd had no idea Luke was coming.

She closed her eyes briefly then carried on.

～

WHEN THEY GOT to the sports bar, Luke led Ava in, giving her the lay of the land as he went. "The bar is to the left," Luke told her.

She nodded as they passed, hearing the sounds of ice shaking against metal. A bottle thunking down on wood. The tempting scents of greasy bar food reminded her she'd missed lunch. The room felt busy and smelled amazing.

"There are tables scattered to the right and a dark wood bar running the length of the room from here," he said as they passed the end. "Bathrooms are down at that end. Let me know when and I'll guide you."

If she could, if she was alone, she liked to run her hand along the bar to see how long it was. To feel if it was slick or rustic. She'd like to walk around the edges of the room to get a sense of the size. When she'd gone places with Maddie, her friend had always given her that information. Having known her so long, Maddie could say the bar is ten steps to your left, or it's fifteen steps long. She did it without even thinking.

She could ask Luke to do that. But she didn't want to be the girl that needed extra.

"Hey, you guys," a voice called out. One she recognized as Hannah. "We just ordered nachos to start."

Ava's stomach clenched. Finger food. *Shared* finger food. The thing was she loved nachos, but it was virtually impossible for her to grab a nacho from a cheesy, chili, sour creamed up pile without touching any of the others.

"Great," Luke said, guiding her to a stool. "You like

cheese sticks?" He gently squeezed her hand, letting her know he was talking to her. "They've got the best in town. I'll get us an order when the waitress comes around. And some plates." He squeezed her hand again, and she got his silent message. *Don't worry about the shared plate of food.*

She ordered a beer and lifted it carefully, each time. Set it back even more carefully, not wanting to spill her own or anyone else's, not touch anyone's food.

"Relax," Luke whispered in her ear then pressed his lips to her temple.

She'd have loved to know who at the table had caught that and what their reaction was.

"How was the honeymoon?" Mia asked.

"Oh, yeah," Hannah said. "I haven't had a chance to get the details."

"There will be no honeymoon detail giving," Ava heard Zach say.

"Eww," Hannah said. "I'm not looking for those kinds of details. I'm talking about the hotel, the island, the food."

"Was there food?" Zach asked. "I don't remember."

Ava heard a thump and smiled when Zach laughed and said, 'Ow.'

"Would you behave? It was perfect," Nora said. "We ate and swam and walked on the beach."

"That's not all we did," Zach said. "Babies don't make themselves."

"What? Are you guys—"

"No. Not yet," Nora said quickly.

Talk turned to kids. Will was cutting a new tooth. Mitchell had developed a bad habit of climbing onto the kitchen table.

"He just stands there and yells," Hannah said dumbfounded. "He doesn't try to get anything, doesn't try to hide it."

"Sounds like your kid alright," Luke said.

"I never did that."

"Yes, you did."

"Absolutely," Nick said.

Zach nodded. "Yep. Every day."

"Ha!" Stephen said grinning and pointing at Hannah. "And you tried to blame it on me."

When the waitress brought the food, she apparently moved Ava's beer over so when she went to reach for it, it wasn't there. Luke must have noticed her groping and slid the bottle until it touched her searching fingers.

"Thanks," she said softly.

"What about you, Ava?" Nora asked. "Any annoying brothers? Sisters?"

"Just one overprotective brother."

"I can relate," Hannah said with an exaggerated sigh.

"I can't imagine having *four*," Ava said. "I bet you've got some stories. Did one of them teach you to drive?"

The group went silent and Ava's stomach immediately seized in a panic. She couldn't see their faces and she hated, *hated,* this feeling. Was it because their parents had died and hadn't been able to teach her?

She knew Hannah had only been two so she'd hadn't thought it'd be a sore spot, just a chance for a funny story. But she couldn't read the room, or the table in this instance.

She couldn't know whose face had fallen. If there was anger, embarrassment, or sadness. Were they looking at each other or looking at her?

Then she felt Luke's arm slip around her shoulders, felt his big hand on her neck and the gentle, reassuring squeeze. She'd never been so grateful. He wasn't going to leave her out there flailing. Before she could think about it, her hand found his muscled, blue jean clad thigh under the table.

"Oh, that's a long story," Hannah said. "I didn't learn to drive until I was older. Just took me a while to work up the nerve."

Luke silently thanked his sister, and thought not exactly a lie. Because no one had taught Hannah to drive, not for a very long time. Being kidnapped and nearly murdered at fifteen had overshadowed getting a driver's permit. Something else Luke hadn't been there for. Not at first anyway. And after... Well, it'd been Nick who had stuck close and been there for Hannah's recovery.

"There *are* some stories, though," Zach said. "Like Luke here setting the Nativity on fire."

"I didn't set it on fire. I didn't," he said again when Ava turned her face to his.

"Here's the truth, Ava," Zach said. "All four of us are messing around the Christmas tree, counting presents, shaking boxes, when Luke pulls a lighter out of his pocket and—"

"Nope. Dallas had the lighter."

"Okay. You stole the lighter from Dallas."

"I relieved him of it," he said to Ava. "It was dangerous."

"How old were all of you," she asked, smiling.

"I was maybe eight, so the twins were six. Nick was ten."

"Anyway," Zach went on. "This nativity was all wood with carved people and animals and Dallas said how when the shepherds were out there with their sheep, they had to build fires to keep warm. And there were already these little bits of straw our mom had put in the manger and scattered around. So one of us—"

"You," Luke said.

"Okay, maybe."

"The look on his face is a clear admission of guilt," Luke said for Ava's benefit.

"And maybe," Zach went on. "I made a little pile of the straw, moved the shepherd and a couple sheep to stand around it. I was just going to pretend."

"Yeah, right," Nick said, grabbing a cheese laden chip.

"Then Luke flicks the lighter."

"I'm sure you were all daring him to do it," Nora said.

"Maybe." Zach, grinned at his wife. "But Luke flicked it and the thing went up in flames."

"Nothing ever lights on the first try," Luke said, shaking his head. "But boy, did it burn."

"Shit," Stephen said, laughing.

"Hey, I've heard some McKinney stories that make us look like angels," Zach said.

"We were angels, every one. Just ask my mom."

"Whatever," Zach said. "Anyway, we're all on our stomachs blowing on it, which just made it spread to Mary and Joseph."

"At which point Dallas said, 'you're going to hell for burning Jesus,' and he starts praying," Nick said.

"Yeah, and then our sitter comes running in, grabs up the whole thing and chucks it right out the window."

"And it lands right at my parents' feet as they're coming home from a Christmas party," Luke said.

"Oh, my gosh." Ava put a hand over her mouth to cover the laugh. "I bet they never left you with a sitter again."

Mia blew out a breath, and looked at Nick. "We should probably go ahead and rid the house of all fire making capability."

"Don't worry, babe," Nick said to Mia. "I'll be one step ahead of them at all times."

"Pfft. It's three against two," Zach said. "You better make it five steps."

"And you, quick as you could," Luke pointed his beer at Nick. "You told Dad *I* did it."

"Hey, I wasn't about to get blamed for your folly."

"Dallas was already crying, afraid he was going to

get his presents taken away, then demanding that we all say the Act of Contrition." With his arm around the back of Ava's seat, he absently ran a strand of Ava's hair between his thumb and forefinger and took a long drink of his beer as he listened to his siblings.

This was the same bar they'd come to to discuss Stephen, back when they'd decided McKinney was no good for their sister. Same one they'd come to celebrate the death of Zach's bachelorhood. He didn't remember ever feeling this at ease.

"And that is why our nativity consisted of a burned-out box and baby Jesus all alone," Zach said.

"Wait," Ava said. "How did Baby Jesus survive?"

"Because every year one of us hid baby Jesus until Christmas morning."

Talking about, thinking about, his parents always brought a bitter twist in his gut and he waited for it to come. But as the story went on, even more exaggerated since the last time it'd been told, he noted the bitterness stayed away.

His brothers' eyes were bright with good humor as they played the blame game. Even Nick was laughing. And the whole time, he was acutely aware of Ava next to him, her hand still resting on his thigh.

"Okay," Zach said. "Time to get serious. Every man for himself or teams?"

"I vote teams," Hannah said.

"Of course you do," Stephen said. "That's the only way you'll get any points."

Hannah drove her finger into Stephen's side as he threw his arm around her.

"I vote girls against boys," Mia said and the other women whooped their agreement.

"Prepare to lose, men," Ava said and the women's cheers died down.

"What?" she asked innocently, knowing for sure they were looking at her this time and knowing why. She liked surprising people. "You don't think I should play?"

"Of course you should." Luke was the only one who spoke. "But, um…"

The fear in his voice at a blind woman throwing darts almost made her feel guilty. Almost. "Don't worry," she said, smiling. "Just point me in the right direction and I'll try my best not to hit you."

They determined the rules and throwing order. When Ava's turn came, she walked to the board hanging on the wall. She felt around it for the size, measured the height against the side of her body. All of it was standard. She walked off the steps, purposefully passing it by four steps.

Luke caught her arm, turned her back. She felt him set an empty chair to the side of the worn tape she felt on the floor.

"There. If you put your left hand here, your toes are lined up just behind the line."

"Got it." Ava waited for Luke to place the dart in her hand, then purposely twisted her body and lifted her arm.

"Wait!" The shout came from more than one, but it was Luke who guided her around to face the board.

"Am I all lined up now?"

"Yes."

"Okay." She raised the dart, took her aim and let it fly.

"How'd I do?"

"Um..." Throats cleared.

She huffed. "Just tell me how I did, where I was off and by how much."

Luke walked over to stand behind her. He laid his hands on her waist, put his lips close to her ear. "You don't have to—"

"Shut up and just tell me where I hit."

"Okay. Missed the board by two inches to the left."

"All right. Back up," she told him. She drew back for another throw and could tell by the sound she'd hit the cork.

"Nice," Luke said, coming up beside her once more.

"I can do better than nice. Where did I hit?"

"Two inches below center, almost dead on."

She threw for a third time, heard it hit then the female squeals and shocked, male curses behind her.

Luke grabbed her around the waist, lifted her off her feet. "Holy shit. It's dead center. You hit it *dead* center."

"Really?" She could practically see the shocked expressions and laughed. "Beginners luck I guess."

"That's amazing!" Hannah grabbed her in a hug. "We're going to kill you guys!"

"Damn impressive," Nick said.

"I think we've just been hustled," Zach added with a grumble.

With a modest smile, Ava lifted her beer, took a long drink.

Luke snaked an arm around her waist, and pulled her a few feet away from the group. "You want to explain that?"

"I've played a lot of darts."

"Really?"

Luke held her close, turning them away from the noise of the group and pressed his mouth to hers. It wasn't much of a kiss, not indecent by any means, but the way his shoulders felt under her fingers, the scent of his aftershave and the faint taste of beer on his tongue made for a heady few seconds.

"My uh... My brother had a dart board in the basement and he taught me. Thought I should have a party trick. I practiced until it became muscle memory. I don't always hit the target, but..." She lifted a shoulder. "You didn't think I could hit it, did you?" She grinned and gave his chest a playful shove. "That's okay. And don't feel bad when we win, just do your best."

18

"I'm going to hit the ladies' room," Ava said after they'd played another round.

"I could use the little boys' room," Luke said. "I'll walk you."

Ava finished drying her hands and pushed against the swinging door. When she didn't immediately hear Luke, she stopped. With Luke guiding her, she hadn't brought her cane. Maybe he was still in the men's room. She turned toward the sound of the open restaurant to her left and took a step.

She liked him. She liked him a lot. And there was no point pretending she wasn't wondering what it would be like to have his big, work-hardened hands on her again. Maybe this time minus the clothes.

"It's good to see you, too," she heard Luke say.

Then a woman's voice. "I'm so lucky we ran into each other. I have a bone to pick with you."

"Oh, really? What's that?"

"We haven't had our date yet."

"Oh. I guess I've been busy. Lot of work on the cabin."

"Oh, I know. But it's been over a week since you promised me dinner."

A week didn't seem that long, but from the tone of the woman's voice she *really* wanted that date. And a week? That was after she and Luke had gone riding. She felt a little stab of disappointment, and shoved it away.

Ava took another step. The voices were coming from just outside the bathroom area to the right. They must be around the corner. Surely Luke wouldn't leave her standing there if he saw her.

"How's Newman?" the woman asked.

"Good."

Ah. The donated horse Hannah had mentioned. She tried to imagine what this woman looked like. She'd started doing that a lot since Blake. How could she not?

Looks didn't matter much to a blind person. But as soon as Blake could see her, he'd decide he wanted to be with someone else. Was it what he saw when he looked at her? Or was it what he saw when he looked at someone else?

The memory of it burned in her gut, in her eyes.

"Ava."

She blinked at the sound of Luke saying her name.

"Ava this is Catherine. Catherine, Ava."

"Oh, well. It was good to see you, Luke. I'm sure I'll see you again," she said, all but purring.

Luke touched Ava's arm. "Ready for another round?"

"You know, I think I'm ready to go."

A beat of silence followed before he said, "Yeah. Okay."

In the car they mostly rehashed the darts competition, the men coming out the winners but just barely. Luke had the radio on a country station and a man was singing about getting a girl's name and number.

She hadn't expected the feeling she'd gotten hearing Luke talk to a Catherine. That stomach ache, homesick kind of feeling. And it wasn't Luke's fault, not at all. But she didn't like it and she didn't want to feel it. Not ever again.

"Thanks for dinner," she said as Luke came to a stop in front of her house, put his truck in park, and turned off the engine. "You don't have to walk me in."

"I do. And I will. But that's not why I stopped." He reached over, slid his hand around hers. "Figured it'd be better to do this here than on your father's doorstep."

Before she could react, his mouth was on hers. Warm and smooth. His tongue eased her lips apart. His hands cradled the back of her neck, then slid slowly up and into her hair.

She was breathless and lightheaded when they

broke apart and as she fought to catch her breath she recognized the feeling beating through her. It was fear. Fear she could fall for him if she gave him the slightest chance.

She couldn't go through that again. Couldn't be sitting in a restaurant listening to her husband talk to a waitress or a friend or a colleague and not wonder if there was more going on. Because she'd known Emily. The three of them had run into each other numerous times in the UN building. How many shared looks had there been between them that she hadn't seen?

How much yearning and regret that Blake was already married, that he had to go home with his blind wife at the end of the day?

As much as she liked Luke, wanted him, she couldn't do it. Couldn't be with a man and wonder, not with Luke, not with anyone. She'd rather be alone with the empty space than have it filled and then ripped out.

She put both hands to his chest and retreated until her back touched the passenger door. "I had fun," she said.

"Me, too," Luke said. "Especially since we won."

"Mmm. You guys got lucky." She turned her face from his to the front windshield.

"Why do I get the feeling you're upset about more than the darts game?"

"What? I'm not upset."

"Come on, Ava. I haven't known you long, but you

suck at hiding it. You went from calling for a rematch to wanting to go home in five minutes."

"Okay." She drew in a deep breath and slowly let it out. "I can't do this. I'm sorry."

"Can't do what?"

"Nothing. It's nothing." And she felt like an idiot for even thinking they were at a point that she needed to put the brakes on. There was nothing *to* put the brakes on.

"No. Not nothing. What can't you do and why? Kiss me in my truck? Go to dinner?"

She didn't want to get into it, but she owed him an explanation. Still, she couldn't, just *couldn't* force herself to say that she didn't know if he was looking at another woman. Not just looking, but wanting.

And what if he was? She wasn't here long term, they weren't exclusive. And that wasn't the point.

"This." She motioned between them. "I'm sorry. I like you, a lot. But this can't go anywhere, not really. And I'm not saying you *want* it to go anywhere. I'm not saying that at all. I just... We have fun together. *I* have fun," she corrected. She wouldn't assume his feelings. "And we're friends. In a lot of ways I feel like we get each other, but..." She drew in a nervous breath.

God, she wished she knew what he was thinking. "Are you still awake? Have I talked you into a coma?"

"Still awake. Not in a coma." Was she kidding, Luke thought? Like he could go to sleep when he was near her. He could barely blink. He sighed and she winced, obviously feeling his frustration from two feet away.

"You know, the first night I met you I thought you were a straight shooter. I thought, this is a woman who doesn't play games."

"I am. I—"

"Then tell me why the sudden change."

"You have a date planned. Which is fine," she added quickly. "It just gave me a weird feeling and more, it reminded me that I'm not going to be here long so this thing really doesn't have anywhere to go, you know?"

"Well, one, I don't have a date planned, and two, we don't have to map the whole thing out, do we? I like you. I think you like me. I like spending time with you."

"I do like you. And okay, now I feel stupid and I *hate* feeling stupid. I really do."

"I can understand that, but you shouldn't." And maybe he should just say, *okay.* Agree with her that this wasn't really going anywhere and cut his losses, but he couldn't seem do it. He'd known her a handful of weeks. She was leaving in a handful more. But... "Is it that you don't trust me?"

"It's not about trust. It's really not. It's my problem. Call it a hang up, call it whatever you want, but it's there. You're a temptation," she said, and followed it with a stiff laugh. "You absolutely are. But maybe we should just be friends, given my hang ups. That's probably for the best, right?"

He wanted to say no, *not* right. Not by a long shot. He almost did. But all the sudden there were tears gathering on her lashes and she was trying like hell not to let them show. That told him that whatever or *whoever* had caused her *hang up*, had done a real number on her.

"Sure," he said, and leaned in, cupped her cheek in his hand and pressed a chaste kiss to her lips. "We can be friends. I'd say we already are."

And call it perseverance or stubbornness, but he wasn't agreeing to anything just yet. They could be friends. But not just.

AVA HELD onto Luke's bicep as he walked her to the door. His other hand, big and warm, covered hers. She was shaking and hoped like hell he couldn't feel it. It was bad enough she'd almost cried in front of him. Her emotions were all over the place.

"Goodnight," he said at the door. "Thanks for going."

"Sure," she said softly, and managed to get inside the house before the tears came. She let herself have a moment to flush out this emotional overload, then roughly rubbed the tears away. It was stupid to cry over a man she hardly knew and she'd had enough stupid for one night. She'd call Maddie, eat some ice cream.

She'd put on a movie, the thought, moving to the freezer, one she'd watched a hundred times with her friend. She grabbed the quart sized container she'd placed in the bottom right corner. Prying off the top, she dug in with her spoon and nearly gagged when she got a mouthful of lime sorbet instead of the Rocky Road she'd expected.

She hated lime anything and spit the bite into the kitchen sink. Time to add braille to the ice cream, she thought with a sigh. Eventually she found *her* ice cream and took it and a spoon to her room. The last thing she wanted was her mom coming in asking her thirty–one-year-old divorced daughter how her date was.

When she was settled on the bed, she directed Siri to call Maddie.

"Hey."

"Hey. What's up?"

She sighed. "Nothing. Eating ice cream."

"Oh, boy. Bowl or container?"

"Container. But there's not that much left."

"Mmm hmm. Hang on. I'll get mine. You know it's pathetic of you to even try to hide it. Just tell me."

Ava sighed again and gave her friend the long and entirely too detailed version, adding in how idiotic she felt and going all the way back to their almost kiss in the tack room and their ride in the woods.

"I can't explain it really. He's such a guy, you know? A former Army Ranger. This is a guy who has hunted down terrorists in the middle of the night and, like, seized airfields. He could probably live in the woods for a month with nothing but a pocket knife and have a log home built by day three."

"Hot," Maddie said around a mouthful of ice cream.

"But there's more to him than that. We talk and he makes me feel... I don't know. Admired. Perfectly able and at the same time he goes out of his way to make things easier for me."

"Sigh."

"Yeah." And when she was with him, she wanted to lean on him. Wanted to have him hold her hand through a crowd or serve up nachos. And in a space jammed with people and noise she'd always been keenly aware of Luke. "I like being around him but..."

"But what?"

But she wasn't so sure she wouldn't fall for Luke, regardless of time.

"You're afraid. Understandable."

"No, I just don't think I'm ready."

"Same thing isn't it? And damn it, I'm out of ice cream. And mine *wasn't* almost empty. That was your fault."

Ava smiled. "I miss you."

"Miss you more." A moment passed. "Have you heard about the job?"

"No."

"Would I be a bitch if I admitted I'd rather you stay in New York?"

"No. You wouldn't be. I'd feel the same way about you. Just don't talk to Rick and Nancy."

"Oh, shit. You told your parents?"

"It slipped out and they reacted about like you'd expect. My brother is being all big brother on me."

"Damn him."

"Luke's the only person that seems remotely interested or excited."

"Luke doesn't love you like we do. He won't miss you like we will."

"True." And she felt a painful skip in her chest at the absolute truth of that. Her parents would worry and make her feel guilty. Her brother would be fine after he gave her some grief. Her best friend would miss her, but Maddie had a huge network of friends and a demanding job. And... that was all.

There was no one who couldn't live without her. No one she couldn't live without. She should be glad about that.

19

Zach made his cut with the circular saw then waited for Luke to finish screwing in the first vertical piece of window trim.

"We've already got his mattress as low as it will go," Zach said. "And he's still getting over the crib rail like it's nothing so Nora's like, we gotta baby proof his room, make it safe for when he climbs out."

"And what if he decided to go rogue around the house?"

"Exactly. And since we really don't want to close him up in his room, I put up a baby gate across the doorway, three feet high. He goes over like it's nothing. And I'm thinking, one day this kid's going to be fifteen, sixteen, and if we can't outsmart him now then we're in deep shit.

"So we put up *another* baby gate over the first one. Now it's six feet high and even though there's no way he's getting over, Nora puts a twin mattress in the hallway just in case. Guess what happened?"

"He went over," Luke said, taking the wood from his brother.

"Damn right. We're in the bedroom, doing... you know and I hear this little voice in the doorway. Scared the shit out of me. I'm telling you," Zach said. "The force is strong with that one."

Luke smiled, picturing his little brother as Daddy and all that went with it. "He's probably laughing at you."

Zach sighed. "Damn it. He probably is."

"What's your next move?"

"We're working on it."

"How about a screen door? With a latch."

Zach paused. "Huh. That's not a bad idea."

They worked another fifteen minutes in silence before either of them spoke again.

"Anything from Dallas?"

"No," Zach said. "Nick is asking around. Quietly. Only thing for sure is he's undercover. And if he can't get word out or if they're too cautious to get word out for him, he must be deep."

"Yeah." And deep was synonymous with dangerous.

"Ava seemed nice," Zach said, taking measurements of the next window.

"Yeah." Luke lined up the next piece, pulled the drill from his tool belt.

"Definitely easy to look at."

Luke looked at him but Zach didn't raise his head from the board.

"Noticed you looking at her quite a bit."

Luke turned again and caught his brother's smirk.

"Anything going on there?"

"Nope." And he'd been expending a good bit of energy trying not to be too disappointed about that. "And don't come off your honeymoon and start trying to pair me off."

"Okay. My bad. Thought you were interested."

"I didn't say I wasn't."

"Okay. Good talk."

Was that hurt he heard in his brother's voice? Frustration? Did his little brother really care that much if he opened up and talked to him? But Zach had always been the one to fill the silence. Luke reminded himself he wanted to connect. If so, he needed to make an effort.

"She put the brakes on." He shrugged like it was no big deal but the gesture felt forced. Because he did care. He cared a hell of a lot which was way past smart.

Zach didn't say anything else for a minute and Luke thought, well, that wasn't so bad.

"Any particular reason?"

Damn it. Should have known Zach wouldn't let that be the end of it. "She had a few, one of which is that she's going back to New York soon. And be careful with that nail gun. She's a little testy."

"I got it," Zach said. "And I guess that's understandable, her going back to New York. Though in my experience, women rarely have one reason for anything. It's not even a list, more like a damn web of reasons and reasonings."

Luke sank the next screw with too much force and had to back it out and do it again.

"So, you just going to let her blow you off?"

"I didn't say she blew me off." Luke wrenched it, tightening it harder than it needed and heard the start of the wood splitting. "Shit." He was too pissed to look up but thought he heard his brother snicker.

"And what difference does it make? She is going back to the city soon. Hell, she's doing her best to get a job in another country."

"Oh. So you want her to stay here and she doesn't want to. Huh." Zach stood there, peering up at the finished window. "Makes sense."

Luke glared at his younger brother. "What makes sense?"

"You want her to stay and she—"

"I heard what you said, you're just so far off base, I'm—forget it. Just drop it."

"Sure. Pass me that tape measure." They worked in silence another few minutes.

"And I'm sure if you *did* want more and she didn't, that would have nothing to do with why you hung half that trim finished edge up and the other half, finished side down. Since I'm way off base, I guess you're just a dumbass."

Luke stepped back, looked at the window. "Fuck."

Zach stopped what he was doing and Luke could feel his curious stare.

"You know, if this isn't about the girl, then... we could... you know. Talk or something."

"What else would it be?"

"Hell, I don't know. God knows a woman is enough to get a guy tied up. But if it was something else... I'm just saying. I'm here. Ya, know?"

Luke stood scowling at the glaring mistake he'd made, trying to take his little brother's offer at face value. It was just an offer, not asking him to unload all his troubles. "Thanks, man. I'm good."

Luke threw himself into the chore of tearing off what he'd done and starting over while Zach made cuts for the window he'd measured.

"Okay, man," Zach said three hours later. "Time for me to call it a day."

Luke stopped, hung the cordless drill in his belt. "Thanks for the help."

"You got it." He paused at his truck door. "Think I'll go screen door shopping on my way home. I'll let you know how it turns out."

Huh. He was going to let him know.

Luke figured that was reconnecting in a way and it hadn't even been that hard. He watched his brother drive off to his wife and baby and daddy stuff. He had a passing thought about what that would feel like. Seemed like a hell of a lot of worry on top of ultimate responsibility.

He didn't let himself wonder about it long, instead throwing himself into the next step which was the front porch. While he worked, he got the idea to hand cut the ladder rungs, make it more rustic and he liked to whittle. He could sit out here at night, keep his hands busy.

The rest of the week passed without seeing Ava and it was driving him crazy. And crazier still that he couldn't bring himself to ask Hannah when she was coming out to ride again. Was she not riding because she didn't want to see him? Or was he just missing her by chance?

He worked until he lost the light. His back and arms ached with the satisfaction of hard labor. Next on his agenda... Shower. Dinner. Ladder rungs. And a long night of quiet. Maybe too much quiet.

20

S he needed to swim. That's what Ava thought as she downed the last of her morning coffee. It'd been a few days since she'd told Luke they should be friends. She hadn't been riding since then, not because she was avoiding him, just...because.

She needed to move, to burn some energy and frustration. Her parents, her growing feelings for Luke Walker.

"Hey, Mom?"

She turned to face the direction her mother sat at the kitchen table. "I was thinking I might take you up on your offer and go to the Y." Her mom had been a member at the YMCA for as long as she could remember. "I've been missing the exercise."

"You're rail thin," her mom scoffed. "You don't need to exercise."

"Well... I'd still like to go. You know exercise isn't

only about losing weight. It's good for the soul, the mind. Gets those happy endorphins flowing."

"Well, I don't know if we should leave your father. And I don't think they have my aerobics class today."

"I wasn't really thinking both of us. I'd really like to swim."

"Oh, Ava. I don't think you want to swim in that pool. For one thing the water is frigid."

Ava stood and went to the sink with her empty mug. It was a straight shot, six steps. "Once I get going I'll warm up. That is why they kept the water cooler, after all. Because the pool was used for swimming laps. Dad's already done his PT this morning," she went on, before her mother could list more reasons she shouldn't.

"How would you get there? I guess I could drop you, but it's all the way across town."

In the city, her gym was two blocks away. And she never had to ask permission or give explanations. She just decided and she went. Maybe it had been a mistake to stay away so much that her parents really hadn't gotten used to seeing how she managed by herself.

"I'll call a ride with my app. I do it all the time," she said quickly, ready for the protest.

"I wish you wouldn't. I just don't think it's safe. I've seen it on the news, Ava. Uber drivers abducting people."

"Mom." Ava turned, smiling. "Do you really see that all the time?"

She heard her mom's chair slide back and the sound of her slippers on the tile. "Okay. Maybe it was once, but—"

"But nothing." She kissed her mother's cheek as she joined her at the sink. "It'll help me to get out and burn off some energy."

"Nance?" Her father called from the other room and Ava made her escape.

She used the ride app on her phone to call for a pick-up and when she got the message back that her ride was only five minutes away, she grabbed a bag, stuffed in her suit and a towel and went out the front door to wait.

Not for the first time, she wished she was home. A gym she was familiar with. With public transportation she relied on. But she hadn't lied, she did use Uber occasionally, but it could be tricky since she couldn't see exactly where the pick up dot was. Here in front of her parents' house shouldn't be a problem.

Using her cane, she made her way down the sidewalk to wait at the mailbox. She heard, then felt a car approach, but she waited for the driver to put down the window and say her name.

"Yes. Thank you." She felt for the passenger door and got in.

"Hello," he said. Bob was his name, according to the app. He sounded middle aged and had a jazz station playing on low.

She took the time to think things through. There'd be a sign in desk. She'd need to show her ID, her proof of parents' membership then find her way to the pool. If she had to ask for help, she would. She accepted that sometimes there was no other way.

It was an eighteen to twenty-minute drive so she sat lost in her own thoughts. Her dad, her job at the UN, and the possibility of a job in Italy. She pictured herself strolling old streets, running her fingers over swirling limestone architecture. Popping into delis for Prosciutto and pastries. She smiled remembering Luke's observation that maybe she loved the city for the food. Then she just remembered Luke.

There was no denying the attraction, the deeper interest. He was an interesting man. But she'd made the decision to step back from whatever was happening between them and it was the right one. She was only going to be here another month, maybe six weeks. No need to set herself up for rejection.

And on the heels of that thought came anger. She'd never expected to be rejected and now she expected nothing else. It pissed her off that Blake had done that. Had changed her. Like the surgery had changed him.

She couldn't blame him, at least not for that. Being able to see after not seeing was a *huge* change. A huge adjustment. Something as simple as walking through a park was new and exciting.

"It's so bright, Ava," Blake had said, a few weeks after his surgery, as they walked through Central Park. "I know I keep saying it, but you just can't understand how *bright* it is. Like a ball of fire that you can only look at for a second before having to look away."

It was winter, but she'd known the sun was out, felt the warmth on her face as she walked beside Blake through the park. She'd been happy to be out with him, her hand on his arm. They used to eat lunch in a park near the UN almost every day. Lately he'd started taking lunch with his coworkers in an adjoining building.

"Oh, my gosh, you should see the flowers. There's already so many more than there were just last week. Yellow and pink and red."

She didn't know yellow. Or red or pink, but she nodded, smiled and let him talk and narrate as he'd done nonstop since the day he opened his new eyes to a whole new world. Like her, Blake had been blind since birth and the joy in his voice was palpable. She couldn't imagine all he was seeing for the first time.

His sight had been blurry at first and a harder, slower recovery than either of them had expected, but it had worked. His employer had given him the time off for the surgery, then more for recovery. And she'd had enough vacation time to take off two weeks to be with him full time.

"It's not at all like I pictured. Just the people. There's so many more, so close together, but not touching.

They paused at a stone railing and Blake went on. "Oh, Ava! You should see these kids. The boy on the end there," he pointed with their joined hands. "He's got the rhythm with his arms but his feet are all over the place." He laughed, and as they stood there, laughed again.

Ava smiled. "What's he doing now?"

"He's—" He broke off with a bark of laughter.

"Is that the cutest thing you ever saw?" A female voice on Blake's other side asked.

"It really is. Look at the one in the red jacket?"

The two of them laughed.

Ava smiled. "Now what's he doing?"

"Oh, he tried to do a spin and landed on his ass—and, there he goes again."

Ava stared at nothing, tried to picture. Tried to *see* the humor.

Blake chatted it up with the other viewer and Ava gradually stopped asking questions and listened to their byplay. It was enough to hear his enjoyment. To be outside with the chilly spring air biting at her nose and the sun warming her back.

She hadn't thought she'd find love. Maybe because she was blind, or maybe just because. Then, in her late twenties, she had. She and Blake had so many shared experiences, growing up blind. And they were the same in a lot of ways, in that one major way. And then they weren't.

She didn't have that in common with Luke, and yet she felt...happy when she was with him. Happier than she'd been in so long. Maybe that's why he scared her so much. Luke took the time to explain things in a way Blake hadn't been able to. And then he hadn't wanted to.

The car she was riding in came to a hard stop, bringing her back to the present. "Are we there?"

"No."

Bob was a driver of few words.

"Almost there?"

"No." The car started moving again and she drew her bag closer to her chest. She pulled up the guide on her phone. Put the direction on speaker.

"We are going there," Bob spat, then mumbled something else under his voice.

"Okay. Thank you." Dread was creeping in.

"Rerouting," her phone said in a cheerful computer voice.

"I'm going to the YMCA," she told Bob in a pleasant voice. The impulse to be pleasant and courteous to a person driving you was instinctual. They did, after all, hold all the power. They had your life in their hands, literally.

She loosened the grip she had on her phone and tried again to refresh the maps app. Even if it did refresh and read out her current location, she wouldn't know where that was. The town had changed a lot in twenty years. There was no way to know if she was where she was supposed to be.

"Can you tell me what street this is?"

He answered her, said something she assumed was a street name but she didn't catch it. Didn't understand him or it wasn't familiar. Nothing was familiar. She missed the constancy of the New York subway system where she could count stops and hear the announcements.

How long had she been in this car? How long was she going to stay in this car? Without audible navigation, he could take her anywhere. He could be driving her out of town and she wasn't familiar enough with the area to know.

And she thought she could move to a foreign country? But in the city, even Italy, she'd be on foot, there would be landmarks. She couldn't remember ever feeling so lost in New York. "Excuse me, I'd like to get out."

"We're not there." The car didn't slow.

"That's okay. I want to get out here." Were they speeding up? "Please. Excuse me," she said again, more forcefully. "I want to get out here."

"I can not stop here."

Why? She wanted to scream. She couldn't see why he couldn't stop. She was at his mercy and she didn't trust him. Maybe an overreaction, but she had a bad feeling and she believed in trusting her instincts. She swiped her finger over her phone, ready to call for help. Her hands were shaking. What would Bob do if he heard her telling Siri to call the police? And what would she tell them?

"Stop and let me out right now," she said more forcefully, unbuckling her seatbelt. "I want you to stop. Right here. Just stop right here."

"Okay, lady. Okay. Fine." The car made a tight, fast turn, slamming her into the door. She was just about to make the call when the car stopped short, throwing her forward. She already had her bag and phone and didn't hesitate. They could be in the middle of a busy road for all she knew, but at this point she'd take her chances.

The relief she felt standing on solid ground was short lived. She had no idea where she was. She smelled the exhaust from the car and heard the Uber drive off, leaving her in the quiet unknown.

Using her cane, she continued with a slow, shuffling step, moving away from where she'd just exited the car. After two small steps she paused, listened, moved her cane in wide arcs out in front of her and felt nothing. A new panic bubbled up and she questioned those instincts she'd followed.

She took another two steps, feeling with her cane and finally hit something. Cautiously stepping forward, she reached a step up, and checking with her cane didn't feel another.

She counted ten steps straight ahead before she reached a wall, assuring herself she hadn't been let out on a narrow median. She took a calming breath, then turning, she walked in one direction, feeling the drop off on her left, the wall continuing on her right. She counted twenty steps, then thirty and still didn't come to a door of any kind.

The sun was out, she could feel its warmth on her face, the heat coming off the brick wall under her hand, but she had no idea how long she might have to walk to reach a place of business. She pulled out her phone and tried again for location services. Nothing. Tried again and got an audio response.

"This app is not responding."

Okay. She should call someone. Not her parents, not her brother.

She asked her phone for the time and tried to estimate. If she was home, she would just walk to the subway. If she was home in New York chances are the app would work. There would be a coffee shop, a souvenir shop, bistro, restaurant, *something*, every ten feet. And people. There were always other people.

Maybe her sister-in-law. She would keep a secret if she asked her to. "Siri, call Connie."

"Calling Connie."

She listened to three rings before it went to voice mail.

"Hey, Connie. It's Ava. Give me a call when you can. Thanks." She ended the call and went to the next person she could think of. "Siri, call Hannah."

Her pulse grew faster with every unanswered ring. Her next option was to call the police but she could just imagine her mother's reaction to her getting dropped off at home in a police cruiser.

"Hey, pretty lady? Looks like you need some assistance."

"No. I'm fine." Her right hand tightened on the handle of her cane as she hung up and tried Connie again.

It seemed unnaturally quiet except for the footsteps getting closer. Where were all the people? The cars? The cabs?

"Hey, baby." Closer this time. There was more talk, she couldn't make out what they were saying, but heard the low rumble of laughter that followed. The feet, multiple feet, approached. And she was a sitting duck.

21

L uke walked into the barn and was nearly run over by his nephew, Mitchell. "Whoa, little guy." He caught him around the waist which made him squeal and kick.

He was just about to put him down when he saw Stephen jogging down the barn aisle from the office. Luke opened his mouth to say sorry. He didn't think he'd hurt him but—

"Damn, that kid's fast. Thanks, man. I thought I'd closed that door all the way."

Luke watched Stephen take his son, still kicking up a fuss, and toss him over his shoulder.

"Little troublemaker is determined to get into one of these stalls. And to be honest I think he's going for the horse shit, not the horse."

"Well." He was still staring at his brother-in-law, not seeming the least bothered by his son's crying. His sister's chocolate lab bounded in from somewhere and came to his side. He gave the dog's head a rub.

"Hey, I was just talking Hannah into running out for some lunch with me and this hellion. Want to come? Or I could bring you something."

"No, thanks. I can hold things down here."

"Thanks, man. I'll just go whisk my wife away for a bit. We'll be back in an hour."

Luke moved on down the aisle, checking the swing of each lower stall door. He'd noticed one was off kilter but couldn't remember which. Hannah and Stephen hadn't been gone ten minutes before the office phone was ringing. Figuring he wouldn't know the answer to anyone's inquiry, he let it go to voicemail.

When the ringing started up again and didn't stop, he stepped in, picked up the receiver from the wall. "Freedom Farm."

Ava closed her eyes in relief. "Hi, could I please speak to Hannah?"

"She's not here. I can take a message, but... Wait. Ava?"

"Yes."

"Hey. It's Luke. What's up?"

"Nothing I... I just needed Hannah. I um..."

"Ava, what's going on?"

"I'm fine, I just... I'm in kind of in a bind right now. I was wondering if..."

If what? If Hannah could come pick her up? She didn't even know where she was.

"Ava what's wrong?"

Luke's voice had gone hard, demanding. And right about now she wanted someone hard. Someone take charge. It didn't make her feel good about herself, but feeling capable wasn't really a priority at the moment. "I don't know where I am. I can open Maps but... I don't know. I don't know what it's saying. I don't know this street."

"Okay. Can you do a screen shot? And send it to me?"

"I think so." Luke repeated his cell number three times and she put it in. Then she went through the steps, going back to Maps, taking a screen shot.

Luke was saying something else but she didn't hear. Her attention was focused on another voice to her right. A male voice. *Talking to her?*

"Hey!"

The voice came again, closer this time, followed by male laughter.

"Is there somewhere you can go and wait?" Luke asked. "A shop or anything?"

"I don't know." Her voice was shaking and now that she was talking to someone the tears were coming. "I—"

"Ava who's that? Who are you talking to?"

Her hands were shaking so badly it took a few tries to get the screen shot.

She heard what she thought was a car door slam

through on Luke's end and a car start. He was coming. She took another deep breath. "Okay. I think I got it. I'll have to hang up to send you the picture."

"Okay. Send it and I'll call you right back from my cell."

The call ended and she felt immediately alone. She managed to get the text sent.

"Hello, madame." The voice drawled out, dripping in fake courtesy. "Could I be of assistance?"

"No, thank you." She tried to estimate how far away Luke was. She thought she'd been in the Uber somewhere between fifteen and twenty minutes. But she didn't know if she'd been getting closer to Luke or farther away.

"No? You look like you could use some help?"

"No. I don't." They knew she was blind. The cane was a dead giveaway and useless as a weapon. She looked in the direction of the voice but it wasn't close enough for her to gauge the height. And he'd said, *I*, not *we*, even though she could feel there were at least two, maybe three. And one was moving slowly around to her other side. A line of sweat rolled down her back.

It was hard to read intentions when you couldn't see a person's eyes, couldn't read their body language. But her instincts were screaming. Their hostile intentions dripping from the fake concern in their voice layered over their obvious glee at finding an easy target.

She couldn't run. Didn't know if there were any other people around to call to. And if they were hunters, if she were the prey, looking weak, looking vulnerable, would only draw them in.

Why hadn't she let someone drive her? Stupid. She knew better. Knew this town didn't have the same resources as the city. Maybe her parents were right to worry, maybe—

Her phone rang in her hand but before she could answer it, it was knocked away. She instantly grabbed her wrist where a hot sweaty hand had touched her.

"Looks like you've got a call. Why don't you let me answer it for you?"

It kept ringing. He wasn't going to answer it.

"This is a nice phone, don't you think?"

She followed the sound of the ringing as it flew from her left to her right.

"Sure is a nice phone."

"Give me my phone," she said in her most assertive voice. *Don't let them think you're afraid. Keep the appearance that you're in control.* "That's my boyfriend calling," she said without thinking. "He's on his way."

"Oh, yeah? I got a car. I can take you wherever you want to go, baby."

His insincerity and body odor permeated the air.

A man yelled from across the street and she thought maybe she was going to get some help. The men around her stepped away but no one came to her rescue. There was yelling, cursing, and she prayed Luke came fast. She could still hear the men nearby. Minutes passed. It felt like hours. Then she heard them mumbling to each other, coming close again.

"Hey, Baby. I'm back. You miss me?"

"I'll hold your bag," another, new voice said, and ripped it from her hands.

She stepped back and recoiled at the feel of a body at her back, the scent of cigarette smoke and sweat.

Where had he come from? How many were there?

She was helpless. She couldn't run. She couldn't fight. Her parents had warned her about this very danger. Had *told* her not to put herself in this position. But here she was.

Ava felt a hand on her shoulder and tried to jerk away, raw fear pounding her ears. Then she heard the low roar of an engine coming fast, a screeching halt, and a door slamming.

"Hey! Get the fuck back!"

It was Luke. In an instant, the hand on her shoulder and the body belonging to it were gone. There was a grunt. The sound of a body falling to the concrete of the sidewalk and her bag dropping beside her foot.

"Hey man, no foul. We were just helping."

"Like hell," Luke said then the only sound was grunting. Pounding and grunting and... crying. There were curses, some Luke, some strangers, and the sickly sound of flesh and body slamming against the pavement near her feet.

"Luke?"

She didn't hear him answer and huddled against the wall, trying to stay out of the way. Praying Luke wasn't overwhelmed by their numbers. Did he have weapons? A gun? She should help. What could she do to help? A body knocked into her, sending her sprawling to the ground on hands and knees. She scrambled up, backed away as far as she dared.

It went on and on, seemed to go on forever, before she heard other voices, then sirens.

"Hands on the wall!"

That command from a male voice was repeated by a female. She didn't know if they were yelling at her but she reached out for a wall. She only felt air.

For a second she felt what she thought was Luke's hand on her arm then, "Hands on the wall," again and the hand was gone.

"Luke?"

"You okay, ma'am? Can you stand by the car?"

She didn't move, but took a step forward, reaching out for Luke. "Luke?"

"I'm here!"

"Stand by the car, ma'am!"

A gasp of surprise escaped when she felt a firm grip on her arm.

"Don't touch her!" Luke yelled. "Keep your hands off of her!"

Then the hand on her arm was gone and she heard Luke curse.

"On the ground! Hands behind your back!"

Then more sirens, more cars screeching to a halt and car doors slamming. She stood there, frozen in place, nothing to ground her.

"Just stand right there, Ava." Luke's steady voice

came to her, giving her something. Wishing she could touch him, that he could touch her. But she could tell by the direction of his voice that he was no longer standing.

There were other voices now, talking over each other, some close, some several feet away. Some coming through a radio. There was a call for an ambulance.

She heard a woman's voice, one she hadn't heard before. "That's the one who was helping. Those are the ones giving this lady a hard time."

"She's blind," someone else said. "They were messing with a *blind* girl."

"I started to come over then this guy came up. He beat the hell out of them, that's for damn sure."

Ava couldn't keep up with the voices, all moving around her. Coming closer then farther away. She had no idea how many people were here now. She rubbed her palms on her jeans, wanted to sit down, was about to, right there on the sidewalk. She jumped when she felt a hand on her arm again. This time it was more gentle.

"I'm officer Dennison."

It was a man, older sounding than the first two police on the scene.

"It's okay, Ava," Luke said, still several feet away. "It's the police."

She didn't shrug the man off, but she didn't feel comfortable being led anywhere. Didn't feel comfortable getting too far away from Luke.

"This your phone?" someone asked.

She held out her hand. Felt for the shape of the pop socket stuck to the back of her case. "Yes. Thank you."

The sound of another car pulling up fast had her taking a step back. She didn't know how close she was to the street. This car had no sirens and the second the door opened there was a string of curses.

Fuck, Luke thought. He was face down on the gritty sidewalk, his blood still running hot and as if things couldn't get any worse, Nick was on the scene.

"Get him up. Get him up," Nick said again, his voice sounding just as disgusted as it had every time Luke had screwed up.

"Get him the hell up. FBI."

With his hands still zip tied behind his back, Luke stumbled against the wall as he stood. "Didn't know the FBI responded to street fights."

"Is that what this is?" Nick's brow shot up. "A street fight?"

His seventeen-year-old self wanted to sneer at his brother. Tell him that's exactly what it was and he could just fuck off. The only reason he didn't was because the look of disappointment on his older brother's face made him feel more than anger now. It made him feel.

Then his brother was giving orders. "Get those fucking ties off my brother."

That surprised him, that Nick would be so quick to claim him.

Nick ripped off his sunglasses, rubbed at his forehead then gave Luke a long, studied once over. "You okay?"

"Yeah. Is she okay?" Luke looked over for Ava, saw where she was standing but couldn't see her face, as there were three cops around her.

"I think so. Let's see the hands?"

Luke held out his hands.

"Not too bad considering the other guys."

Luke took his first look at the assholes, all on the pavement. Four men, all early to mid-twenties, in sagging jeans and T-shirts. And all in various degrees of hurt.

Another officer, the one who seemed in charge, left Ava and came to him.

"Sounds like, from the lady, it was a straight up Good Samaritan deal. We'll get your statement, then you can go."

Luke told him in as few words as possible what had happened. He answered the officer's questions, repeated himself when prompted.

"Any idea how she ended up on this end of town?" Nick glanced around. "Not much around here. No shopping."

"Said she got spooked," the officer said. "Told the driver to let her out." Garbled radio speak came through the officer's radio on his hip. He pulled it off and stepped away.

Nick looked at Luke. "One of them's wanted for questioning in a case I'm on."

"Oh." So Nick hadn't peeled out of work like his ass was on fire to come see his little brother's latest screw up.

"You're free to go. Take care of her. I'll take care of this." Nick looked at the four in cuffs and his partner taking a facial of one of the guys with his phone. Nick clapped a hand down on Luke's shoulder, a purely brotherly gesture. He gave his brother a tight smile and went to Ava.

"Ava." He held out a cautious hand. "Hey. It's me."

Ava turned toward his voice and reached out with shaking hands. She looked so damn scared. What if he hadn't answered the phone, or made it in time? Then his arms were around her and she was clinging to him. Luke closed his eyes and held her as much for himself as for her. He buried his nose in her hair, inhaled, assuring himself she was okay as he moved one hand up and down her back.

Too soon, she pulled back. "I'm okay," she said, and wiped a shaky hand over her face, smoothed her hair back.

Still holding her shoulders, he looked at her a long moment, then led her to his truck. He put her in, drew the seatbelt across her body. Even if she was perfectly capable, he needed to take care of her right now. He set her bag in her lap and closed the door. More like slammed it, as his entire body was still vibrating. He quickly rounded the hood and got in.

Ava didn't say anything, but he could hear her breathing. Her face was pale, her fingers gripped so tightly on the edge of her bag he thought they might snap.

"Are you all right? Are you hurt?"

"No. Everyone's asked me that. I'm not hurt. Are you?"

"No." He'd been pinned down under heavy fire. He'd had teammates pinned down, which was a thousand times worse. But even then he'd maintained a steady calm. This was different. This was Ava and seeing her in danger, seeing the fear in her eyes—that had struck a particular nerve. He'd known he had the capacity to kill. Knew he would kill to protect his home, his family. But this felt different.

He started up his truck, backed out and headed away from the scene before he went back and killed someone. The world didn't need scum that preyed on the helpless. Thinking what could have happened, what they could have done to her, to Ava, if he'd been just a minute later—

He tried to relax his grip on the steering wheel, then thought to hell with it. To hell with deep breathing. He slammed his palm hard on the steering column. Hard enough he felt the zing up to his elbow and hard enough to make Ava jump at the sound. *Shit.* "Sorry."

"It's okay. How many were there?"

"What?"

"How many? When you got there?" she asked, her voice still shaky.

"Four," he said. She hadn't even known how many. For some reason that scared him more than anything as it demonstrated just how helpless she'd been. And Nick hadn't said right there what case the perp was wanted in, but he'd find out.

"Thanks for coming. If you could take me home, I'd appreciate it."

Luke heard her, but he had no intention of taking her home. Not yet. Not until he'd recovered from seeing her standing there like a lamb surrounded by wolves. And made sure she'd recovered.

"I'm fine," she said, when he gave no sign he'd heard her. "Nothing happened to me."

He took a turn too fast and Ava's hand shot out to the console between them to brace herself. "Slow down. You're making this into way more than it is."

"I don't think I am." And from the way her voice shook he knew she may be telling herself it was no big deal, but she wasn't feeling it. But he eased up on the gas and at the next light made a right onto a quiet, empty street. He pulled the truck over to the side, put it in park.

Her paper-thin veneer of composure didn't fool him. She sat rigid, her hands clenched, one still on the console and the other on her bag. Her eyes were closed and closed tight and her brow was pinched so hard it looked painful.

He was a man of action. His natural inclination was

to funnel anger and fear into a plan. Something tangible he could do. When he'd gotten there, seen the men surrounding her, he'd known what to do, without hesitation. But now...Now he didn't know what to do for her.

He reached out, put his hand on her neck and felt her jump. "Sorry," he said, but didn't remove it. He just touched her, felt her rapid pulse, gave her a gentle, what he hoped was a reassuring squeeze. "Take a breath."

She did, blowing it out on a shaky exhale.

"Nice and easy. That's it." He rubbed his hand slowly up and down the back of her neck. "What the hell were you doing there by yourself, anyway?"

"I..." She swallowed. "I was going to the gym. To swim."

"To swim," he repeated, looking at her then realized she didn't know. "You ended up on the wrong side of town all alone because you wanted to *swim*?"

"I like to swim. I didn't know I was on the wrong side of town. I don't know if the driver got lost or was going a different way. I usually pay better attention if I'm in a cab or Uber. But then I usually know exactly where I am and where I'm going and..."

She rubbed her hands over her face then dropped them to her lap. "Traffic moves so slowly in the city it's not that hard to keep up. I panicked and I asked to get out. I shouldn't have."

"Don't do that again."

"I won't. That was stupid."

"I mean, don't go swimming."

"What?" She turned her face to his.

"Don't take an Uber, a cab. Go by yourself. Whatever. Just... don't."

"Excuse me?"

There was a snap in her voice and he noticed some of her color was coming back.

"Don't treat me like that. Don't make me feel like I'm not capable."

"I don't mean to do that. I—"

"Never mind." She held up a hand meant to stop him from speaking. "Just take me home."

"I'm not taking you anywhere just yet."

Her eyes were open now and narrowed right at his. "Are you trying to make me mad?"

"Maybe." Better mad than shaky. He didn't like the uncertainty he saw or her pale face. She'd had a scare but she wasn't crying. Hadn't leapt into his arms when he'd arrived, not that he'd given her a chance. He laid his hand over hers, tightening his grip when she would have pulled it away. "Just hang on. If you don't need a second, I do."

She sighed, leaned her head back to the headrest.

When he felt he was more in control, he put the truck in drive, then took her hand back in his.

They drove in silence ... Until he turned onto the road leading to Freedom Farm.

"Wait. Where are we?"

He stopped at the top of the hill. "How do you know we're not at your house?"

"Because there's no hill just before my parent's house for one thing. I want to know where."

"Amazing," he murmured, shaking his head. "We're at the barn, or almost."

"I told you to take me home. I don't want to go for a ride right now."

"I know. I'm sorry. Look, I can take you home, but you're pale as a ghost and you're still a little shaky. If you thought your parents were overprotective before, well... they're going to know something happened the second they see you. I thought we could just take a minute. Let you calm down a bit, get some water, something to eat."

She wasn't the only one still shaken. He didn't particularly want to run into his sister either. Which reminded him he should probably tell her he'd run out after saying he'd stay put.

But it was more than that. Ava's guard was back up, he could see it in the set of her face. If he wanted her to trust him, and he did, this hadn't been the best way. "Ava. I'm sorry. I thought maybe we'd go for a walk, or a ride. If that's doesn't sound good, I'll take you home right now if that's what you want. Whatever you want."

She blew out a breath, turned her head to her side window. "I don't like not knowing where I am."

"I know. I wasn't thinking. I'm sorry." He put the truck in park and put his window down, then hers. "We're at the top of the hill. You were right about that. The road rises just a little after you leave the main road then takes a steady roll down to the front of the barn. You can just see the top of the barn from here."

She lifted her face to the open window, the warm breeze fluttered blond strands around her face.

He reached over, took her small hand between his massive ones. "Do you want me to take you home?"

"No."

She didn't say anything else for a long moment. Then she looked at him, her eyes full of unshed tears and he felt a hammer blow to his chest.

"I hate thinking, *knowing*, that I can't take care of myself."

Luke caught her chin, tilted her face up to his. "That's just bullshit. How long have you lived in New York?"

"Ten years. Twelve."

As much as he feared for her, his fear was not what she needed from him right now. "I'm thinking that's long enough for you to have heard of women being abducted, murdered? Hell, not just there, but anywhere."

"Sure."

"Were they all blind?"

"No." She wrapped fingers around his wrist, slowly lowered his hand from her chin. "That's not my point. I'm not one of those people who think, oh, I can do anything despite my disability. I don't. I know there are things I can't do."

He rubbed his hand across his mouth, unsure what to say. Was she waiting for him to agree with her?

Maybe to chastise her again for getting a ride to go do something she had every right to do? He closed his eyes a moment, and chastised himself instead.

He focused on the dark behind his lids. He didn't know if that's what she saw. The absence of light. Of anything.

"Name one," he finally said after a long silence.

"What?"

He turned to take in her profile. She was so strong and vulnerable, so smart and beautiful. And her usually stubborn chin that was dropped toward her chest just now. "Name one thing you can't do."

A wry laugh left her lips and she frowned. "There's more than one and I'm not complaining or fishing for compliments. I'm not looking for you to feel sorry me."

"I don't feel sorry for you. That's ground we've already covered."

"Well, then I don't need a *'pump up, let's look on the bright side'* talk."

"In case you hadn't noticed, I'm not a pump up, bright side kinda person. And I'm just asking you to name one."

"Fine. I can't drive." She turned, gave him a triumphant look. "That's one. I'm also not great at puzzles. Probably wouldn't make a great sniper," she added, seeming to relax a bit more. "Movie critic. Art Critic."

"Pfft." He waved those off. "Critics are full of shit." He started the engine and put the truck in gear. He didn't want her feeling like she couldn't do things. He wanted her safe and he wanted her smiling.

"What are you doing?"

"It's what we're doing and we're about to knock off number one on your list."

22

"What are you talking about?"

"Driving," Luke answered. "You're about to learn." He drove down the gravel that led to the cabin, then beyond to an open field.

"Are you *crazy*?" She grabbed onto the side as they hit a dip in the ground and bounced over.

"Maybe a little," he said, smiling at her shocked expression. He drove on until he felt they were in the perfect spot, then put the truck in park. "Come on," he said leaning in, stopping just short of her lips. "It'll be fun."

She shook her head at him, but her lips twitched.

"That's my girl." He pressed his lips to hers. "Climb over here," he said, giving her a little tug as he climbed out.

"What? Wait! Where are you going?"

"I'm not going anywhere. Trust me."

As she moved into the driver's seat he maneuvered the seat back as far as it would go.

"I can't believe I'm doing this," she said, getting behind the wheel. "I can't believe *you're* doing this. I'm going to get us both killed, or at the very least kill your truck."

"If you do, I'll get a new one."

"Just like that."

"Just like that. Scoot all the way up on the edge of the seat. Little more... Yep." It was tight but he climbed in behind her. Damn near pulling his groin, getting his right leg up and around her.

He continued getting them situated until his feet were over the pedals and her bottom was on his thighs. "Lift your feet a little." With his hands on her hips he pulled her back against him. "Now, we're going to take it real slow. Just listen to my voice and follow my directions."

"Okay. Now what?" She ran her hands over the steering wheel, feeling the shape of it, touching the buttons for radio and volume lightly. Excited now, her hand veered over to the levers on the side of the wheel. "What does this do?" She pulled and pushed them.

"Don't—" The wipers scraped over the dry glass with a squeak. "That's the window wipers. We only need those when it rains."

She adjusted herself, pulling the tail of her shirt from under her bottom and leaning on the horn in the process. It blared and she screamed, and jumped back, damn near crushing his nuts.

He groaned, but she was laughing. He was happy to take a little pain if she was laughing.

"Now... you put your hands at ten and two, like on a clock. Do you know—"

"Yes, I've felt a clock." She put her hands in the right place.

"You're going to use this to steer, just like you do a horse. I'll do the gas."

"Okay, let's do it! Turn it on! Can I turn it on?"

"Yes," he chuckled and took her hand, placed it on the key. "Turn this," he mimicked the movement over her hand, showing her the way to turn it.

"The engine turned over and rumbled."

Her dainty hands flew back to the position and he was reminded again of just how small she was, and how helpless she'd be against a pack of men who wanted to hurt her.

"What's next?"

"Next we put it in gear. There's forward and backward and ...well those are the important ones."

"Oh, God. Do we have to go backwards?"

"Not today. We'll save that for your next lesson." He put the truck in drive, with his foot on the brake. "Okay, I'm going to give her a little gas, nice and easy. You just hold us straight."

"Okay."

He gently got them going at ten miles an hour but there was nothing gentle about a field.

"Oh, my gosh. Oh, my gosh." She repeated it like a mantra. Or a prayer.

"You're doing fine but you don't have to grip the wheel quite that hard. It's not going anywhere. I'm going to speed up a little. Turn us a little to the right."

At his direction she yanked the wheel to the right, slamming them both to the left.

"A little!" he said laughing and covered her hands with his own.

She was screaming and laughing. "This is nothing like riding a horse!"

"Okay, drive. You're in control."

"What! Where do I drive? I don't know where I'm going!"

"Anywhere you want. I'll tell you if you're going to hit anything."

He kept it slow rolling over the uneven ground.

"I want to go faster! Can we go faster?"

"Always wanting to go faster." He gave it a little more gas.

"More," she demanded, driving them in a serpentine pattern across the field of grass. "I'm doing it! I'm driving!"

"You're a natural."

She laughed. "You're lying and I don't even care!" She leaned over, stuck her head out the window and let out a wild woo weee, letting the truck veer off to the left as she did so.

He put his hands on the wheel to correct them and she swatted them away. "Let me do it! No helping!"

"Yes, ma'am." They drove and drove, serpentines

and big, wide circles, him giving her gentle instructions.

When they came to a stop and the engine was off, the keys safely in his hand, he lifted her hips from his lap. He maneuvered his way out from behind her and got out.

"Okay, Nascar, let's get some air." He took her hand, held it as she climbed down. "Oh, my heart," he said dramatically. "I've had a grenade dropped in my lap and not been so scared."

"Stop it." She slapped at his chest. "You said I was good."

"You were." Then she surprised the hell out of him by throwing her arms around his neck.

"Thank you," she said, smiling up at him, once again as bright as the sun.

"You're welcome." He wanted to kiss that smiling mouth, but he was afraid to push too hard. And he wanted her way too much.

"You want to know what else I can't do?"

"I'm almost afraid to ask."

"Baseball or softball. Neither. But it was baseball that I wanted to play." She dropped her hands and moved to stand beside him, but he eased her over until he could wrap his arms around her from behind.

"I begged my brother to give me one chance so he did," she said, relaxing back against him. "And busted my lip. It scared my mother to death. My brother got in so much trouble. Want to play with me?"

"Absolutely not." He wrapped his arms around her

waist, rested his chin on the top of her head. Tried to figure out what the hell to do with what he was feeling toward this woman.

"Doesn't feel like it's going to rain today," she said, her head resting back against his shoulder.

"Nope. Sun's out. No clouds. What's your fascination with rain, anyway?"

"I already told you, I like the feel of it. It's maybe one of my first really clear memories as a child. Sitting outside, listening to the steady patter. I stuck my feet out and then that patter was hitting my skin, coming from... Well, I had no idea where it was coming from. It felt like magic."

"That's a good memory," he said. "I should have brought some food out here."

"We weren't really thinking of food."

"No. I guess not. Next time. Unless you're hungry. We could go get something."

"Nah. I'm good."

But now that the thought was there, it took hold. He'd bring her out here one day, to this exact same spot, with food and drinks. Maybe a blanket to sit on. Maybe he'd even let her drive.

He laughed softly at himself. Making picnic plans, for God's sake.

"Ahhh." He drew in a deep breath of the clean air, let it out. "A beautiful girl, a truck, and an open field."

She laughed. "Is that every boy's dream?"

"A lot of them."

"Just what did you do with girls and trucks and open fields?"

"Wouldn't you like to know," he said, kissing the side of her neck like it was the most natural thing in the world. Like they'd hung out like this every day for years. "What about you? I bet not a truck in a field. Back of a car?"

"Uh, no. I didn't get many dates. It was camp for me."

"Camp?" Ava felt Luke's arms tighten around her. "Jeez. What kind of camp did you go to? And wait. How old were you?"

She laughed at the outrage in his voice. "It was blind camp. *Teen* blind camp. And I'll bet I was older than you were."

"Please don't tell me it was a counselor."

"No! Good grief. It was another camper. I was seventeen. The blind leading the blind, you could say. You can laugh. It wasn't pretty."

He didn't laugh, but slid his arms even tighter around her, pulling her back against his chest. "Should I be jealous?"

"Of...well, shoot. I can't even remember his name so I guess not."

"Good." He dipped his head, kissed the side of her neck.

"Should *I* be jealous?"

"Yes. Sally Sutherland." He nodded slowly as if he was remembering her fondly until she smacked his arm.

"Did you concentrate on school at all or just girls?"

"A lot of girls. A little school." That got him another light smack. "How was school for you? I'm going to bet you were straight A's. Probably Valedictorian."

"Salutatorian, and it was good. I was a good student. I liked school."

He nodded, his head moving on the top of her head. "I'm betting it wasn't all easy."

"No. Not all. Kids can be cruel no matter who you are or how you're different. I learned to be... not paranoid, but..."

"Cautious?"

"Yeah. Cautious. But I had my friend Maddie."

"And she had you."

"Yeah. But she never needed me like I needed her."

"Mmm. You might be surprised." He'd known Ava three weeks and already felt a pull, a need.

She turned sideways to face him, her smile slipping. "Are you okay?"

"Why wouldn't I be? I just survived the most dangerous ride of my life."

"I mean from before." She lifted one of his hands, feathered her finger over his knuckles.

As much as he didn't want her feeling that, imagining that, he couldn't make himself pull his hand away. It was the first time he'd wanted to do something. And by do, he meant, hurt, kill. Gary was going to love this.

"You were really mad," she said, and lifted his hand

to press her lips to his scraped skin. Her lips curved up in a small smile against his skin.

"I wasn't mad. Well, not at you. I've spent the past twenty–two years protecting innocent against evil. Today seemed to fit the bill. But this isn't Afghanistan. I have to adapt, change tactics. I look at you and I think..."

"What?"

"I think..." *That I'm falling in love with you.* "I think God, you've done a lot of adapting."

"Maybe, but not really." Still holding his hand, she turned, leaning against the truck, beside him. "I started out this way so I haven't really changed anything. And for the record, I think you're adapting just fine."

He closed his eyes. "Am I?"

"Why would you say that? Because of today? You were upset. Anyone would have been."

"Would they have wanted to kill four men with their bare hands?" There. He'd said it. And he braced himself for her retreat. She didn't move.

"I'm sure my brother would have wanted to. Not sure he could have," she said with a small laugh, surprising him. "But he'd have wanted to. And calmed fast enough. You calmed me."

Luke opened his eyes, looked at Ava. He had to touch her. When he stroked a finger down her cheek, she turned her face to his, smiled. Then the smile faded and doubt replaced it.

"I like to think of myself as self-sufficient and I'm usually confident. But today I was—"

"Amazing."

"How can you say that?"

"Brave. Bold. Strong."

She shook her head. "Sounds like you're describing yourself."

Part of his charm with women was his ability to smile his way out of a situation without giving up anything. Without analyzing it too deeply. It was different with Ava. "I don't think so. I was scared."

"What were you scared of?"

He might not have answered, certainly wouldn't have answered Gary, but because she seemed to have her own fears, because she seemed to need to hear his, he did. "Letting the team down," he said. "Making a mistake that got someone else killed."

"Did you? Ever make a mistake?"

"A couple. No one died because of them, but good men did die. Men that had families to go home to and I think after, or maybe even before Hannah's wedding, I started thinking maybe I've dodged enough bullets, you know?

"My commanding officer asked me what I was waiting for? Coming up on twenty years and he asked me point blank, are you going to stay in until you get killed? Is that your goal? Not long after that, I had a close call. RPG hit close, too close. And for a second I laid there, ears ringing, trying to feel if I still had all my limbs because I was too scared to look, and for just a second I thought, I should have gone home.

"Then the close call was forgotten. A week, a

month, went by and if I ever thought that again, I pushed it out. I didn't have the guts to go home. What kind of person needs guts to see his family? Would my parents be proud of that?"

"I'm sure they'd be proud of you."

It made his throat dry, the way she looked at him, as if even without seeing, she saw something in him. Something great even, something absolutely worthy. And it rocked him. *She* rocked him.

"I'm about to kiss you," he said, just before he took her face in his hands. He gave her half a second to say no, then touched his lips to hers. On a quiet moan, she shifted toward him and everything in him sighed.

His thumb stroked over her jaw and when she parted her lips, he slipped his tongue past. He tasted her, drew her in and he thought he'd be content if there was nothing else in the world but right here, right now. Just Ava and a country field. No other sound but their combined breathing, their lips moving together. The slight movement of air over grass.

A long, slow rush of pleasure rippled through him. There was heat between them. A toe tingling, impossible to walk away from heat. With a grip on her hair, he pulled, exposed the long line of her throat. He dragged his teeth down and back up. Nipped at her ear, her jaw. "I have a confession."

"What's that?"

"I'm not really sure about this friend thing."

"No?" Her breath trembled out. Her fingers dug

into his arms as she held on, pressed her body closer to his.

"No. Not *just*. Is that still what you want?"

"Not right at this second, no."

Then his mouth was on hers. His hands raked through her hair, held her face to his, bringing her in and up onto her toes. He hooked one arm around her waist so that her body was plastered to his and the kiss deepened to a level of desperation. "You know this isn't going to be enough."

"For who?"

"Both of us. Either of us."

She didn't pull away, not physically, not out of his arms, but he felt her shields come up like ten-foot barriers. "It'd probably be a mistake," she said softly.

"For who?"

"For both of us," she said, and now she did step back, just enough to let him know he'd pushed too hard. "It's getting late. I should get home before my mother decides I'm dead on the side of the road."

"Not funny."

"It is if you knew how many times she's been certain I've been murdered, hit by a bus, or fallen down a manhole."

"So call her. Text her, whatever. Tell her you'll be late."

"I'm already late. Probably really late. Shoot." She slipped from between him and the truck, used her hand to feel her way to the passenger side and her bag. She pulled out her phone, clicked it. "Dead."

"I'll take you home. Or we could check out the cabin. It's right over there." He lifted her hand to point with his in the direction. "About two hundred yards. You could see how I'm doing. Or not see...exactly. Sorry."

Ava linked her fingers with his. "It's okay to say see and watch. I say it too."

"Okay then. We can see what tips you can give me and you can charge your phone. Let your mom know you haven't been murdered." He held his breath. This felt like a hurdle right here and now. One he hadn't known how badly he'd wanted to get over until just this second.

"Okay."

"Okay," he said, tightening his fingers around hers. "Want to drive?"

"Nah," she said with a teasing grin. "I'll ride."

23

They parked in front of the cabin and Ava stopped just outside the truck. "Can you tell me what it looks like from here. I don't really have my bearings."

"Oh. Yeah, sure. So straight ahead is the cabin. There are two steps up and I'll be building a ramp on the right side. Or maybe one on both, I'm not sure yet."

He drew her hand to the right again, angled up. "Hannah's house is that way, up a slight hill in the wood. You can't see it from here. The cabin is straight ahead, then..." He took her hand and lifted it to point. "The plan is to build another one to the right, and two more to the left. Each spaced about forty yards apart."

"Are there trees here?"

"Lots of trees back behind, maybe thirty yards from the cabin and a few pines sprinkled around."

"So they'll be nestled at the edge of the woods. That's nice. It'll feel like they're camping."

"Yeah, I guess that's the idea. Hannah's full of ideas."

Ava smiled. "She is. I love that about her. Cookouts with campfires and s'mores. So it's not just about the riding, but the whole camp experience. Not with riflery and swimming, I mean it's a riding camp, but they can't be riding every second of the day. You could have a camp fire, but there'll need to be some kind of a guard rail.

"What about around the cabin? You could maybe have something different than grass. A path? Maybe gravel for the walkways so they can hear and feel if they go off track."

"Hannah had mentioned paved for wheel chairs."

"Oh, right. Shows what I know. But maybe both." Hmm. She pursed her lips, running the problem around in her mind. "It'll have to be wide enough for people to pass and walk in groups. That way you could keep the walkers on the gravel, chairs on the pavement, that kind of thing."

"I can actually picture that. Want to check out the inside?"

"Lead the way," she told him, and smiling, took his arm again.

"Stick close. There's no railing yet." And looking around with Ava here, he saw a lot more things that needed to be changed, improved, altered, reworked.

"You and your brothers built it?" He opened the door and she stepped inside.

"We helped. Hannah's husband Stephen and his brother Matt did most of it. We were extra muscle."

"And you're going to build all the others?"

"Not just me, but yeah. I guess that's the plan. Hannah wants to have four cabins that would each house four campers and one counselor. Here. I'll give your phone some charge."

He took her phone and moved a few feet away. "Now that I've seen them do it, I think with a little direction I could do the rest. Or at least frame up the walls then get some help putting it together. The money is an issue. We're all chipping in and Hannah's trying to get a lot of the lumber donated. Matt helped her out with the plumbing and electrical with his contacts."

He came back to her, laid her hand on his arm. "The style is simple and the layout is mostly a square. Main room here, just big enough for seating and a table for games."

"What kind of seating?"

"Right now there's a couch and a coffee table, thanks to Zach and Nora consolidating their furniture. Probably need to add a couple of roomie chairs."

"Wood floor?" She said, walking across it.

"Yeah. Wide planks. I need to do another round of sanding then a couple coats of poly. The walls are tongue and groove."

She slid her hand over the wall as they walked. "I like it. You can feel each piece of wood."

"Yeah. Each one is quarter rounded. Then off this

room on the right, a bunk room for the campers and to the left the counselors room."

He led her to the campers' room, stopping in the middle. "It's tiny, but it's mainly just for sleeping. Two sets of bunk beds, one on each side. Hannah said some kids she'd have here would be able to sleep in a top bunk. They'll get a kick out of it. Don't know what it is about a top bunk, but some kids really get a charge out of it."

"It's different, if they don't have one at home." She let go of his arm and walked to the bed, running her hand along the smooth side. "And it's independence. I always felt more freedom when I was away at camp. I'm sure my parents signed some kind of waiver in case I got hurt, and I know the counselors were careful, but they didn't hover, you know? There was more room to be a kid. Get some bumps and bruises."

"Sounds like you're an expert. No wonder every other word out of Hannah's mouth lately is, I'll run that by Ava."

Ava turned in the room, running her hands along the side of the upper bunk. "Did you build these beds?"

"Yeah."

"They're amazing."

She kept touching it, more like caressing it. It made him proud and also made him think thoughts of her hands caressing him.

"I um... I always wanted a bunk bed. Dallas and

Zach got bunk beds. There was a constant battle between them for the top."

She smiled, made a wistful sound.

On their way out, Ava paused with her hand on the door jam. "You know, you could hang some little information plates here. Just something simple like, *bunk room* or *bunk room one,* if the cabins are numbered. Or maybe a cute name for each one instead of a number."

He could kind of see it, being here in it with her. He could see kids actually using it. Benefitting from it. Ava made it feel like more than busy work for a man who had nothing else to do. She made it seem important.

He led her out, passing the bathroom on the way to what was now his room. "The bathroom needs a lot of work. Just the basics in there now. Toilet, running water."

"Basic is good, from a blind standpoint. Simple. No rugs out in the middle to trip on."

"I'm trying to decide on tile in the bathroom or if I continue the wood."

"Different floorings are good. An easy way to instantly know where you are. Again, from a blind standpoint."

"That makes sense."

He continued on to his room, stopping for her to put her hand on the door frame. He'd noticed she liked to feel her way, get her bearings. "This will be the counselor's room. It's about the same size as the bunk room. Just big enough for a full bed which I have now. There's a bedside table and a dresser, more cast offs from everyone getting married lately. I was thinking I could make some simple tables, add a dresser or close in a section over in the corner and make it a closet with shelves."

"You're pretty handy."

"Just wood and nails mostly. Measuring and planning. Plus YouTube."

"I think it's more than that. You have skill."

"I'm good with my hands."

"Good with your hands, huh?" Ava huffed out a laugh at that and turned to face him, surprised when he was right there, so close.

"Pretty good."

She felt those skilled hands slide onto her waist, felt his fingers tighten just the slightest bit when he pulled her in a little closer.

"Ava."

He brought one hand up to her face, cupped her cheek, then combed his fingers through her hair from her face and all the way down to the ends.

She teetered on the edge of what he might say as he ran his fingers through her hair again, and once more before catching her face.

"I don't know what's going on, but I can't get you out of my head. I tried."

She scoffed, started to turn but he held.

"What? You don't believe me?"

"I don't know whether I believe you or not. I don't know if it matters."

"Why wouldn't it matter?"

"Because... Because..." Her hand flitted up to her hair, touched his hand there and dropped away. *Because I never want to go there again. Because I don't want to give you the chance to hurt me.*

It was on the tip of her tongue to tell him about her ex but what would be the point? If she told him she was divorced, he'd ask what happened, probably say he was sorry. And if he did, she was greatly afraid she'd do something stupid like cry.

It was hard enough to have someone tell you you weren't enough for them. But saying that to Luke? Telling him that and why? "Because you're afraid?"

"I'm not afraid," she said too quickly. "I'm... careful."

"Cautious."

"Yes." And she didn't want Luke, or any man to say those things to her again. That he couldn't get her out of his head, that she mattered. So why could she barely breathe when Luke said it?

"Ava, I wasn't planning to be with the woman you heard me talking to."

"It's not just that."

"I know." He pressed his cheek to hers, planted a kiss just below her ear. "I know."

Something snapped inside her, a desire and need for this man that overshadowed fear. She drew his face down and kissed him with more abandon than she'd ever felt. That seemed to give Luke the freedom to take what he wanted as well and their kiss exploded.

Luke's mouth was wild on hers, fierce and possessive. Ava felt herself turning, felt the edge of the mattress against the back her legs. Her head was spinning when her fog–kissed brain registered she was on her back, Luke over her. He grazed his teeth along her jaw, dragged his hot mouth down her throat. Found a spot just below her ear and spent some time there driving her crazy.

She wanted him. She'd been so sure she'd never feel this again. And it'd been so long since she'd felt wanted. But Luke's erection pressing like steel against her thigh said he did. He wanted her.

She couldn't think. It was all she could do not to be swept away on the tide of passion Luke was raising in her. Her hands went up and around his shoulders.

She felt the power there, the bunch and movement of muscles under his shirt. She ran her fingers into his hair, gripped the back of his head as if to hold him right there.

He found her breast, gave teasing nips through her shirt and bra. She shivered when he slipped warm fingers under her sweater and she felt his rough hands sliding their way up her side.

Then his lips left her throat and before she could think she felt them again on her bare stomach. He kissed her there, tasted, pushing her sweater up and out of his way as he went. The feverish assault on her senses was almost too much. Almost.

She moaned his name when his tongue stroked across the slight slope of her breast. Her breath hitched when his lips closed over her nipple through the satin bra. She gasped, gripping his shoulders, feeling the tension in them, the bunch and flow of muscles.

With a curse, he rose up, and with both hands, stripped her sweater up and over her head. Then, as if he didn't have the patience to remove her bra fully, he tugged down the top edge, took her nipple into his mouth, sucked hard. She arched off the bed, gripping his head, silently begging for more.

He moved to the other side as one hand slid down between her thighs. She closed her eyes, willing him to touch her where she needed it most. Her center pulsed and throbbed, until she was desperate for him to touch her there. When his hand went between her legs she sucked in a cry.

He cupped her, pressed the heel of his hand in just the right spot. She lifted her hips, desperate for more, and he gave it. His mouth at her throat, his hand rocking, rocking.

The blast of her ringtone beside the bed was ignored. Then it started again. The notes of the Star Wars Storm Trooper's theme edged in to her haze. Her brother.

"I should get it," she murmured against Luke's mouth now back on hers.

It stopped and started again.

"Shit. I have to get it." She reached out. Luke leaned

over her, pulled out the charging cord and put the phone in her hand.

"Hey."

"Hey? What the hell, Ava? Where are you? Mom's a wreck. We've been looking for you for hours."

"What?" Her heart was still pounding, her head still swimming. "I'm sorry. I'm fine." *I'm in a man's bed.* She sat up, losing that delicious, pulsing climax she'd been so close to.

"Where are you?" Ryan demanded. "I'll come get you."

"No. I'll come home. Now." She was already searching blindly for her sweater. "I'll call Mom."

"No. I'll tell her. Just come home." The line went dead and she set her phone down on the bed.

"Uh, oh," Luke said, sitting up beside her.

"Yeah. Shit. *Shit*." She shook her head and covered her face, a nervous laugh escaping. She'd gone from a woman on the edge of ecstasy to helpless child in seconds. "My brother strikes again, huh?"

"Hey. I get the family thing. God knows I get the brother thing."

With her face turned from his, she scooted to the edge of the bed and stood, wondering how the hell she was going to find her clothes. Damn it. She couldn't even make a grand exit. Couldn't avoid Luke's gradual withdrawal she knew would come, his easing back to avoid hurting her feelings.

She swept her hand in an arc over the bed and

rapped her wrist on the wooden post. *Shit*. She shook it out.

"Hey. Relax, okay? Let me help you."

"Don't you know not to tell a woman to relax?" Truthfully, she did need to relax. She was an adult. Her parents knew she was fine now. No need to panic. But need or not, her heart was racing and not in a good way as it had just minutes before. Thank God she didn't have to crawl over the floor searching for her underwear.

"Ava."

"What? *What*?" She stopped, stared in the direction she thought he was. "I'm thirty–one Luke and I can't even drive myself home. I can't—"

"Hey." He took her face, pressed a kiss to her lips. "You drive pretty good."

She wanted to laugh, but felt more like crying.

"Arms up," Luke said.

She felt her sweater brush her stomach as Luke lifted it then he pulled it down over her head. "I can dress myself."

"Yeah. Maybe I like doing it." He let the back of his hand brush over her breast, back, and again. He straightened her sweater, spent more time than necessary getting it situated.

When she was dressed she stood awkwardly beside the bed. "Well." She bit her lip wishing she could make a hasty exit.

"You know, Ava. I can see just fine and I have no idea what you're thinking right now." He slipped his hand around her neck, lifting her hair out and letting it fall down her back. "Is it just your parents or is it me?"

"No," she said after several seconds. "It's not just my parents and it's not you. It's nothing to do with you." She laid her palm on his chest, thinking how close she'd been to getting that shirt off, feeling his bare skin. "I like you, Luke. Maybe I'm afraid of just how much."

"Well, maybe that makes two of us."

24

Gary leaned back in his ergonomically correct chair as Luke walked in. "Don't you look slightly less morose," Gary said, sliding his mug amongst piles of papers.

"Good morning to you, too." After three sessions, he had to admit the guy was growing on him.

"Want coffee?"

"No, thanks. I've had my quota of coffee for the day. Moved on to Diet Coke." He raised his hand to show the plastic bottle of liquid caffeine.

"So what are we talking about today?" Gary asked as Luke took his seat.

"You tell me, Doc."

"Okay. Well... why don't you tell me everything that's happened since the last time I saw you?"

"Okay." Luke drew out the word as a million things passed through his mind. Ava's lips. Ava's eyes. The confidence and pride as she'd hit the center of the dart board. The men he wished he could bloody all over again. Her squeal of laughter, sitting in his lap, driving his truck.

"Wow," Gary said. "Based on your face I'd say you had a hell of past two weeks. Some good, some bad. I'd say it ended on a good note if I had to guess."

"Yeah. Maybe."

"Okay. Then why don't you do more than think about it and say some of it out loud."

"Okay. I went on a family outing you could say."

"Voluntarily?

"As a matter of fact. But don't call me a success story yet. It would have caused me way more grief if I'd refused. But still, I should get points for that. Go ahead, write it in my file." He pointed to Gary's desk. "But then I beat the shit out of some people, so I guess I lose points. Maybe I come out even for the week."

The concern on Gray's face was so grave, Luke almost laughed.

"Did this happen on the outing?"

"No. I made it through that fine. It was... later. A few days." His hands balled into fists. "They deserved it."

Now Gary did find some paper to write on.

"I'm going to have to make a note of this. You know that."

"Sure, go ahead. The cops came and everything, it was quite the scene. Oh!" Luke snapped his fingers and pointed at Gary. "And my brother Nick showed up from the FBI. You don't want to miss that part."

Gary stared at him for a full minute. "I have to wonder why you're telling me this, Luke? Or is there some reason I was going to find out?"

"I don't know about that." Luke sat back, shrugged, smiled. "You asked me about my week. That came to mind."

"Okay, why don't you back up and tell me the circumstances."

"Some assholes that don't deserve to live were hassling someone. A woman."

"And you just happened along? A good Samaritan?"

"I didn't just happen. She called me."

Gary laid his pen down. "Then you knew the woman?"

"Yes."

"Was she hurt?"

"No."

"And the... assholes?"

"I didn't kill them, so they weren't hurt as badly as they should have been."

"So you're clear with the police?"

"Yep. Clear as glass."

"You could have started with that." Gary sighed. "How did you feel after? Or during?"

"Mad."

"Out of control?"

Luke thought about that. "No. I knew what I was doing. Where I was and who I was doing it to."

"Could you have stopped?"

"I'm not sure. I didn't want to. She's blind, this woman. They had their hands on her, they—" He stopped, closed his eyes. When he opened them Gary was watching him over the rim of his mug.

"So..." Gary said after another minute. "The police came, the perpetrators were arrested?"

"Yes."

"And your brother?"

"One of the perps was wanted in some FBI case. Or they wanted to talk to him."

"Wow. You saved the girl and helped the FBI at the same time."

Luke didn't know what he'd expected from Gary, but it wasn't that. "This doesn't... concern you?"

"Does it concern you?"

Luke laughed. "How did I not know that would be your answer?" He shook his head.

"No, it doesn't concern me," Gary said. "That's my answer."

Luke looked down at his mostly healed knuckles and nodded slowly.

"How about the woman? Did she have anything to do with the rest of your weekly reflections?"

"Yes."

"Anything else you want to say about her?"

"No."

"Okay. Fine. Keep the good stuff to yourself. Selfish, but fine." Gary got up with his mug, took the silver thermos from the top of this file cabinet and poured himself a refill. "You sure you don't want some?"

"I'm sure."

Gary waited to speak again until he'd doctored his cup of Joe with sugar and sat back in his chair.

It took so long Luke started thinking his next question was going to be a big one. He wasn't disappointed.

"You still think you made a mistake? Leaving the military?"

"I never said it was a mistake."

"You said you weren't sure or you didn't know."

"Exactly. I don't know. What do you think?" Luke asked, picking at a splinter in his thumb.

"It doesn't matter what I think."

"Oh, give it a rest Gary. Of course you want to tell me what you think. That maybe I should have thought it through, shouldn't have left a life when I had no plan for another one."

"Is that what you think?"

Luke closed his eyes against the headache pulsing over his left eye.

"Okay, I'll tell you what I think," Gary finally said.

"About damn time."

"I think you knew that you couldn't know what kind of life you might have unless you left the life you were in. It's difficult to see the clearing when you're in the forest."

"So the Rangers was a forest and now I'm in a clearing? I gotta tell you, that not only sounds like a crock, but it sounds wrong. Being an operator, a Ranger, was the clearest fucking thing I've ever done. It's *now* that I'm in the forest. It's *now* that I don't know what I am."

"I think you do know, but it wouldn't do any good for me to tell you. Have you thought any about the jobs we went over?"

"Not too much. I've been pretty busy helping my sister. What about money?"

"What about it?"

"Do I have to make it?"

"Well, most people do. Have you won the lottery? If so, I could start being a lot nicer."

"I have some money. I could invest it, move it around. I've got a brother-in-law who's pretty good at that stuff. Anyway, what if I did something that didn't make any money?"

"You mean like volunteer work?"

"God, no. Like building."

"Builders can make quite a bit of money."

"I mean building for my sister. She needs the help. I can do it or most of it. I'm good at it."

"You like it."

Luke shrugged.

"It's okay to admit you like it. It's okay, even preferable to be happy in your work, in life."

And Gary knew that was perhaps the greatest hurdle. To accept and allow one's self to be happy. "Satisfying work doesn't always have to earn a lot of money, or any. Your sister runs a non–profit, right? And she's productive, wouldn't you say?"

"Yeah." And he thought of Ava. Her job. What she wanted to do, her goals. Her need to be in New York or

Italy or wherever the hell she'd be a couple months from now.

"Uh, oh," Gary said. "Care to share your thoughts?"

"No. Not really. And times up."

"No, it's not. Not even close."

"I say it is. I'm picking up lunch for myself and my sister. Write that down." With that, he waved a goodbye to Gary and left.

s soon as Ava got in Luke's truck she smelled it. Pastry. Chocolate. She sniffed, wanting more. "Have you been to a bakery?"

"I have."

She reached out, felt the paper bag, but didn't open it.

"Go ahead. It's for you."

"Are you serious?" But she was already diving in, pulling it out. "Oh, my gosh! It's still warm! How did you get this?" She bit into the chocolate croissant, closed her eyes, and moaned.

"I have my ways." Luke started the truck and backed out of the driveway. He looked over at Ava when they stopped at the end of the street. "Good?"

"So good," she mumbled around a mouthful. She licked a bit of chocolate off her fingers then paused. "Did you want some?"

Luke smiled. God she was pretty, her hair pulled

back in a pony tail, a smudge of chocolate on her cheek. "No, thanks. I'd like to keep my hand." He watched her eat the rest in three bites then pushed a cold bottle against her hand. "Careful, it's already open. Water."

She took a long drink.

"How did the return of the prodigal daughter go after I left yesterday?"

"Fine." She said, making a face. "You'd think I was eighteen. I do feel bad, I shouldn't have made them worry, but my mom was actually about to call the police."

"Yikes. Guess I'm in the dog house, too."

Ava waved it off. "Just ignore them."

Hard to ignore, Luke thought, what with Ryan shooting daggers at him from a few feet away and Ava's mother eyeing him like a creepy kidnapper. Or like he'd just deflowered her daughter after the prom. It'd been even harder to ignore the change in Ava. She'd looked so forlorn, repeatedly apologizing, reassuring. There'd been nothing of the laughing girl who'd driven a truck through an open field.

"Now do you see the appeal of the city?"

"I'm beginning to," he said.

"Thanks for getting me out today. You were right, I needed it. Dad did great with his PT this morning so I don't feel so bad."

They pulled into the YMCA lot and Luke parked. Seconds later he was opening the passenger door. "Come on. Let's see that world class swimmer."

"I don't need you to walk me in. And I'm not swimming with you watching me."

"You've still got a little chocolate right... here." He leaned in, kissed her, stroked his tongue over her bottom lip. "And I'm not going to be watching you. I'm going to be swimming."

"You're not a member."

"How do you know? Okay, I'm not but I am a citizen. They've got to let me use the Y don't they?"

"It doesn't work like that. You have to register and pay a fee or come as a guest."

"Great. That's what you're for." He grabbed her bag and took her hand. "Come on. You're not afraid to swim against me are you? Afraid you'll lose?"

Her lips were pressed together, pursed, but she was cracking. He could see it.

"*If* I raced you, I wouldn't lose."

"Huh. Care to have a little wager?" This time when he tugged on her hand, she climbed out of his truck.

"Do you even have a bathing suit?"

"No. But I have on shorts."

"They're not going to let you swim in shorts."

"Why?"

"I don't know." She sighed like she was annoyed but she couldn't hide the smile.

She didn't speak to him as she signed in then signed him in as a guest. Didn't speak to him as she used her cane to go to the ladies' locker room. He found himself a suit at the counter, had to pay fifty dollars for it as it was an extra swim team suit, but he considered himself lucky.

He still had to wait and began to wonder if she was going to hide out in the locker room. She wouldn't sneak past him would she? Called a cab and left without telling him? She might have. She was just that stubborn he thought, with a smile.

He was striding toward the locker room when he saw her come out and it stopped him in his tracks.

A bold, red one–piece that fit her body like a glove. Molded to her body. She held a towel in one hand, her stick in the other as she made tentative steps toward the pool side. He knew she could do it without his help, but he went to her.

"Hey," he said just a fraction of a second after he touched her arms and made her jump. "Shit. Sorry. I'm sorry. I'm going to stop doing that. I promise."

She laid her hand on his arm. "Why do you move like a ghost anyway?"

"Bad habit." He walked beside her, following her lead as she went to put her things on a chair. Using her stick, she counted the distance from the chair to the edge of the water, then walked along the edge, drag-ging her stick until it hit the corner of the pool. Marking her location.

She made her way back to her chair and when she was satisfied, laid her stick down and counting her steps, went back to the pool. And that's when he saw it. A stark, brownish–green mark on her upper arm. He drew in a long breath through his nose. "You said you didn't bruise easy."

"What?"

"There's a bruise. On your arm." He lightly ran his finger over it. "Those men. They hurt you. Touched you."

Goosebumps broke out on her arm and she rubbed at the bruise. "It doesn't hurt and I'm fine. Can we just forget about it? Please?"

"Okay." Because how could he say no? He didn't think he'd be able to say no to anything she asked.

She squatted down, went over the edge to stand in the chest high water. He followed, thinking they'd talk a minute, get used to the water because it was damn cold, but no. She was off the wall and swimming toward the other end.

He waited for her to swim down and back, watching her long, fluid strokes. She had the grace and strength of a true athlete. Perfect form, her toned arms rising out of the water then slicing through it. Her legs and feet churned a wake of force behind her. She only turned to breathe every third stroke.

On her third time back, he stepped to the center of the lane to intercept her and nearly got smacked in the face.

"Hey! I'm swimming here."

"I see that. I thought you might want to take a break for a second."

"Nope." She didn't want to take a break, didn't want to stop and talk to him or think about the two of them in the cabin yesterday. The fact that he'd brought her her favorite pastry. She just wanted to swim and swim and swim. She didn't need to see when she was swimming.

"Ready for that race?"

"You really want to race me? You haven't even warmed up."

"Don't need to," he said, reaching for her under the water.

"No, no, no," she said, skirting back from his hands. "What's the bet?"

"How about dinner?"

"Meaning what? If you win I go and if I win I don't go?" That didn't sound like a win for her and she was confident she would beat him.

"No," he said, moving in again, stealing a quick kiss from her wet lips. "Meaning if I win you pay."

"You're so sure of yourself aren't you?"

"So are you. In fact you look smug."

"I never look smug. I'm always gracious, win or lose. But I do need my own lane." She pointed. "Get your own."

He ducked under the rope, put his hand on the wall behind him. "Okay. Ready?"

She nodded. "On your mark, get set, go!"

He had to admit he hadn't expected them to be so evenly matched. But where he had a longer reach and more power, she had technique. She also didn't seem distracted by him as he was with her.

She touched the wall a full stroke ahead of him.

Her chest was heaving as she stood in the chest deep water.

"You cheated."

"What? I did not!"

He ducked under the lane rope and came up beside her. "You did." He shoved his wet hair back, slowly moving into her space. "That little flip thing you did? That wasn't agreed upon."

"It didn't have to be agreed upon. It's a common skill."

"For competitive swimmers maybe." He slipped his hands around her waist under the water.

She slid her hands up his bare chest and over his shoulders. The man was built, she thought. "Any ten-year-old can do it."

She splayed her fingers over his back, soaking up the feel of his bare skin under her hands. His thumbs teased over her hips and she remembered how his fingers had done just that the day before. Her heartbeat was up from her laps, but she shouldn't be this short of breath. Shouldn't feel like she couldn't breathe, hear her blood thundering in her ears.

When he went in for the kiss, she met him. Stroke for stroke, rising up on her toes to get closer, linking her arms around his neck. He moved from her mouth, over her jaw and nipped at her ear.

He had her pressed so tightly to his body, she felt him grow hard against her stomach. When she pressed her lips to his wet neck, licked a drop of water there before sucking lightly, he groaned and she felt the power surge through her.

She heard the shrill sound of a whistle, ignored it. The whistle blast came again, closer.

"Hey! You can't do that."

Luke lifted his head, but didn't loosen his hold on her. "Sure. Sorry."

"Oh, my gosh. Did we just get busted for PDA in a YMCA swimming pool?"

"We did. And the kid who busted us doesn't look old enough to drive."

She laughed, hid her face against his chest. "Please tell me there's no water aerobics going on. My mother will never be able to show her face again."

"No aerobics, but there is a group of ladies staring at us. Come on. Let's go again."

"I'd like to do a few more laps, but the race is over. I won. I'll just be thinking of where I want dinner." She pushed off the wall ahead of him.

When she went to climb out twenty minutes later, it took everything in him not to help her to the chair where she'd left her things. She didn't need him so he stepped back, dripping on the tile pool deck.

She dried off, rubbing the towel down her legs so slowly he would swear she was doing it just to torture him.

"I'll go change and then we can go."

"Okay."

"You didn't bring a towel did you?"

"I'll air dry."

She rolled her eyes, and pushed her damp towel at him. "Wash off the chlorine. It's bad for your skin."

He was waiting for her when she came out of the ladies' locker room. This time he remembered to give her some kind of cue before he touched her. And this time she put her hand on his arm and let him lead her to the car. "You sure that flip thing is legal?"

"I'm sure."

He opened the door for her and went around the hood as she buckled into the passenger's seat. He cranked the engine, noticed the chill bumps on her arms and cranked up some heat. "Did you decide where you want to go for that dinner?"

"Um...I was thinking we could order in."

"No way. I pay my debts. I said I'd take you out and...Oh."

"Yeah. Oh." She leaned over the center console and met his lips.

"I'm slow."

"We already knew that. Thus, I am the winner."

26

Ava's nerves jittered on what seemed like an endless drive to the cabin. She was a grown woman, she knew what she wanted, but this was Luke and there were nerves.

When they finally, *finally* arrived, he turned off the truck. He made no move to get out, but she heard him shift in his seat.

"Hey," he said.

"Hey," she said back. She could tell by the sound of his voice he was facing her. Looking at her. Waiting for her?

"We're here."

"Yeah. I figured that," she said with a shaky laugh.

"Ava. We don't—"

"No." She faced him. "I want you. I'm scared to want you as much as I do, but I do."

"Then we're on the same page."

There was no cabin tour this time. There was only

one goal and they both knew what it was. They'd fought it as long as they could. The second the door closed behind them, Luke pressed her body back against it, took her mouth with the same ferocious need that she felt. The kiss was hot, wild, his hands possessive and strong as his hard body pressed into hers.

She gripped his shoulders as he took her mouth like he was starving for her. Like he couldn't get enough. Neither could she. She raked her fingers through his hair, moaned into his mouth when he slipped a heavy thigh between her legs.

"Ava." He said her name roughly, his lips streaking a hot path down her throat. "I want you under me. Over me. I want to move inside you and watch those eyes when you come apart."

His hands skimmed up her body, thigh to breast, setting every nerve on fire. He held there, molding her breast in his hand.

Ava sucked in a breath when Luke lifted her, wrapped her legs around his hips, bringing his erection against her core. Her mind blurred as they hit the bed still wrapped around each other. Rolled, kissed as they stripped off clothing, fighting to free themselves. Her top then her jeans. His shirt and shoes. She was going for the button on his jeans when he pulled back.

The warmth of his chest was gone from hers and she felt a chill of air. She could hear his rapid breathing, feel the weight of his body on the mattress beside her.

"Luke?" She moved to cover herself and he stopped her hand.

"No. Don't move. Please. Just give me a second."

She couldn't read his eyes, had no idea what he was thinking, feeling. And she hated the little gallop in her heart that wanted to run. "Luke." She reached out, felt his wrist on the bed beside her. She ran her hand up his arm, felt the tension there. "You have to tell me what you're thinking."

"What?"

"I can't see your face. I don't know what you're thinking. If you're changing your mind or—"

"Ava, baby." He cupped her face and maybe now more than ever he felt what it was to be her. To not see, to not know. He leaned over her, took her mouth again mixing tenderness with heat. "I'm looking at you ... dumbstruck. There's no other word for it." He trailed one finger slowly down her chest between her breasts. "I've wanted you since the first minute I saw you."

"No, you didn't," she said breathless. "You thought I was drunk."

"Since the first second. You in that dress, your hair that I was dying to touch. And your eyes. Damn when you looked at me with those eyes..."

He cupped one breast, grazed the rough pad of his thumb over her nipple. She gasped and he did it again, then it wasn't his thumb, it was his mouth, hot and hungry.

He moaned as his hands cupped and stroked, his hungry mouth moved from one to the other and she felt that burn of pleasure rising inside her. Felt the heat like a tide and distantly heard him moaning, felt the hard erection pressed against her leg.

"It's been awhile," she said, as his teeth grazed the line of her throat.

"For me, too. Afraid you forgot?"

He pressed smiling lips to the skin of her throat, stayed there a minute and she shuddered.

"Forgot? No," she said, on a shaky breath. "Remember it feeling like this? Never."

LUKE WATCHED the desire in the rising color on her cheeks. Elation filled him as Ava opened for him and he delved into the sweetness of her mouth. How long had he known her? He couldn't think clearly enough to do the math, but it felt like he'd been waiting forever to kiss her like this. Touch her like this.

Her breasts were small, pale and so perfect he may have whispered a prayer. He cupped one in his hand and watched her eyes close, heard her sigh. He wanted her trembling with need. Wanted to watch her face when he took her over the edge.

Every touch with his hands and mouth was pure heaven. And she managed to hold off any thoughts that would darken it. Luke was her friend, her lover and she wanted him. And for the first time in a long time felt very much wanted in return.

He came over her, took his time, using lips and hands. Going back to her mouth again and again, moving down her body until she was hot, wet. Until she was begging.

"Now," she said. Her hands pulled at his hair, his shoulders. "I want you inside me."

He grabbed a condom, then he was over her, her soft legs parting for him. The wild need he'd tried to bury burst to the surface. With his own blood roaring in his ears, he drove into her. Her fingers dug into his shoulders, clutched there. When she rose to meet him stroke for stroke, his heart rammed into his throat.

He could have gone over, could have driven them both, but she slowed, drawing it out, driving them both mad with it. But he gave them just enough before pulling back then filling her again. He'd wanted women before but he'd never felt this razor-sharp edge of need. He fought for the patience and control he'd honed the past twenty years.

He watched her. Her face, her breasts swaying, the flush on her chest. Her legs were open to him, wound around him. Her body gripped him, dragged at him, then pulled him back in. But when he felt her tighten around him, heard her strangled cry of release, all this violent need he felt for her erupted. He drove into her, thrust deep and went over.

When he came back to himself, his face was pressed into the side of her neck. Strands of her hair stuck to his cheek. He shifted, took in her closed eyes and slack, satisfied expression. Rolling, he brought her limp body into his side, stroked a hand down her back over smooth, damp skin, and felt pretty damn satisfied himself.

Ava lay there, trying to recover from the mind-blowing sex she'd just had. She felt each beat of Luke's heart under her hand. He was so warm, so hard, her hand moved over his chest savoring the warmth. She'd needed this, hadn't known how much until it had happened.

Her fingers touched something small and cool and metal. She rubbed it between her fingers, felt the raised grooves on the small oval shape.

"Saint Christopher," he told her. "Hannah gave it to me years ago. Figured it'd be bad luck to thumb my nose at the saints by not wearing it."

She moved her fingers over the medal again, thought about all the moments Luke must have needed a saint on his side.

"Hungry?"

She smiled against his chest. "Are you asking me if I am or telling me you are?"

"Both."

"I am actually. The swimming and then the..."

Luke sat up, snagged his jeans from the floor and tugged them on. Then he turned, leaned over her. "I still owe you dinner."

"You do."

"I have frozen pizza and maybe a casserole Hannah's always pushing on me."

"What kind of pizza?"

He slipped a hand over her side and up to her breast because it was right there and he wasn't done touching her. Not by a long shot. "Barbecue chicken and a pepperoni and sausage."

"I like either."

"Then I'll make both."

Ava's phone chimed with a message from Maddie. She'd listen to it later but it did remind her to text her parents.

Luke found her in the bathroom, speaking into her phone.

"Your message to mom says, I went swimming and now I'm at Luke's. Ready to send it?"

"No!"

"Okay."

Luke stood just outside the open door listening to Ava talking to herself and he smiled.

"Don't wait up, I'll be having sex with Luke all night. Yeah, that's a no."

"I kinda liked that one," he said, feeling only a little guilty when she jumped.

"What are you doing?"

"Coming to ask if you want me to run out for salad or something. I didn't want to interrupt your messaging."

She scowled at him. "Thanks."

"Hey, Siri, text Mom."

"Texting Mom."

"Hey, Mom, I'm with Luke. Don't wait up."

Siri repeated the message Luke had given, then asked, "Ready to send it?"

"No!" Ava said. But Luke said *yes* louder and held the phone out of her reach.

"There. Done. Now we can eat." He slid his hands around her, cupping her bottom. "Then we can do other things."

Ava woke in Luke's bed to the scent of coffee. She hadn't meant to stay, didn't know if he'd meant for her to stay. Sex between adults was one thing. Sleeping together was something else entirely. After a night of mind blowing sex, she should feel loose. Instead she was tense and uncomfortable. She hated not knowing where things stood, where she stood. She'd spent too many months not knowing where she stood with Blake.

But she was a big girl. She'd get up, get dressed, and face whatever it was. Get the answers she needed. It could still be simple. They'd let the fire smoldering between them catch and burn. Now things would probably cool off. Nothing to be uncomfortable about.

Although the room was a square and not a circle, Ava pictured the room like a clock, putting herself at six. The chest of drawers was to her left, at nine. The door out to the kitchen at ten or eleven.

She didn't know where her clothes had ended up. When she felt around with her foot, she touched cloth, picked it up, felt Luke's jeans. She brought them to her face and felt a little foolish for smiling. Making her way around the room, using her feet for feelers, it didn't take her long to find her bra, shirt, and pants. Took a while longer to find her underwear hidden in the sheets.

Dressed, she went in search of that life-giving liquid. She wasn't sure where Luke was. Maybe he was already out doing stuff. She hadn't asked her phone for the time.

She used her cane and one hand on the wall to find her way to the kitchen. "Hey," he said, when she reached the corner.

"Hey." She was more tense than she'd been before. Those insecurities she'd had as a teen, then overcome with Blake only to have them come roaring back tenfold bombarded her.

Was he looking at her, at his watch, his phone? Was he frowning? Scowling? Wanting her to leave but not sure how to say it?

"You breathing over there?"

"What?"

"I asked if you were breathing. You stopped, froze like a statue. Need help?"

"No. Yes, I'm breathing. I was just thinking." She held her hand out to use the wall for guidance.

"I could tell."

"Do you know where my phone is? I need to call a ride. I could start yelling, 'Hey, Siri', but it might be awkward since you're standing right here."

Luke didn't answer but she heard his footsteps, felt the vibration of the wood under her bare feet. He stopped right in front of her.

"Trying to run away?"

"Nope. Not running. Just going. I've got things and...you've got things."

Luke couldn't get inside her head, no matter how much he wished he could. But the unsettled, uncomfortable feelings were vibrating off of her loud and clear. Because they'd had sex? She certainly hadn't seemed uncertain or uncomfortable during that part. Was it the morning after? Regrets? Because of him specifically or just in general? He wanted time to figure it out. Figure her out and himself. Them.

Luke caught her fingers in his and stepped into her. "You're thinking too much," he said slipping his arm around her waist. He brushed the hair from her neck so he could kiss her there. "I made you breakfast. You think your things can wait until after that?"

"Um...sure. Sounds good. Smells good."

"You know, if I wanted to rush you out the door I would have only made enough for one."

It made her heart jerk to know he read her thoughts so easily and she didn't care for it. "Maybe you're too polite to only make breakfast for yourself."

"And maybe you're looking to get the hell out of dodge. Planning to call Hannah and cancel any scheduled rides." He pressed a kiss to her lips. "I don't know what you're thinking either, Ava. Just feeling my way here."

CLAUDIA CONNOR

He led her to the little table Hannah had added to the room last week. "And what if I was too polite, which I'm not. Would I ask what you were doing later? And I'd be asking for the purpose of seeing you again, in case you didn't get that."

Ava heard the teasing note in his voice, heard the smile in it. She grinned and forked up a bite of the eggs he'd placed in front of her.

"Are you gonna tell me what you're doing later?"

"Maybe. I think I'll try the eggs first."

27

Two days later, Ava had a very early and *very* long phone call with Maddie to confess her recent bedroom deeds with Luke. During which her friend tried her best to finagle all the sexy details.

Following that, and a rushed cup of coffee, she put her dad through the paces of his physical therapy until he cried uncle. "Okay. You did good," she told him. "I'll get you some water."

She came back and got him comfortable in his recliner then handed him a cup of water.

"How's that new man of yours?"

The question was so out of nowhere, so surprising she choked on her own water.

"He's not— I mean...he's fine. He took me to the pool the other day. I beat him in a race."

"That's my girl."

She took the empty cup from him. "Let me get you

a cool towel." His breathing was still heavy.

"You know I'm not so old that I don't know why you didn't come home the other night, or why you were so late that day."

"Daddy! I—"

"Ahh." He gave her leg a pat. "Forget it. Just make sure he's good to my girl."

Good grief? Was her dad really commenting about her sex life? Her face was hot when she came back with a damp dish towel and handed it to him.

"That's nice, honey. Thank you. I'll just cool off here a bit."

"Okay. What about some juice?"

"That'd be fine. Thank you."

Ava took a glass from the cabinet and was just getting ice from the door of the refrigerator when the front door opened. She heard Ryan walk in. He had an unmistakable way of slamming the door. There was also a certain rhythm to his walk as his dress shoes moved over the kitchen tile.

"Hey," he said, stopping across the room from her. She hadn't talked to her brother since he'd stormed out yesterday. "Mom here?"

"Yeah. I think she's in the bedroom, changing sheets maybe." Ava moved around him to get to the refrigerator. She felt around for the Cranberry juice she'd labeled for herself with a sticker from her braille label maker.

She poured the juice, using the tip of her finger over the edge of the glass as a guide.

"That for Dad?"

"Yeah."

"Here. I'll take it in to him. Hey," he said, stopping on his way out of the kitchen. "Don't be mad at me, okay?"

"Is that an apology?"

"I don't know," he said, his tone getting hot again. "Should I be apologizing?"

"Well, I apologized about a hundred times yesterday, so yeah, I think so. And," she said before he could interrupt. "I clearly remember you staying out all night when you came home from college for the holidays. And I clearly remember Mom and Dad being worried. What I don't remember is it being a big problem. Is that because you're male or because you're not blind?"

"Wow. How many brain cells did you use coming up with that?"

"Don't be an asshole." Even as she said it, she felt a little twinge of guilt because really, they *had* had reason to worry, considering what happened.

"Okay. So I ask again, are you still mad at me?"

She heaved out a breath. "Fine. No." She knew that was her brother's version of an apology and since she still felt bad for worrying everyone, she'd take it. She poured a glass of milk for herself and was popping a piece of bread in the toaster when her mom came in.

"Ava, I've been thinking."

"Oh, boy," Ryan said, coming back into the room. "I can't wait to hear this. Pop a piece of toast in there for me, will you? And add some Nutella."

"Don't be a smart mouth," his mother told him. "And don't either of you make a mess in this kitchen. I just wiped down the counters."

Ava had already canceled her toast, added his, and started it again.

"As I was saying... I've been thinking and I think you should invite Luke to dinner."

Ava choked on her milk in mid swallow. "No. A major no."

"Ava Lane." Her mother paused her banging of dishes as she unloaded the dishwasher. "You're seeing a man. You should have him over."

"That's not what this is. Mom. I've known him a few weeks. And we're not..."

"Not what?" Her brother asked and she could hear the smirk.

"None of your business," she snapped in his direction. "And I'm not seeing a man, Mom." *I'm just ... having sex with him.* She liked the sound of that. Not seeing, not dating, not planning. Just enjoying. "I'm not asking him over for dinner, and especially not on your birthday."

"Why not my birthday?"

"Because that's like a family thing and..."

"It's *my* birthday. I should get to have who I want. I barely got a chance to talk to him the last time he was here."

"Because you were too busy yelling at me."

She knew her brother was standing there, sipping

coffee, probably grinning like a fool. "Shut up," she said to him and threw the dish rag in his direction.

"Missed me," he said and heard the door open and close as he left.

Damn it. Every single time.

LUKE MET up with Hannah outside the back of the barn at the horse shower. Standing off to the side, he watched her work. "Does he really need to be clean?"

"Of course. Makes him feel better about himself, doesn't it, Al?"

The little tan and brown horse bobbed his head as if agreeing.

"He took a roll in the mud and I have a client coming later for ground therapy."

He'd learned ground therapy meant petting, feeding, touching. He supposed that went better with a clean horse. "I've got some errands to run," Luke told Hannah as she sprayed off the soapy horse.

"Oh, yeah? Don't tell me you're buying more building supplies."

"Nope." He hadn't told them about Gary. He didn't particularly want to talk to Gary much less talk to people about talking to Gary. And wouldn't that make them worry more? Or maybe it would make them worry less?

"Luke?" A light spray of water hit his legs and he looked up to see his grinning sister.

"You really want to play that game?"

"No." She quickly cut off the water. "I really don't. Oh, hey. Did you ever talk to Nick about the guy he arrested?"

"Yeah. Turned out he didn't have any information that could help."

"I still can't believe that happened to Ava."

"I know." And he still wasn't over it. Had in fact dreamed about it last night. Dreamed he hadn't gotten there in time.

"Where are you going?"

"Grocery," he said. "Milk, bread. Just the basics." He walked beside his sister and the horse into the barn. Hannah tied his lead rope to a ring outside his stall. "Need anything?"

"Nope. We're all set. It's taco night so I'll expect you around six."

They had established that Luke loved tacos. Another get to know your siblings thing, he supposed. "Thanks, but I'm not going to be able to make that."

"Luke." She turned and gave him that pitying look. "There's no need for you to eat alone. We love having you."

"I won't be eating alone. I'll be eating with Ava." He smiled at the thought and turned his head so his sister couldn't see the love–sloppy grin.

Ava didn't know it yet, but they were going out. He still owed her dinner.

∼

LATER THAT WEEK, after a very nice dinner date and another night with Ava in his bed, Luke stood at the fence rail watching Ava and telling himself he had other things he needed to be doing. Even as he went through the mental list, he didn't move away. He had this constant need to be near her even when he wasn't touching her.

Of course, touching her was always a good option. Even now he imagined unzipping that vest, unbuttoning all those little buttons on the shirt she wore underneath. He needed to get a handle on seeing Ava and whatever these feelings were going on inside him every time he saw her.

Ava walked Winnie past Hannah, listening to her directions on her seat, her leg and hand placement. Ava adjusted, listened, made adjustments. Again, he thought how good she looked up there.

She worked Winnie into a trot and over a few rails laid out on the ground. Now she was cantering around the ring. How in the hell she did that without seeing was still beyond him. The woman had courage in spades.

He watched her go by again, then watched as his sister set the rails into a low bar jump. No way was she setting that up for Ava. He started to climb over the fence, make his way into the ring, and just stopped himself. *Don't be like her parents. She's got this.*

Damn it. He stood, breath held, as Ava came around and made a wide turn. He felt the muscles of his stomach tighten in fear. A simple, razor-edged fear.

She raised her butt up out of the seat and she and Winnie were up and over.

Hannah called out instructions and more praise. Ava pulled Winnie back into a walk and stopped beside Hannah. He couldn't hear what they were saying but Hannah did all the talking and Ava nodded.

Luke watched as Ava moved away from his sister and picked up the canter again. She went down the straight outside of the ring, passing the jumps set up in the middle. She did that three times and every time Hannah called out something but he couldn't make out the words.

On the fourth pass Ava made a turn, going right down the center of the ring where the jump was set up. Ava and Winnie sailed over the jump on the first pass and Luke let out the breath he'd been holding. After a quick pow wow with Hannah, Ava repeated the exercise.

Picking up a trot, then a cantor, then lined up for the jump. Only this time they didn't sail over. Winnie stopped short, sidestepping to the right and Ava went over the horse's head, hitting the rail with her shoulder before her body hit the ground.

With a hand on the top rail, Luke leaped up and over and raced across the sandy riding ring. He got to her seconds before Hannah did.

"Ava?" His heart was in his throat as he ran his hands lightly over her arms and legs. "Where are you hurt? Don't get up."

For a few seconds she obeyed, then sucked in a

deep breath of air. "I'm fine." She pressed her fist to her chest, she drew in more air. "Just— Knocked the breath out of me." She started to sit up, dusting the sand from her arms.

"Just be still, damn it. You're bleeding."

"Luke, I'm fine."

"Bleeding? Where?" Hannah gave his shoulder a shove. He didn't move but she squeezed her way in. "Let me see. You sure you're okay," she asked Ava.

Ava reached up, touched a finger to her forehead. "I'm sure. I must have scratched myself. It's nothing," she said, standing but Luke still had a hold of her arm. "It was my fault. I lost concentration and she didn't know what I wanted her to do."

"Well you made it over the first one beautifully," Hannah said.

Luke stared at the women. "Are the two of you crazy? She could have broken her neck."

"Luke," Hannah said, with what he read as false patience. "We're in the middle of a lesson. Maybe you should go find something else to do."

Luke looked from Ava to his sister and back to Ava.

Hannah touched Ava's other arm. "If you're sure you're okay, let's go back to that first cross bar we did today, and have you and Winnie end on a high note."

Hannah looked at him. "We'll just finish up and you can cool down."

"I'm fine," Ava said. "Really."

Well nice that someone was, Luke thought and turning on his heel, made his way back to the barn. He wasn't going to the cabin to work. Not yet. He wasn't finished with what he wanted to say. Not yet.

The second the women entered the barn he straightened from the wall he'd been holding up for the past fifteen minutes. Ava had already dismounted and was leading the horse.

She went right to Winnie's stall, running her hand over the braille name plates, no help needed from him. Just one more impressive thing about her. She took the halter and lead rope and with a few flicks of her fingers had unbuckled the bridle.

He waited until she'd slipped the halter over Winnie's ears before he stepped forward. "For God's sake, don't do that again."

She turned her face to stare at him, or seemed to. "Excuse me?"

"Look, you can ride in the ring. You can—"

"I can ride in the *ring*?"

Her tone hit something scary which was punctuated by his sister's abrupt departure. Damn it. The women had already conspired against him.

"So," Ava said. "Tell me again exactly what I can and can't do? Maybe you should write it out. Oh, wait. I wouldn't be able to read it. Maybe you should put a leash on me so you can be sure I do as I'm told."

"Now hold on."

"No, you hold on." She was standing close enough that when she poked out a finger it hit its mark dead center in his chest. "Didn't I already tell you I had my family breathing down my neck, worrying about me?"

"Yes, but—"

"And didn't you say you understood?"

"Yes, I said that." He took the finger poking him, wrapped his fingers around her entire hand. "But I sometimes forget what I've said when my heart stops."

Her expression lost some of the anger, replaced by confusion.

"My heart stopped when I saw you hit the ground, Ava. I'm not even sure it's started again."

Now she smiled at him, soft and sweet. "The ground is sandy." She laid her other hand on his chest. "I didn't fall that hard."

"I know." He'd meant the kiss to be quick, an apology, a period, but it wasn't quick. Nor was it a period at the end of anything. He kept right on kissing her as her hands came to his shoulders. Her fingers slid around to the back of his neck and up into his hair.

When Luke finally managed to release her, Ava was breathing hard which was a relief considering the way his own heart was pounding. A sexy flush tinged her cheeks and there was a just–kissed look to her mouth. Both made her eyes look even bluer. "I'll see you later?"

"Okay."

He ran the back of his hand down her cheek, then made himself step back. There was something going on here, new territory, no map. But he was pretty sure he knew which way he wanted to go.

28

"I think if you just labeled the shelves, that would be enough," Ava said. She'd hung around this morning after riding to help Hannah with some camp details. "Like brushes and picks. The individual items wouldn't need to be labeled."

"Okay," Hannah said. "Got it. And I had this thing I was going to ask you about. It was an app people could download and use when they're here. Hang on. I've got it somewhere."

Ava heard Hannah opening her file drawer then closing it.

"How was your date with Luke?"

"It was good."

"Yeah? Anything else?"

Ava heard more shuffling and also the teasing friendship in Hannah's question. "It was *really* good," she said, smiling. And it had been.

He'd taken her to a quiet restaurant with cloth

table coverings and a candle in the center. She had an app on her phone that could scan and then read the menu to her which he'd thought was cool. But leaning in, their heads together, he'd read it to her. With her.

Deciding and debating on what each of them would order, what they might share. And for more than two hours, they'd shared food and wine, tasting from one another's plates, talking about everything and nothing.

She started to take another sip from the cold can of Coke she held, then stopped. "You know, on second thought, labeling each one wouldn't be a bad idea and they're not expensive. Children or even adults who've recently lost their sight could use the practice. Like anything, it's better to practice with a purpose. Feels less like a chore."

"Absolutely." Ava heard Hannah's pen hit the pad. "You know, you're really good at this."

"Happy to help."

"No, I mean you're *really* good at it."

Ava smiled. "Well, thanks."

They went over the app Hannah had found and in the end decided it wouldn't be that helpful and the money could be better spent.

"What else is going on? How's your dad?"

"Good. Better every day. We've been doing the home therapy for four weeks now and he's starting to get around more."

"Do you know how much longer you'll be here?"

"Not exactly." She busied her hands, flicking the

tab at the top of the can. "I'm supposed to be back in three weeks unless I ask for more time."

Ava flicked the tab again and decided to take the plunge. "My mom has it in her head that Luke has to come to her birthday dinner. I mean, she's insistent and it's ridiculous that I even feel pressured about it. But she's all like, 'it's my birthday and if you're going to...' I won't repeat exactly what she said as it's just too embarrassing, but she's insistent."

"Well, I don't know about parents, but I do know that no matter how old I am, my brothers, especially Nick, can lay down the pressure. And the guilt. And oh, my gosh. Before Stephen? He was like a lunatic."

Ava smiled.

"I take it you don't want Luke to come."

"No. No, it's not that. It's just... It's weird, right? Like guys say, don't take a girl to a wedding unless you want her to get ideas. Asking him to my house for a family event definitely seems like I'm getting ideas."

"Are you?"

"No. I mean...I'm..." *I'm deathly afraid I'm going to fall in love with your brother.* "I'd rather have him there than not, but I don't know." She blew out a breath thinking she seemed to *not* know a lot lately. Especially when it came to Luke.

She thought about their date again. How thoughtful Luke had been, how at ease she'd felt. He made it easy. He handled it. He'd handled everything.

"I don't want to mess things up," Ava said, pulling her thoughts back. "We're having fun. It's temporary."

"If it's just temporary how messed up can it get?"

"Mmm. Good point."

There was a knock on the door then it opened.

"Hey," Luke said. "Hey, Ava. Didn't know you were here."

"I didn't know you were here," she said with a smile in his direction. "We were just going over some camp stuff."

"Right. That's good."

There was something in his voice she thought as he came farther into the room and closed the door behind him.

"I found something. I really hate to tell you this, either of you, but I found two of the kittens. Just outside the barn. Looks like something got to them."

"Oh, no," Hannah said. "Did you see Tom?"

"No. No sign of Tom or the others."

He crossed the short distance and Ava felt him beside her just before he laid a hand on her shoulder. Sadness filled the little room.

"Could have been a raccoon," he said. "Or a weasel. Probably something small or there'd be nothing—well."

Ava reached up and covered his hand with hers.

"I'll bury them, okay? Then look around again for the others."

"Okay," Hannah said. "Thanks."

"Sure." He gave Ava's shoulder a squeeze then he left.

"Well, that sucks," Hannah said.

"Yeah," Ava said, staring after Luke. "Maybe Tom took the others somewhere."

"Yeah. Maybe. Shit."

Ava heard Hannah's office chair squeak as she sat heavily, heard her sigh. "Not all the kids know about the kittens yet. The ones that do, well... I guess I can answer honestly and say I don't know where they are."

"I wish I could help you look," Ava said.

"If they're anywhere around, Luke will find them."

Ava sat a moment with her thoughts then stood. "I better get going."

"Yeah. Me, too. I've got a rider coming in ten minutes. Ava."

She stopped at the door. "Yeah?"

"I think you should ask Luke to dinner. I think he'd like to go."

LUKE KNEW ENOUGH NOT to go empty handed, so when he entered Ava's parents' house he had flowers in hand. He'd gone back and forth over one bouquet or two. Flowers for Ava's mom was a no brainer. It was her house, it was her birthday. But Ava had invited him. Should he take Ava flowers too? In the end he'd decided on the one, pulling out a single rose for Ava. He left it in the truck to give to her later.

The second Ava opened the door he regretted his decision. She looked like a dream, standing there in a dressy white top and dark jeans. Her hair was brushed to a curtain of fine silk that framed her face. There was a touch of nerves in her eyes.

"I brought flowers for your mom," he said, when he leaned in to hug her.

She sniffed and smiled. "Mmm. Roses. That will get you major points. Might even get you extra cake."

"I'm hoping. I pulled one out for you. It's in the truck."

She smiled and he turned his head so that his lips slid from her cheek to her lips. She was so damn sweet, he had to kiss her.

"Luke."

Mrs. Bennet's voice had him jerking back. "Hi, Mrs. Bennet. Happy birthday." He held out the flowers to the thin woman with a silver bob.

"Yellow roses. How lovely. Thank you. Come in, tell Ava what you want to drink."

With Ava's hand on Luke's arm, they moved into the kitchen. Ava's father, a stout man with a full head of gray hair, bushy gray eyebrows, and a smile much like Ava's sat at the table.

"Luke, good to see you again."

"You too, Mr. Bennet. How's the knee?" he asked, coming over to shake the man's hand.

"Good, good. Better every day. Ava's a slave driver."

"Hey, man." Luke shook hands with Ava's brother, who sat near his father, some type of magazine between them. "This is my sister-in-law, Connie," Ava said, leading him toward the kitchen counter.

"Hi." A slim brunette, several inches shorter than

Ava turned to him. She had wide brown eyes and a kind smile. "I'd shake your hand, but..." She held up hands dotted with chocolate icing. "I'm just putting the finishing touches on the cake. Leave it to me to wait until the last minute."

"Well, when it comes to chocolate icing, I say better late than never."

"Good answer," she said, going back to the triple layer round cake.

"I'll get a vase for your flowers, Mom."

Ava let go of his arm and using her cane, went to the cabinet below the sink and retrieved a tall, clear vase. "In case you're wondering why my mom is cooking her own birthday dinner, it's because she's stubborn."

"I like to cook. And I told you, going out is too much trouble. There's some snacks here, Luke," her mother said. "And tea, beer, water, soda. I think we have a bit of everything."

"Thank you."

Luke took a glass of sweat tea and took a seat at the table with the men as directed. He watched Ava move around the kitchen.

"I hope you like lasagna," Mrs. Bennet said to him.

"Love it."

Twenty minutes later, grace was said and they were seated.

"This is amazing," Luke said. "The salad, the lasagna. All of it."

"Thank you. Ava made the salad. Though I always

worry when she uses a knife," her mother said, frowning at Ava.

"Seriously?" Ryan pushed the lettuce around on his plate. "Am I going to find a finger in here?"

Luke slid a glance at Ava, noted the small smile on her lips as she shook her head while her mother scolded her brother.

"You know when Ava was seven, she cut her finger off," Ryan said.

"Would you stop?" Connie elbowed her husband.

Luke lifted Ava's hand, held it up. "Looks like she's got all her fingers to me. Unless you started out with six?"

Ava turned her head, sent him a smile that went all the way to her eyes. "Nope just five." For a second everyone else disappeared. "And I didn't cut it all the way off," she said to her brother.

"Nearly," her mother said. "So when she tells me she's taking this cooking class in the city and learning how to make all these fancy things and chop faster, it makes my heart race."

Luke looked at her again. "I didn't know you could cook fancy."

"I haven't told you everything," she said, with a smirk.

"Did she tell you how she used to hit me with that stick she carries?"

Luke eyed Ryan, might have taken offense but he heard the teasing in his voice and saw Ava's mouth twitch.

"Ryan James," their mother admonished mildly. "That stick," she muttered.

"No, I didn't," Ava said. "I also didn't tell him how you used to take broccoli off your plate and sneak it onto mine."

"Did not."

"Did, too. And I'm not sure but... Dad, did I ever tell you how Ryan took your rental car one night when he was *fifteen*?"

"Ryan!"

Mrs. Bennet seemed shocked, while Mr. Bennet kept eating like he'd known all along. Reminded Luke of his own dad. For all the stuff he'd pulled, he'd never fooled his dad. He wondered what his own parents would be like now. Imagined them sitting around a table, enjoying the sound of their grown children squabbling like kids.

Ryan pointed his fork at his sister. "I can tell some stuff on you, too."

"Ignore them, Luke," Connie said. "In another few minutes they'll start throwing food. They revert to childhood whenever they're around each other for more than ten minutes."

Luke smiled. This didn't seem so bad. Just some good-natured ribbing between siblings. Not nearly the awkward event Ava had warned him of when she'd asked him to this dinner.

"Maybe you could help us, Luke." Ava's mother was looking at him pointedly.

"Um…" Luke looked up from his nearly cleaned plate. "You want me to stop them from throwing food?"

"Heavens, no. They know better than that. I meant help us talk Ava into staying. At the very least talk her out of this idea of moving to Italy. I mean really."

"Mom, please. Not today."

"I love the city," Connie put in. "I miss it."

Ryan swung his gaze to his wife. "I thought you liked it here."

"I do," she said quickly. "I do. I just said I miss it. I can see why Ava would rather live in a city and Italy? Who wouldn't jump at the chance to live in Rome?"

"Me, for one," Ryan said, making a face.

And oh, boy, maybe they were just getting to the family undercurrents. "I think it's cool," Luke said, taking Ava's hand under the table. He might not want her to go on a personal level, but he'd have her back. "It's a great job opportunity. And you know, it's easier for her in a city. I'm sure she's told you."

"Well, I don't know how that could be possible," her mother said.

Luke shrugged. "I'm not sure either, but then I'm not the one who's blind. Ava's more than capable."

Mrs. Bennet's face took on a sour look, but the little squeeze Ava gave his hand made it worth it.

"Well, it's dangerous," her mother said. "New York is bad enough but a *foreign* city?"

"Well." Luke swallowed his last bite and took a sip of tea. "Nowhere is completely safe, not for anyone.

What happened to Ava on the way to the pool could have happened to anyone, anywhere."

Ava's mother lowered her fork. "*Excuse* me?"

Her dad also stopped eating as did Ryan and Connie. Ava tensed beside him. *Shit*, Luke thought to himself.

"What happened on the way to the pool, Ava?" Ryan asked.

"Nothing really."

"Ava Lane?" her mother said.

Ava mumbled a curse under her breath and tugged her hand from his. He'd definitely stepped in it here. He'd clean it up.

"Her Uber got lost," Luke said, taking a another sip of tea, going for casual. "It happens. You know, they think they know where they're going and then they don't." He shrugged. "She even drove my truck," Luke added, hoping to change the subject.

Bad idea, he thought when Ryan fumbled his garlic bread and both Mr. and Mrs. Bennet simultaneously choked.

WHEN THE *DRIVING his truck* comment was adequately explained, Luke slipped off to the bathroom. He was kicking himself for putting her on the defensive again. If he'd thought it would help, he'd be in there right now explaining to her family how absolutely capable Ava was. Of course, if they didn't see it, nothing he said would make a difference.

Part of him understood. He saw it, and didn't he still worry about her?

He did his business and noted a bedroom across the hall. One with a white iron bed covered in a white bedspread with small pink flowers. Curious he stopped in the doorway. The matching bedside tables were also white, as was the dresser. The walls were painted a pale gray and were decorated with art and a large mirror hung over the dresser.

"Get lost?"

Luke turned to find Ava nearly beside him. "Didn't hear you. And sorry, I was just looking. Your room?"

"Yep."

"There's a mirror over the dresser."

"I know. My mom said the wall looked bare without it."

Ava stepped into the room and Luke followed. There were sheets of papers stacked on a desk. They looked blank and his eyes almost passed right over them before coming back. "Is this braille?" He picked up a sheet and felt the raised dots.

"Yep."

"How do you—?"

"Braille printer. I have one at work and love it so much I broke down and bought one. These are some papers I brought with me."

He ran is finger over the sheet. To him it felt like someone had glued tiny gravel all over a sheet of paper. "You can read this?"

"Yes. Obviously."

"Sorry. That wasn't a question, just a..." He had a million questions. How did she learn it? How long did it take? Questions she probably got all the time. "Could you teach me?"

"You want to learn how to read in *Braille*?"

"I don't think I'll live that long. Just tell me how it works."

"Okay. It's a grid system, each cell has six positions, two across and three down. The first letters of the alphabet are made up by changing around the top four positions. Then by adding the bottom row, you can make the rest."

"So everything is spelled out? Letter for letter?"

"That would be level one. There's a more advanced short hand. Combinations and contractions for words, other short cuts to decrease the length of a document."

"Very cool. It's like invisible ink and you're the only one who can see it."

"I guess. I like the way you say *see* it. Because I do see, I just do it with my hands instead of my eyes."

He smiled, put the papers down on the desk and put his hands on her waist.

"Thanks for coming," she said, running her hands up his chest until she held his face and drew him down for a kiss.

It was short and incredibly sweet and even so, it had his blood heating. "I like how you do that," he said.

"You like how I kiss?"

"That too, but I like how you take my face."

She smiled. "I do that so I can find you, make sure I hit the mark I'm aiming for."

"Doesn't matter why," he said, his arms banding around her. "I just like it."

THEY RETURNED to the kitchen and Ryan offered to show Luke the deck he'd helped his dad add on the back. He'd gone about it under the guise of asking for advice. Luke had a feeling he was about to *get* some advice of the brotherly kind.

Luke went out ahead of Ryan. He took in the roughly ten by twenty-foot deck. It was pretty straight forward and didn't look at all new. Ryan came out, leaned his forearms on the deck railing.

"The deck looks good to me," Luke said. "Feels solid. Level."

"Yeah. It's good. Wasn't too hard."

An awkward moment passed between them and Luke got the distinct feeling Ryan had come out here to give him the don't hurt my little sister or else warning. Luke understood that and was happy to let him say it, but he wasn't going to open the door for him.

"She was a warrior growing up," Ryan finally said.

Not at all what he'd expected and Luke looked over at the man.

"So strong, so damned determined. Everything and anything. And it didn't matter, nothing was going to stop her."

"She told me about the baseball."

Ryan groaned and his face looked pained. "That was awful. Seeing her face bloody was worse than the punishment I got. Anyway..." Ryan leaned his forearms on the iron railing. "I guess I've worried about her more since her divorce."

Luke straightened. That was news to him. All the times they'd talked and she hadn't mentioned it.

"You didn't know. Well." Ryan, dropped his chin to his chest and slowly shook his head. "I've stepped in it now, might as well keep going. Look, to say she wouldn't appreciate this would be an understatement, but... he did a real number on her." Ryan shifted, the set of his jaw harboring a lot of anger. "He came here, my wife and I went up there. I didn't think he was such an asshole."

Luke watched Ryan's fingers tighten around the glass in his hand. "But he was."

"Yep." Ryan took a drink, then slowly turned his head, blue eyes, darker and not as clear as Ava's stared at him. "I hope you're not an asshole."

So do I, Luke thought. And somehow, for maybe the first time, he didn't think he was.

After the cake was served and the handful of birthday presents opened, he led Ava through the cool night air to his truck.

"Well that was fun," Ava said, pulling her seatbelt across her. Her face was tight as she dropped her head back against the head rest.

Luke started the truck, put it in drive. "It was fun. Sorry for spilling the beans. I didn't intend to."

"I know. It's okay. You covered it pretty well." She blew out a long breath. "I think I talked my mom off the ledge. For now."

When they stopped at the next light, Luke looked at her profile. "But they'll use it to pressure you into not going back."

"Maybe. Doesn't matter. They have plenty of ammo. What did you and Ryan talk about? And please don't say me."

"Okay. I won't say it."

"Good grief. Did you guys draw swords? Have a standoff over my virtue?"

"Nah. It wasn't all that bad. He actually… Well—"

"What?"

It was right there, this need to confront her. To ask her why she hadn't told him she'd been married. "I was just going to say he handled things with a lot more finesse than I did in the same situation."

"Ahh…" Hannah mentioned something about over-bearing brothers. "I thought she meant Nick. I didn't think she was talking about you."

"Well, let's just be clear. Nick *was* the worst. But I… I had my own moment. But we had our reasons for not trusting McKinney. Anyway—"

"Oh, no. You started down this path. What did you do?"

He made a face she couldn't see.

"Did you hit him?" Her face swung around to his. "You *did*, didn't you? Oh, my gosh. You actually fought him." She laughed. "What is it with you guys?"

"We look after our baby sisters. It's code."

"It's code." She scoffed. "More likely you're all just a bunch of head-butting rams."

He laughed along with her but what Ryan had told him weighed heavily.

What had happened? Maybe it was none of his business but she'd been hurt, damn it. If Ryan had it right, and Luke had no reason to think he didn't, Ava had been hurt. And didn't that have something to do with him? With them? Had he hurt her physically? His hands tightened on the wheel at the thought.

Had she left him? Kicked him out? Had he left her? Broken her heart? He couldn't imagine anyone walking away from her.

It wasn't that he was bothered by it, but he wanted her to tell him. To let him in.

"So whatever he said wasn't too terrible? Luke?"

They stopped at a light and he looked at her, looking at him, saw the question in her eyes with a hint of worry.

"Nah. Just the basic threats a big brother gives the man who's..." Dating his sister? Sleeping with his sister? Falling in love with his sister?

"Seeing his sister?" Ava offered.

"Exactly." He turned up the song on the radio, another country tune.

"I'm so completely stuffed," Ava said, as they pulled up in front of the cabin. "Why did you let me have two pieces of cake?"

"Am I supposed to answer that?"

"No and I don't think I can concentrate on braille right now. Okay if we do it later?"

"Sure." He parked in front of the cabin, turned off the engine but made no move to get out. When Ava did, he stayed her with a hand on her arm. If they went in, they'd end up in bed and as much as he wanted that, he needed to get this out of the way first.

"Ava, I have to ask you something."

"Okay. You want to do it here?" she asked when he remained silent.

"Yeah." He took her hand, thinking this was harder than he'd thought but he was in it now. What if she said she was still in love with him? That wasn't something he'd considered. The possibility forced him to face some uncomfortable feelings.

"Luke?"

"Okay. So here's the thing. I wasn't going to ask. I thought, nah, she'll tell me if she wants me to know, but..."

"What?"

"Something your brother told me, and you can tell me it's none of my business, but..."

"But what? What is it?"

"He told me you'd been married."

29

Fighting for calm, Ava closed her eyes, slowly shook her head. "He had no right to tell you that."

"Maybe not. What I'm wondering is why you didn't tell me."

"Why would I?"

"Why *would* you? *Seriously*?"

"Seriously." Ava sucked in a breath and turned so she wasn't facing him anymore. She pressed a hand to her stomach. "It didn't work out. Why does it matter?"

"Why? Because it's a part of who you are? Because we're sleeping together? Because I care about you? There's a few," he shot. "Take your pick."

Ava wasn't being fair and she knew it. But damn it, she hadn't wanted him to know and right at this minute she welcomed the anger, the indignation.

"Did he tell you why? That Blake was blind and after he got his sight back he decided he didn't want to be with me anymore? Because I was too much trouble? Did Ryan tell you that he didn't want to be married to a blind person?"

When Luke didn't answer, she went on, turning to him, a smile trembling on her lips. "I'm sure you've heard the expression 'love is blind,' well, turns out it's true."

"Why are you making a joke about it?"

"It *was* a joke! *I* was a joke because I never saw it coming. Is that what you want to know?" She waved her hand like she could wave it away. "It was over a year ago, and really, it was over long before the papers were signed." She reached for the door handle.

"Is it? Is it over? I think you owe me that much, because if you're still hung up on him, if that's why you need a change and Italy and—"

"*What?* No! No." She let go of the door handle and turned back to him. "That's not it. That's…" She closed her eyes, pressed her fingers against them. "I didn't want to air my dirty laundry."

"Sounds like it was his dirty laundry, not yours."

"I guess it seemed like he got mine dirty by association. You know what they say. It's not just one person. It takes two."

"I don't believe that. What if I married a serial killer? Would that be half my fault?"

She stared across the truck. "Well, that was a weird place to go."

"Sorry. I just watched the Ted Bundy thing and it happens. And for the record, those women could see, and they didn't *see* it. And even though you didn't ask, I'm forty–two and I've managed to slip around, avoid and evade any serious sort of relationship with a woman. I figured I always would. You're making me rethink."

"Luke." Ava shook her head because she honestly didn't know what to do with this man and how he made her feel.

"Just tell me why," he said more gently.

"Because the man I thought loved me decided I was too disabled to spend his life with. Or maybe it was just that as soon as he could see me, he..." She raised her hand, let it fall. It still hurt, Ava thought, just to say it. Not because it was Blake, but it hurt, not being wanted.

"You don't really believe that," Luke said, touching her cheek. "Not the disabled crap or the other. You're too damn smart for that, Ava."

"I don't have to believe it," she lifted her face toward his. "I just have to remember."

"Oh, baby." He drew her hand to his lips. "Come on. Let's go inside."

"No. We should finish it. Just because I don't have feelings for him anymore doesn't mean I can forget it. It doesn't mean I just forget the hurt. And I'm not looking to feel that again, I'm really not."

"Well," he said, still holding her hand. "That's a problem because I know I'm falling in love with you."

"You... Don't—Don't say that. You can't."

"I can and I am. And I can see that shocks you

which tells me I need to work on my communication skills. It also maybe makes you want to run which makes me wonder why you'd be so opposed to hearing that."

HER HEART WAS POUNDING in her throat and she wanted to run. To just get out of this truck and run from the pain his words could bring somewhere down the road. She tried to pull her hand away but he didn't let her go.

She shook her head. Wanted to say, please don't make me fall in love with you. "You don't. If you're thinking about a future with me, you'd be asking for a lifetime of frustration and trust me, it would get old. The novelty wears off."

"Did you just refer to yourself as a fucking novelty? You could give me and yourself more credit than that."

She hadn't expected the anger. Or the hurt she heard under it, and shook her head again. "You're right. I'm sorry."

"Ava, your ex obviously had a problem. And it was *his* problem, not yours. But I don't care about him. I care about you. I see *you*."

"But I don't see *you*," she said. "And maybe that's the problem, will always be my problem. Because how can I trust, *really* trust if I can't see?"

"I don't know, Ava. I don't know." His thumb rubbed over the back of her hand. "But for someone who's brave enough to step off, literally, into the unknown every single day, I think you'll figure it out."

"And if I don't? I don't know if I can have sex with you, sleep with you, and then go back to New York like it was nothing. I don't think I'm the fling type. And see?" she said before he could respond. "Even now I don't know if you're smiling or frowning, if you're frantically looking for an exit, trying to think of a way to untangle yourself. I can't see if your face is shocked or amused."

"I'm not shocked," he said, taking one of her hands and laying it on his cheek, just over the edge of his lips. He took her other hand and held it to his chest just over his heart. "I'm not amused. And I don't know that I'd categorize this as a fling. A fling implies you can take it or leave it and that's not how I feel when it comes to you." He guided her fingers over his lips, turned her hand and pressed a kiss there. "You can feel this, trust this."

"And if I can't?" Her lips trembled. So did her heart. "Because if I'm honest Luke, I don't know if I can or if I even want to."

"Ava," Luke started.

"I don't *want* to want you," Ava said, cutting off whatever he might say. "I don't want to need you. Does that make sense?"

"Yeah. It does. But how about we work on the *want to* for now?" He leaned in, kissed each cheek, then her lips. "And we tackle the rest later?"

Ava started to say something else but Luke was kissing her, drawing her in inch by inch. Even with the console between them, maybe because of it, she suddenly just wanted to be closer. Wanted to lean on him, be comforted. Once again Luke had taken it. She hadn't exactly thrown it out there, the news of her ex, but he'd handled. More than handled it.

He thought he was in love with her? She shivered at the idea of ever believing in that again. And she wouldn't dwell on it. She couldn't dwell on anything with Luke's mouth making love to hers, his hands sliding up and into her hair.

He held the back of her head with one hand, deepened the kiss, and something inside her opened and she didn't have the strength to stop it. His scent filled her, swamped her and pulled her under as his lips cruised along her throat while his fingers traveled seductively over her breast.

"Let's go inside," he said.

"Let's."

"It's dark," Luke said, as he carried her across the cabin back to his bed. "Just the smallest bit of moonlight."

It was something he'd started doing, describing what he saw, what he didn't see. His mouth hovered a breath from hers. "I can see the outline of you, a hint of shadows."

Luke laid her on his bed and came over her. Before she could reach for him, he snaked his quick and clever hand up and under her lightweight sweater.

"Mmm. Are these the moves you were telling me about?"

"Some of them. But I've got new moves just for

you." He leaned in, brushed his lips over hers, retreated, then brushed again.

"You don't need to see for this, Ava," he said, lifting his head. "You don't need to see me. Just feel me. Feel me touching you."

No. She didn't need to see for this. She was feeling everything. The hot smooth skin of shoulders, his back. The man and the muscle. How was she supposed to form a coherent thought when this man, vibrating with strength, gently ran his rough hands over every inch of her body? While he touched, kissed, and stroked, all the while telling her what he saw and all the ways he wanted to touch her.

It was a slow, skillful seduction and different than other kisses they'd shared. This kiss was knowing what was coming. Knowing what he did to her body, what he could make her feel. Knowing what their joining would be. It aroused her as much as it scared her. But little by little, the arousal overtook everything else. Her need to get closer, to touch him, to feel him inside her.

"Get it off," she demanded and frantically tugged at his shirt.

He stripped it over his head and she sighed as her hands raced over him. His shoulders, his back. All that power and strength. Just for her. At least for now, it was just for her.

Laughing, they struggled to get off each of their jeans. Tugging, bumping hips and hands, and eventually going over the edge to land with a thump on the floor.

"Ouch," he said, landing under her and rapping his elbow on the night stand in the process.

"Thank goodness for the rug."

"Yeah. Not feeling so thankful for the table here."

"Aww. Poor, baby." She nibbled at his throat, glided her hands down his chest, his abs. She stroked his erection still caught under the fabric of his jeans and smiled when he groaned.

As if she weighed nothing, he lifted her up, flipped their positions so that he was on top. He wouldn't rush, Luke thought. Not this time. Tapping into whatever patience he'd developed, all the skill he possessed, he would use both tonight. He would take it slow until they both lost themselves in each other.

"I wish I could see you," she whispered into the dark. "Not to see what you look like, but I wish I could see your eyes looking at me."

"You see me, Ava. Maybe more than anyone else ever has." Luke stroked her skin, shoulders to thighs. "This is me looking at you. You can feel that."

He lingered over every dip and curve, filled himself with her taste. Used his lips, his hands, driving her mad. Her breath hitched and her eyes closed when he tugged, then slid her underwear down and away.

He was mad for her, for Ava, as he came over her, took her mouth in a long, greedy kiss. There was a shocking flash of heat as their bodies joined. Like a fiery arrow, it shot right through him. Her arms came around him and she arched up to meet him, locking their bodies even more tightly together, making them one. And then there was no slowing down.

Slick with sweat, they moved, flesh slapping flesh until he felt her tighten around him. He filled his hands with her breasts, moved his body in time with hers, fitting himself to her like a key in a lock. Yes, she saw him, he thought. And when he slid inside, when their bodies were joined, he saw himself too. He made love to her slowly then fast. Both were perfect. Both were more than he'd ever had before. More than he'd ever felt before.

He hadn't known, really known, what he'd been looking for when he came here. Peace maybe. Resolution with the family. But looking at Ava sleeping beside him he knew whatever it was he'd been looking for he'd found it in her. And more than anything, he wanted to be the man she needed.

The flash of his own orgasm was so staggering he rode on the high thinking he might not survive it and in the moment didn't care. It snagged the air right from his throat and he collapsed, unable to move, and lay with his face buried in Ava's hair.

When they were finally breathing evenly, he took her into his side and held her against him. "We should get off the floor."

"We should. In a minute."

"Yeah. In a minute," he said, happy where he was.

She traced her finger over his shoulder, down his bicep. "Do you have any tattoos?"

Luke rose up slightly and looked down at her. "What do you know about tattoos?"

She smiled. "I've read about them. So do you?"

He brought her hand to the inside of his arm, sliding it along the length of his forearm. "I have one here."

"What is it?"

"Just words. Yea, though I walk through the valley of the shadow of death."

She traced her finger along his skin as he read.

"What about the rest? I will fear no evil?"

"Would you believe they ran out of ink?"

"Hmm."

She continued touching him, not challenging him on the ink, not pressing him on the why. She never looked at him like he was broken and he was coming to realize she wouldn't think of him as broken or weak even if he did tell her. That he hadn't wanted the rest of the verse because he had feared evil.

"Are all the memories bad?"

"No. Not all." He took her hand and put it to his cheek so she would know it. Her thumb moved the slightest bit to brush over his bottom lip. And it seemed like Gary was right. Because here he was talking to Ava, saying things he'd never said to anyone and feeling lighter.

He drew her hand higher, held one finger to a spot where his forehead met his hairline. "There's the scar from that clothing rack I ran into. It's just there, above my hairline."

Ava felt for it, found it and traced her finger over it. About an inch long, barely there. His skin was warm under her hand, warm and smooth and she moved her fingers over his face, felt the sandpaper of a day's growth on his jaw and around his mouth. "Do you have any others?"

"A few." He guided her hand to his shoulder. "One there. A bullet. Just a graze. Another on my leg. Nothing too bad."

"I'm glad."

"I do trust you, Luke," she said after a long moment. "In a way I never thought I would trust again. You're good and honorable and kind. You are," she said when he tried to interrupt.

"You care about your family, you care enough to bury a kitten and search for the others. But...I was lost for a while. Really lost. I couldn't find my footing, my happiness. I felt robbed somehow, and misled. He made me uncertain of myself, that was the worst part. But little by little, I got it back. I don't want to lose it again."

She said the words so softly it nearly broke his heart. And at the same time he felt a strike of jealously that she'd felt so strongly for another man. "No. I wouldn't want you to lose it. Wouldn't want you to lose anything." He pressed his lips to her shoulder, gathered her in.

"I don't want what happened before to happen again and at the same time I don't want my past to dictate my future."

"Then don't let it."

"It's not that easy," she said.

He knew it wouldn't help to make promises. To tell her he'd never hurt her. It actually shocked him that he was so sure he wouldn't.

Luke's heart broke with the pain and anguish in her voice. He wanted to beat the man he knew had hurt her but at the same time knew if he hadn't that she wouldn't be here with him now.

"I was with someone for five years and he walked

away like I was nothing, like none of it meant anything. And you expect me to believe this is different in five weeks?"

"I do. In five weeks. Five days. Five minutes. But I don't think it would matter if it was five years or fifty if you've decided every man is just like him."

"I don't think you're like him. But I'm afraid. Afraid I'll take the chance, that I'll reach out and take hold and you'll be there. And then one day, you'll be there wanting to leave but not leaving exactly because of who you are. And I won't even see it. I won't even know. I'll never know if I'd been able to see his face if I would have known he didn't love me anymore."

"Would it have changed things if you'd seen it?"

"I don't know. Maybe. Maybe it's impossible to trust, to really *know*, if you can't see a person's eyes."

If someone had asked him a week ago, a month ago, if he wanted someone to trust him, to depend on him, he'd have said no. Hell, no. But now...

"He actually said that," she said. "That there was a different kind of connection looking into someone's eyes and having them look back at you."

"And you believed him?"

"Why wouldn't I?"

"Well believe me, Ava, when I tell you he was wrong." He moved over her, settled between her legs. "I'm looking at you, right at your eyes, and I'm feeling everything. All."

He kissed her, taking his time, loving her, wondering how he could make her believe he'd never hurt her? And more, how could he convince her she had more power to hurt him?

Ava woke hours later to an empty bed and the steady sound of sand paper sliding over wood. She got up and made her way toward the sound— the bathroom. She stopped in the doorway. "Hey. I fell asleep."

The sanding stopped. "I noticed. Sorry, I didn't think this would wake you up."

"I don't think it did. I just woke up. What are you working on?" She took a step to move farther in.

"Hang on. I've got stuff everywhere."

She waited for him to move it then walked in and leaned back against the sink. "What are you working on?"

"Ah. Sanding the baseboard trim before I put a final coat of clear coat on it."

"Such a perfectionist. Can I help?"

Luke laid down his tool, looked at the sleeves of his T-shirt hanging well below Ava's elbows. The bottom edge hung to the middle of her thighs and the neck was so big and stretched out it hung off one shoulder. "That's very sexy night wear you have on."

"Is it? It's soft." She pulled the V-neck up to her nose and sniffed. "It smells like you. Can I help or not?"

He stood and moved to her. "I'm not really in the mood to work anymore."

"No?"

"No." He took her face in his. "You're so beautiful." When she said nothing, he ran his thumbs over her cheeks, slid his fingers in her hair. "You really have no idea, do you?"

"No. And it wouldn't mean much if I did since I have nothing to compare it to."

He continued stroking her. Her hair, her face. Down her arms. "Your eyebrows are like these delicate little feathers," he said, coming back to her face. "Your eyes are so blue, the exact shade of a summer sky. Your cheeks are like cream then they get these splashes of pink when you get embarrassed." He brushed his lips over her cheek. "When we make love."

He traced a finger lightly down her nose. "Cute little nose. Rosy lips that I can't look at without wanting to kiss. They move a little when you're counting steps. It drives me crazy."

"You're very observant."

"Not much I haven't noticed about you." He leaned in, nuzzled her neck, then made a slow, lazy path to her breast. "But I'm up for more study."

With one of her hands still caught in his, he brushed a strand of hair back from her shoulder. The touch led to a kiss and the kiss to her leading him back to bed where they made slow love and after, he slept until morning.

When he woke, Ava was beside him. Her hair lay wild, half off her pillow, over her shoulder. Something had happened to him the night before. Something much more than sex. He craved her like no other woman. He knew that with a certainty that shocked him. Something had clicked into place when he hadn't been looking for it. Hadn't even wanted it. But here she was and he wasn't sure he could ever go back.

Yet the look he'd seen on her face when they'd talked in the car, all that heartbreak and distress so plain to see in the slant of her brows and downturned lips, it made him wonder if he would have a choice.

31

Two days later, Luke picked Ava up for dinner at his sister's and they decided to park at the cabin and walk the new path. It was really coming together. The gravel had been delivered and spread. Soft rope served as a guide with braille plaques every so often.

Luke showed her the finished pathway with the rope and the braille. Still needed a few more. "Still needs some smoothing and maybe a warning edging of a different stone so you'd know if you were off track."

"You could, but I think with the rope it's enough. It's wonderful, Luke. I feel like I could run."

"Go ahead." With the rope in her hand she walked faster, then picked a light jog. When she went back to a walk and he caught up with her, she was breathing hard and wearing a bright, broad smile.

"That was fun. I don't feel comfortable going all out

like I do in the pool but I could definitely get some exercise with something like that."

Something *like* that, but not *that*? Was it too much to hope that she could see herself here? "Glad you like it."

When they stepped into Hannah's they were assaulted with sounds and smells and movement. Everyone seemed to be talking at once. The space felt large and open, the kitchen voices blended over other voices a little farther in front of her, along with the sound of a basketball game.

Greeting them, Hannah touched her arm and took the pie from Luke.

"You can loosen that grip you've got on her," Stephen said, from across the room. "Unless you're afraid she'll get away."

"Maybe he is."

Nick, Ava was pretty sure.

"Hey, Ava." Hannah hugged her, then heard her kiss her brother's cheek. "I love you, but get out. Boys and babies are in the other room."

"What? You think y'all are the only ones who can cook?"

"No," she said sweetly. "But we *are* the only ones who can cook without eating it all in the process. Now get out."

"We've already lodged a protest," a male voice yelled from the adjoining room.

"I'm good," she said when Luke didn't move. She gave his hand a squeeze. "Go."

Ava felt the loss of his big warm hand around hers but she smiled. It was nice to have the touch of a man that you missed when it was gone. More than nice.

"Here. We can put you to work." Hannah guided her to a bar stool at a waist high counter.

She heard someone open and close a refrigerator to her left, felt the cool air just before someone set a dish on the counter near her left hand.

"Here's the salad. Just need to add the strawberries and the pecans."

"I can do the strawberries," Ava said.

"Thanks," Hannah said.

She heard clatter of a wooden cutting board being placed in front of her, then the slide of a plastic carton and the clunk of a knife. And she went to work.

She enjoyed their company. All of them. And she'd often thought she could see herself becoming more than just friends with Hannah, but *really* good friends. If she was going to be here long term.

BY THE TIME they said the blessing and got all the kids served or tied down in high chairs, Luke was starving.

He dug into the parmesan covered chicken. "Mmm. This tastes just like..."

"Mom's?" Hannah said. "I know. I got her recipe box. I made some copies for Nick and Zach."

"Lot of good that does us," Mia said, grinning at her husband.

"One day we won't be outnumbered and we'll both

be cooking up a storm. Until then?" Nick scooped up a forkful of rice covered with the creamy cheese sauce and toasted his sister.

"I can make some copies for you too if you want," Hannah said to Luke.

"Oh. Well, sure. I guess I could try."

"Whenever you want. No pressure."

Luke noticed the little look his sister shot Ava. Did she think he and Ava were going to be cooking their mom's recipes together?

It was a nice thought.

Nora unbuckled Will from his highchair and handed him off to Zach. She must have said something only he heard because he laughed and leaned over to kiss her cheek.

Luke smiled watching the two of them. Obviously in love and riding the high. Just five short weeks ago and he hadn't been able to relate. Now, he looked at Ava and... She had him, he thought. She could wring every beat from his heart with nothing more than a look, a smile. And he didn't even know how in the hell it had happened.

He tried to picture her working in New York. Sliding her stick side to side, as she made her way along crowded sidewalks at a clipped pace. Busy like all the other people in the city with things to do and places to be. She probably wore a suit to work. Long slim pants with a tucked in blouse or a skirt that no doubt had men taking advantage of the fact she couldn't see them staring. He sincerely hoped there was someone there at the UN ready and able to pop the lookers on the head.

No, he'd rather be the one to do it. To walk her to work, not because she needed him to but just because he liked the feel of her hand on his arm. He'd listen to her voice rise and flow in a foreign language and it wouldn't matter a damn that he had no idea what she was saying.

She had a gracefulness that just screamed for a suit and heels and it all fit. Her job, her look, the city. But, he thought, watching her now, she also fit here. Wearing jeans, a casual shirt and boots. Riding horses, listening to the creek, helping a child like Kylie. Spending her nights in his bed. Waking up beside him.

"Here. If you're done eating, take him." Before he could resist, Mia handed him his nine-month-old nephew who promptly stomped on his balls. "Dude, your shoes are too hard to be doing that." He held the baby up, removing kicking feet from crotch range. "Is this the spitter?"

"No, that was Sam," Nick said. "Max has a tiny birthmark near his right eye."

"Huh." Luke examined the kid he was holding then he stood to save the glass of water the baby was going for, and to save his balls.

"I can help clean," Ava said, standing.

"Nope. You're our guest. It's not much. Stephen is the resident dishwasher loading expert."

"Because there's a right way to load a dishwasher," he said.

Hannah waved her hand. "Have at it, expert."

Luke went to Ava's side. "Come one, you can help me with this one." She took his arm and he led her to the couch.

Nora carried dishes to the kitchen while Zach wrangled Will into submission. Nick held two babies while Mia made bottles.

Hannah rescued Mitchell from his highchair while Stephen tackled the kitchen.

"Bottles coming," Mia said over her shoulder.

"Here," Luke said as soon as Ava was seated beside him and passed her the baby.

"Wait," she said but already had her hands on the baby.

"You don't have the same parts as me and he's intent on kicking my balls off."

"I don't have much experience with babies."

"I guarantee you've got as much as me." The baby started crying and Ava lifted him higher so that he stood on her lap.

"Hi, baby," she said, in that voice people used when they talked to babies. "Your dinner's coming. Yes, it is. Luke, what's he doing? Help me."

The crying had stopped and though he still didn't look happy, he was watching Ava intently. "He's just looking at you. That talking thing is working. I hope none of you is thinking of having any more," Luke said as the chorus of crying from the others reached a peak.

"We only have one," Zach said in defense.

"And we only have one," Hannah added, walking out of the room with Mitch.

Everyone looked at Nick.

"What? So we did ours all in one bang. One day you guys will be jealous."

Mia handed Luke a bottle.

"What do you want me to do with this?"

"Just hand it to him. He knows what to do." Luke was skeptical as he held the bottle to the kid's hands but sure enough, he took the bottle, plopped down in Ava's lap, then kicked back like he was in a lazy boy.

Mia handed out the other two bottles and in seconds there was silence.

Talk turned to the new Star Wars movie releasing soon and that led to an old debate.

"Of course Luke always insisted he got to be Luke," Zach said, still holding a grudge.

"Well, duh," Luke said. "That's my name. I sure as hell wasn't going to be Han or Chewy and call you Luke. That doesn't even make sense."

"It does make sense," Zach argued, "because Dallas made a rotating schedule."

Mia rolled her eyes. "You know you guys sound like you're ten."

"Thanks, babe."

When the babies were all asleep or nearly so, Hannah got a roaring fire going. The women got into a deep discussion about an HBO mini-series, and the men took the heat of the fire as long as they could before escaping outside to a comfortable sixty degrees.

Luke stood at the wooden porch railing, trying to broach the topic of asking Stephen to do something with his money. It wasn't that he didn't like the guy. He did. But after punching him in the face, it was still hard to ask his brother-in-law for a favor.

"So. McKinney," he finally said.

"Yeah?" Stephen turned his head.

"I was thinking... I've got this money, just kind of sitting around and..."

Zach snickered from his seat on the swing.

"What?" He asked, tossing a look at his brother. Then he noticed Nick's matching smirk. "*What*? Not like I can't figure out something. Just thought I'd get some tips from the money guru. Forget it."

"Relax, bro. We're not laughing at you," Zach said. "We're laughing with you."

Stephen smiled, hooked a thumb over his shoulder. "These two gave me their money a long time ago."

"Huh. Well. I'm not *giving* you my money. Just maybe some advice."

Stephen shrugged. "Whatever."

"Man knows what he's doing," Zach said. "Why make it harder than it has to be."

"It's not like I can turn it into gold or anything," Stephen said. "But I can give you some ideas, depending on what you want to do with it."

"Well, it's not doing anything sitting in the bank, that's for damn sure."

"What? You don't have it buried in the yard?"

"Bite me," Luke said to Zach. "I was also thinking

that maybe Hannah might need some help going forward. Even after the cabins are finished. By the time everything is finished, things are going to start needing repairs. Then there's the horses. You've got your own stuff going on, plus a kid. I just figured maybe she could use someone for the heavy lifting full-time."

"Then you're thinking you're going to stay around here?"

"Yeah. I guess I am. Definitely need to talk to Hannah about it. It's not like I'm looking to move in on you guys. I'll get a house, or apartment. Something. But there's still ramps to be built everywhere. Basic upkeep. Just that windstorm we had last week brought down limbs and pinecones all over the area I started prepping for the wooded path.

"I don't know. Maybe there's not enough stuff, but anyway that's just what I was thinking." He took a sip of his beer. Nobody said anything and he finally got so uncomfortable he looked back over his shoulder at the other men. "What? You want to say that's a stupid idea? Go ahead." He shrugged. "It's not like I'm married to it I was just throwing it out there."

"Hannah's been wanting to ask you for weeks," Stephen said, slapping a hand down on Luke's shoulder. "She was afraid to mention it. Said she didn't want you to feel obligated."

"No, shit?"

"And the animals. You know she was thinking about getting donkeys? Rescue donkeys?"

"Rescue donkeys?" Zach said. "I didn't even know that was a thing."

"I've heard about the donkeys," Stephen said. "And the goats and the rabbits. Newest thing is chickens."

Nick lowered his beer. "Is she building a riding camp or a petting farm?"

"Little of both, I think. She wants the kids to have a lot of experiences."

"Well, there'll be upkeep for sure," Stephen said. "And it's a lot of land. Lots to do and plenty of room. From what Hannah said, you've pretty much paid for the cabin you're in now. Plus the labor to build four more— and you know four is going to turn into eight."

Luke nearly groaned at the thought of building seven more cabins. He was going to have to bring in some help to get all that done. He knew some guys who didn't mind physical labor. A few of them might even benefit from it as he had. That was an idea.

"Ava's always giving me these ideas, and they're good ideas. Ways to make things more tactile, as she says."

And he was starting to see the world as Ava did. Thinking through things like people who had different needs than he did. He'd noticed the path debris walking here with Ava. Things he would have stepped over or around, or simply kicked out of his way, were a hazard. Stepping on a pinecone you didn't expect was like stepping on a rolling log. Not to mention making it impossible for kids in wheelchairs.

"I think it sounds like a solid plan," Stephen said. "Talk to Hannah. She's the boss."

"Yeah."

"Also sounds like Hannah might not be the only reason you're thinking to stick around."

"I don't know what you mean."

"He means a woman, dumbass," Zach said. "The one in there right now who I guarantee is fielding questions from our wives about you."

AN HOUR LATER, they said their goodbyes and started the walk back to the cabin.

"Thanks for going," Luke said, taking her hand as they walked back.

"You're welcome. It was fun."

"And now look at you. City girl walking in the woods."

"I'm getting used to the change of pace. Kind of liking it."

"You were good with them. The babies. Their faces lit up every time you held them. It's the eyes. I'm telling you."

She smiled, tilted her head up to the sky as they walked. The smooth rope slid through her left hand and she was confident Luke wouldn't let her fall. It was nice. So nice that she knew she needed to deal with these feelings she had for Luke instead of trying to ignore them. Especially since ignoring them wasn't working.

"I never did much babysitting, or any, obviously. But I used to think I might have children, then I was with Blake, but two blind parents..." She shrugged.

"We decided that wouldn't have been fair even if it had been feasible. Then when he got his sight back, I thought maybe, but... It wasn't meant to be. He called me not long ago, to tell me he was getting married. To the woman he'd starting seeing while we were still together. Wanted me to hear it from him. And that she's pregnant."

"Asshole." Luke pictured how Ava had looked, stroking Sam's head. Running her finger over his small hand, over each finger. It was a beautiful sight and at the same time he tensed with anger at a faceless man who'd dared to hurt her.

She shrugged again and he was sure she didn't know how much pain was written so clearly on her face.

"I'm not bitter. Not anymore. He showed his true colors and I wouldn't want to be with him, have children with him or anything else. What about you?"

"I don't know. Don't know that I've ever thought about it, but..." He let out a short laugh. "It's hard to be around them for more than five minutes and not think about it."

"Your family's great, you know. Feeling better about coming back?"

"Yeah. I am," he said, letting her shift away from that topic. They walked on a bit farther along the wooded path under a canopy of new tree growth. "I'm starting to think, to realize that all that friction when we were younger was more my fault than I ever admitted. And at the same time that they blamed me a lot less than I assumed they did. Hell, I'm not even sure they've been as concerned about me going over the edge as I thought they were."

"Maybe you were concerned about you going over the edge."

"Maybe so."

"I've been thinking also. That maybe my parents don't worry about me so much because I'm blind, but just because they worry."

"Sounds like we're making progress."

"It does."

"Maybe we should—" She froze. Cocked her head.

"What?"

"Shh. Listen. Do you hear that?"

It was a high, pitiful, mewling. Ava was already moving toward it, off the path using her cane.

"Wait."

The mewling got louder. Ava tripped but he was there to catch her. Then she was kneeling next to the cabin porch.

Luke dragged out his phone from his pocket and hit the flashlight feature. "Well, I'll be damned."

"Is it kittens?"

"It is. Kittens and Mama Tom. She must have thought this would be a good safe place." Luke reached in, pulled out one of the kittens. It squirmed and mewled. "This one seems strong. Here." He held it out to her.

Ava took the tiny body of fur, holding it close to her chest just under her chin. "She carried them all here? One by one? But it's so far." She continued to cuddle the baby while Luke reached in to check the others.

"Here." Ava held out the kitten. "Better put her back with mama. You think it's too cold?"

"It's a little chilly, but no." He reached in slowly, rubbed his hand over Tom's head. "They feel toasty warm in here. I'll bring out some blankets just in case."

It hit her. The mother cat who'd lost her babies and the little kittens violently killed in the chain of nature. And then for another reason she couldn't name, maybe Luke. Maybe talk of babies, but she felt tears gathering, hot and stinging in her eyes. "How did she know this would be safer?"

"I don't know that she did," Luke said. "But she took the chance."

Ava could tell by his voice, he was looking at her, not the kittens. "If I knew I could have something real, something *really* real, with you, of course it would be worth the risk, worth anything. But how would I ever know that?"

"I don't know, Ava. How do you ever really know?"

I know, she thought, because I've been there. *And I know even more because I never loved him like I love you.*

32

Luke woke from a dream, a slight variation on the standard. This one morphed from running through smoke in Afghanistan to running toward his Hannah teetering on the edge of a building, to running toward his parents. He never made it to any of them in time.

He looked at his watch. He'd only slept an hour. He reached for Ava but she wasn't there. He found her standing outside on the porch. "Hey. You sleep about as well as I do."

"I get days and nights mixed up sometimes. It's worse here, not being on a schedule. New York might be loud, but its night noise is different than its day noise. I thought I heard it raining."

Little droplets dripped off the roof. "Looks like you did."

"Yeah. I missed it."

"You know you could go stand in the bathroom

shower." He slipped his arms around her from behind, pulled her back against him and rested his chin on her shoulder. "I'll even stand with you."

"That's very generous of you. But it's not the same."

"No. I guess not." He'd spent plenty of days and nights in the rain. It didn't appeal to him, but for her, he'd stand in a soaking shower.

They stood together in a comfortable silence, listening to the light sounds of insects and intermittent dripping off the porch overhang. He ran his hands down her arms to her waist and around to hold her close from behind.

Ava drew a finger in absent circles over his bare arm. "I checked my email while I was up."

"Oh, yeah?"

"Yeah. I didn't get the consulate job. They decided not to fill it."

"I'm sorry. I know you wanted it." He was sorry, for her. But knowing she wouldn't be so far away...

"Thanks."

"You'll go back to the UN?"

"Yeah. That was in the email, too. A subtle nudge."

"To get your pretty ass back up there? Solve world peace?"

"Not my boss's exact words."

"Better not be." And God he wanted to ask her to stay, was figuring out a way to do that without asking her to sacrifice her life. Maybe he should offer to go to New York. He was sure he could do it, but for her? He'd be a fool not to try. Maybe he'd be smart to think on that, on all his options, before he posed them to Ava. She was a smart woman, a woman with a career and plans and fears on top of that.

And he didn't just think he was falling in love with her, he *was* in love with her. And he knew without a doubt she wasn't ready to hear it. A change of tactics was in order.

He slid his hand up her thigh, under the edge of the shirt. "You have anything on under here?"

Laughing, she batted his hand away. "Maybe."

He held her tight, finding what he was searching for and finding she did in fact have something on underneath. "A shame, but probably for the best." He took her hand and stepped down two steps. "Come on, I want to show you something."

"What? *Now*?"

"Yes, now."

"In the dark?"

"It's not any darker for you now than it is in the day, right?"

"No, but you—"

"Come on. I have excellent night vision."

She sighed. "Okay, but, wait. I need shoes."

"Don't need 'em."

"You might not, but I do."

"Nope. This is full service." He turned his back to her, guided her hands to his shoulders. "Let's go, Bennet. Hustle up."

. . .

Ava hopped on his back, and held tight around his neck as he loped across the grass. It wasn't more than a few minutes when he stopped.

"Okay. Here you go."

Her feet landed in soft, cool, grass; little droplets clinging to her ankles.

"Right around here. That's it. And put your hands here."

Rope. She felt thick, rough rope in both hands as her fingers closed around it. "A swing. You made a swing?"

"Yeah. Had some extra wood, some time. Thought the kids might like it."

She scooted back until she felt the solid line across the back of her upper thighs. "And you thought I might like it." She rose up on her toes, scooted her bottom onto the smooth, wooden seat.

Luke stood in front of her and covered both of her hands with his. "Do you?"

"I do."

Luke leaned in until his forehead touched hers. Did he know what that made her feel? Then he was gone, backing up and pulling her feet with him.

"Hold on."

She held tight as he drew her and the swing up and up then let her go flying back.

When she swung back toward him, he pushed her feet to keep her going, making her go higher.

"You know most people push a person on a swing from behind."

"Most people aren't looking at you."

Her heart dipped into her stomach. It wasn't just the swing, though there was a sweetness in that that struck her. It was more. It was the things he said, the way he said them. Blake had never said those things. Because he hadn't been able to see her? Because he didn't mean them? Did it even matter why? No, it didn't. Not when she was with Luke. Not since the first time Luke's lips had touched hers.

Nothing else mattered when she was with him. Luke could see her and he wanted her. They both knew he could still have her in his bed without carrying her out for a midnight swing. But here he was. Here they were.

Luke watched her tilt her head back, her hair float behind her. A soft smile rode her lips, as soft as the night air around them. The dream that had woken him slipped away under the night sky with Ava.

"Can you really see out here?"

"I can. The moon is out, bright enough to cast shadows on the ground."

"What's it like? The moon? I've always tried to imagine it."

Luke caught her feet and brought her and the swing to a stop. Then it was just the sound of the night.

"Hop up." He smoothly switched their positions, then pulled her down in his lap. "Now. The moon. It's a circle. Here, give me your hands. Put your thumbs together." He moved her fingers until she was making a circle with her thumbs and forefingers. Then he held it up until the circle she'd made matched the moon in the sky.

"It's there. Yep. That's it. Of course it's bigger in person, or so I've been told. Haven't actually been there. You can stare at the moon as long as you want and it doesn't hurt your eyes. I'd call it a silvery light. It's a fact it's cold in space, and it looks kind of cold; it doesn't blast heat like the sun. It's not a yellow light. Did that do anything for you?"

"Maybe." She lowered her hands, rested them on his arms. She mostly just liked hearing him talk. The way it made her feel knowing he wanted to give her something.

His legs were long enough he could hold onto her and still move them back and forth with his feet on the ground.

"How would you describe yellow?"

"Yellow. Hmm... Happy. Maybe because a lot of flowers are yellow. Lemons. Summer. Awake. And if it's a bright yellow, then hot, because of the sun."

"Red?"

"Ahh, red," he said with a hint of wistfulness in his voice. "A woman in a tight dress or a fast car. A little dangerous."

She laughed. "Why dangerous?"

"Oh, I don't know. Because dangerous women wear red? Long red nails that would cut a line down a man's chest."

"Seriously?"

She craned her neck back, shot him a grin over her

shoulder, and damn it, he felt that clutch in the belly again.

"Not me, personally. Just an impression. I'm giving you my impressions. And maybe dangerous because blood is red."

"Okay. That makes sense. Pink."

"Okay. Pink...A little girl laughing? Twirling in a dress. Your lips after I kiss you."

"Green?"

"Spring. Moss, grass, life. Leaves before they turn yellow and brown."

"I thought yellow was flowers."

"It can be. But this is a softer yellow. A gradual shift from green to yellow and orange, and sometimes red. Then brown and the leaves fall. Not all of them, but most of them."

"So brown would be leaves?"

"Sometimes. And a horses muzzle. A leather jacket. A saddle."

"And your eyes?"

"Yeah. How'd you—"

"My sister in-law told me. What about blue?"

"Your eyes," he said without hesitation. He didn't think he'd ever think of blue and not think of her eyes. "Like the sky. A clear blue sky on a summer day. Or any day really when it's bright and clear. Makes me want to fall in, swim around."

"Why swim?"

"Ahh... Maybe because water is blue? Not all water, but the most beautiful water, in my opinion. Water that's cool but not cold. Warm but not hot. The kind of water you'd want to dive into, float around in. That's your eyes. Makes me want to dive in, stay awhile."

She turned in his lap, caught his face in her palms. "I don't know what to say to you sometimes."

He didn't reply and she didn't need him to. For a minute she just held him there, his face in her hands, her fingers spread over his cheeks. When she leaned in, put her forehead to his it was like seeing, or she imagined it was. Like having that moment she'd read about when two people looked across a room and their eyes met. It was that. Except it was their hearts.

That's how it felt. Like she was seeing him, like they were seeing each other.

33

A week later, Ava was in the barn. So was
Luke. She couldn't be sure, but he seemed to
always be here when she was. Making sure
she didn't get hurt? Looking out for her? Instead of
getting her hackles up about him being overbearing
and overprotective, she smiled.

Especially when he ran a hand down the silky tail
of her hair as he had the habit of doing. She was still
getting used to it. To him and whatever was happening
between them. It seemed so easy, so natural. It fright-
ened her and it made her want to sing. It was as if she'd
crossed some boundary into the normal she'd always
yearned for. She didn't know how it could possibly last,
how every moment was so easy and natural.

Now that her dad was getting around a bit, she
spent most every evening with Luke. Sometimes she
cooked, sometimes he picked up food. They might sit
outside or take a walk over to the pastures to visit

with the horses. They talked about Hannah's camp, going over what he'd done that day, tossing ideas back and forth. And he was always, always touching her. Letting her know he was there. Holding her hand, not for the purpose of leading, but just holding.

He talked more about his childhood. Camping out in the backyard. A trip to Disney World. The night their parents had sat them down and dropped the bomb that they were having another baby *and* it was girl. Every time, she heard the love in his voice for his family, for the parents he missed. And sometimes she could feel the weight of his guilt and regret.

One night he pulled out a deck of cards, nearly making her cry when he slid one into her hand and she felt the raised bumps on it.

Special order from Amazon, he'd said. *You can show your gratitude by not beating me too badly.*

They'd played Gin then Gin Rummy and she had beaten him more than he'd beaten her. He made her laugh, made her smile. And when they came together in the dark, all her worries, all her doubts, that had grown inside her for the past year just dropped away.

Every time she woke with him beside her, she felt a jolt of happiness that stayed with her for hours. If he was trying to convince her she could trust her heart to him, he was doing a damn good job.

He used the hand he had around her ponytail to pull her in. Then kissed her in that way that never failed to make her limbs weak. She gripped the front of his jacket, for balance, and because she didn't want to let him go.

"Once again, harassing my students," Hannah said, passing them in the barn aisle.

Luke broke the kiss but didn't let go of the hold he had on her. "Just a little pep talk," he told his sister.

"Right. I didn't hear a lot of talking."

Ava gave him a playful shove. "Go find something to do."

"I like doing this," he said, sliding his hand down to give her bottom a light squeeze. She laughed and slapped at his hand.

"I'll see you later."

He pressed his lips to hers again, and then one last time. "Okay. Now I'll see you later."

Smiling, she listened as his boots clumped down the aisle until she couldn't hear him anymore.

"Well," Hannah said coming to stand beside her.

"Yeah. Well. Um..." Ava dropped her hand where she'd been touching her still tingling lips. She didn't know if Hannah was still looking at her and wondered if what she was feeling was written all over her face.

She also wondered what Hannah had seen on her brother's face, but shoved that small insecurity aside. "So, the lesson today," Ava said. "We're going to...um..."

"Jeez," Hannah said laughing. "Take a second to get your feet back under you. I don't think you'd be safe on a horse just yet."

"That obvious? Well, no offense, but your brother knows how to kiss."

"I'll take your word for it."

Ava listened as Hannah moved down the length of the horse, heard her patting him softly. Was she getting a vibe from Hannah? Was there something there? It hadn't occurred to her that Hannah would mind her being involved with Luke. "Hannah, if this bothers you at all, Luke and I…"

"Then what? You'll kick him to the curb?" Hannah asked in a teasing tone. "Relax. I'm totally joking when I tell him to leave you alone."

"Okay. I guess I'm just realizing I haven't thought about how you would feel about me sleeping with your brother." She closed her eyes. "And if you didn't know, I just told you."

"Oh, wow. *Really*? I never would have guessed it," Hannah said, her tone light and fun.

"Right."

"I just don't want you to get hurt. Or Luke. Either of you."

"I care about him. I think, no, I know, he cares about me. I'm not sure either of us is looking to go beyond that."

"Hmm. Well." Hannah patted Ava's shoulder. "If you're steady enough, let's get going."

As Ava walked into the tack room, Hannah thought, if you could see my brother's eyes when he looks at you, you'd know that whether he's looking for it or not, he more than cares.

34

"Will you just tell me where we're going?"

"Nope."

She growled and he laughed. She huffed and he reached over and took her hand.

"How's your dad?"

"Good. Itching to get up and around with Mom fighting him every step of the way. He took five steps this morning. I'd say if he doesn't start to move faster, my mom may kill him. They may kill each other."

"What about Maddie? Anything up with her lately?"

She started to tell him that asking her questions wasn't going to take her mind off where they were going, then remembered. "Oh! There is some gossip. My sister-in-law told me she was going to tell my brother she wanted to stop working and have a baby."

"Wow."

"Yeah. It's weird. I mean I'd be excited for them to

have a baby, but it's weird. I never thought Connie would consider not working. Not being a lawyer."

"Does that bother you?"

"No. It doesn't bother me, it's just... It's surprising."

"Well, like you said, things change. Our paths change."

"I guess." Thoughtful, she turned her face to the wind coming through the open window. Luke turned up the radio to a song she knew he liked.

"Well, look at that."

"What?"

"Someone knows the words to a country song."

"Do not."

"Do too. Unless you talk to yourself in the exact same words as Luke Bryan."

Ava put the window of Luke's truck all the way down. Luke turned up the music. Still holding his hand, she smiled to herself, and listened to Luke sing the tune in his deep voice. On the next chorus, she gave up and sang along making Luke laugh.

Several songs later, his truck stopped. Even with her window down, there wasn't much she could tell about where they were from the sounds because there weren't any. She opened her door and when Luke led her out of the truck a strong wind buffeted against her back. Wide open space? "Just tell me where we are."

"You're about to find out."

With her cane in one hand and the other on Luke's arm, they walked across cement. Maybe thirty steps then a short pause and they went through a door into a building. No more wind. More voices.

"Hey, what's up?" a male said in greeting.

"Not much," Luke replied and Ava heard hands slapping together.

"Glad you called, man. And you must be the birthday girl."

"Yes." She held out a hand that was sandwiched between two thick, hard palms for a quick shake.

"You ready for this?"

Luke's hand at her back gave the smallest tap, telling her the man was speaking to her. He did things like that. She couldn't really say when or how he'd started. How he even knew to do or how she knew how to read him. But he did. And she did.

"I don't know. Luke won't tell me what it is."

"Ahh, you son of a gun." The man chuckled. "You know she has to sign a waiver."

She swung her face to Luke's. "A waiver for what?"

Luke slid the hand on her back down to take her hand, reached around and took her other. "We're going skydiving. Happy birthday."

"We're going *what*?"

"You're not scared are you? You said you wanted to try it."

"Might," she said but her stomach was all kinds of butterflies. "I said I *might* want to try it. I can't believe you didn't tell me."

The man still standing close cleared his throat.

"Sometimes it's best not to think too much about it beforehand, you know?"

"See? And Harley here is an expert."

She huffed. "And maybe you told him to say that." The truth was, she did want to go skydiving. No way was she going to tell him that now. Not yet. "Fine. Where do I sign?"

An hour later they were in the air. The vibration of the plane was like nothing she'd ever felt and she'd flown plenty of times. It was enough to make her teeth rattle. And the way they were dipping and rising, this plane felt more like a toy than something that should actually be in the air. She figured it was good that she couldn't see the ground beneath her.

"You okay?" Luke yelled over the noise and adjusted the goggles on her face.

"Yeah."

"You're going to love it. Trust me."

Nerves mixed with excited anticipation as a line of sweat trickled down her back. Luke held her hand that she knew was sweaty. "I guess you've done this a few hundred times."

"A few thousand." Luke grazed the back of his hand over her cheek. "Turn around." Not waiting for her to move, he turned her the way he wanted. He tugged on the straps on her back and the ones around her thighs. He spoke calmly next to her ear, telling in precise language each and every step he was taking. What he was checking then going over the steps of the jump with her again. His care and patience loosened another something inside her.

When he was satisfied, they sat again on the metal bench seat. "Talk to me. Tell me something."

"You look hot in goggles. And this jumpsuit..."

She shook her head at him then was immediately distracted by the whine of the door as it lowered. She wanted to say, *wait, time out*, ask one more question but before she could make her mouth work, they were scooting on their bottoms toward open air. Another second and her legs were hanging over the plane edge into the unknown. The force of the wind ripping at the fabric covering her legs and her heart tripled.

"Meet you at the bottom," Luke said, giving her hand a squeeze and then his hand was gone. Was *he* gone? She no longer felt him beside her. The thought sent a jolt of fear through her. Luke gone, falling through the sky. But there was no time for worry. The instructor's voice was in her ear.

"Three, two, one. Bombs away."

And then she was falling. If she'd tried to scream, and she wasn't sure if she did, nothing came out. That initial plunge shoved her breath right back down her throat. Then she was weightless. Arms and legs out like a starfish. The man strapped to her back was forgotten and all she felt was air.

She'd heard of birds flying, always tried to imagine what it looked like. Was this how it felt? Was this what Luke felt every time he jumped? No wonder he missed it. But Luke would have been thinking about the danger below. Where was Luke?

Too soon she was jerked up and back. That time she did manage a squeak. Then a long easy glide.

"Three, two, one. Run," her instructor said and she felt the earth beneath her feet then her butt did a gentle bump on the ground.

Her landing was textbook, at least she thought so after hearing how it was supposed to be. She heard the clicks of latches being undone then Luke's whoop as he came up.

"Nice landing! You're a pro! "

The second she was released from her tandem, he pulled her to her feet and into his body.

"What did I tell you, man? Didn't I tell you she would rock this?"

Then he had her face in his hands and was kissing her. Her heart was already racing, her entire body tingling and trembling. When he finally lifted his head, she grinned up at him. "Can we do it again?"

Luke's laughter rumbled against her chest as he tightened his hold and lifted her off the ground.

AVA PEPPERED him with questions all the way back to town.

"Where have you jumped? How many times? What's it like at night? What was your longest fall? Did your chute ever not open?"

He answered all her excited questions, leaving out

the less desirable details. Her cheeks were still pink from the wind, the excitement, and the sun. He'd have to take care when she was in the sun, her skin was so fair. Even with the band holding her hair at the base of her neck, plenty of pieces hung tangled around her face.

Her eyes were lit with excitement and happiness. He should take her skydiving every day. Seriously. He should buy a plane and take her. There was plenty of room on Hannah's farm for a small runway and... he was crazy. But maybe not. Maybe he'd take some of Hannah's campers. Would that be allowed? The ideas ran around in his head.

They drove the rest of the way with the windows down. The sky above was cloudless and blue. The wind coming through the open windows blew the scent of spring and sun and Ava around the truck. He wondered if, like him, she'd begun to see this place as home and if she did, what that could mean for them. "Why don't we stop for food?"

"Sure. I'm starved. Does adrenaline make you hungry?"

He laughed. "Burger place?"

"Definitely."

He knew of a place they were coming up on and pulled into the lot. With Ava's hand in his, they waited at the hostess stand, it was that kind of burger place.

"The fries and onion rings are great."

"Mmm. Sounds good."

When they were seated, they ordered drinks and he ordered a mixed basket for them to share.

Luke watched her dip her battered and fried onions in the special sauce and take a bite. She smiled around the bite, moaned her enjoyment and it hit him. He wasn't ready for her to go. He wasn't ready for whatever they had to end.

He'd pursued her, he could admit that. He'd seen her, gone after her, even if he hadn't been entirely sure what he was doing in the beginning. But he'd figured it out. They spent nearly every free moment together, day and night. And all the while the clock was ticking toward the day she would move back to New York.

This thing with Ava was well beyond anything he'd planned on and they'd shot into much deeper territory much faster than he would have thought possible. He thought about what she'd said about her dad and his steps. He wanted to take some steps of his own. Would Ava be like her mother? Would he have a fight on his hands? He wasn't afraid of a fight. Had no reservations about fighting for her. But he was still watching his step, not wanting to scare her off.

"I guess you'll be going back to the city soon," he said, trying for casual not to give away his feelings.

"Yeah." She spun the fry in her fingers but didn't put it in her mouth. "Pretty soon."

She sighed and he kicked himself for throwing a shadow on their perfect day. "Hey, maybe you'll stay for the burgers," he said going for light. "No way do they have burgers like this in NYC. Well, tofu burgers maybe."

She gave a small laugh but the mood had definitely changed. "People do eat meat in the city. But, no. I've never had a burger like this." Her eyes were on his face.

"Knew it." A few minutes passed, both of them eating. Luke watched her every move intently.

Ava hadn't mentioned that Hannah had asked her to stay on and help with her students. Hannah had told him, thinking Ava would have already done so. Wondering why she hadn't. Or maybe he knew why she hadn't. Because she'd already decided that's not what she wanted.

She put her burger down, grabbed a napkin. She wiped her fingers. Then wiped them again. "I could visit," she finally said. "You could visit."

"Yeah. That could work. Or you could stay." *Damn it.* He wasn't going to ask, had *told* himself he wasn't then the words were out.

Her head came up, her blue eyes nearly meeting his dead on. He watched her wipe her fingers a third time, effectively shredding her napkin. "Of course it wouldn't be safe if you couldn't breathe."

"No, but maybe..." She slid her hand across the table and he covered it with his. "Maybe it's getting easier to breathe."

"nd that's where we went. That was my birthday," Ava told Hannah, sitting on the edge of Hannah's office desk, swinging her feet.

"I can't believe he thought that was a good surprise."

"But it *was*," Ava said, smiling. "It was the best way to do it. I barely had time to obsess over everything that could go wrong before we were up in the sky and then— shewwww!" Ava made a diving motion with her hand. "We were falling!"

"Better you than me," Hannah said. "I'm all about adventure as long as it's on this earth. I'll leave the sky to the birds."

Ava hopped off the desk. She was still wired, energized by the day she'd had with Luke. "Oh! I know what I was going to tell you. There's a braille label maker that makes these little peel and stick labels. I actually have one."

"Great idea," Hannah said. "Making a note."

"I meant, I could do it for you. I use it all the time. Every spice is labeled, some of my make up. It's fun to use and I could do it in a fraction of the time."

"Hey, if you're offering, I'll take it and say thank you very much."

"Okay. Want to make a list now?"

"Okay. Let me grab a pad."

"Or, if you dictate it into my phone, then I can have it read back the list and make the labels tonight."

"Seriously? Okay, but you have to tell me if I'm getting out of control or asking too much."

"I will, but really, it's so easy, I can do as many as you want."

Ava opened her note taking app, handing the phone to Hannah. Then, with her cane in one hand, they worked their way through the tack room. Done with that, they made their way outside to the inclusive play set.

Ava thought about summer here, then the fall when Hannah was hoping to have her first campers here. "I wish I could be here to see them." Not sure when she starting seeing herself here instead of city.

"You could come back. I'd love you to come back. I couldn't pay you much but—"

"You wouldn't have to pay me. It might be hard to get the time off work though." She'd never wanted to get what she'd thought of as a blind job, teaching the blind or typing dictation notes. But really, she just hadn't wanted to do what people might expect of her because they saw her options as limited.

"Sorry. That's dumb. Of course you wouldn't want to do that. You've got more important things like world peace."

"No, I was just thinking. I don't really have anything to do with peace." It sounded really cool, a translator at the UN, but really she was just repeating what other people said. She wasn't actually changing lives. Not like Hannah.

"I told Luke about my ex," she blurted, then wondered why on earth she would bring that up.

Hannah stopped walking. "I'm listening."

Ava recapped the details for Hannah, and thought how odd that it didn't hurt in the retelling. It felt like history, a sad history, but history none the less.

"How did Luke take it?"

"About like I thought he would. He was angry on my behalf and I was embarrassed. But then..." She lifted a shoulder. "I don't know. It felt like more than pity."

"Why would he feel pity toward you?"

"Seriously?" Ava tilted her head and gave Hannah a look.

"Okay. I know about pity from personal experience. And I also know that there's a difference between pity, the kind that makes you feel like you're less, like there's something wrong with you, and the feelings that someone who genuinely loves you feels. It took me a long time to learn the difference. Even longer to *accept* the difference."

Ava nodded, taking in what Hannah said. "I've been thinking about it, about a lot of things while I've been here. And what I realized is that Blake did. He always saw himself as broken. Thought of *both* of us as broken. And I think, more than anything, I reminded him of that."

Hannah wrapped an arm around her shoulders and squeezed. "Then it sounds like even with his sight, Blake's the one with the problem. It also sounds like you know that."

Ava smiled. "Yeah. I do." They turned and walked back into the barn.

"Okay, one more thing and then I'll shut up. I get wanting to prove yourself. And not just prove to others that you can, but proving to yourself. And I'm not saying that has anything to do with you going back to New York or taking the job in Italy, but—"

"I didn't get the job."

"Oh. I'm sorry."

"Yeah." Ava toyed with a leather lead rope hanging on a hook beside her.

"Are *you* sorry?" Hannah asked.

"Honestly, not as much as I thought I'd be. I applied for it a few months after my divorce. I wanted to be running toward something, something better, and not running to get away. I wanted a fresh start and I wanted a good reason for it. Italy was a good reason, a good opportunity. And, I don't know." She shrugged, let the leather slide through her hand. "I really did want to move there but not as badly as I thought I did."

"Or maybe you don't have the same need to run now," Hannah offered. "Maybe you already found something better. Sorry, I'm being a pushy sister."

Ava laughed softly. "No. You're not. I was just thinking... maybe I have." *Now I just have to figure out if I'm brave enough to do anything about it.*

She'd wanted to prove she was just as qualified and capable but maybe on some level, she'd wanted to prove herself to Blake. Since Blake regained his sight, had she lost her way and ended up on a path to prove herself rather than go after what her heart truly wanted? Love, a second chance, a family.

"Can I ask why you aren't staying with the cowboy tonight?"

Ava smiled at Connie's reference to Luke and shrugged. "I don't know. I guess I figured I should spend the night at home, you know? Plus, I wanted to go to dinner with you. And *plus* plus! You're pregnant! I still can't believe it!"

"I know. Guess we know I'm fertile, right? I also can't believe Mom didn't spill the beans."

"Only because she didn't have a chance."

"True." Her brother had told her parents right before their friends came over, leaving Connie to tell

Ava. "I'm really glad we got to do this before you go back to New York."

"Me too."

"You are going back to New York, right?"

"Of course. Why? Don't tell me they've enlisted you too."

"No. And I wouldn't try to convince you even if they'd asked. Your brother knows better. And really, Ryan doesn't have a problem with it. He trusts you."

"Thanks."

"I was just asking, well, because of the cowboy you're *not* with tonight. You've been spending a lot of time together."

"Yeah. We have. Maybe that's why I'm not with him." Because the truth was, she hadn't *wanted* to come home and sleep alone, but she'd decided she *had* to. It couldn't be a good idea to sleep with Luke *every* night.

She was falling for him, *had* fallen, she knew that. Even worse, she'd done it after vowing to never let that happen again. She needed to consider the price she would pay if she let things continue.

"I don't consider myself weak, or needy, but with Luke, I feel—"

"Safe?"

"I do. Is that wrong? I shouldn't need him to make me feel safe or protected. But he also makes me feel strong."

"I'd say that sounds about perfect. A man that makes you feel safe and strong. Have you ever thought you do the same for him?"

"What?" Ava turned her face toward Connie in the driver's seat. "Why?"

"I don't know because I don't know him. But even if you can't see it, I can see the way he looks at you. Like a man going from freezing cold to standing in the sun."

She didn't know what that looked like, but she knew what it felt like. To stand in the sun, feel the warmth. "I love him," she said softly.

"Well, there's a news flash."

Ava's face crumpled as her throat clogged. "I love him and—"

"Oh, honey. It shouldn't make you cry. No, I take that back. It might make you cry. It can be scary and overwhelming."

"Overwhelming—there's a word for it. I love being around Luke, I like the way he makes me feel." She shook her head. "I wasn't supposed to feel this. This wasn't supposed to happen." She blew out a long breath. "I turned it off, you know? And I was determined not to turn it on again."

"And let Blake win?"

"There's no winning."

"Maybe moving on, being with someone better, is you winning. And by better, I mean someone who loves you, *really* loves you."

"And if I'm too afraid of having my heart broken a second time? Because I don't know if I could take it. I really don't know if I could it take with Luke."

"Well. Sounds like you have some decisions to make."

"Yeah." They rode in silence a few minutes.

"Would you ever consider staying here? I know your reasons for living in the city," Connie said quickly. "I get it, I really do. But if things with Luke are serious…"

"I don't know. And that's a huge leap from *hell no, never.* He loves it here. I know what he's doing with the camp means a lot to him. He came here to reconnect with his family and he's doing that." She sighed, turned her face to the window. "I guess the only answer I have is, it doesn't sound as crazy as it used to."

LATER THAT NIGHT, Ava got up for a glass of milk before bed and found her mom in the kitchen.

"Hey, honey. Can't sleep?"

"I haven't really tried yet. Just feeling like a snack."

"Now that you mention it, a snack sounds good. How about sugar cinnamon toast?"

Her mom had always made her cinnamon sugar toast as a child, extra sugar. "I'd love that. I'll get the milk."

Ava poured two glasses and turned the oven on broil while her mom spread two pieces of bread with butter. She knew her mom would give them a generous crumble of brown sugar topped with a sprinkle of cinnamon.

"How was your dinner with the Simons?"

"It was nice. Sharon made that prosciutto wrapped chicken dish your dad loves. Between the four of us, we polished off an entire bottle of wine. We even played cards."

"You party animals," Ava said smiling.

Her mom brought the warm toast to the table and they sat. Ava bit into the sugary crunch. "Just right every time." She heard her mom eat. "On a scale from one to ten how excited are you about Connie being pregnant?"

"I'd say somewhere near a hundred. You know the Simons have *three* grandchildren. All in town. They talk non-stop about taking them to the park, having them over for Nanny and Poppy days."

"You're going to make a great grandma," Ava said and meant it. Her mom might be overprotective but she was attentive and giving.

"Well, I'll be counting the days right along with them. Now if *you'd* just come home, my life would be perfect."

Ava closed her eyes mid bite, but before she could get up her defenses, her mom covered her hand.

"I'm sorry, baby. I tell myself not to say things like that, but then it just comes out before I can stop it. I'm trying to be better. I really am."

"It's okay mom."

"It's not," her mom went on. "You don't deserve me laying a guilt trip on you, and really that's not what I'm trying to do, I just... I miss you. I love Connie like a daughter, but you're my baby girl. I feel like I hardly see you."

"I'm sorry, mom." She squeezed her mom's hand.

"No. Don't be. I'm so proud of you, Ava. So proud. My baby girl, working at the United Nations."

"You taught me I could do anything."

"And then when you achieved it, I tried to hold you back."

Ava smiled at the truth of the statement.

"It's not that I didn't want you to succeed. I *did*. I just worried."

Ava clasped their joined hands. "I love you, mom."

"I love you, too, so much. You know, when you were a baby, I read all the books. I read them over and over again. The ones about babies and stages, the ones about babies without sight. I tried to follow everything, to do everything just right."

"Mom. You were great. You did great. I mean look at me." Ava grinned at her mother. Her *Mommy*. "I turned out pretty okay."

"You absolutely did," her mother said. "And I am sorry about the consulate job. I know I said it was too far and all," she said when Ava looked shocked. "But you wanted it, so I'm sorry."

"Thanks, Mom. I appreciate that. But I like New York. I'll be happy at the UN."

"Will you be happy so far from Luke?"

"Umm..."

"Oh, don't pretend, there's nothing there. A mother can sense these things."

"I don't know that I have a choice. His life is here. Mine is there."

"I've seen the way he looks at you. What about Luke moving to New York?"

"No." Ava shook her head. "He would never do that. I would never want him to. He came home to connect with his family and that's what he's doing. He's good here. The quiet is good for him after being in the military..." She shook her head again.

To Ava's great shock, her mother didn't push, or make suggestions. She stood, came over and squeezing Ava's shoulders, kissed the top of her head. "You'll make the right decision for you. You always do." And then she walked out, leaving Ava to mull over choices she'd never considered.

36

"Hey, you home?"

"In here," Luke answered his brother from the bedroom.

Nick took one look at the bed and froze. "Going somewhere?"

"Yeah, I am." He surveyed what he had, still feeling like he was forgetting something. He'd decided to attack his picnic plan like a mission. Figured he needed to lay out all the gear before he starting packing.

Nick came farther into the room, looking closely at what was laid out. His gaze moved over the wine, the glasses, the blanket. "Ahh. Setting the stage for a romance. Chocolate covered strawberries? Bro. I didn't know you had it in you."

"I know where the specialty markets are."

"Huh. That's interesting."

"What's so damn interesting about it?"

"Nothing. Here. I brought you some stuff."

Luke looked at the box tucked under his brother's arm. "Thanks. What's in it?"

Nick shrugged and set the box on the floor. "Just some stuff. Stuff I saved."

"Like what?"

"I don't know. Shit from your room."

Luke straightened and went to the box, opened the flap. The first thing he saw was his high school yearbook. Under that was a stack of cards with a rubber band around them. His throat felt thick. He didn't need to look at each one. The only people to ever give him cards were his mom and dad. "Thanks man." He had to clear his throat and swallow hard to get that much out. Lucky for him his older brother was also a man of few words.

He straightened and went back to the bed. Damn, he wanted to dig through the box but no way would he do it with his brother here. Couldn't do it now anyway. He had a date to make. And damn it, he knew he was forgetting something. He cursed under his breath.

Nick stepped up beside him.

"Don't give me any grief."

"Wouldn't dream of it. Let's see... Bottled water, little champagne bottles, nice. What's in the foil?"

"Half a chocolate cake. Hannah made it."

"Good choice. Napkins, plates, blanket."

"I've got everything I can think of. Cheese and grapes in there," he pointed to a small plastic container. "Bread in that other foil."

"Condoms?"

"Shut up. Knife for the cheese. A three ounce can of bug spray."

Nick picked up the small first aid kit, raised an eye brow.

Luke grabbed it back. "I like to be prepared, okay?"

"Yeah. Fine."

Luke frowned at the supplies. "I'm missing something. I know it."

"Well, if you're missing it so am I. You've got everything there but the kitchen sink. If you're going to take this much stuff you might as well stay home." Nick picked up the bug spray, read the label like he was inspecting it and laid it back in its place. "You know, I had something I wanted to say."

Luke stopped his packing to look at his brother. "Okay."

"I wanted to say that... well...I'm glad you're here."

Luke huffed out a laugh. "Well, thanks." He started to turn back to his pack.

"I mean really glad. And not just that you're here. I'm glad you're out." Nick sank onto the edge of the bed, ran his hands over his face and into his hair. "I should have gone after you that night. I should have stopped you, and all these years, every damn day, I thought, 'if he dies, if my little brother dies it'll be my fault.'"

"Nick. I..." Luke was so taken aback, he sat on the bed next to his brother. "That's just bullshit. It was my choice. My only choice, or the only one I could see at the time. And really, if I'd gotten killed, I kind of would have deserved it."

"That's ridiculous."

"No more so than you thinking it would have been your fault. I forged your name to do it," Luke added, sliding a grin at Nick.

"Figured, you little shit."

They sat another minute. "You still thinking you're gonna stay?"

"It's looking that way. I talked to Hannah."

Nick nodded. "This picnic have anything to do with it?"

"Maybe."

"Well... don't forget your condoms," Nick said with a snicker as he left.

LATER THAT AFTERNOON, Luke stood on a ladder, hanging fascia. It was more of a two-man job, but Luke whistled as he worked. He hefted another board over his head, straining to hold it in place as he nailed it in with the air gun.

The picnic had been a success. The lovemaking on the blanket he'd spread on the ground had left him loose and in a whistling kind of mood. He was relaxed enough to go inside and coax Ava onto the couch. They could close their eyes, talk, listen to music. Or do nothing at all. But he wanted to get the outdoor electrical strung for the call box and the fascia needed to come first. With the electrical done, it'd be a simple thing to hook up call boxes along the way from cabin to barn.

He wanted Ava to see that, experience that, and all the possibilities that would make her living here possible. He thought maybe she was starting to change her mind about New York. Maybe. And if not... Could he move to New York? The bigger question was could he live without Ava? He already knew he didn't want to.

Even now she was inside, prepping dinner for the two of them. By the time they finished eating the sun would be down and they'd go for a walk. Tell her about the lights, let her feel her way to the call boxes.

"Hey, Luke. I just—"

He turned from his spot on the top of the ladder, saw Ava walking toward him and shit. He'd left the miter saw on the ground, not wanting to take the time to drag out sawhorses and plywood to make a table surface. "Wait. Stop!"

Everything happened at once. Ava was one step from disaster and in his haste to get to her, he missed a step on the ladder, fumbled the tool in his hand. The nail gun went off twice in quick succession. "Ah, shit."

"What is it? Luke? What happened?"

"Just stop. There's—" His words were cut off when he reached the ground. He groaned and looked down at the inside of his upper thigh. Not good. His tan cargo shorts were already wet with blood. He knew that before he even looked at the wound. Before he saw the blood already pumping down his leg in a ribbon of red. "Ava. Get my phone."

"Okay."

"It's on the porch, I think. Ava..." He was already light headed and lowered himself to sitting, then laying.

"I can't find it! Luke? Where is it? I can't find it!"

Ava was screaming and there was already a roaring in his ears. "It might be inside. Ava. Forget it. Come here. I need you to come here."

He watched her coming toward him, her arms out in front of her. "Stop. Go to your left, little more. Okay. Feel around with your hands. I'm here."

Luke looked at his hand, at the blood squeezing between his fingers. It was a lot. Maybe too much.

She reached him, grabbed for him, touching his left shoulder. "What happened?"

"I shot my leg."

"*What*?" She reached out, searching for the wound.

"With the nail gun. Listen." He reached out for her hand. "I need you to put your hand right here and press down hard, okay? Take my shirt." He stripped his T-shirt over his head, balled it up and put it over her hands. "Okay. Press down on that. Hard."

Her breath caught on a sob.

"It's okay. We'll tighten the belt around it and you'll find the phone. It's all good."

He fumbled with the buckle, sliding it from the loops as best he could. Levering up so she could get it from the back.

Her hands were shaking when she got it loose. He

tried to help her with one hand, keeping the other pressing on the wound.

Her hands, covered in his blood were shaking so badly they slipped on the leather. "Ava. Hey. Stay calm here, okay?"

It was good she couldn't see him at that moment. He knew his face would be losing color. "Okay. Take the belt. You're going to have to wrap it around. I'll hold onto this end and every time you wrap you pull. Tighter. Do it tighter, Ava."

"Okay! Tell me what to do!"

"I'm telling you. You're doing fine. Go around again. One more time. Okay. Good. Now stick it through the buckle." Her fingers fluttered over the square buckle. "Okay. Now you're going to pull and pull hard."

Luke sucked air— in through his nose, out through his mouth. *Keep it slow, keep it even*. A rapid heart rate wouldn't help right now. He knew enough to know he wouldn't stop the bleeding but needed to slow it down.

And also knew that if the nail had severed his femoral artery he'd already be dead. The fact that he was still conscious, still seeing clearly, told him it was most likely nicked.

"Okay. Now I need you to find a phone. Yours, mine, whatever. You can do it. Stay calm. We've got time here." Honestly, he didn't know how much time they had. And if she couldn't find the phone...

"Okay. Okay. I'll find it. I'll get it."

Ava was up and moving over the grass to the cabin,

too fast and not at all careful. He couldn't afford for her to be too careful right now.

He turned over, using his hands and his uninjured leg to make his way to the porch. He hadn't made it halfway when he let his eyes close and fought the darkness pulling at him.

37

Ava moved through the cabin, using only her hands to feel for obstacles.

"Siri, call Luke!" She stood still, listening for her iPhone to follow the command. For a ring or vibration that would help her find it. Nothing. She moved around the room as fast as she could. She didn't have her cane, didn't know where it was. Couldn't see.

If she could just *see*. The phone could be right in front of her. She felt around, swiping her hands that were sticky with blood over furniture. Over the kitchen counter. She screamed for Siri again, relying on a machine to save the life of the man she loved.

She couldn't find it. She couldn't *find* it! Frustrated, terrified tears ran down her face.

I can't find it.

She'd go for Luke's, she thought. She'd find Luke's phone. Outside.

She didn't know how much time had passed but it

felt like hours. She made her way back, moving as fast as she dared. "Luke?" She crawled on her hands and knees toward the spot she thought she'd left him. Her hand pressed down on something jagged and sharp and she cried out, but kept moving.

"Luke!" She sobbed when she felt him. She thought he was closer to the porch now but he wasn't moving. She pulled at his arm, her voice breaking. "Luke!"

She felt for the wound. Warm and wet. His blood had soaked through his shorts, his shirt. She put her hand over it and panic roiled in her gut as she felt Luke's blood well between her fingers. The belt wasn't working. She touched his face, his chest. "Luke? Please. Say something!"

"I'm here," he said, but his voice sounded funny. Tired. "My phone's on the porch. Get it."

"Okay." She was already standing. "Okay."

She stumbled, tripped, went down hard. She made it up the steps then moved her hands in a wide, sweeping motion. She knew it was a chaotic search, knew that she could be within inches, centimeters of what she was looking for and miss it.

It was here. It was on the porch somewhere. She started at one end, feeling along the edges, making sure she went all the way across side to side. She scooted back, repeated the blind sweep side to side.

"Luke?" She called out to him when she was thought she was nearing the end. "Luke? Luke! I'm looking! It's not here! It's not *here*!" But he wasn't answering her. "I'll get help. Okay? I'll get help." Where was she going to get help?

The truck? She scrambled down the porch steps, missed the last step and fell, but she was pointed in the right direction. She was almost sure. Hadn't they gotten out of the truck and walked straight to the porch? To the left, then straight?

She half ran, half crawled until she felt the front fender. She got in, thanked God Luke had left the key in the ignition, and turned over the engine. She knew how to put it in drive, knew which side was the gas. She pressed her foot on the gas and the truck lurched. She cried out and hit the brake. She couldn't do it. She couldn't get help.

She had to. She let up on the brake, let the truck roll slowly over the ground and laid on the horn. Someone would hear. Someone would see. They had to because she didn't know what else to do.

She slammed her hand down on the steering wheel again and again, stopping in between to listen for any sign someone had heard. She wanted to go back to Luke. She was just about to abandon the horn blowing to look for the phone again when she thought she heard yelling.

She froze. It was distant, faint, but there was definitely something. She pressed the horn again, three quick blasts, hoping and praying whoever was close enough to hear would get the message.

When she heard a car horn call back to her, she

heaved a sobbing breath and crawled out of the truck cab and back to Luke.

She heard a car coming up fast, heard doors open and shouts. "Over here! He's over here!" Her knees gave way and she sank to the ground.

Everything happened in super slow motion after that.

She heard Hannah and Stephen, heard Hannah saying her brother's name over and over, more frantic every second that she didn't get an answer.

"What happened? Ava, what happened?"

She heard Stephen call 911 then heard him say, "No time."

"It was... I don't know. He... He said it was the nail gun."

"Get him in the car. Hang on, buddy."

Then Luke's silent body was being lifted away.

She felt the movement around her. Heard shouting to get his legs. She stood, reached out to help but only found air. She heard the grunts of effort and the sound of breathing. And Hannah continuing to say her brother's name over and over.

She never heard Luke's voice. She stood there, frozen. She couldn't run to him, couldn't help carry him.

"Ava!" A hand grabbed her arm, pulled her. She felt the side of a car. Felt for the door handle, felt another hand swipe hers away.

"Get in." Then the door was opened and she climbed in. There was no time. No time. Then Hannah was gone and Stephen was yelling instructions. The back door closed.

The engine revved and Hannah laid on the gas. Ava had to brace herself against the dash.

"Luke? Luke? Open your eyes, damn it."

It was Stephen, Ava knew his voice.

"Come on man!" When she heard flesh on flesh, a hand slapping a face, she pressed both hands over her mouth. To stop herself from vomiting or screaming. She didn't know what was happening. Were Luke's eyes open? Had the bleeding slowed? She wanted to ask but couldn't make her lips move.

She wanted to cover her ears so she wouldn't hear people calling out to Luke and him not answering.

What seemed like a lifetime later she was standing in a cold hospital hallway. Luke had been taken into surgery. That's all she knew. That's all she'd been told.

Luke's blood that had coated her hands had dried. She could feel it cracking. She could smell it. She tried to hide them, crossing her arms across herself. She didn't want to wash it off. Not yet.

There was other family there now. Mia and Nick. Zach was there too. Nora was coming from a different hospital as soon as she could. Ava heard their voices, trying to be quiet but the sound carried.

"Why didn't she call for help?"

"She couldn't find the phone, I think. I don't know."

"He goes off to God knows where and does God knows what and comes back here and *this* happens?"

Hannah's voice was nearly shrill and someone shushed her.

Ava swallowed back a sob and bit her lip. There'd be no stopping the tears once they started.

"Hey, Ava."

Mia. The woman's arm came around her shoulders. It didn't help the twisting in her gut. An alarm went off over the speakers and a voice echoed *code blue*. The soles of feet slapped on the floor as people moved quickly past her.

"Don't worry. He'll be fine."

If he was, it'd be no thanks to her.

Ava heard the door to Luke's hospital room open from where she sat in a plastic chair next to his bed. Mia had been right. He'd made it through the surgery.

"What the hell, bro?" Zach asked, coming into the room. "You done with your near death experience?"

"Pfft. Near death my ass," he said. "Pass me some water, will you?"

Ava heard Zach slide the plastic pitcher, heard the water pouring over ice. Luke hadn't asked her to get him more water.

"Do I need to take away your power tools?"

"Nah," Luke said, his voice softer than usual. "Just me being an idiot, not paying attention."

"What do you think, Ava? Is he too old to climb a ladder?"

"I wasn't climbing, I was coming down."

Ava's stomach clenched as the realization hit her. Luke had been coming down the ladder, hadn't been paying attention. Because of her. Because she'd come outside while he was working and he'd yelled at her to stop. To keep *her* from getting hurt. So that's what had happened. She'd been about to run into something and Luke had yelled at her to stop. He'd stopped paying attention to what he was doing and... And he'd almost died.

He could have died. She distantly heard Luke offering her fries over the roaring in her ears. She'd stupidly thought that she would end up needing him too much, that he'd expend all his energy watching out for her and assisting her until he grew tired of it. She hadn't considered that he'd be hurt because of her. Had never thought there would be a time he would need her and she wouldn't be able to help him.

Was he already thinking about how to get out of this? How to take back what he'd said? If he wasn't thinking it now, he would. And she wouldn't go through that again. She wouldn't put either of them through that.

She slid her hand from the edge of his bed and stood.

"Hey. You okay?" Luke caught her hand and she trembled at the feel of his big hand around hers.

"Yeah." She slid her hand from his. "I... I um..."

"Hey." Zach touched her shoulder. "You sure you're

okay? You look kinda pale. Want me to grab you something to eat?"

"No. Thank you. I'm fine." Were the two brothers exchanging a look? When she walked out of the room would Luke ask his brother for advice on how to get out of this? She shivered with a sudden chill. "I just need to go the bathroom." She had her cane and her other hand out, feeling her way.

"Use this one," Zach said. "I can step out."

"No, really. I'll be back. It's fine." She managed a smile and prayed it was believable.

She made it out the door, her insides trembling. Because her blindness and Luke trying to protect her had nearly gotten him killed.

38

L uke wasn't in the best of moods, laying flat on his back. His leg ached and he was bored while Ava bustled around, asking him every two minutes if he was okay, did he need anything. And that's about all she'd said to him since he'd come home from the hospital two days ago.

"Are you sure I can't make you something to eat? My mom's going to be here any minute."

"I'm good. But you could come sit down for two seconds." He didn't consider himself particularly sensitive, especially when it pertained to the moods of women. But he knew when something was off. And something was off with Ava. He'd give her a little time to work up to telling him and if that didn't work he'd pull it out of her.

"Luke?" She sat down on the coffee table in front of him. "I've been thinking."

And here it comes, he thought.

"I think I should go back to New York. It's just... It's the best place for me and..."

She shrugged and he wondered if this was what she'd been working up to saying for days now. "I see." Of course she had a right to do what she wanted, to live and work where she wanted. But she was acting like it was a foregone conclusion that her life wouldn't include him. And that was a punch.

Luke's voice was calm. He didn't sound angry or upset. Didn't sound shocked or hurt. There was nothing Ava could discern in his tone that made her think maybe she was making a mistake. *Because he knew she wasn't.*

"I don't know what you're thinking," she whispered.

"Well, that makes two of us."

"Luke—"

"You know the first thing I thought when we met? Brave. I thought, that's one brave lady. No way is she a coward."

She pulled back. "And now you think I am?"

"You're running. Again."

His words struck true and hard and she nearly rubbed at the sting in her chest. "You almost died."

"That's just bullshit."

"It's not! Your blood was on my hands! I called your name and you couldn't answer me. I couldn't get you help!"

"You did get help!" He matched her anger with anger of his own.

"I couldn't drive you to the hospital."

"It was my own damn fault and if I was unconscious you wouldn't have been able to get me in the car anyway. What if I'd been alone? Then what? There would have been no one to tie the tourniquet, to put pressure."

"It wouldn't have happened if I hadn't been there."

He cursed under his breath. "It could have happened any time."

"But it didn't. It happened then. Because you had to look out for me because I couldn't look out for myself. And sooner or later something will happen again."

"So what?"

"So *what*? Would you say that if the tables were turned?"

"They're turned now aren't they? I'm flat on my back. You're sitting there."

"It's not the same thing."

She wouldn't cry, Ava thought. She wouldn't back Luke into a corner where he felt he had to convince her, and himself, that this would work. Because it wouldn't. If he didn't know that now, he would.

But for a moment, she'd allowed herself to imagine what might have been. What she might have had with Luke. Even now, *maybe* if he said, *No. Don't go*, she might cave. She might let him convince her and give in to what she wanted more than anything. But he didn't. Because he knew she was right.

And one day he would look at her, regret where he was and who he was with and she wouldn't even see it. Even now, she felt that he knew this was the best thing for both of them.

So she quickly slammed the door on *maybe* and didn't look back.

LUKE SAT on the porch listening to the sounds of the country. There weren't many at the moment. No insects, no power tools, not even a whisper of breeze in the trees. Just silence. He looked at horses, the grass, taking in the scene and thinking he would have given it up. He didn't know how it would go, him in the city, but he'd been willing to try. Would it have made a difference if he'd told her that?

He'd overdone it and now he was paying the price. He couldn't even call his sister for more ibuprofen because she'd no doubt tell Nora and then he'd get the wrath of both of them. All three of them, since they'd probably bring Mia over just to make sure they had him good and outnumbered.

With nothing else to do, he sat in a chair on the front porch, eyes closed. It'd been a day since Ava had walked out of the cabin and he'd replayed their conversation to the point his head ached with it. He'd wanted to push back and push hard, because, Jesus, she'd ripped his heart out.

He opened his eyes when he heard the sound of a

car coming, imaging it might be Ava. Unless she'd gotten a ride from Zach, it wasn't. Oh, well. He closed his eyes again. It was either Nora, coming with food and TLC, even if she did badger him with her nurse rules, or it was his brother. Probably no food, no TLC, but maybe he'd hang for a while, pass the time.

The truck stopped and he watched Zach get out of the driver's side, then Nick from the passenger.

"Hey, bro." They climbed the steps of the porch, gave him a good once over. "You look like shit."

"Thanks. Hand me a beer."

"Uh, uh, uh." Zach wagged a finger at him. "Never mix alcohol with pain meds."

"Haven't taken any today so pass it over."

Zach and Nick exchanged a glance before Zach handed Luke a bottle. "Just one. Guess I owe you for the night you showed up at my door."

Luke smirked at that and twisted off the top. "The night you were crying."

"I wasn't crying and holy fuck. Is that a kitten in your lap?"

"What's it to you?" He moved his hand over the sleeping black and white kitten he'd named Night Rider.

"Man, I knew things were rough, but... wow." Zach made himself at home in the chair to Luke's left. Nick sat on the top step. "How's the leg?"

"Better."

"How's everything else?"

Luke took a drink of the beer. He definitely wasn't

himself because it tasted like shit. "I don't know what you're talking about."

Nick shook his head. "Told you he wouldn't admit it."

"Admit what?" Luke asked, feeling pissy and sounding the same.

"Ava. Unless you're such a pussy that you're sitting here pouting and talking to a cat because you got a scratch on your leg."

"You know what? You can both go now."

"Pretty sure I told you to tell the woman how you feel," Zach said. "That's just how it is, right Nick? You gotta man up."

Nick shrugged, lifted his beer in agreement.

"You don't want to screw around as long as this guy." Zach pointed at Nick.

"Watch it," Nick said.

"Or you can sit here with your cat. Be the crazy cat man. That'd actually be funny for the campers. The crazy old army guy who lives alone with his cats because he has no balls."

Luke closed his eyes and let his head fall back. "You know, at least Night Rider keeps his advice to himself."

"You sure you don't want us to walk you in?" Ava's mom asked for the third time.

"No, Mom." Ava stood outside the car in the airport's drop-off lane. She hugged her mother, held on tight. For once, not minding the protectiveness. Her emotions were raw. "I'm good. You wouldn't be able to walk me to the gate anyway."

Her mom squeezed her tightly. "You know you can change your mind. But I understand," she added quickly and brushed Ava's hair back on either side of her face. "I understand. If you want, I can go by, check on him. Take him some cookies."

Ava bit her lip so she wouldn't cry at the thought. "That'd be nice," she said, turning her face away and reaching for the handle of her roller bag. She hugged her dad goodbye. She'd already been through the goodbyes with her brother and Connie the night before. Had fought back tears throughout her confession, her explanations, as to why she was leaving the way she was.

And had tried miserably to put on a brave face, telling herself not to be surprised, not to be disappointed.

It's for the best. She'd repeated that, hoping if she said it enough it wouldn't hurt so badly. She hadn't eaten much of her mom's going away dinner, and barely gotten down a bite of toast this morning.

A heavy fist of tears clogged her throat as she sat on the Norfolk runway. She sipped on a Coke she'd bought in the airport, her lips quivering as she tried to suck on the straw. She could be grateful for the ties she'd strengthened with her parents. And maybe, after time passed, she'd be grateful for the time with Luke.

She couldn't regret what she'd found with Luke,

but she wasn't too grateful yet. Not for the pain in her heart. She shouldn't have let herself fall so hard. So deep. Now she'd have to crawl out of that hole and she wondered how long it would take.

Her flight was delayed due to weather. Even now, rain pelted the little window she shared between her row and the row in front of her. Of course it did. Of course it would rain now.

She'd come here to help her parents, but it'd also been for her. A little break, a little space from the memories of her old life. She'd thought she'd go back to New York renewed, more settled. Or maybe not go back at all, maybe go to Italy. She'd never considered she'd be going back even more unsettled. In love with someone else and even more heartbroken.

39

Walking into the barn and knowing he wouldn't see Ava was another small ache. There were so many aches these days aside from his heeling leg, it seemed his entire existence was made up of them. Waking without her. Knowing he'd be going to bed without her.

He'd had no idea he would want to be tied to somebody in that way. Not one damn bit of an idea. Then there she was and... that was it. Everything changed. And now she was gone.

He'd wanted to yell, to tell her to save her sorry. But he couldn't. He loved her. He'd always love her. He'd known she wasn't one hundred percent in. He'd told himself she was just afraid of being hurt, but now he wasn't so sure.

Maybe she wasn't sure of him. Maybe she didn't feel the same. If he'd had more time to convince her... That she could live here, that they could live here together and be happy. Kind of hard to convince her of anything when he was flat on his back.

Leaning heavily on a cane, Luke limped his way to the tack room, thinking he'd find his sister. He did find her, and Kylie.

"Hey," his sister said, turning to him.

"Hi," Kylie said shyly.

He looked right at her, saw the little girl she was. She wore pink today, what he'd learned was her favorite color. A pink T-shirt with a brown horse covering most of the front.

"Kylie and I were just finishing up. Did you need me?"

"No. Just getting out, getting some exercise."

The office phone rang, and he jerked his head in that direction. "Go ahead. Kylie and I can hang."

If his sister was surprised by his offer she didn't say anything.

"I'll be right back Kylie. You can show Luke here, where everything goes."

"Okay."

Luke walked farther into the tack room, made a slow awkward turn and dropped his butt onto the trunk. Same one he'd sat on beside Ava not so long ago. But Ava had left, he thought mustering up the anger which was better than the emptiness.

"Ava left," Kylie said, as if reading his thoughts.

"Yeah. She did."

"I wish she didn't."

"Me too," he admitted to the little girl, more than he'd admitted to anyone else.

Kylie sat down beside him. "You hurt your leg."

"Yep."

"But it's getting better."

"Yeah." He smiled at her. "It is."

Kylie sighed. "She was pretty."

Luke knew she spoke of Ava and his chest tightened. Then he looked at Kylie again. Her gaze was down, where her feet hung a few inches from the floor.

"Yes. She was. So are you."

"Thanks." She raised her head, looked at him. "You're sad."

He blew out a breath. Nothing wrong with the kid's eyes. And somehow it didn't bother him so much to be seen. Not when it was the truth. "Yeah. I am."

"Maybe she'll come back."

"I don't think so."

"Maybe you could go get her?"

He wanted to. God, he wanted to.

"Hey, guys," Hannah said from the doorway. "Your mom's here, Kylie."

"Okay." She hopped down from the trunk. "Bye, Luke."

"Bye, beautiful."

She smiled bigger than he'd ever seen her and skipped out. Hannah watched her from just outside the doorway, waved goodbye. He heard car doors slam and wheels on gravel and tried to imagine where Ava was, what she was doing. Back at her favorite deli? Eating croissants and sipping fancy coffees?

Hannah came in, picked up the bridle Kylie had left on the trunk and hung it on the wall. "She'll remember that," Hannah said. "Later, when Kylie's older, somewhere that memory will be with her when the world tries to tear her down."

"Anyone tries to tear that kid down, I'll end them."

Hannah smiled, kissed his cheek. "You know... Kylie's a smart girl."

"Yeah."

"You *could* go get her."

"It's rude to eavesdrop and don't start." He started to stand, but the soreness in his leg had him staying where he was. "She's got a life in the city. It's better for her there, easier. It's what she wants."

"Women want all kinds of things, different things, when they know a man loves them. When the man they love loves them back."

His eyes narrowed in on his sister's. He couldn't, wouldn't deny that he was in love with Ava. But did Ava love him?

"And need... You'd have to be blind yourself not to see that she needs you as much as you need her."

Not true, he thought. Otherwise she'd be here right now. "Yeah, well, she left. I get a stupid cut on my leg and she runs."

"Just a cut, huh? You almost died."

"I really wish people would stop saying that."

"You know, before Ava left, I was thinking, wow, Luke's not as surly as he used to be."

"I was never surly. I was... pensive."

She moved around the tack room, not addressing that, then she stopped, turned to him. "Can I ask you something?"

"As long as it's not about Ava."

"Why did you leave? All those years ago when you joined the Army?"

The question was sudden and shocking and he stared at her, seeing a grown woman, not a little girl. Her hair was in its customary braid, pulled around to hang past her collar bone. She wore jeans and a long sleeve shirt with the sleeves pushed up to her elbows. A few of her scars from her ordeal when she was a teenager were still visible.

Was she asking in general terms or about that last night specifically? Either way, she'd given him the opening to get it off his chest.

"I thought Nick would have told you."

Hannah lifted her hands in an empty gesture and leaned against the wall across from him, waiting.

"We were at a football game, for the twins. I was supposed to be watching you. I didn't. Nick got there and... well he was the one that found you. Teetering at the very top of the bleachers. The chain link guard behind was broken. You almost fell. You almost..." He shuddered unable to finish the sentence.

"But I didn't. Luke, you were a teenager. Do you

know how many teenagers are supposed to watch their siblings and don't?"

Didn't matter. And she was making excuses for him.

"So you felt guilty and you left. Or you felt afraid something would happen again, even worse."

"Yeah. Maybe. That and the fact that I'd been screwing up in just about every other area. Nick told me more than once if I didn't cut it out, DHS would step in, take you, split everyone up."

"Mmm." Hannah nodded and straightened the saddle blankets, taking them off the shelf, refolding and putting them back.

"What?"

"Just thinking that sounds a lot like what Ava said to me, the day before she left."

"What? That she was afraid she'd get hurt here? I made the path. I strung the rope. Damn it, I put in the wire for intercoms."

Hannah turned. "Would that be the wire you were working on when you shot yourself in the leg with a nail gun?"

"I didn't shoot myself. The damn thing misfired."

"Uh huh. So while you were doing something for Ava, because she's blind, you had an accident that could have killed you—" She put up her hand to stop his argument. "Could have *killed you*. I was there, thank you very much. And so was Ava and she couldn't help you. Can you imagine what that was like for her? The helplessness? Feeling your blood and not being able to get help?"

He shrugged, not wanting to picture Ava afraid and helpless. "Would have been the same if I'd been alone."

"Oh, that's a nice thing to tell your partner in life. Hey, if I'm ever hurt, being alone won't be any worse than if you're with me. Very nice."

He felt like he was being scolded by his CO instead of his little sister.

"So you had the accident because you were looking at her about to walk into a table saw instead of watching what you were doing. Is that about it?"

"It was my fault for leaving it out."

"And if she could see, you wouldn't have had to put it away. Do you want to go round and round with the blame game?"

"No. I don't. I don't blame her, damn it."

"But she blames herself. You made mistakes that night at the football game, and fine," she added when he raised his hand to argue. "You made mistakes before that, but I wasn't even hurt, didn't have a scratch on me. And you still left, afraid you'd continue to act like the teenager you were.

"You made a choice. I wonder how Ava feels, knowing it's not a choice for her. You grew and matured. She can't change what she is. She'll never see. She'll always need a certain amount of help. And she knows that anyone who cares about her will always have to be on the lookout, trying to keep her safe. Just think about it."

"Okay, brat." He stood, and for the first time in too many years, he reached for his little sister, pulled her into a long hug. "I love you."

Her arms wrapped around him. "I love you too."

"I didn't fight for her," he said after a moment.

"No, you didn't."

"I'm an idiot."

Hannah laughed. "Yes, you are. But you can change that."

He could. And he would.

AVA HAD BEEN BACK in New York for a week and still felt like she was just going through the motions. She got up, dressed for work, walked to the corner coffee shop, and ordered her usual skinny mocha latte. She worked, answered questions about her dad and accepted everyone's warm greetings on her return. Then she walked home, picking up take-out that she didn't feel like eating.

She'd texted Luke, asking how he was. He'd answered *better*, asked how she was, but obviously, nothing was the same between them. She missed him. And even though she tried not to miss him to the point of misery, she did, on top of second guessing her decision to end things.

But even if he hadn't said the words now, he would

eventually. Something else would happen. She was right to end things now instead of later.

She skipped the bagel, she hadn't been that hungry lately, and took her coffee to go. Using her cane, she made her way two more blocks then into the UN building.

"Hey! Ava!"

She cringed, not in the mood to run into her ex. She was tired. She hadn't been sleeping well since she got back either. But she stopped, turned, with a pasted on smile.

"Hi."

She knew by his voice he'd been a few feet away when he greeted her, but the next thing she knew, he was wrapping her up in a hard, shocking hug. She didn't hug him back, was barely getting her balance back when he let her go.

"Wow! So good to see you. I heard you were back."

"Yep. Here I am." She didn't know what to say to him, it was so odd, but she felt...nothing, really. Maybe a mild irritation at being grabbed without warning. But that was all. She felt nothing like the warm tingles she felt when Luke touched her. Her heart didn't flutter and swell when she heard his voice.

"Ava?"

"What? Sorry."

"I asked if you had anything interesting on the schedule today."

"Oh. I'm not sure. I was just going up to my office."

Before, she'd always known what was coming up.

Always checked and researched who she'd be sitting in with on what meeting. She still liked her work, but maybe it had lost a little of its glitter.

So had Blake. He smelled the same in his dry-cleaned suit, the same splash of cologne he never left home without. As he went on about his latest project in the IT department, she imagined he was wearing his black leather dress shoes, and had a tie cinched up to his throat. Luke would never work a job in which he wore a tie every day.

She'd been so afraid to lose this man in front of her. And because of him she'd been so afraid to let herself take a chance with Luke. Because even though she did worry that she'd be a hindrance to him, and even if there was a niggling fear about losing the independence of the city, that's not why she'd left. She'd left for the exact reason Luke had said. She was afraid.

Being alone was safer. Living in the city was safer. But it didn't feel as safe as it once had. Or maybe safe wasn't the right word. Maybe it just didn't feel right. Not without Luke, she thought, and her throat closed up so tightly it threatened to choke her. The truth was her life wasn't so good without him. It had nothing to do with where she lived.

Blake went on a bit more about the changes that had been made to the lounge area. Paint color changes, new furniture. It was all about how it looked, sleek and updated. Nothing specific that she could readily imagine. Like he didn't even remember that she couldn't see.

"Blake, can I ask you something?"

"Um... Sure," he said, sounding almost surprised that she'd stopped him mid-sentence.

"Did you really hate being blind so much?"

"What?"

"Did you hate it? Hate your life? Or were we happy?"

"Well, I'm not sure, Ava."

"Yes, you are. It's a simple question. What if the surgery hadn't worked? Would you have moved on? Continued on as you were?" She already knew the answer, she just didn't know why it was just occurring to her.

"If you're asking if I would have been happy if it hadn't worked, I think the obvious answer is, no."

"Not happy that it didn't work, just happy. With me, with yourself, with life."

"I'm not sure I see the difference."

That's what she'd thought.

"Look," he said. "I hated knowing people were looking at me, at us. Then after... people still looked."

"Because of me."

"Yes. I don't want to hurt you, but yes. Only then I could see them and it was worse."

"But they weren't looking at you, they were looking at me. I assume."

"Yes, but I was with you."

"Ahh."

"Ava, I'm sorry."

She smiled. "You don't have to apologize, Blake.

Don't apologize for being who you are." *And I won't apologize for feeling sorry for you.*

A man so self-conscious, who cares so much about what other people think, that he'd leave his wife.

Luke wouldn't care. Luke was the type of man to do what he wanted, be who he was. And the world could take it or leave it.

And she'd left it.

"Have a good day, Blake," she said, happily walking away from her past, and bitterly regretting walking away from what might have been her future.

40

L uke missed his friend, his lover. He hadn't seen Ava in exactly nine days and it felt like a lifetime. He wanted to show her the guide ropes that had been added in front of the cabin. The wooden braille name plates he'd made to hang outside the cabin doors.

He made his way down the city sidewalk with irate honks and exhaust from the taxis following him. His steps were lighter today, stronger and more sure than they'd been since the accident. He'd spent the entire flight to New York working out what he would say. Now that he was here, he wasn't sure anything he'd come up with would be enough.

He stopped at the corner, waiting for the blinking red hand to turn to green. He could barely hear the beeping Ava had mentioned over the noise of the city. But if this worked out the way he hoped, it'd be his city too, so he'd better get used to it.

The scent of a sidewalk cart selling hot dogs filled his nose and followed him six more steps. Yeah, he caught himself counting steps.

Nothing was familiar so he double checked the map on his phone, as he headed to the address Ava's brother had given him. How in the hell did she find her way around here? He crossed another block and took a right. His plan was to be there waiting when she got home from work. It was four-thirty now, so he might have a few hours to kill.

He hadn't told Ava's brother why he was coming, or even exactly when. Hadn't told him he was *coming* at all. For all Ryan knew Luke was adding Ava to his Christmas card list.

But Connie, the sister-in-law, she knew. That female sixth sense, he thought, reading the incoming text.

AVA'S AT TRATTORIA. Friday drinks. 5-8 Corner of East 44th and Second Avenue. Don't be an idiot.

HE SMILED, feeling a slight bolstering to have someone on his side. He checked the restaurant address on his phone and changed course.

When he saw the name lettered on the black and white striped awning up ahead his heart skipped. And as he drew closer and scanned the outdoor tables, he could see that she'd held to tradition. He stopped short, causing a man to curse behind him and a woman to bump his shoulder with her bag.

He didn't care.

The woman seated with her, Maddie he assumed, sat with her back to him and Ava couldn't see him so he took a minute. She wore a heavy navy coat over a white top. The coat hood was down and the fur edge curved around and under her chin. Smiling at whatever her friend was saying, she gathered her hair in her hand and pulled it around, holding it at her shoulder to keep it from blowing in her face.

This was it, he thought, as another rushing New Yorker skirted around him, cursing under his breath. This was how it fit, how it felt. What he hadn't understood at his brother's wedding just weeks ago. But it didn't matter how long ago it was. He hadn't known Ava then, so it might as well have been a lifetime.

And just a few weeks ago, when he was making that terrifying slide toward love, he'd thought he needed time. Just enough to get a handle on it, to get the details of his life ironed out, but he didn't, he realized. He didn't need time. He only needed Ava. And if she needed time... Well... If she did, he was about to find out.

Luke had to go through the restaurant to get to the outside seating and as he made his approach, he saw the female he assumed was Maddie catch sight of him and do a double take. As he continued in their direction she raised her eyebrows at him and he gave her a tight smile.

When he reached the table, the friend whispered something to Ava then gathered her purse from an unoccupied chair and stood. "I'm guessing you're the cowboy," she said, staring him down.

He nodded. She touched his arm as she passed and in a low voice said, "If you hurt her, I'll kill you." Then she flashed him a slightly scary smile and left.

"Hey," he said and his heart pounded in his chest.

Her eyes were wide and her mouth had dropped open as she cast those blue, blue eyes directly at him. Damn, she was beautiful.

"I can't believe you're here. How are you? How's your leg? Here, sit."

He pulled out the iron chair her friend and just vacated and sat. Unable to help himself he leaned in, simply letting his lips linger on her forehead a moment until he felt steadier.

"Luke? Are you sure you're okay?"

"No. Not really. But I will be." He scooted his chair in, angling closer to Ava until their knees were touching. "And that's not where I wanted to start, but I guess it's got to be covered so I will."

"Ava," he started and took both her hands in his own. "I know you were scared, baby and I understand why, but what happened was a fluke. An accident. I was damn lucky you were there. I might have tried to drive. Might have fainted. Anything. Things happen."

He looked at her small hands in his, stroked his

thumbs over the back of them. In the beginning, he'd taken her hand for her, then later for himself. Then somewhere along the way he'd started taking her hand just because.

"Ava, I know you think being blind brings challenges, but I come with challenges too. I still don't sleep like a normal person. There'll be times I forget and leave stuff out but I'll try my damnedest not to. I don't think I'll ever have a conventional nine to five job. You'd have to take all those, just as I take you. And I wouldn't have you any other way, because that's who you are, and you are exactly who I want.

"And there's more than one way to help someone, Ava. To lead someone. There may be times I lead you physically, but you know as well as I do that you don't need much leading. But you lead me, too."

"I don't think I've been leading—"

"You're wrong. Physically or emotionally? Who's to say which is more important? I was looking at the past. You made me want to look at the future. And now I only want to look if that future includes you. I have my sight. You don't. My eyes are wide open on that one and I'm sitting here, choosing you. Choosing us."

"I'm asking you to choose me Ava, to choose us." He gathered her hands close to his chest, forcing her to turn in her seat. "I don't care where we are, but I don't want to spend my life without you. I love you." He said it gently. "I won't go away and I won't stop loving you. Even if I have to navigate this circus all alone."

"You'd hate it here and you love the farm."

"I love you."

"But you're helping Hannah. And you said you needed to be there. That it was good for you."

"I need to be with you. *You're* good for me."

"Luke."

She drew in a long deep breath before speaking. It was no more than a second and yet he felt like a man, standing on the block, waiting for his execution, praying for a reprieve.

"I've always wanted to make a difference," she finally said. "To leave a mark. To do something that I felt was important, and honestly, that made me feel important."

"Ava—"

"No. Let me finish. I wanted to feel... I don't know, accomplished maybe? I wanted to contribute something because I was so worried I didn't have enough to contribute, or that I had to contribute more than other people for it to count. To prove I was more. But my mom was right. As much as I hate to admit it, she's been right all along. I could work as an interpreter at a hospital or a clinic. And you, you made me feel like I was enough even if I did nothing at all."

"You could sit in a field and pick daisies and you'd be more than enough."

"It's crazy that you actually make me believe that. I don't need what I thought I needed. I already knew that. I can help people and make a difference without having my UN clearance badge. The work Hannah's doing, helping her with that, that might make the

biggest difference of all, but then you got hurt and..."
Her face dropped.

"That can happen anytime."

"It's more of a risk with me," she said.

And when she raised her face back to his there were tears clinging to her lashes and it nearly killed him. "No. No one knows what's going to happen tomorrow. I could lose my legs tomorrow, my sight, my arm. It would be a commitment. Good or bad. What-ever happens."

"I thought you might be relieved."

"Relieved? No. I've been sitting outside on my porch with a kitten in my lap and—"

"Wait. Did you say *your* porch not *the* porch?"

"Yeah. Hannah's given up on the camp this summer. Says there's too many codes and details and, anyway, she also decided that if I was going to stay on that I should take that cabin and build the others a little closer to the barn and— Look. None of that matters.

"Ava, you're the first woman I've ever loved and you'll be the last. I spent most of my life convincing myself I didn't need anyone. I thought I wanted to be alone, that I was better off alone. Or other people were better off."

"Luke—"

"I used to think that. And then you came along and..."

She put her hand to his cheek and just that simple gesture nearly did him in. Without warning, Luke caught her face in his hands, covered her mouth with his and all but inhaled her. He lifted his lips from hers, looked into those blue, blue eyes. "Marry me, Ava."

She jerked back as far as she could with his hands still holding her face.

"I know you said it was the last thing you'd do. But that was before. At least I hope it was before because I'm serious. I want it all. Marriage, an entire life, with you. A family, if you want it. And don't say we can't because we can. We can do anything we want. Together. Marry me."

She was still staring, her mouth opened, but no sound came out. All the emotions he'd been carrying for years, decades, climbed up his throat until his eyes and nose burned with the effort of holding it back. He took one of Ava's hands, laid it on his cheek.

"Do you know the last time I cried? No? Neither do I. But you can feel this Ava. Even if you can't see it. Just like you can feel the rain. Here's your rain."

"Luke." Her chin quivered and her eyes welled with tears, making deep, blue pools. "Don't."

"It's okay and a long time coming. Though I can't believe I'm actually crying at an outdoor table in the middle of the city. But it's okay." He smiled.

Ava shook her head slowly. "I can't believe this is happening. I can't believe I would even consider it."

"But you are. Considering it."

"More than. I'm more than considering it. I'm saying yes."

"Yes?"

"Yes." She threw herself at him, taking a strangle hold around his neck. "Yes. But it won't be here," she said, loosening her grip, easing back. "I love you, Luke. Let's go home."

He kissed her, a long, slow, sweet kiss and thought she heard clapping in the background. Wondered absently if it was for them.

She brushed her fingers over his damp cheek, and rested her forehead against his. Everything she wanted was right here in her grasp. And she could trust this. She could trust him with her heart and she would give hers to him, without reservation, without fear. Forever.

Four months later...

L uke walked with Ava on his arm down a floral scented cobblestone street, the scent of fresh baked pastries guiding them. The sun had set and now lights lit the ancient streets, reflecting off the water on lamp posts and draping strings.

Yesterday, she'd become his wife, he'd become her husband, on a centuries old bridge crossing a narrow waterway in Venice. They hadn't planned it, not exactly, and it wasn't legally binding, they'd take care of that when they got back to the states, but it had been perfect.

Ava in a white summer dress flowing around her knees, her hair long and loose and fluttering around her cheeks. They'd promised to love, to honor, to remain faithful. They'd exchanged rings they'd found in a little shop on a street they'd only gone down because they'd gotten lost. And just as the sun dropped into the horizon, as a gondolier sang as he floated under them, they'd said *I do*.

So now they walked, his *wife*—and Zach had been right about the sound of that— on his arm, their bellies stuffed with pasta and prosciutto. His phone buzzed and he pulled it out of his pocket, slowing his steps as he read the text.

Ava drew to a stop beside him. "What is it?"

"Dallas is home." He shook his head almost not believing it.

"Wow. Is that all he said?"

"Yeah. That's all Zach said." But it sounded like there was a load of words behind the simple statement.

"Do you need to call him?"

Luke thought a minute and started walking again. "I'll call him later. Right now I promised my wife a chocolate croissant and that's what she's going to get."

AVA GOT HER CROISSANT, Luke a cannoli, and they shared a cappuccino as they walked into an open piazza. She heard slow, moaning notes of a lone violin, heard people nearby speaking in English, French, and Italian. City sounds without the cars.

As they neared the violin, Ava felt the stone under her feet change to grass. Luke slowed his steps.

"Dance with me."

"Now? Here?"

"Why not?"

Laughing she went into his arms, even kicked off her sandals. The grass was cool under her bare feet and Luke's hand was warm wrapped around hers, holding it over his heart. His other hand moved slowly up and down her back. "It all started with a dance," she said.

"Funny, I thought it started with cookies." He dipped his head, kissed her neck. "You in this dress is making me crazy."

"It's just a sundress."

"It's a sundress that needs to come off." He nipped her ear.

"Don't rush me," she said, smiling. "It's our last night." But she sifted her fingers through the hair at his neck, knowing it made him crazy.

"You know it's damn sexy listening to you speak in Italian. We're going to have to figure out a way to continue that at home."

"I think that can be arranged."

"Are you sorry you won't be living here?"

"Not even a little." She lifted her face to his. "And Italy would have been so much less without you. You've made me see it." There was sultry and romantic music, food, scents, and Luke touching her, always touching her. Her hand, her face, skimming his fingers through her hair. "But I'll also be happy to be home. I'm sure Night Rider misses you."

Luke lifted her hand to his face, laid her palm over his smile then kissed her fingers. He gathered her close again, resting his chin on the top of her head.

There would be a dinner with her family when they returned. Thankfully her parents hadn't been too disappointed at the elopement news. The impending birth of her nephew helped. She imagined there would be a Walker dinner to celebrate the return of Dallas. She knew Luke was anxious about Dallas and his dark years of working undercover, but also knew Luke would do whatever it took to help him through it.

The cabin was finished and Luke had added on a

room which he was sure would become a nursery. They hadn't been trying long, but it was a thrilling thought. Four other cabins that would house campers were nearly complete about fifty yards away. They'd talked about moving into town, or maybe hiring a builder to build something bigger on the farm, but for now they were content.

She helped Hannah and volunteered as an interpreter at the hospital. And she had a garden. She and Luke walked and rode. Sat on the porch and sometimes on the swing. Sometimes in the moonlight, sometimes in the sunlight, either way Luke painted a picture, a feeling, in her mind. And if there was rain, she knew and she painted her own.

She knew everything she needed to know. Her heart and his. Sometimes there was light, sometimes darkness, and then sometimes, if you were lucky, you got rain.

TURN the page to read an excerpt from WORTH THE WAIT

ABOUT THE AUTHOR

Claudia Connor is an award winning New York Times and USA Today bestselling author of Contemporary Romance. Claudia attended Auburn University, where she received her undergraduate and masters degrees in early childhood education. When she's not writing, she enjoys movies, reading, and travel, with a heavy dose of daydreaming during all three. Claudia lives near Memphis, Tennessee, with her husband and three daughters.

You can find out more about Claudia's books at Claudi-aConnor.com. Join the reader fun on Facebook HERE!

A
MCKINNEY/WALKER
NOVEL

Worth THE WAIT

NEW YORK TIMES BESTSELLING AUTHOR
CLAUDIA CONNOR

WORTH THE WAIT

Chapter One

Present day...

Nick Walker leaned his shoulder against the weathered wall inside the barn. Sturdy and solid, a good place for his sister. A safe place. Through the open back end of the barn, he could see a patch of dry grass blowing in the wind. Farther in the distance, a dark line of green pines met a hazy blue sky.

Hannah's hair hung in a long braid down her back, the exact color of the blowing grass, and he watched her carefully as she stabbed the pitchfork into the hay bedding then dumped horse manure into the wheelbarrow parked next to his feet. As she went back for more, he continued to lay out all the pitfalls of dating, all the reasons to be careful, every precaution an overprotective FBI agent could think of. For all the good it did.

He should be glad his sister was spreading her wings, but thinking about her with McKinney only amplified that sick feeling in his gut. Part of him said that fear was irrational. A bigger part knew it wasn't. He hadn't protected her before. He wouldn't make that mistake again.

He sighed, noting she was going about her work without comment. "Are you even listening to me?"

"Are you even saying anything worth listening to?" she countered sweetly.

"Stubborn."

His baby sister, who admittedly wasn't a baby, shook off the extra straw then swung around for another dump in the wheelbarrow beside him. He'd hung around after bringing Hannah lunch, his excuse for checking in on her more than she'd like. But she was his little sister; that was his job. The fact she was dating had his threat level dialed up to the highest setting. DEFCON one on the big brother scale.

It didn't help that he still saw her as a two-year-old with corn-silk, barely-there pigtails and eyes too big for her face. "The guy is trouble."

"The *guy* has a name. He even has a family and everything."

"Yeah." *Stephen McKinney.* As an FBI agent, Nick had run the guy through the system and found things in his past that might or might not be legitimate cause for worry. The fact that he was a millionaire playboy was enough. That his photo was recently on the cover of a magazine as Norfolk's most eligible bachelor would have made Nick roll his eyes in any case. But McKinney was sniffing around his sister. Definite cause for a lot more than eye rolling. Hannah was not a player, and she sure as hell was not going to be played with.

Tall and lean, she had an inner strength, but she was also fragile. Breakable. Even with the heat thick enough to swim in, she wore jeans, which made sense for riding. But not the long sleeves she wore, as she always did, to cover the scars of her past. The marks left by a man Nick hadn't protected her from. Faded after twelve years, but he still saw them, still heard her crying in his nightmares.

That was the bitch of regret. It kept the past in the present, right on top of you, so you couldn't forget, so it could keep eating at you until there was nothing left. Until the woman that was holding all your pieces together walked right out the door.

"Nick, you know I love you," Hannah was saying, "even if you are a pain, but I'm twenty-six years old. I can make some decisions for myself."

"I didn't say you couldn't."

"You didn't have to." She sent him a meaningful look before turning back to her task. "You know, if you have time to watch me work, you have time to *help* me work."

"And get yelled at? I don't think so. You've told me more than once to stay out of your way."

"Hmm." She leaned the pitchfork against the wall. "Well, you're in my way now, so move you and your fancy self back."

Dressed in his standard khakis and button-down, he stepped back into the barn aisle not to save his scuffed brown boots but because he didn't put it past his sister to dump horse shit on them.

Hannah lifted the handles of the wheelbarrow and marched it out to her dumping pile. A breath of summer air blew through the breezeway, sweeping tiny bits of hay to the sides of the aisle, offering a little relief from the Virginia heat.

Freedom Farm was a physical therapy riding facility for children with various special needs, from amputations and paralysis to severe burns and visual impairments. Even five years ago, he couldn't have imagined it, and seeing her happy was like a balm to his soul. And McKinney was ruining that, he thought with a scowl.

"Where's Luke?" he asked as Hannah walked back, pulling off her work gloves. "I saw his truck."

"I don't know. He went for a walk, I think. We talked, then he left."

He wondered what they'd talked about. His younger brother wasn't much of a talker. A Special Forces officer, Luke still hadn't said why he was home. That worried him. He worried, about all of them, had since the day they'd stood like soldiers in the front row of the church, struggling to keep their gut-wrenching shit together.

Luke, a sullen seventeen, the twins, Zach and Dallas, just fourteen and forced to take the sudden death of their parents like men. And then two-year-old Hannah in his arms, quiet, observant, confused. Not yet twenty, he hadn't been ready for the responsibility of his siblings. It hadn't mattered.

The service ended; a pause between music pieces followed as the organist flipped pages in her book. The air was sticky with the scent of too many lilies. The only sound came from the squeaking wheels as two identical caskets were rolled to the back of the church. You could have heard a pin drop until Hannah's scream split the reverent silence in two.

It pierced every ear, so high and sorrowful it rattled the organ pipes. She lunged toward the aisle with a desperate cry for *Mommy* that tore through all of them. Again and again until her voice gave out. She understood more than he'd thought. Solemn music played over her while women around him wept. Luke and Dallas watched the scene in horror. Zach slumped to the pew and buried his face in his hands.

Since that moment, she'd been his.

He'd like to think he'd done a decent job. He knew he hadn't. The screams that had come years later were far worse than those in that church twenty-four years ago.

"Don't you have any real detective work to do?" Hannah bent to scatter the pile of fresh hay she'd set inside the doorway. "Someone else to bother?"

"It's more fun to bother you," he said lightly, even if he didn't feel it. He did have two hot cases going, both related to drugs and possibly to each other. He checked his watch. He'd only meant to come for lunch. "I do need to go, I just—"

"Wanted to hover? Typical." She blew out an exasperated sigh. "I wasn't kidding when I said you should think about settling down. If you can't find that special someone who'll take you, God bless her, at least get a dog." She added that last bit with a smile as she turned.

Then her expression grew serious, her probing eyes studying him until he wanted to squirm. But he was a federal agent. It was his job to make *other* people squirm.

"In all seriousness, I've been wanting to talk to you about—"

"Right." He kissed her cheek, tapped a finger lightly on her furrowed brow. "I'll catch up with you later." He knew better than to get into this with his sister. If she was getting it into her head that he needed to settle down, she'd be like a dog with a bone.

A dark cloud of rain was blowing in fast. He almost turned around to see if Hannah needed help but resisted the urge. All the horses were in, and her assistant, Lexi, was in the office. If she needed help, she had it.

As he drove his standard black Suburban up the rise and away from the barn, the first giant drops hit his windshield. He paused at the end of the gravel drive then took a left for the Norfolk field office. On the long stretch of empty country road, Hannah's words about settling reverberated painfully through his chest.

He couldn't settle, not like his sister had in mind, probably not ever. Because he'd found that special one. The only woman who'd ever owned him.

Found her. Lost her.

Chapter 2

Twenty-four years ago...

Nick pressed two fingers into the headache pounding in his temple and tried to concentrate on professor Jenkins's explanation of ideal gas law. He circled a line of notes, ignoring the knock on the auditorium door until he heard the familiar cry: Hannah, who he'd left in the university daycare two hours before.

The high-pitched wail wasn't his two-year-old sister's hurt cry. It was her scared cry, with a touch of pissed off. In the six weeks since their parents' death, he'd learned to tell the difference. He'd learned a lot of things. If he didn't take her to the bathroom, she'd wait too long and have an accident. Green beans made her throw up, but she'd eat them if he told her to. And she would never, ever, go to sleep without *the song*.

He was up, out of his seat, and halfway down the auditorium stairs before his professor laid his pen down. Nick's eyes narrowed on the young blonde in an oversized sweatshirt with silk Greek letters sewn on the front. She held a sobbing Hannah dressed in the white sundress with little pink flowers he'd picked out that morning. She hadn't been crying when he'd left her. Now her eyes were red, and snot mixed with tears dripped into her mouth. She lunged for him, and he caught her against his chest. His heart squeezed like it always did when she held on to him, but especially when she cried.

"I stay you," Hannah said, each word tumbling out of her with a jerk of her tiny shoulders.

He eyed the coed coolly. "What happened to her?"

"Nothing happened *to* her. She hasn't stopped

screaming for the past hour, and she bit three other kids. We can't keep her like that."

Several responses came to mind.

She's just a baby.

She missed her nap.

And the loudest of all, *It was my fault for leaving her.*

Hannah raised her head to look at him, giant tears hanging from golden lashes. "I bite."

"Well, at least she's honest." Professor Jenkins turned his questioning eyes to Nick. "She yours?"

He hesitated for only a second. "My sister. But yes, she's mine." And at that moment, she became even more his, which seemed to be the case every day. Every day, a little more his.

Understanding dawned, and the man's hard features softened a bit as Hannah shuddered and quieted in Nick's arms. He figured Professor Jenkins, like most of the professors at the University of Virginia, was aware of his parents' recent passing over the summer.

Hannah sniffed and wiped at her running nose. "I st... stay you," she said again, and her little chest jerked with a hiccupped breath.

*Continue reading Worth The Wait

ALSO BY CLAUDIA CONNOR

Worth The Fall

Worth The Risk

Worth It All

Worth The Wait

Waiting For You

Waiting On The Rain

Love At Last

Where I Belong

Made in the USA
Coppell, TX
01 February 2021

49335434R00252